GREEN

KRISTIN ANDERSON

DEDICATION

This book is dedicated to my husband Arie Jan who encouraged me to pursue my lifelong dream of publishing a novel and gave me the time to do so; to my son Ezra who brings laughter and joy to my daily life; and to my mom and dad, who brought my brothers and I up in the countryside and through exposure to literature and storytelling, helped form a lifelong interest in creative expression.

ACKNOWLEDGMENTS

I would like to acknowledge my amazing friends Jesse Wedmore, Antara Hunter, Dr. Kathy Gruver, April Wethe-Palencia, Delilah Poupore-Drummey, Karna Hughes, Cheryl Adam, Crystal Najera, Roger K. Jones, A.J. van der Bom, Lisa Hickling and Janita van Nes (by order of reading) who read through drafts and provided valuable feedback in making my first novel a better book for all of you. I would like to thank my inner critic for lightening up and allowing me to write contemporary romantic fiction. And finally, to Catrin Welz-Stein for permission to use an altered version of her beautiful painting *The View* for my cover.

Chapter 1

Ellie found a parking space three blocks from La Maison café large enough for her SUV to cruise into without gaining any new paint samples from surrounding vehicles. After checking her lipstick she hopped out for a brisk walk to the café. She ran on the early side of punctual, but was it a good idea to be early to a blind date? She decided that five after seven would be more appropriate and began to slow her pace. As if announcing that spring was in full bloom, all of the little boutiques and storefronts were open late. Ellie saw a tall, sophisticated blonde in the window of a candy store, and for that split second before self-recognition kicked in, she saw herself as a stranger might see her; and she had to admit, she was pleasantly surprised. The last three years had been good to her; at least where her physique was concerned.

She mulled over what she knew of her e-date James Hadley: Dentist, 31 years old, tall with blonde hair, blue eyes; rather handsome, or at least photogenic in his profile picture, and he had an interesting write up on e-Connect.

Despite the time of 6:59 p.m., she headed into the busy café. She glanced around for Mr. James Hadley, but they apparently did not share the promptness gene. To her dismay, she spotted Soo Jin and Bethany, co-workers at Duomo.

"Ellie!" Bethany called. "Join us!" She waved Ellie over with an urgency that turned a handful of heads away from their drinks. Ellie walked over and sat in one of the two empty chairs at their table. Bethany's sleek black dress accentuated her milky skin and model-like frame and Soo Jin looked stunning in white pants and a floral top. With a nearly empty bottle of Pinot Grigio on the table between them, the two women were clearly relaxed.

"Happy Tuesday," Ellie said awkwardly.

"Are you here alone?" Soo Jin questioned, a bit of concern in her voice.

"I don't know yet," Ellie responded playfully. All three women laughed. "Not quite like that," she defended. "I'm supposed to meet someone here and I don't see him yet."

"Emilio?" asked Bethany.

"No. That was over before it began," Ellie admitted.

"What happened? He seems like such a catch." Bethany asked curiously.

"Well, he's one of those guys that think all they need is a few dates to get you in the sack. I don't work that way." Although Soo Jin nodded in agreement, Bethany raised her eyebrows as if Ellie had just said something amusing. She should have known better than to go out with Emilio. She'd had her fill of set ups with friends of friends, however well intentioned. Despite some winning quality, they were too pushy where sex was concerned; and personally, she wasn't giving it up unless she considered a man worthy of a serious relationship.

"So who's the lucky guy you're meeting tonight?" Soo Jin quipped in a friendly tone, lightening the mood.

"James," Ellie responded vaguely, hoping he would arrive before she broke down and admitted she was meeting an e-date. She knew people met like that all of the time, but she wasn't ready to announce it to the office. Although she could count on Soo Jin's discretion, she wasn't so certain Bethany could keep her mouth shut.

"I've got to use the little girl's room." Ellie hurried to the restroom before either woman asked more about her date. She adjusted her cashmere sweater, pleased that the corn powder blue brought out her eyes. She remained in the bathroom long enough to warrant the trip and then gazed around the restaurant. She spotted a tall, lean man at the bar. He looked very confident, yet out of place in his jeans and green woven shirt among all the young professionals still in their business attire. Their eyes made contact and a shimmer of color dappled her cheeks as she took in the bright green of his pupils. He raised his eyebrows flirtatiously, and Ellie couldn't help but smile back before turning away.

Just then, a man walked into the restaurant that looked remarkably like his e-Connect profile picture, except that James Hadley was shorter than he claimed. She could tell already that she was at least his height, and in heels, would have a nice aerial view of his hairline. He scanned the restaurant and his eyes landed on her. She waved, prompting him to head toward her.

"Are you Ellie?" He asked formally as he reached her.

"Hi. Yes. You must be James." They shook hands and she was surprised by the warmth of his hands. Perhaps he had just run the last few blocks.

"Um, restaurant looks full. Want to sit at the bar?" he asked.

"Sure," Ellie responded. Clearly he hadn't made a reservation. Maybe he was plotting a quick getaway, or maybe that was the strategy for e-dates; no reservations, no commitments, she thought to herself.

She peeked over her shoulder toward her friends, and not surprisingly, caught them gawking as she followed James to the bar. She glanced at her watch. 7:11p.m.

"What can I get you?" he asked, once again in a very formal tone.

"Triple Scotch," she replied. "Joking. A glass of Chardonnay." James didn't laugh, or even smile.

"So what would you prefer? Scotch or Chardonnay?"

"Chardonnay." Great Ellie, start off with a stupid joke, she chastised herself. She glanced in his direction, but he was trying to get the attention of the bartender. James was definitely a head turner. He had a friendly, symmetrical face, pearly whites that were a testimony to his profession and he clearly put regular time in at the gym. His hair and clothing were meticulous, and based on the starchy scent in the air, he donned a freshly pressed shirt. They sat for a long minute in silence. Ellie opened her mouth to ask a question but James spoke first.

"What do you do for a living again?" He questioned.

"I'm the advertising manager for Duomo magazine."

"Never heard of it. Italian?" His fingers went to his watch, which he stroked three times before letting it go.

"No. Not really. The name is of course. It's a design and fashion magazine with a splash of high adventure and travel."

"That's pretty broad. What's the circulation?" he questioned, his fingers returning to the watch. Ellie shifted in the barstool uncomfortably.

"453,000 and growing," she answered, trying not to get too distracted by his movements.

"Sounds interesting. I'll have to get a copy." He said in a slightly accusatory tone. "And how does that circulation compare to say, Cosmopolitan?"

"Cosmopolitan has over 3 million subscribers," she stated. Am I on a date or in a business meeting? She wondered to herself.

"You know your magazines." The corners of his lips turned upward for a brief moment before flatlining. Usually conversation came easily to her, but his solemnity threw her off.

"And how long have you been a dentist?" she asked, not knowing what else to say.

"Five years." Another stretch of awkward silence passed until their drinks arrived. He twirled his beer mug in his hand, methodically wiping off the last bits of condensation.

"So Ellie. Why are you here?" he asked suddenly, turning toward her.

"Excuse me?"

"Can I be frank?" Without waiting for an answer, he hastened forward, his words spilling quickly out of him. "I get a lot of women who want a wealthy man. And they think, you know, because I'm a dentist, and rather good looking, well. I'm looking for someone who wants more than my money or status." Ellie's eyes opened wide.

"I don't know how to respond to that," she quipped defensively. Was he accusing her of being a gold digger? What on earth was this?

"We met on e-Connect, remember? The sight for *upwardly mobile professionals?*" he pointed out, aggression edging his words.

"Okay. Yes," she started, feeling strangely cornered. But then she remembered something she had read. "But if we're going to be frank, James, the national average for a dentist is just over 170k per year. That's reasonable, but not exactly *wealthy*. Especially not in Southern California. So you have nothing to worry about." She tried to keep the growing anger out of her voice. Keep it professional, she told herself. You never know who might be a future client, or stalker, for that matter.

"And why would you know that?" he asked accusingly. Ellie wondered how it was possible to get into a fight within the first few minutes of a date. Wasn't that when you were supposed to be on your best behavior? Out to impress?

"There's a finance and economy section in the online edition of Duomo. That statistic was in the February issue."

"Oh. I see," he responded as his eyes fixated on the beer mug once again. At least he wasn't tapping his damned watch anymore. As he spun the glass mug methodically in his hands, all she could think of was figuring out the best way to leave. I have to finish my drink, she told herself. Then I'm free to go. In the meantime, she could at least strive for normal conversation.

"So. You said online that you like hiking. Where does one hike around here?" she ventured.

"Actually, I have a few more questions to ask you before I talk about myself," he announced, clearing his throat. "What is your favorite jewel?"

"My favorite jewel?"

"Yes. It tells a lot about a woman's personality." He had no interest in getting to know her, but in pigeon holing her with formulas more trite than a Teen Magazine personality quiz. Ellie revised her plan; no need to finish the drink after all.

"What, do you think you can just conduct an interview?" She asked as she reached for her handbag and stood. "I'm not applying for a job, or to be your wife."

"Everybody's applying for a position, Ellie," he responded. She draped her lightweight overcoat over her arm before standing to go.

"Thank you for the drink James. This isn't going to work out."

"I'm sorry," he listlessly replied, not bothering to stand up. It seemed clear he was having some sort of date meltdown déjà vu. "You're an attractive woman," his words casted weakly after her. "Sophisticated. Damn shame."

As she bee-lined it for the front door she glanced toward the table where Soo Jin and Bethany had been sitting, discovering a young couple in their place. Thank God, she whispered. At least she had been saved that round of humiliation. When she was certain she was out of view of the restaurant, she looked at her watch. 7:23p.m.; perhaps the shortest date she'd ever had. Well at least so far. She hadn't tried speed dating yet. No more e-Connect dates for me, she told herself. By the time she reached her car, her stomach growled. She texted her roommate Gillian as she got into the car.

12 minutes of e-date hell. Headed to Ono.

Chapter 2

Jake looked both ways down the alley before lifting the lid of the large black dumpster behind the Do-it-Yourself Mart.

"You're clear man. Here. I'll help you in," Conrad offered. He turned on his headlamp before cradling his hands together, creating a step for Jake. Jake ignored the offer and deftly sprung onto the edge of the large metal dumpster, climbing inside.

The dumpsters of Los Angeles are filled with perfectly useful, brand new items. Not all dumpsters, but those strategically located behind office stores, nurseries, home improvement centers and the like. Like all extreme sports, dumpster diving has its risks—like stepping on glass and nails, or a wayward bag of dog shit or rotting fast-food leftovers. Not to mention the potential for a negative interaction with police or security guards. Some stores lock their dumpsters in the evening, but most leave them open all night. And that knowledge is what brought Jake Tillerman and Conrad Wright out on this particular Tuesday evening.

Jake rummaged in the dumpster with the beam of his headlamp helping him separate useful items from those that were unsalvageable. The portion of his socks that came over the top of his boots was suddenly wet, and he looked down to see hunter green paint one might use for a tool shed pouring out of its dented canister. He kicked the can away, and kept digging.

"Score," he whisper-yelled as he handed out a sealed box of nails and a case of drill bits in a cracked plastic box. The salvaged items were plentiful: a pack of sandpaper with a small tear in the cover, three measuring tapes, four wooden picture frames with slightly dinged corners, a dented staple gun, three brass doorknobs, six plastic pots and a handful of other useful home improvement items, all tossed because the packing was a bit beat up.

"We already have about ten measuring tapes. Leave em," Conrad insisted.

"No way, man. The kids in my program can use them," Jake responded as he crawled back out of the dumpster and sprung to the ground. He pulled the paint-covered plastic bags from his feet, throwing them back into the dumpster.

"Hair," Conrad said. Jake ran a hand through his thick curls to pull out bits of packing material. The two men divided up the loot into their oversized duffle bags, looking about them as they did so. Last week they had recovered a perfectly good Fichus plant behind a commercial nursery, as well as a flat of slightly haggard looking yellow Alyssum and two 20-pound bags of organic fertilizer, tossed merely because of a few rips in the packaging. They'd had a steep learning curve through their weekly dumpster diving activities, and now knew to bring heavy plastic garbage bags for just such a find.

Another lesson Jake and Conrad had learned was not to go dumpster diving in the day, especially not before something important. The last time they did so, Jake had shown up at his office flecked with shards of fiberglass in his clothing, which caused him to itch incessantly throughout a client meeting.

"Want to grab a beer at Reds after we drop off the goods?" Jake asked as they fitted in the last few items. He was always wired after rifling through the dumpsters, and it took him a while to come down from the thrill of breaking the law by the very act of taking someone else's throwaways.

"Maybe a quick one, but somewhere in the neighborhood. I can't stay out too late. Stephanie's heading out tomorrow for two weeks in the Sequoias."

"Camping or another research trip?" Jake asked.

"Research. But I have some research I want to conduct myself before she leaves, if you know what I mean," he smiled. "So I gotta get home before ten."

"Ah," Jake replied quietly. Conrad still gloated over his wife of six years like they were newlyweds. Jake found it both annoying and quaintly charming. "I suppose we could head back to that yuppie French bar," Jake suggested. "At least they had some decent beer on tap." Not to mention some beautiful women, he thought to himself.

"Ssh! I hear someone!" Conrad whispered. Sure enough, a guard stepped out the rear door of the Do-it-Yourself Mart and shone his flashlight down the alley. He glanced toward the streetlamp, which was mysteriously burnt out, and then down the alley in their direction. Jake and Conrad flattened themselves against the cold metal of the dumpster, barely breathing. The clicking of the guard's shoes suggested he wore wing tips cased in metal that not only protected his toes from impending danger, but could also double as some sort of tap-dancing gear. Not the most subtle shoes to wear as a guard, Jake noted. The two men slowly exhaled as the tapping made its way back to the rear entry of the building, followed by the suction sound of the door firmly closing. They soundlessly fled the scene, dropping their spoils in their bike trailers before cycling away.

Chapter 3

Ono was Ellie and Gillian's favorite neighborhood sushi bar three blocks from the house, a place they often came when one of them needed a bit of cheering up. Based on the number of times Ono appeared on her credit card bill in the last few months, Ellie was on a need-to-be-cheered-up streak.

"You're favorite jewel? You've got to be fucking kidding me!" Gillian howled as Ellie gave her the low-down on her e-date. "I bet the girls at the magazine would love that juicy detail for a column."

"We don't really write about bad dates—at least not yet. But I know who they'll come to for first-hand information if we decide on the topic," Ellie sighed.

"Hey, don't be so hard on yourself," Gillian chided.

"Easier said than done."

"You'll meet the right guy, Ellie. Don't worry." Even as the words left Gillian's lips, she knew she was spewing comfort words. When it came down to it, Gillian worried about Ellie. Sure, she was a sharp shooter when it came to her career—smart as a whip and driven. But when it came to men, she either attracted complete assholes only after her curves, or major fixer-uppers, like the "favorite jewel" guy. Plus, there was that little traditional dream Ellie fostered; marry by the time she was twenty five; kids before thirty. She would be turning thirty in a few months and there was not a boyfriend on the horizon, let alone a reasonable date.

"I don't want to meet my future husband in a bar or online, and I don't go to church anymore. What's that leave me?" Ellie pondered, as if responding to Gillian's inner thoughts. Gillian tapped her manicured fingernails on the table top from pinky to thumb and back again.

"Weddings," she responded distractedly. "Hey, at least you got to wear that new cashmere. That color really brings out the blue in your eyes."

"Thanks," Ellie exhaled. "But I don't need a guy as an excuse to wear it." At least that much is true, Gillian thought. Ellie's clothing didn't exactly scream sexy and single; more like sophisticated woman on the climb with no time for a man.

Their food arrived and Ellie dove in. Gillian, who usually savored each bite of sashimi, barely responded. It was then that Ellie noticed her twisting a lock of her long brown hair, something she always did when she was fretting. She had been so caught up in her own pity-party, she hadn't even bothered to check in with her friend.

"Everything okay?" Ellie asked gently. Gillian didn't answer. Instead, she used her chopsticks to line up her sashimi into a half moon. An almost imperceptible tremor made its way across Gillian's smooth composure; the type of disturbance only a good friend could pick up. "Something with work? With David?" Ellie pressed.

"David," she finally replied, the picture of calm. Ellie knew better than to trust the calm; that smooth surface was something Gillian often displayed before the storm.

"What's happened with David?" Ellie questioned, keeping her voice even.

"Nothing, really, But. I don't know." Gillian turned her palms upward. It probably wasn't the best time to broach the subject considering Ellie's state of mind, but Ellie was a good listener, and she really needed a sounding board right now. "You know how I'll be spending three weeks with him starting weekend after next," she began.

"Yeah, of course," Ellie responded. She wasn't sure what to make of Gillian's Ivy League boyfriend. He was certainly in love with Gillian and that counted for something. Yet she looked disturbed by the thought of going to see him.

"I'm feeling weird about it," Gillian stated as her nails began to beat out a staccato rhythm on the lacquered wood table.

"Like you don't know if he's the one for you?" Ellie probed. She had come to that conclusion on several occasions herself. He was the type of man who grew up devouring the Wall Street Journal for breakfast and sported an extensive collection of cuff links. Sure. Gillian also had an uppity streak in her that came from growing up with money, but she was a free spirit, opinionated, even obnoxiously so at times. Ellie just couldn't see such a conservative man handling Gillian's character. But then again, love conquers all, right?

"No. Not like that. David and I are meant to be together. It's just this damned geographical problem we have. I mean, I love it out here. I can't imagine being back on the East Coast." Ellie looked at Gillian's low cut fuchsia dress with sparkly sequins and knee-high boots. She couldn't quite picture it either.

"And no chance of him coming out here? If he's the one for you, and you end up getting married, you'll have to live in the same state, in the same house," Ellie glibly pointed out. Gillian was quiet for a few beats too long and her lips puckered at the corners just like they always did when she was trying on her poker face.

"What?" Ellie asked.

"What do you mean what? Hey, want to split a bottle of Sake?"

"Come on Gillian. Don't try to change the subject. You're holding out on me."

"Okay. Okay," she relented. She pushed her long brown hair away from her face once again and started massaging her neck before continuing. "David's been strangely mysterious the last few phone calls. And he told me to bring my passport along, like he's planning to whisk me away somewhere exotic."

"Oh Gillian!" Ellie's voice tilted upward. "I bet he's going to propose!"

"I'm thinking that's a distinct possibility," Gillian replied, an uncertain smile breaking over her face.

"Oh my God! Are you excited?"

"I'm all mixed up. I'm excited. Afraid." Her voice waxed louder with each response before just as suddenly waning into a whisper. "I mean, I know I want to be with him, but there was something in his voice; guarded; not quite himself."

"I bet he's nervous as hell, Gillian. I mean, you started out on the premise that neither of you believed in marriage, plus that whole kid, anti-kid debate. So if he's going to propose, he might fear that you'll laugh in his face."

"I haven't ruled that out either," Gillian mused. Her hazel eyes sparkled under the low light, and Ellie wondered if those could be tears making them shine. "I just wish he hadn't said it so soon. My trip's still a week and a half away, and now it's all I can think about." The low light illuminated the pink sequins of her dress, giving Gillian an ethereal-like quality.

"Maybe that was intentional," Ellie suggested with a smile.

"Yeah. Drawn out suspense. That's just great."

"Wow, did we have different days!" Ellie laughed. "You're practically engaged, and I'm practically throwing in the towel on men."

"There are a lot of beautiful women in Southern California," Gillian teased. It was Ellie's turn to roll her eyes.

"Yeah. Wouldn't that be nice if I could just change teams? I don't think biology works that way." Ellie took a long sip of her wine and smiled at her friend. "You know what? I'm just going to stop dating and focus on other things."

"Yeah, right," Gillian chortled. "Our whole evening, besides a brief respite on clothing, has been about men. In fact, it seems to be our number one topic and you're just going to drop it all? What will we talk about?"

"Art, theater. Ah, and your wedding!" Ellie responded gleefully.

"Let me get engaged first, okay?" she smirked. Ellie saw a curtain go down over Gillian's face, signaling that the topic was now closed. "So, what are you going to do without me for three weeks?" Gillian mused.

"Dye my hair black and join a rock band," Ellie responded dramatically, giving her best rock star kiss into the air.

"You have to be musically inclined to do that," she quipped.

"Actually, I sang in a band in college," Ellie announced. Gillian raised her eyebrows in surprise.

"Well then, you can have a practice run without me this weekend. I'm going down to San Diego Friday night to visit my cousin Jenny. I should be back Sunday afternoon."

"I can manage just fine without you."

"Yeah. I'll bet you a case of my Carica Syrah that you stay home the whole weekend, or if you go out, you just go to a movie with Arno."

"I'll bet you a case of 2009 Forager Pinot Noir that I do something extraordinary."

"You're on," Gillian smiled.

Chapter 4

There was never a time when the streets of Los Angeles were empty, but Jake Tillerman had worked out a route where the traffic was a little lighter for his cycling commute. He noticed the air felt crisper, more breathable if he began before 6:30 a.m., as if the smog wasn't awake yet. Just after 7:00 a.m., he arrived at the run-down office building he rented on the edge of the industrial district and shook his head.

"Shit," he muttered as he looked at the metal roll-ups over the windows. One had been tagged in bright green and red spray paint, and despite the fact that it livened up the ugly gray building, he knew he had to clean it off before it drew more graffiti. He unlocked the large metal roll-up doors and windows and brought his bike inside. His muscles pulsed with warmth from the ride over, but tension whizzed through his body, an unfortunate byproduct of cycling in a city made for automobiles.

Still in his cycling clothes, he rolled out his yoga mat and began to stretch his six-foot-three-inch frame through a rigorous series of yoga poses until the tension dissolved. The sun shone through the windows onto the frayed office carpet, and he sat in its warmth, doing a short meditation before pouring his first cup of tea.

Jake glanced over the checklist he kept on a thick yellow pad of lined paper. Bills that needed to be paid were mixed in with phone calls that needed returning and a long list of tasks for Gaia Eden. But on the top of his mind was a talk he would be giving at West Los Angeles College to his buddy Kyle's Environmental Studies class. He had asked him to give an overview of the

Deepwater Horizon Oil spill and the environmental impact it would have on ocean life and the estuaries along the coast.

"Great chance to introduce the contest. Potentially high conversion rate," Kyle had added as a blatant attempt to enlist Jake's help. He was referring to the Seven Eco Steps, an online campaign Jake and his team would be launching this Friday in protest of the oil spill. And since they wanted the protest to take off, and take off fast, they needed as many sign-ups as possible. If that meant Jake had to prep for and give a lecture to sixty college students, so be it.

He doodled in the margins of the notepad as he thought about his speech. Before long, his thoughts materialized as a series of sketches, word bubbles and arrows about the oil spill: death and destruction, long term impacts, a stereotypical oil-drenched seagull. Then he worked in the bigger picture of the campaign; enacting change. He drew two paths. Two students emerged with different approaches to life; one stepped out of his oversized car, the other stepped off the bus. One threw a plastic cup onto the ground, the other sipped from a reusable mug. One ate mangoes, shipped from over 5,000 miles away, the other bit into an apple grown on a local farm. One path spiraled downward, digging a gaping hole in the earth in the form of an oil well, the other spiraled upward into a wind turbine, bringing renewal and health to the planet and the student.

A delicate profile of a woman made its way into the sketch. At first he wondered if she had anything to do with the speech. Her vague features begged to be filled in, and as he selected colored pencils off his drafting table, she came alive; her large, gray-blue eyes staring flirtatiously off the page. Long brownish-blond hair surrounded rounded cheeks, prominent forehead and short chin. He looked at the sketch with amusement. The mouth wasn't quite right, but he couldn't put his finger on it.

Just then the entry bell rang, causing him to glance at the clock. Ten minutes after eight. That would be Natalia.

"Morning Jake," she said as she wheeled her bike through the shop. "Ethan'll be here in a few minutes. He's running late."

"That's cool. Want some tea?" he offered as he took one last glance at his sketch.

"Sure. Working on a speech?" she asked as she flipped her hair away from her deep brown eyes, stealing a glance at his notepad.

"Yep. For Kyle Peterson's Environmental Studies course."

"Who's that sexy thang?" she intoned with a fake Texan accent.

"Don't know," Jake responded as he worked on the sketch. "But she's hot."

"Well. I'd do her," Natalia licked her lips, as she took in her features.

"I probably would too," he responded. "But unfortunately, she's just a figment of my imagination, crossed with a fleeting impression of a stranger."

"You need to get out more often," Natalia said with more emphasis than intended.

"Yeah. That'd be nice," Jake admitted as he stretched his shoulders back. But as the rest of the contents of his list caught his attention, he couldn't imagine how. The bell rang again, and a thin young man entered, removing his tri-colored beanie before bringing his bike inside.

"Hey man. Hey Natalia," he mumbled.

"Hi Ethan," they responded in unison.

"See that latest tag?" he asked indifferently.

"Yeah. Looks like Christmas in May," Jake noted. "We gotta clean it up before it draws more." It was already getting warm in the office and Jake got up to crack open a window.

"Is that the speech for Peterson's class?" he asked.

"Yeah," Jake responded. "I wouldn't mind doing a practice run with you two before the afternoon program." They both nodded in agreement.

"Hey. The compost bin is totally full. We'll need to take it to the garden site today," Natalia said. Jake took in the curves of her tiny form appreciatively; didn't hurt to have a good looking co-worker. "Where should I put these tea bags in the meantime?"

"I have a worm box out back, if no one's stolen it," Jake grimaced.

"Still bitter over that solar oven disappearing?" Ethan asked, scratching his goatee. Jake couldn't beat the rent or the spaciousness of their industrial office, but the location he'd chosen for Gaia Eden headquarters had its drawbacks as well; theft and graffiti being among the minor problems. The landlord, now that was another story. He thought about his solar oven again.

"Bitter? Well, if whoever stole it actually planned to do some solar cooking with it, then I'd be over it. But I bet they don't even know what they've got."

"Perhaps they're using it to cook up some crystal meth" Ethan quipped, getting the intended rise out of Jake, who shook his head from side to side.

"Yeah. That would put a whole new twist on the L.A. drug industry: solar baked eco-meth," Natalia chimed in, causing both men to laugh.

"Now there's a solid fundraising idea!" They bantered back and forth for a while before settling in behind their computers. Jake went back to his yellow-lined pad. Fundraising wasn't on there, but it sure as hell needed to be. As he fiddled with his speech, Natalia and Ethan plugged in and started working on the online campaign for the Seven Eco steps. Jake pulled at his curls, a telltale sign of frustration. Ethan caught the movement out of the corner of his eye.

"Lay it on us," he suggested.

Jake went through his speech, which was still clearly rough around the edges, but nonetheless compelling with a good balance of facts and appeals to the conscience. He covered the basics of why they had started the Seven Eco Steps, talked about the oil spill, and how the eco-steps give people daily tools to reduce their oil dependence.

"Why not say 'to empower people with daily tools," Ethan suggested. "College students love anything that empowers them." Jake scribbled it down.

"Good tip. And then I'd go through the list: buy local, organic produce; 2) cloth bags instead of plastic; 3) reusable cups; 4) launder in cold water . . ."

"Boring!" Natalia cut him off mid list while putting her hand over her mouth, feigning a yawn. "The rest was great, but this part. You can't just rattle off a list. You need drama here." Jake knew she had a point.

"Better to have the list all printed out in 72 point font that you can hang on the blackboard. Unveil it step by step." Ethan suggested. Jake nodded his head in agreement.

The three of them worked in the office until it was time to load up the van and pick up the kids for the after school program. Today they were working on an urban organic garden in Pico Union, one of the poorest areas in central Los Angeles. Two of the kids in Jake's program lived in the neighborhood and would have first dibs on the fruits, vegetables and flowers growing there.

Sharp coils of barbed wire topped the chain link fences surrounding the garden, which could only be entered through a locked gate. Despite the prison-like exterior, the garden itself was a paradise of lush vegetation, the rows of plants and rich soil creating an oasis in the concrete desert. The garden project replaced a vacant lot. Although it wasn't considered a brown field, it had its own version of a toxic background; it had served as a rendezvous point for drug dealers and pimps.

Jake pulled weeds around a section of tomatoes and peppers that would be ready by the end of August, early September. It felt good to work his fingers into the soil. Rafa, a young man who was turning fourteen next week, worked beside him. The kids had grown the seedlings at home on their windowsills, and were now transitioning them to the outdoors.

"Mama's gonna love these jalapeños," Rafa said. "She makes chili just like mi abuela used to."

"Back home in Ecuador?" Jake asked.

"No. She lived here with us."

"She doesn't live with you anymore?" Jake questioned gently.

"No. She died last winter."

"I'm sorry Rafa. Were you close to her?"

"Of course. She was mi abuela," Rafa responded quietly. There was a long silence as Rafa planted the little seedling, breaking apart the compact soil and placing it in the small hole he had dug. Jake made a mental note to call his grandmother over the weekend.

"What was her name?"

"Carolina."

"We'll dedicate this chili pepper to Carolina," Jake suggested.

"Dedicate. What's that mean?"

"That means to do something to honor someone. Pay them tribute. Many great men have dedicated things to their wives, mothers or grandmothers. It's a sign of respect for those who teach you about life."

He handed him the watering can. Rafa poured the water gently into the earth, holding onto the small seedling with his other hand. He set the can down and patted the earth upward, forming an earthen wall around the plant. He looked at the bright green leaves of the jalapeño pepper and a faint smile spread across his face.

"To Carolina," he said.

"To Carolina," Jake responded.

Chapter 5

As five o'clock finally approached, Ellie finished her last sales call before calling it a day and heading out the door. Her SUV was parked in the basement, and she took the elevator down with a few women from the office.

"Hey Ellie, some of us are heading over to Antonio's for a drink. Want to join us?"

"Thanks Melissa, but honestly, I'm beat. I'm going to call it a night."

"Its Friday night, girl, and the sun hasn't even set!" Melissa declared.

"I didn't mean it literally," Ellie responded. "I'm just tired. I'm going to stay in this evening."

"Okay. I understand tired. Have a good weekend!"

When Ellie sat down in her car, she rolled her shoulders back and took in a long breath. With Gillian away this weekend, she looked forward to having the house to herself; watching a movie online and cooking up something tasty—leaving the dishes exactly where they landed until morning. After thirty-five minutes behind the wheel to go eleven miles, she pulled into the driveway of a large Westwood home that she and Gillian rented. She changed into her running clothes, started a pot of brown rice and set her stopwatch for a thirty minute run.

The roads were wider in this neighborhood and she appreciated the tree-lined streets. She often ran with an iPod, but this evening she cherished the awareness of the sounds all around her and the time with her own thoughts. I'm going to do something different this weekend, she mused as she locked into her eight-minute mile pace; nature; a hike even. It had been a few years since her feet had hit a trail, rather than asphalt or the gym. The different scenarios ran through her head as she approached the intersection of Elm and Fresno. She ran her route through a neighborhood park, around Harvard Elementary School and back along a strip mall before popping back into her neighborhood. She reached her front door, taking in the warm breeze and the red-gold of the approaching sunset before going inside.

She turned off the rice, and prepped the rest of her dinner before hopping in the shower. As the hot water massaged her shoulders, she lifted her left arm and started her monthly breast check, feeling for any lumps in her arm pit before circling around her breast tissue in an inner spiral until she reached her nipple. Methodically, she switched to the other breast. Ellie lingered at her left nipple, which stirred something inside her. It had been a while since she'd been with a man; a long while. Maybe I just need sex, she thought.

Despite a sturdy build, her full breasts and rounded hips provided her with curves that brought a lot of male attention her way—but not from the type of man she was looking for. She let the water wash over her as she explored her body. If it hadn't been for the kitchen timer, she might have stayed in a state of shower trance for another twenty minutes.

The house felt calm and quiet. Although she loved her roommate Gillian, she was a talker, and always had something on, whether it was the television, the stereo, the radio or YouTube videos on her computer, and tended to leave a combo of them on whether she was home or not. Gillian and Ellie usually ate dinner together two or three times a week and got into lengthy conversations about work, art, men or politics. During summer, they sat at the table out by the aquamarine pool, lazily dipping their feet in the water as they drank tea. Perhaps her days with Gillian were numbered, she thought with a mixture of sadness and excitement for her friend. She wondered how David would pop the question this summer, and smiled at the idea of Gillian actually settling down and having a wedding ring on her finger.

She thought of her comment earlier in the week to Gillian— *taking a break from men.* Perhaps that's what she needed, a mental break from even thinking about the topic. Clearly that would take a little mind retraining on her part. Wrapped in a pale blue bathrobe, she headed into the kitchen and opened the refrigerator. On the door next to the tartar sauce she noticed an unopened bottle of Zinfandel from Frog's Leap winery she had been saving for a special occasion. No time like the present. She retrieved the wine and the tartar sauce, lit a candle and poured a tall glass of Zin. Aware of the calming silence around her, she bent her head to say grace before starting dinner. Ellie couldn't remember the last time she'd said grace at her own table. Gillian got a little freaked if there was any mention of God unless it was directly followed by Damn it.

After dinner she went online in search of hiking trails within an hour of her neighborhood in Los Angeles. To her surprise, she discovered a plethora of trails fewer than ten miles from her front door. The idea shocked her. She had the sensation of being surrounded by only concrete, asphalt and vertical mass, when in actuality, that backdrop of mountains was not a Hollywood set, but bona fide nature at the edge of the concrete. Why, in three years, had she never even thought of hitting a trail, or even looking one up? Perhaps her shortest date ever was just the universe's peculiar way of telling her to break out the hiking boots.

She decided on Temescal Canyon, just off Sunset Boulevard, at the entrance of Temescal Gateway State Park. According to the write up, the five-mile hike offered mountain and ocean views, a waterfall, and a curious feature called Skull Rock. Ellie checked her online calendar that merged her work life and private life in a series of color coded obligations, and Saturday was open until her 2:00 p.m. hair appointment with Arno, one of her best friends and favorite stylist at Coco's Salon in Santa Monica.

She tuned in to her favorite online music site and typed in the Avett brothers. For the next hour, she listened to the sweet ballads and jams of the North Carolina boys while opening up plastic storage bins in the back of her closet looking for her hiking gear she had moved to California with her three years ago, but hadn't had reason to access until now. She found a treasured pair of lightweight hiking pants that zipped off below the knee to convert into shorts. She tried them on and they were at least two sizes too big. Her hiking boots, on the other hand, slipped on like long lost friends. As she touched each item, remnants of her old life before moving to California popped into her mind. She picked up a water canteen with "Grace Falls Church" written on the outside. It both amused and disheartened her. She had been so naïve back then. A small round object caught her attention.

"My compass!" she said out loud as she retrieved it from the box. Memories flooded her; hiking in the forests, up mountains, skiing into the wilderness. God; how can a person change so much in just a few years? She questioned. Another box held a lightweight backpack, portable first aid kit and compact lunch bag with freezer blocks. Since she hadn't been out in a while, she decided to err on the side of caution, and packed all of the safety items she had. It was only 10:15 p.m. when she'd finished prepping her backpack, but she couldn't stop yawning. After changing into her pajamas, she climbed into bed and was asleep before she could even finish one article in the New Yorker.

Chapter 6

Ellie re-checked her backpack, which was ridiculously over packed for a three-hour day hike: lightweight sweater, extra socks in case of blisters, first aid kit, compass, water bottle, journal and pen, enough snacks to feed a small army and freezer blocks to keep it all cold. Although she'd racked up thousands of miles in the wilderness and had more outdoor experience under her belt than most women her age, she couldn't bring herself to lighten the load. She chalked it up to re-entry jitters, pulled it on her shoulder like a life insurance policy and headed out the door. Within 10 minutes she turned her SUV onto Temescal Canyon road and followed it to the park. A half dozen cars and a school van were already parked in the lot, and she sat for a few moments in the car while sipping her latte and listening to the news. The stock market had crossed below the 10,000 mark yet again. It was approaching week three of the disastrous oil spill off the Gulf of Mexico and the oil was inundating the delicate wetlands along the coast of Florida and Louisiana.

"Entering week three of the disastrous Deep Water Horizon debacle, the oil leak is still not capped, and thousands of gallons of crude oil are inundating the coastal wetlands of Florida and Louisiana," the reporter said gravely. "The eleven employees who lost their lives on BP's Deepwater Horizon are not the only victims; thousands of birds and other wildlife are being poisoned and dying, and fishermen who rely on the sea to make their living are also victims of this disaster," the reporter went on. The news is so depressing, she thought as she snapped off the radio and hopped out of her vehicle.

Ellie shifted her attention to her surroundings, taking in a deep breath. The slightly astringent scent of Eucalyptus filled her nostrils. The park itself was expansive, with vast open spaces, picnic areas and Oak and Eucalyptus trees providing ample shade. As she started up the trail, she breathed in the crisp morning air, and marveled at the dew still decorating the vegetation. Within 10 minutes Ellie was in her stride, and her old hiking sensibilities merged with the thinner, urbanized version of herself. The trail was steep, gaining 1,000 feet in the first mile, and despite the fact that she was more physically fit now than she had been since high school, she felt herself breathing a little more quickly.

A few minutes passed before the trail flattened out and followed the edge of a ravine at a much more gradual ascent, shaded by small, overarching trees along the trail. She could hear the trickling of the waterfall before she came to it. The gentle splashing of the water created a cool mist as she crossed the bridge. It was strange to be taking in such beauty so close to the city, and to be alone in what felt like a spiritual place. So far, she hadn't seen any other hikers on the trail, and she reveled in the idea of being in nature on her own so close to home.

Even though she had read about it online, Ellie was surprised when the ravine gave way to a sandy ridgeline trail through the chaparral, with panoramic views of the city and surrounding mountains. In the distance she spotted a group of kids, their chatter breaking the spell nature had cast upon her just moments before. As she headed up the Skull Rock trail, she looked down upon the city, sparkling in the morning light. The Pacific stretched into the horizon to the south and layers of mountains presented a palette of navy blue dappled with brown to the northwest. Ellie could feel the stress she hadn't been aware of in her body letting loose. She plucked a few leaves from a sage plant and rolled them between her fingers, holding her hands up to her face and inhaling the sharp medicinal smell.

She was closing in on the group of children, which she could now see were all boys led by a man. *Gaia Eden Los Angeles Summer Camp* was emblazoned in bright green across the backs of their t-shirts below a stylistic drawing of the earth. These kids were not only out of their beds on a Saturday morning, but unplugged and out in nature. She made a mental note to Google Gaia Eden Los Angeles after her hike.

"Dude, look at the view," one boy exclaimed to another, as if he might not have noticed.

"Super cool," replied a boy with braids poking out of his ball cap.

"Check that out. I think that's the Pacific Coast Highway."

"Word."

The highway glittered like a sinewy snake in the distance. Ellie slowed her pace so as not to startle the boys in back when she heard the leader speaking.

"Okay guys. Hiker coming through. Step to the right side of the trail." As the boys willingly made way for her, she issued a series of soft spoken thanks and smiled at each young man as she passed, excited to see the variety in their features. That was one thing she loved about California; diversity. Besides an occasional Native or Central American, Idaho offered up a monotonous stream of skin as milky white as her own. The boys smiled appreciatively as she passed, their eyes clearly taking in her curves with adolescent curiosity. As she passed the last of the children, she looked into the deep green eyes of the leader, who returned her gaze without hesitation. It was her turn to feel a surge of appreciation for the opposite sex. He was at least four inches taller than her, with the wiry build of a cyclist. His yellow bandana was clearly more worn than the boys in his summer camp, and she figured him for a seasoned camp leader. As she held his gaze, she had the uncanny sensation that she had seen this man before.

"Good morning," he said.

"Morning," Ellie responded.

"How far are you going today?"

"I'm in for the four mile loop," she reported, her eyes still staring directly into his.

"Well this is a side route up to Skull Rock, which adds another mile round trip." A thin scar ran up his right cheek like a poorly drawn cat whisker. She wanted to study his curious features long enough to figure out where she had seen him, but it wasn't coming to her. Oh God. I'm staring, she thought.

"Yes, I know. I'm planning to take in Skull Rock as well." The boys had already started talking amongst themselves; their moment of courtesy expired.

"Beautiful up here," he commented, without taking his eyes off her. She felt heat rising in her cheeks and knew they were turning crimson. She only hoped that they were already flushed a bit from the hike so it wouldn't be too apparent. His wide set eyes and high cheeks bones reminded her of the robed men of the Italian renaissance who gazed pensively from centuries-old paintings toward an imaginary audience.

"Yes, it sure is," she returned, matching his gaze. What had gotten into her? She was acting more like her promiscuous colleague Bethany than herself. Although the subtle creases around his eyes suggested he was in his early to mid thirties, his freckled cheeks gave him a boyish look.

An oak leaf was tangled in his curls, and she had to resist the temptation to pull it out—not like he was the type of guy who would care about a leaf caught in his hair. For some reason, she found this thought refreshing. She realized she was still staring and quickly broke eye contact.

"Have a great hike," she said confidently.

"You too," he returned. She headed up the trail without an answer to her question of where she had seen him. Had he been on TV? Perhaps in the news talking about his summer program? She'd never heard of Gaia Eden, and that name would have stuck with her. Gaia was a Greek Goddess described as the feminine earth, but the name was also related to theories of the earth as a living organism and self-regulating entity. She figured by that name, Gaia Eden had to be either an environmental camp or some sort of new age camp. Why am I obsessing about this? She asked herself, annoyed. Just some guy who's not even my type. She set a good pace, putting some distance from the group of boys.

Something moved in her periphery vision and she turned to see a red fox darting through the chaparral. It had been years since she'd seen a fox. The scene reminded her of hunting trips with her brothers and father. She'd basically lived outdoors growing up, tagging along with her older brothers, learning the lay of the land. She stepped more lightly on the trail, relaxing her pace in hopes of spotting a few more animals. A rabbit darted across the trail ahead of her, rewarding her silence in its dainty yet nimble speed. As she breathed in the cool morning air, she felt a sense of invigoration. Nature had been right here all this time, just a stones throw from all that concrete. She smiled to herself as she headed back down the trail.

It didn't take long before she could hear the boys talking loudly, and the group leader was doing nothing to hush their tones. As they huddled around a boulder taking turns looking through field glasses at something off in the distance, she passed the group of boys without much notice.

She continued up another curving trail for thirty minutes at a good clip, passing other hikers until she reached a stretch where she was once again alone. Ellie found a cluster of small boulders beneath a tree and sat down to rest. She referred again to the map and retrieved the small notebook she had brought along out of her pack. She jotted down some notes about the trail before writing down Gaia Eden. As she gazed around her, she recalled *Adoration of the Magi*, a Botticelli painting she had loved during her college years. It depicted a group of royal figures paying reverence to the Madonna and baby Jesus, with members of the Medici family painted in the crowd. Perhaps it was the earthen tones of the boulders around her that brought the image to mind. Botticelli had actually worked himself into the painting as well, and she had always been taken by the features of his self portrait, especially the broad green eyes that stared out to the audience. She sketched a pair of broad set eyes before returning her notebook to her pack. Just then, a couple on their way up called out to her.

"Excuse me. You don't happen to have any first aid stuff with you, do you?" they asked.

"I do, is there a problem?"

"It's that troop of young boys back there. One of them twisted his ankle."

"I have a wrap and an ice pack. How far back are they?"

"About ten minutes down the trail. It's nice to know someone is prepared back here." The couple looked at her approvingly as she headed down the trail at a good clip. She found the students huddled around a young Latino boy sitting on the ground, his foot elevated awkwardly on a rock as the man spoke to him. Several boys glanced in her direction as she approached.

"Hi again," she greeted the leader as she got closer. "I heard you're looking for a first aid kit?" He glanced up at her with a solemn expression, his first aid kit open, but missing any sort of ankle wraps or disinfectants. He gave her a nod as she got out her first aid kit. The young Latino boy's ankle was quite swollen and he winced in pain. A scrape on the side of his leg speckled with bright red blood.

"Mind if I . . ." Ellie began, as she approached the young boy.

"Yeah. I mean, no," he responded nervously.

"What's your name?" She asked in a sweet voice.

"Ignacio."

"Hi Ignacio. I'm Ellie. I'd like to clean up that scrape you have on your leg and then look at your ankle. Is that okay?" she asked calmly. He nodded. It had been a while since she had addressed a field wound, but years of experience kicked back in as she slipped on plastic gloves, disinfected and dressed his scrape before moving onto the ankle.

"Ignacio, can you try rotating your ankle a little bit for me, like you're spelling the letter C?" she asked.

"Good. You have quite a bit of movement. That means the sprain isn't too bad, even though it hurts a lot right now. Once we get you fixed up, it's going to be just fine," she reassured him. She affixed the icepack from her lunch bag to the swollen area of his ankle with an extra bandana.

"Once you've iced it for a few minutes, you'll need to wrap it with this bandage with just enough tightness to give him added support, without cutting into the swelling," she explained to the man.

"You've done this before," he responded appreciatively. "Thank you so much." He was standing close to her, and she liked his presence. Seeing this strong, able bodied man concerned about one of his charges cast him in a more humble light than the over confident, flirtatious man she had encountered an hour ago. The boy had a slight frown on his face, mingled with embarrassment.

"Ignacio, how is it feeling?" the man asked.

"Better since she came along," he responded, a smile forming on his face. All of the boys broke into laughter, releasing the brewing tension.

"Good!" Ellie said enthusiastically. "You'll need to get a walking stick for the journey back down the trail, and proceed with caution down that steep incline," she advised. Several of the boys in the crew scattered, looking for something that would work as a walking stick.

"Whoa. Whoa. Careful guys. Keep your eyes out for snakes and no more jumping off the rocks!" he called after them.

"Okay boss. Sure thing," came their replies.

"Elevate that tonight and alternate between ice and heat. If it doesn't feel better by morning, make sure to have your family call the doctor." The boy nodded his head.

"Are you a doctor or a nurse?" asked the man.

"No. Neither. I just used to spend a lot of time in the outdoors and this sort of thing comes with the territory," she explained.

"Well. My lucky day. I'm Jake Tillerman, by the way," he said, offering her his hand.

"Ellie Ashburn," she responded. He had a firm grip, and as their hands touched, the flush came back into her cheeks. The scar on his right cheek intrigued her. How long did people wait before asking him about it? He motioned for her to follow him out of earshot of the boys.

"Ellie. I'm grateful that you came along just now." His voice trailed off. She could see a strange mix of guilt and genuine thankfulness playing its way across his features. "I got a call at 6:00 a.m. this morning asking if I could fill in," he explained, almost apologetically. "I don't usually lead the hikes and I didn't have time to check the gear that was in the van."

"It's okay. It's not a bad sprain. He's going to be fine."

"Yeah. I know. It's just shitty not being properly prepared."

"It seems to me you had it pretty much under control," Ellie offered.

"Except the ice, the ankle wrap, bandage, calm demeanor, and knowing how to assess the seriousness of the sprain," he listed with a downcast look on his face.

"Well. Um, do the other hike leaders usually carry ice packs?" she asked.

"Come to think of it, no. But I'll add that to the list," he answered.

"So, what is Gaia Eden?" she questioned, giving into her curiosity.

"It's an environmental education program for inner city boys, ages nine to sixteen." Jake was thankful to change the subject, and began to relax as he talked about his program. "We do mainly urban environmental work, teaching kids about cause and effect of their actions in response to the environment. In the summer, we get them out in nature."

"Sounds noble," she commented. Two boys returned with a sturdy looking piece of wood and gave it to Ignacio.

"Thanks man," Ignacio said. Jake looked at Ellie and then to the boys.

"Ellie, would you care to join us for a mid-morning feast? The boys made a mean batch of PB & J on whole wheat and there are extras to go around."

"Yeah. You can have some of mine," one boy offered.

"You should totally join us!" another chimed in. Ellie started laughing. A curiously handsome man and a troop of cute boys for a brunch date of peanut butter and jelly sandwiches.

"PB & J, how can I refuse that!" she smiled.

"Keep your eyes peeled for snakes," Jake warned as they headed into a clearing off the main path. As they settled into the grass, the boys removed their backpacks and several PB & J sandwich halves arrived like offerings at Ellie's feet on a metal plate.

"So are you some sort of lady ranger?" one of the boys asked. Ellie laughed. She hadn't been out in nature for three years, and on day one of re-entry she was being deemed a lady ranger. Good thing I was over-prepared, she told herself.

"I used to lead high adventure camps before I moved to California."

"Where did you live before here?" another boy asked.

"I used to live in Idaho."

"Where's that?" he responded.

"In the Northwest," she explained, finding their blatant curiosity both amusing and refreshing.

"The Northwest?" he asked.

"My cousin Joey's from Montana. That's in the Northwest," a boy explained.

"Exactly. Idaho is right next to Montana," she confirmed.

"Idaho's where they grow a lot of potatoes," another boy added.

"Yeah, and they have those crazy white supremacists in Idaho," threw in the boy with tightly woven braids in his hair. "I read about that on the internet. I sure as heck wouldn't want to live there." They had just summed up what most west coasters thought of Idaho.

"Not all people from Idaho are white supremacists," Ellie explained gently. "There are just a handful of people who think that way, and unfortunately, they get a lot of news coverage because it's a sensationalist story. But that's not how everyone else in Idaho thinks." Based on the large grin on Jake Tillerman's face, he was enjoying the show. Ellie smiled at him as the boys started talking about the Lakers.

"So Ellie from Idaho," Jake began.

"Yes, Jake from . . . "

"California. I grew up here in Los Angeles."

"Really?" She responded, slightly surprised. She had him pegged as a more outdoorsy type. He zipped off the bottom half of his cargo pants, exposing rather developed leg muscles and tanned skin. Perhaps he was a tennis player or cyclist, Ellie thought.

"Yeah, really." There was something innocent about their exchange. The flirtation was back, but it was friendlier, more playful.

"Ever been to Idaho?" she asked. He shook his head no. "Northwest?" she tried.

"I've been to Vegas. Does that count?" He pulled out a cloth bag filled with tortilla chips and offered her some.

"There's a whole lot more to Idaho then they're teaching your kids here," she commented while taking a few chips.

"Oh yeah? Like what?" he chided.

"In addition to potatoes and white supremacists, we have cities, universities, museums, spots of culture. And thousands of acres of wilderness and open space." Ellie flicked a spider off her arm, not missing a beat.

"Sounds awesome." He smiled again. "But you like it here?"

"I do. Most of the time."

"So what town are you from in Idaho?"

"McCall. It's a really small town. I'm sure you've never heard of it."

"You got me there. How small?"

"About 2,100." She re-crossed her legs in the opposite direction.

"Whoa. That's about the size of my senior class in high school!" Jake leaned back onto his elbows, extending his legs onto the warm, earthy soil. She couldn't help but glance at his body, laid out before her. She did her best to concentrate on the conversation.

"Yeah. Tiny. Not a lot going on there."

"So that's why you moved?" he asked. "Opportunity? Life in the big city?" Ellie thought it through. The entire morning, memories of Idaho triggered by the pungent smells of sage, prairie grass and heated earth had been plucking at her heartstrings.

"Opportunity. Yes. But a small town has its charms too. You know what to expect from people and it is perhaps the friendliest place I've ever been." If she didn't know better, she might even be experiencing home-sickness.

"So why'd you leave?" His question was open, nonjudgmental. She felt like telling him all about McCall, families that went back generations, the incredible outdoors and safety of small town living. But to be fair, she'd also have to mention the small-mindedness, the lack of diversity and employment opportunities for that matter.

"That's a long story for another time," she said.

"I'd like that," he responded, massaging his calf muscles while keeping his eyes on her.

"Like what?" she asked, completely distracted by his hands.

"Another time."

"I . . ." she thought about her idea of taking some time off from dating.

"You have a boyfriend?" His lips turned downward, suggesting disappointment.

"No, I . . ."

"You have a girlfriend?" The playful arch of his eyebrows suggested he was more accepting of this scenario.

"Sheesh, can I finish my sentence?" she laughed. "I don't have a boyfriend, and I'm heterosexual, thank you very much. And I'd love to have a conversation with you some other time," she admitted, surprising herself. "I'm just in a really busy period right now."

"We could exchange emails," he suggested. "Make contact when time allows."

"Okay. That'd be great. And you? No girlfriend?" She decided to check; hard to tell with these California boys.

"No. And an affirmative check in the hetero box as well." They were giggling now, and the boys, who had been enwrapped in talk about the Lakers team, seemed to hone in on the shift between their camp leader and lady ranger Ellie. They whispered amongst themselves and started their own round of giggling. As Ellie got ready to go, Jake extended his hand.

"Thanks again Ellie. It was a pleasure meeting you." They exchanged emails as covertly as possible with six boys looking on. Ellie said her goodbyes and walked down the trail with seven sets of eyes upon her.

Chapter 7

It was just before noon by the time Ellie got home. After a long, hot shower, she put on a floral dress and headed to downtown Santa Monica to do a little shopping before her hair appointment. She had only been to a few shops before she felt hunger pangs in her stomach. She was famished, but it was too late to sit down to lunch. She went to a juice bar and ordered a tropical smoothie to go before heading to the salon.

As she entered Coco's, she spied Arno sweeping up his station. Based on the long red curls filling the dustpan, his previous client had gone for a drastic change. She loved looking at Arno. A tall, well-built Dutch man with smooth skin, pale blue eyes and bleach blonde hair, he had a flair for clothing that put her fashion sense to shame. As if feeling her eyes on him, Arno turned in her direction.

"Ellie, darling, how are you?"

"Great!" she responded enthusiastically. He raised his eyebrows twice at her as he beckoned her to the chair with his hand.

"You look more than great! You're glowing," he noted, looking her over from head to toe as she settled into the chair. "I sense romance in the air."

"No, no, I wish." She let out a sigh. "I went on my first hike in Los Angeles."

"A hike in Los Angeles? Whatever do you mean?" he asked.

"I went to Temescal Gateway State Park. Have you heard of it?"

"I've heard of it, but I've never been. So you just hiked around the park?"

"No, there are trails that head out from the park. I actually got out in nature—did a four mile loop. Saw some wildlife."

"Mountain lions?" Arno joked.

"Three of them," she countered. "No, squirrels, a fox, rabbits."

"You saw a fox?"

"Sure looked like it."

"How adventurous!"

"Well, not really. Even though I went for an early hike, there were already people on the trail, including a group of kids." And a particularly handsome man, she thought to herself.

"I have to say that nature has certainly put a glow on you. And that dress is sizzling. Is it new?" Ellie nodded as he continued. "Perhaps you should get out there more often."

"You could go with me next time," she suggested. She tried to picture fashion God Arno on a trail.

"I'll stick with city pavement and the beach for my walks, thank you." He began to play with her hair as he looked at her through the mirror. "So, what are we doing for you today, darling? Trim and highlights?"

"Sounds perfect." He led her to the shampooing station and rubbed her neck and shoulders. As he massaged a vanilla almond shampoo into her scalp, she began to relax. She knew her love life was in trouble if a short massage from her hair stylist gave her so much pleasure. It was over too soon and she was back in the chair in front of the mirror staring at her wet mop of hair flowing over a purple gown. She didn't look nearly as sexy as she'd been feeling just moments before. As if sensing her thoughts, Arno launched into an all too familiar topic among friends.

"So Ellie, I met this fabulous guy last weekend, and unfortunately, he's straight." Ellie laughed as Arno sighed in disappointment.

"But, I figure my loss could be your gain." He started combing out her hair.

"That's very considerate of you Arno. But I'm taking a break from men just now."

"You know, that's just like asking the universe to provide you with a court of suitors. It's when you're not looking that the right guy will come along."

"You may be right about that," Ellie confessed

"Aha! So you have met someone!"

"Well, sort of." Ellie thought about Jake Tillerman. "I encountered a rather friendly man out on the trail this morning."

"You met some nature boy out there huh? Love and hiking boots."

"Sounds like the title of a terrible film!" Ellie laughed.

"So, do tell."

"Not much to tell, really." She pondered her morning and felt a rush of heat rise through her body. "I just happened to be on the trail at the same time as a teacher taking a group of kids hiking."

"A teacher, huh? I always had a thing for teachers. I'll never forget my high school math teacher, Mr. Bouma. Talk about a hotty!"

"I know what you mean about teachers. I had a crush on my high school English teacher, Mr. Jacobs. In retrospect, he wasn't that hot, he was just, brainy sexy."

"So about this teacher on the trail," Arno prompted.

"Well, he was more like a camp counselor, environmentalist type. I happened to come along when a child in his troop hurt his ankle and I had my first aid kit."

"Ellie. You have a whole other side you've been hiding from me! Hiker girl with a first aid kit. You're the heroine in the story! What, was it a Boy Scouts troop?" Ellie laughed inwardly.

"No, some sort of environmental program for kids."

"That's sexy. I mean, not the kids of course, but the idea of a guy who's out there saving the planet and educating kids."

"Yes. Definitely. I only spoke to him briefly, but I didn't get that he was an extremist or anything. He was just . . . nice."

"Nice?"

"Nice and kind of handsome, in that rough, unkempt sort of way." Ellie pictured his eyes again, and the heat of attraction that had run up her arm as they had shaken hands.

"A nice, handsome, environmentalist. Sounds like a trap, girl."

"Trap?" Ellie thought of his eyes again; somewhere between jade and emerald green, she decided.

"You never know with those types. He could be all uptight about the fact that you drive a car, highlight your hair, or grab a Starbucks."

"I didn't get that impression."

"Believe me, Ellie. I dated this guy once. What was his name? Oh yeah. Devon. He was a total environmentalist. Extremely idealistic. Gorgeous and all, but really difficult." Arno rolled his eyes as he started mixing colors. "We went shopping together once and he was appalled that I wanted to go to the mall. He rattled off facts about each store, citing their crimes against the environment and the use of sweat shops and child labor. I mean, of course I want to do the right thing, don't get me wrong, but sometimes, you just need a Nike sweatshirt, know what I mean?" Ellie started laughing.

"I know. It's just way too complicated to try to figure out what's okay and what's not. There are so many reports out there saying contradictory things."

"Exactly. Kind of leaves you feeling like you can't even use toilet paper without contributing to the planet's demise," he mused.

"That's where I draw the line," Ellie arched her eyebrows, sipping her smoothie. "But, really, I didn't get the sense that he was an extremist or anything. But, you know. Someone's got to be an extremist to pull us all off center a bit, and make changes."

"Yes. I suppose you have a point there. So did he get your phone number?"

"Email."

"Aha," Arno said, as he started to paint highlights into her hair, wrapping foil sheets in-between sections of color. "Speaking of environmentalists, what are you wearing to the big opening next weekend?"

"I have no idea. It's not really my type of show. I mean, I know it's important to support the arts, but I'd rather we go to the Getty than see this over the top eco stuff."

"I'm counting on you, girl."

"Are you sure you still want to go?" she asked Arno gently.

"I do. I don't care if I run into him or not. There's no guarantee he'll even be there."

"But Arno, if Javier is there, it might really hurt to see him; especially if he's with the new guy." Arno focused on Ellie's hair, working in silence. She wondered how long it would take him to get over his ex. He and Javier had gone out for over three years. Their break up, now four months old, had been the topic of their last three get-togethers.

"I think I'm ready to see him in his new life. And besides, with you by my side, it will feel just fine." This was Arno's not-so-subtle way of letting her know she wasn't getting off the hook. "So, we're on?" he asked as he moved on to the other side of her head.

"We're on," she replied. Arno let out a sigh of his own before launching into another topic.

"So about this guy I met. The straight one."

"I'm listening."

"His name is Joseph Santos. He's a gorgeous Latino man—lean, clean cut and muscular just like you like them."

"I've been telling you way too much Arno!"

"No darling. You're a mouse compared to most of my clients."

"He's thirty-two, never been married, and he's an author."

"What sort of author?" Ellie asked, mildly curious.

"I don't know. I think fiction. Could be wrong. But he's published."

"Yeah. Go on."

"Well, he's going to be there next weekend as well, and I'd like to introduce you."

"Like I said, I'm sort of taking a break from dating."

"So if nature boy asks you out for a shot of wheat grass are you going to say no?"

"Absolutely!" Ellie laughed. "But if he asked me out for a glass of wine, on the other hand," she started.

"Okay then. Then you can at least say hello to Joseph as well."

"I suppose I can."

By the time Arno was finished with her, she looked like model material.

"Is there a dress code beyond fancy for an eco-artist?"

"I suppose if you find a cocktail dress made out of recycled water bottles, you would be a total hit!" he teased. Ellie looked at him with dread. "No. Just wear something fancy. With all those functions you attend with the magazine, I know you have something to wear."

"Too bad the opening's not tonight. You really made my hair look fabulous." Ellie gave him a hug before leaving.

"I'll see you next Saturday and I'll pick you up at six o'clock sharp," Arno said, giving her a kiss on the cheek.

Ellie ordered Chinese take out and while she ate, thought bleakly over the collection of dresses in her closet. William's, she thought. After tossing the to-go box in the trash, she hopped in her car and headed to one of her favorite boutiques. But when she tried on a size-twelve black dress and looked in the mirror, it looked like many other dresses in her wardrobe.

"Do you have anything else black in my size? Something striking?" Ellie asked the salesclerk. Ellie waited in the dressing room while the saleswoman found another option.

"I know it's not black. But what about this?" she offered. Ellie pulled the deep emerald dress into the fitting room, gazing at it in surprise. Made of silk, the low cut dress was decorated with green and blue vines brocaded into the three quarter length sleeves. The vines wrapped around the bodice. A diamond cut in the front exposed a fair amount of cleavage, but a black pearl clasp pulled the dress back together, adding elegance.

"Well . . ." she hesitated, "I suppose I can try it on." A few moments later, she looked at herself in the mirror and was surprised at how flattering the cut was on her shape. Far sexier than she would usually dare, but still, the color was fabulous.

"How is that working out for you?" the salesclerk asked. Ellie stepped out of the dressing room hesitantly.

"That looks stunning on you," commented another woman in the dressing area. Two other women in the store turned around, marveling at Ellie. She looked at the price tag and swallowed.

"Any chance this is on sale?" Ellie asked quietly.

"I'm afraid not," responded the saleswoman. Ellie turned around in the dress, seeing herself from different angles. It was like it had been made for her and the color made her eyes sparkle, accentuating the green flecks mixed into the blue of her irises.

"That dress fits you like a glove," the saleswoman sighed. "How about ten percent off?"

"Okay. I'll take it," Ellie responded with resolve. She might not have a man in her life, but that didn't mean she couldn't look fabulous in the meantime.

Chapter 8

Jake walked into Castella Nursery, receiving a series of nods from the familiar faces of the employees as he headed back to the flower area. He walked casually up and down the rows, eyeing the rainbows of color nature had to offer up this time of year. He stopped in front of a crate filled with light pink Peonies. On the subtle side, but she would appreciate these, he thought. But then the vibrant yellow flowers on the next table pulled him in. According to the tag, these star-shaped beauties with a fiery red center were called Asiatic Lilies. He picked one out and headed to the check out stand.

"Time for your monthly date?" asked Jesse, the young blonde behind the counter who had been shamelessly flirting with him over the last couple of years. She had to be at least legal by now, Jake shamelessly thought. Just as quickly, he pushed the idea out of his head; way too young.

"Date, well, I suppose you could call it that," he responded, looking directly at her. He watched her cheeks flush over, just as they always did when he made eye contact. He couldn't help but smile at her response. He knew he had a decent enough build and a somewhat attractive face, but he had learned early on in life that it was his eyes that had such a strong effect on women: heart melting, hormone pumping responses that had given him easy access time and time again--all from an eye color. He wasn't complaining, but he found it hard to grasp. He could understand if it had been a particularly strong build that attracted them. Then it would at least make sense on a primal level—woman seeks strong man to provide for her and her offspring. But eyes? What did they have to do with attraction and reproduction of the human species? But then again, he understood it perfectly.

As he loaded the flowers into the trunk of his Toyota Prius and started his drive, he thought about a rather well-built woman he had met on the trail yesterday. Though not his usual type, when he looked into her baby blues dappled with green, she took his breath away. Funny thing was, he had seen her earlier that week; had looked directly into those eyes at that yuppie bar he and Conrad had hit up before dumpster diving. But he'd gotten the color wrong. Gray blue, he had guessed. And now he had the color down, as well as a name; Ellie Ashburn.

She clearly hadn't recognized him on the trail. Or if she did, she hadn't let on. Now that he thought about it, he hadn't recognized her at first either in her casual hiking gear, but when their eyes met, recognition, as well as instant attraction kicked in. And the email in his wallet proved the attraction was mutual.

He wondered if he should make use of Ellie Ashburn's email. He was so damned busy. And even though she was a beauty, there was something reserved about her that he couldn't quite place. On the other hand, she had a natural confidence that piqued his interest. She had graciously saved his ass by bandaging up Ignacio and dissipating the entire situation with her calm demeanor. And unlike the nineteen year-old at the nursery and countless other women, she didn't melt in his presence; a slight flush, maybe, but her confidence remained intact.

He crested the grade and dipped down into Thousands Oaks. The traffic was heavy, but he still had a chance of being on time to his "date" with an older woman. He'd have to save his ruminations on Ms. Ashburn for later.

He finally pulled off the freeway and made his way through the maze of the residential neighborhoods that had gone in over the last thirty years before reaching Orange Lane. Each house on the street boasted the gracious architectural craftsmanship of the late 1930s and early '40s. Their elegance and detailing were in stark contrast to the tight and boxy pre-fab houses just a few streets away that shot up during the post World War II building boom; or the uniform McMansions a few blocks further up. Silk Oaks reached forty feet into the air on Orange Lane, and their branches lined with silver gray leaves created a canopy of shade over the wide sidewalks and streets. Each ample front yard presented landscaped gardens that rivaled any landscape magazine cover shot—especially the front yard at 37 Orange Lane.

He hopped out of the car, retrieved the Lilies and walked along the stone path. The bright fuchsia flowers of the Hummingbird sage next to gold and orange poppies gave the garden a festive look. He stepped up to the wooden, screened in porch. She was waiting for him, gently swaying in the love seat. He noticed a loose board on the porch and made a mental note for his fix-it list.

"Hey Grandma," Jake smiled through the screen.

"Hey yourself. Late as usual." She unlatched the screen door and let him in.

"Flowers for you. They're called . . ."

"Asiatic Lilies," she filled in. "Beautiful, Jake. They'll look fantastic next to my desert bluebells over there. You can help me plant them this afternoon if you're game." He bent down and kissed her on the cheek before serving himself a glass of iced tea from the pitcher beside her.

"Of course I'll help. Need a refill?" he asked.

"No. But I do need to stretch my legs. And judging on the traffic report, you could use a stretch as well." Jake smiled. Leave it to Grandma to monitor my drive over, he thought to himself. Grandpa wouldn't be home for another 45 minutes, so they began rambling along Orange Lane and headed slowly into the surrounding neighborhoods. He liked to think of this area as the sedimentary rock of architecture; one architectural style gave way to another, creating a timeline of housing styles over the last seven decades. Perhaps this was why Jake had gone to architecture school; he had spent years walking and cycling through these very neighborhoods, developing tastes for different architectural vernaculars.

As they cut through Mr. Hanson's property that ran along the back of all the neighbors' lots, she asked Jake numerous questions about Gaia Eden and the boys in the program, and about his architectural work. After she was satisfied with all of his answers, she broached the topic of women, wanting to know if there were any in Jake's life that he was serious enough about to bring by for a visit. Not yet, Grandma was all he could muster. She brought him up to date on her life the last five weeks; the progress of her garden, what gramps had been up to, her consulting work on the charter flight business she had sold for a mint last year.

"And yes, I implemented your carbon offsetting idea for all international flights," she winked at him.

"You're fantastic grandma."

"So does this mean you'll take me up on my offer on a free flight now and then?" she asked. "Now that I've greened it up?"

"Yeah. Maybe," Jake smiled. As they settled back into their usual banter, Jake felt himself lightening up, letting go. Most of his friends dreaded the occasional visits to their grandparents, but Jake had the opposite problem; he loved visiting them, and it was getting harder and harder to make the time. The passing of his student's grandmother had been a wake-up call for him, causing him to keep his monthly appointment, despite how busy he was. They settled back on the front porch and sat, listening to the chirping dialogue between two Blue Jays in the Oak tree.

"You're staying for dinner aren't you?" she asked. Jake ran his fingers through his curls.

"I'd love to, but I have a lot of work to do this evening."

"Working on that online campaign against big oil?" she asked.

"Yeah. And there's a few grant applications due at the end of the week, and I have to talk to the city about the watering system for a pocket park we're designing, and . . ."

"Oh Jake. You can't do all of that tonight. I'll tell you what. You can put in an hour in my office while I get dinner together."

"What were you planning to make?" Jake asked, his mouth already watering as he thought over five of his favorite Grandma Jeanne recipes.

"Vegetarian pot pie and a salad fresh from the garden."

"That's entrapment. I'm in." Jake winked. He headed to the office, booted up his laptop and started plugging away. One item that had been on his mind on and off throughout the day should only take a few minutes to address; sending an email to ask Ms. Ellie Ashburn out for a date.

Chapter 9

Sunday morning, Ellie participated in her usual ritual of heading to Starbuck's with a copy of the Los Angeles times, a pair of scissors and a shoe box. She leisurely read through the paper. After working her way through the headlines, she opened the fashion section, cutting out Aidon Mattix dresses, bags by Gucci and a beautiful pair of wedges by Derek Lam. Originally $780, they were on sale for $276. Usually Gillian sat at the table across from her, and her reading and clipping was often interspersed with conversation. Gillian's absence enabled her to read the entire paper.

She devoured the art and culture section, noting a few plays she wanted to check out. Next she perused the classifieds with mild curiosity. One opening grabbed her attention: Public Relations Manager for The Literary Child. She wouldn't be where she was today if she hadn't been exposed to literature. After reading the short write-up about the non-profit, she clearly knew it was something she would like to support. She felt a wave of excitement as she imagined herself helping promote literature to children across America. She knew from experience that non-profit paid a fraction of what she could earn in the private sector, but she clipped it out anyway, throwing it into the shoe box. The little ad landed on top of one of the Aidon Mattix dresses she had clipped out, and she had to laugh. If I worked there, that would be the end of my fashion days, she thought.

When she found herself flipping through the real estate section, she realized it was probably time to give it a rest and decide what to do with the rest of her afternoon before Gillian got home.

Just then, a small article about Pacific West Holdings and a new industrial loft project caught her eye. There were so many trendy loft projects in L.A., she couldn't imagine the city needed another one, but nonetheless, this bit of information could come in handy. She clipped it out and threw it in the box.

When Ellie got back from her early evening run, she noticed a text message from Gillian; *Ono? 7pm?* I guess my quiet, contemplative weekend is over, Ellie sighed. She showered, changed and headed out the door.

◊◊◊

"Still alive I see," Gillian purred when she saw Ellie come into the restaurant.

"Of course," Ellie intoned, slightly annoyed. Gillian was joking, but sometimes it seemed like she really thought Ellie wouldn't survive without her.

"How's Arno?"

"Good." Ellie replied.

"Ha! So I'm right! You two went to a movie. You owe me a case of wine!"

"We didn't go to a movie. He did my hair."

"That's not out of the ordinary."

"No. I suppose not," Ellie reacted. Earlier, she had been eager to tell Gillian about the curiously handsome man she had met out hiking. But now she hesitated. Was it worth a case of her 2009 Forager Pinot Noir to keep it to herself? And then she realized she could keep her Forager and have Gillian's Carica Syrah if she played her cards right.

"Looks like I'll be transferring a few bottles to my side of the cellar," Gillian teased.

"But I did go hiking in the mountains of Los Angeles by myself Saturday morning," Ellie announced casually. Ellie noticed a spaghetti strap of white around Gillian's collar bone, suggesting she had spent the weekend sitting by the pool—not the most adventurous of pursuits.

"Hiking?" Gillian asked with a look of confusion on her face.

"You know: hiking boots, walking along a path through the chaparral, gazing from high-mountain vistas that make PCH look like a little silver ribbon along the coastline."

"You're not kidding, are you?"

"Do you think I could make something like that up?"

"Possibly, with your journalistic background. But wow, I'm impressed. I thought you had to break in hiking boots before you went out in them."

"I have an old pair," Ellie announced in a serene voice Gillian didn't recognize.

"Who are you and what've you done with my roommate?"

"She's right here," Ellie smiled confidently.

"Looks like I'll be transferring wine bottles after all, but not in the direction I was hoping," Gillian laughed.

As Ellie talked, she seemed calmer, more at ease. Usually she went on about some charity event, work, or men. But this evening, she talked about how good it felt to be out in nature again, and although she mentioned work a few times, she didn't say anything about men. Perhaps she was serious about taking a break from dating, Gillian mused.

"Oh. I wanted to let you know. I might extend my trip by a week or two," Gillian commented.

"You're going to be gone a whole month?" Ellie responded with surprise.

"Yeah. One of the benefits of being self employed. Flexibility," Gillian quipped.

"I'm afraid flexibility doesn't come with my benefits package," Ellie admitted.

"Oh. Did you get a chance to swing by the dry cleaners?" Gillian asked.

"Yes. Don't worry. I think the two of us alone are keeping that place in business," Ellie laughed. "And I also picked up some groceries at Safeway, including a crate of bottled water for each of us."

"Thank you! Such a good little house wife!" Gillian teased.

After they finished dinner, they both hopped in their cars. As Ellie drove home, she was amazed that she had kept so many of the details of her weekend to herself. She was so used to her routine with Gillian, but even a few days apart had given her a little breathing space she didn't even know she needed. A month was a long time, but perhaps it would do her some good to be on her own.

Chapter 10

Arno arrived on Ellie's doorstep at 5:54 p.m. Saturday night, ringing the doorbell his characteristic seven times.

"Come in!" she called. As he crossed the threshold, he gazed at Ellie.

"You look fantastic, darling! Where did you get that dress?"

"At Williams. Last one in the store." Arno let out a slow whistle.

"It gives you fairy princess eyes, like that shade of green was designed just for you! Not to mention that gorgeous cut."

"Thank you. Not too sexy?"

"It's classic and sexy all at once. Did Gillian make it to the airport all right?"

"Yep. I dropped her off this afternoon," Ellie reported. It felt strange already to have her gone.

"Then I get dibs on Thursday nights while she's away," Arno declared.

"Deal," Ellie agreed as she put on a shawl and placed her keys in a small black clutch.

"Oh no you don't!" Arno reprimanded, pulling at the shawl.

"What?" Ellie asked.

"Don't cover up your sexy self! You're on fire! You have a spark this evening. Embrace it!" Ellie bit her lower lip. She hadn't planned on going for sexy. "And to hell with your moratorium on men," Arno added. "You need to live a little."

"Live a little," she repeated aloud, mulling over the words. They drove in silence for a few miles as Ellie wondered if she lived enough. Her life felt pretty predictable: working hard, shopping and eating out, exercising, socializing, art openings, theatre, charity events. Life was pretty good, if she compared it to her upbringing. She could buy just about anything she desired. She had friends that adored her. She was surrounded by art and culture, and she was working her way up the ladder at work. What more was there? Volunteering? Spirituality? A wild fling? Love? Love. She looked over at Arno and wondered how he was doing.

"You are one handsome date," she surmised, admiring his elegant pinstriped suit replete with a yellow pocket square. "I think you're going to meet someone special tonight."

"How cliché," he retorted. "I certainly hope so." They headed to Studio City and pulled up in front of a contemporary building of steel and glass.

"Where's the valet parking?" he asked an employee.

"There's only valet parking for bicycles this evening, sir. However, there is a secure automobile lot two blocks away," the attendant explained, pointing.

"Oh this is going to be interesting," Arno chuckled as he turned toward Ellie. "You wait here while I go park my evil little gas-guzzling Carmengia."

Clearly the artist was popular as they had to wait in line to get in. When they finally reached the entrance they were greeted by two glamorous women in green sequined dresses with matching stilettos. They handed Arno and Ellie cloth napkins with a forest design signed by Earl Diamond, the artist.

"These are for your use this evening, and yours to keep. This is a waste-free event and Mr. Diamond encourages you to switch from paper to cloth," they chirped in unison.

"I hope there's t.p. in the bathroom," Ellie whispered to Arno mischievously.

"Multi-purpose cloth in your hand there, dear," he clamored.

A jazz quartet situated around a grand piano played a slow ballad. Ellie and Arno entered the room as the tenor sax player began a solo, his melancholy notes mingling with the din of conversation in the glass box gallery. Ellie wondered where the art pieces would be hung, considering there were no solid walls within view. Perhaps the entire show was the grotesque sculptures on four foot columns in the center of the room.

"There must be 200 people here," Ellie guessed as they maneuvered through the crowd.

"At least," he agreed. They noticed a sign made out of tree bark that said Locavore appetizers & Fair-Trade Wine with an arrow pointing to the hallway.

"What does Locavore mean?" Arno asked.

"I don't know, but I'm guessing it means locally made. Something like that?"

"Yeah. Something eco-chic, I'm sure. Talking about appetizing; check out that hunk in the crimson shirt, three o'clock." Arno gestured with his shoulder. Ellie casually turned her head, as if looking in the distance for someone she knew, and her eyes landed on a gorgeous African man with skin so black you could get lost in its velvety richness.

"Beautiful," Ellie agreed. "Ah, ring on his left hand."

"Doesn't hurt to look." In their ongoing game, it was now Ellie's turn. She scanned the room, taking in a crowd that was overwhelmingly younger in demographic, with pockets of 40 to 60 year olds. Ellie's eyes landed upon a fit man, perhaps in his mid to late thirties, with deep olive skin, medium length, black hair, a goatee and wire rimmed glasses. He looked like an Italian tennis player: athletic, handsome and kept, yet bristling with energy.

"By the grand piano with the red handkerchief in his breast pocket." Arno looked over, taking in the man Ellie had been studying.

"Oh my Goodness," Arno quipped. "Yes. That will do." They both laughed.

"Now there's a piece of art I could live with," Arno added. "In the corridor, next to the bathrooms, black suit. Ah. He just turned away."

"Where?" she asked.

"The one next to that beautiful Latina woman." Ellie followed his gaze. The tall man had a sleek yet muscular frame from the back, topped by an unruly head of dark curls. As he turned around, Ellie inhaled quickly. There was Jake Tillerman, the curious hiker man all dressed up, deep in conversation with the sexy woman at his side. She couldn't help but watch for a moment longer as the woman leaned in to kiss his cheek. Single, huh? Ellie sighed as she turned away.

"You sure know how to pick them, Arno."

"Hot. Huh? But taken. Lean and tall like you like them. But, a little on the wild side for your taste."

"That's nature boy."

"You're kidding me."

"Unfortunately, no." The disappointment burning in her cheeks caught her off guard. "He had asked me out for this evening. Perhaps to this very event," Ellie realized. "But obviously when I said no, he quickly moved on." A promising romantic seedling stomped upon, she thought.

"Oh, darling. He's just on a date; nothing wrong with that."

"I guess so," Ellie responded downheartedly.

"Upward and onward."

"Okay. I need to find a restroom and then we should go see this art collection," Ellie responded with resolve.

"Absolutely. Shall I get you something to drink?"

"Absolutely," she returned. "Something strong, if they have it."

"That's my girl. Have a drink and then we'll find Joseph."

"Who?" Ellie asked.

"That beautiful man I told you about last week? The author?"

"Arno. Let me get over my short-lived fantasy about hiker boy before you throw me so easily to someone else."

As she stood in the long line to the women's restroom, she concentrated her attention on the fluorescent painting right in front of her. Bold geometric shapes in neon green and hot pink intersected with random raindrops of burnt oranges and deep reds that cascaded across the canvas, creating a strange tension. A small sign near the base of the painting gave the title, Sunset Ex Machina. She looked back at the painting, trying to make the title and the artwork jive in her mind.

Ex Machina pulled at her memories of courses on Greek Tragedy and a technique used in the theater to lower a God or Goddess from the heavens onto the stage.

"Hello Ellie," a voice came from beside her. She looked up to see an all too familiar face too close for comfort.

"Hello," she replied, surprised at the coldness in her voice.

"James. James Hadley. We met last week at La Maison."

"How could I forget?" she pulled upon her acting skills to conjure up a smile. First the attractive hiker with a girlfriend and now her shortest date ever. What was going on with this opening?

"What a coincidence to see you here," James noted cordially. She had seen enough of what lay beneath his pleasant veneer to know she wanted nothing more to do with him, but her silence did nothing to discourage him. "Ellie, I just want to apologize for my behavior the other night," he demurred. "I don't know what got into me. I think I was just nervous." He paused for a moment, clearing his throat. "You're a very attractive woman. Certainly, I'm not the first guy to go stupid in your presence." Ellie felt herself blush. Part of her wished for her shawl to cover herself up.

"Well, no, I, well, thank you," she stammered. A woman in line turned slightly toward her with a smile, clearly pleased to hear a man saying the right thing.

"So, a fresh start then?" he asked, with a slight pleading in his eyes. Ellie knew with certainty she would never date this man. She raised her eyebrows, giving him no further response. James Hadley hovered awkwardly before her, uncertain of how to proceed.

"Okay. So," he stammered. "What do you think of Earl Diamond's art?"

"I just arrived, and I've only had a chance to look at a few pieces here in the hallway. But, I really like this one," she said, pointing to Sunset Ex Machina.

"That's a demanding piece," he responded. She didn't want to start a conversation with him, but his comment made her curious. Was he into art?

"Demanding. How so?" she asked tentatively.

"Well, it feels so incongruous it's hard to look at. It grates on your nerves."

"I actually like the tension in it," she countered, looking at the painting again. "It feels like a Wednesday evening."

"A Wednesday evening?" he asked, looking at her curiously with his bright blue eyes.

"Yes. I can't really explain that." She couldn't help but smile.

"Try."

"Try. Okay. I'm just going to wing it, here."

"Please!"

"Here goes. On Wednesday, you're halfway through the week and there's forward momentum to sensing freedom and creativity. That's the red and orange splatter there. And there's this structure that underlies your existence—you know, patterns in life, work, responsibilities—that's represented in the neon shapes." She paused for a moment and he didn't interrupt. "But the tension of course is about our contemporary lifestyle and the conflict with the natural world." James stared at her, dumbfounded.

"I think that's brilliant."

"Brilliant?" she smiled. A group of women came out of the restroom and the attendant waved Ellie and three other women in.

"To be continued," James suggested hopefully as she disappeared into the restroom.

Four wooden outhouses stood in the middle of the bathroom, two labeled solids, the other two liquids. Ellie looked on in dismay.

"Outhouses?" an older woman exclaimed as she brought her hand to her mouth.

"This sign explains it. They're composting toilets," her friend responded.

"You've got to be kidding me," a young woman in a cocktail dress chimed in. Like four women caught in a catastrophe, they seemed to bond together in trying to take the best plan of action.

"I guess this is an interactive art experience," Ellie commented. The women laughed nervously in response. The only standard flush toilet stood by itself in the room. Mirrors ran the length of the bathroom, which left you in the rather awkward position of being seen half naked by everyone in the room if you chose the standard flush toilet. No wonder the line was so long. They had to make decisions. Ellie wasn't about to go in an outhouse in a four hundred dollar dress. She swallowed her pride and went to open the seat of the flush toilet only to realize it was sealed shut. Another round of nervous laughter filled the room as the women realized they had no choice but to *experience the art.*

When Ellie entered the stall of the compostable toilet, she was relieved to discover toilet paper. And it was surprisingly clean inside; not like an old outhouse in a campground covered with flies. The "seat covers," however, made her squirm. Not paper seat covers, but long strips of compostable eucalyptus bark. After she washed her hands, she searched for something to dry them with, displeased that there were no paper towels. Several other women had retrieved the custom printed cloth towels, and Ellie pulled hers out of her purse. She noticed the metal d-ring on the towel, which was obviously meant to loop onto a bag. Now that would look lovely hanging off my five hundred dollar clutch, she thought to herself as she left the restroom. James hovered by the entrance.

"Ah, there you are. Can I get you a drink?"

"No thank you," Ellie replied calmly, "My friend is already getting me a drink."

"Oh," James said as Ellie started back into the grand room. He walked beside her tentatively, as if asking permission to follow. She did nothing to encourage him. "Did you study art in school?" he asked.

"No," she responded. How could someone be so different? Last Tuesday he was stiff, accusatory, defensive. Tonight he was all charm. Had he forgotten to take his medication last week? Either way, she certainly didn't want to encourage him.

"Oh, that's right. You must have studied advertising or a related field?"

"English Lit and journalism, actually. Double major."

"Brilliant. That's why you have a way with words." More flattery, she noted.

"Well, I do talk to people all day long and I used to be a journalist." Why am I sharing anything personal with him? She asked herself. But it wasn't in her nature to hold a grudge either.

"That makes sense," he concluded. Ellie looked around and saw Arno in rapt conversation with the sexy Italian tennis player guy.

"There's my friend. Nice to see you again James. Have a nice evening," she said politely before bee-lining it for Arno. Luckily James took the hint and didn't follow.

Even from a distance she could see the clear chemistry developing between the two men, and she didn't want to disturb them. But Arno waved her over. The handsome man named Pierre was French and not at all Italian, but, it ended up, was a tennis player and extremely knowledgeable about wine.

"Ellie and I met at a wine tasting three years ago," Arno remarked by way of introduction, "and we've been fast friends ever since." They talked about wine for thirty minutes before the sculptures right in front of them all but demanded their attention. Large tree stumps covered in forest moss balanced precariously on the pedestals, the ringed surfaces polished to smooth perfection. Puddles of bubbling red liquid spewed from the center of the stumps like fresh blood spurting from a wound. The crimson waterfall spattered down the side of the trunks and circulated back through with the soothing sound of a fountain. Paper products, from tissues and throw away cups to greeting cards were stapled to the tree stumps. Post-it notes created a pattern on another side. It was both gruesome and intriguing.

"Clearly, he wants us to never print out another email," Ellie commented.

"I never thought I'd feel guilty about a Post-it note. But here I am," Arno commented.

"Or a tissue," Pierre said. "Speaking of which; where are the restrooms?"

"Over there," Ellie pointed. "Enjoy the compostable toilets," she winked.

"Love is in the air," Ellie announced once Pierre was out of earshot.

"There you go with that sappy talk again. But keep it up, girl. Remember what you said earlier about me meeting someone special tonight? I think I just did."

"Pierre is a beautiful man, Arno. But, please take it slowly. You're still fragile."

"Don't worry about me sweetheart. I can take care of myself." Arno gave her a cheerful, elated hug before continuing. "Oh. I also got a text from Joseph. He's not coming tonight after all."

"Not a problem, Arno. I'm not in the mood to be set up on a date right now anyway."

"Okay. Fair enough. But Ellie, I have a favor to ask you. And please, if I'm a rude bitch, you just say so."

"Go on."

"Any chance you can catch a cab home?"

"A cab? You rude bitch!" she laughed.

"No. It's just that . . ."

"I get it. I get it. He's hot. You go for it."

Chapter 11

Her day had been such an emotional roller coaster that Ellie decided a little time in an anonymous crowd might be just the thing to soothe her nerves. No conversation, no expectations, just the sensation of being part of the something bigger. As she searched for the appetizer table, she did something out of the ordinary and indulged in a third glass of wine. I'll be taking a cab home after all, she justified to herself. The crowd was still growing and the gallery staff had clearly not ordered enough *locavore organic appetizers* as the food table was decimated by the time she found it. She placed the remaining three carrot sticks and two crackers on her napkin— hardly enough food to combat the wine swimming through her veins.

As she moved on to another painting, she looked up and her eyes fell upon the environmentalist Jake Tillerman. This time he was standing by himself. The wine had numbed away any apprehension she had experienced earlier and she took in his form as if looking at another piece of artwork. The top button of his shirt was undone, exposing the contours of his chest. She felt the heat of attraction rising in her body mingling with the alcohol; a dangerous combination. As if feeling her eyes on him, he turned in her direction and when their eyes met, he gave her a simple smile. As if sizing up the situation, neither of them moved for a moment. It was Jake who finally broke formation and headed toward her. She took a deep belly breath as he approached, exhaling slowly.

"Hi Ellie," he greeted, reaching for her hand. As they shook hands he smiled sheepishly. "This is the very event I wanted to invite you to, and here you are. What are the chances?"

"Hi Jake."

"You look fabulous," he added, taking in her curves accentuated by the deep emerald dress.

"You brush up pretty nicely yourself," she responded, surprised at the slowness of her words. Jake laughed at her comment.

"The only suit I own," he admitted. The ease of their conversation returned, but Ellie couldn't ignore what she'd witnessed earlier.

"So Jake. Where's your girlfriend?" she asked slowly.

"My girlfriend?" he repeated, puzzled. She inhaled, trying to clear the fog in her head.

"Remember, that beautiful Latina girl that was kissing you?" she clarified.

"Oh, you mean Natalia," Jake responded, breaking into a broad smile. "No. Not my girlfriend, but yes, I did come with her tonight. She's a co-worker, a friend."

"Oh." Ellie looked at him, thinking about the kiss she had witnessed. She'd heard about those types of friends. Just then, Natalia appeared and headed toward them.

"Natalia, I want you to meet Ellie Ashburn." She was impressed he had remembered her last name.

"Nice to meet you Ellie!" Natalia bubbled in a peppy voice. "Beautiful dress!"

"Thank you," Ellie responded warily.

"We're having a little debate, and I was wondering if you can clear something up for us."

"I can try," Natalia said, flipping her long black hair away from her eyes.

"Ellie thinks you're my girlfriend," Jake casually announced. Natalia squealed.

"Sorry to disappoint. But, no way. Not Jakey." She leaned in and kissed his cheek, just as Ellie had seen her do earlier that evening; "gorgeous, but not my type." She ran her hand across his chest playfully. "Jake, I'm going to take off. Mary just texted me and we're going to go to the rally workshop over at UCLA."

"Great. That's awesome." Jake hesitated, stealing a wistful glance at Ellie before finishing his sentence. "How late are you guys working tonight?"

"No. You're not coming. You've done enough good work for one day. For God's sake Jake, take a night off!" She gave him a slight nudge in Ellie's direction.

Natalia leaned in toward Ellie. "He's a good guy. Go for it," she whispered with a wink. She was gone before Ellie could respond. Jake looked her over, and led her to a bench in the middle of the main gallery room, just as a couple vacated it.

"I think you're a little tipsy, Ms. Ashburn," he surmised.

"I think I am too." She took a deep breath, exhaling slowly. "Listen, I'm sorry if I was a little rude just now," she said, pointing vaguely toward the hallway.

"You weren't." His smile was hypnotizing.

"How is Ignacio, anyway?" Ellie asked, changing the subject. The shrill laughter of two women behind them prompted Jake to lean in closer to hear.

"He's doing just fine. Thanks for asking. And, thanks again for having it so together out there last week." He took a sip of wine as the women behind them raised their conversation another decibel.

"Oh. Well. It was just luck, really," she began to explain before her voice trailed off. Jake looked at the plate in her hand, which held one tiny carrot.

"I think you could use some real food," he half shouted. Ellie knew he was right. Not only was she hungry, but she knew she was more than tipsy. And based on the hoots and hollers, the crowd around them was getting smashed.

"Yes. I'm starving."

"You want to get out of here and get some dinner?" Jake asked suddenly. Ellie was caught somewhere between speechless and dizzy at the prospect of dining with Jake Tillerman.

"Yes. That would be great," she managed.

"Did you drive?"

"No."

"Are you on a bike?"

"On a bike?" Ellie asked, confused. She was in a silk dress and three inch heels and Jake was asking if she was on a bike. "Do I look like I am on a bike?"

"No. Absolutely not. Sorry."

Then she remembered the bicycle-only valet parking. Cycling to posh events was a new sort of trend, she guessed, but pretty impractical in the city.

"Oh, I'm planning to take a cab home," Ellie explained.

"Gotcha," he responded as they headed for the door. "I know a great restaurant within walking distance."

Chapter 12

A few hours ago, Ellie had written him off as another slippery L.A. man. Now, leaving the gallery with Jake Tillerman seemed like the most natural thing in the world. Even though she didn't know Natalia from Eve, she felt comfort in having another woman deem Jake a good guy, something she already instinctively felt.

They headed to a neighborhood restaurant and sat down at a small table in the back. Conversation flowed easily between them and Ellie learned that he was the founder of Gaia Eden, and had three employees, Natalia being one, who helped him run a series of programs and environmental actions. He asked her about herself in the same non-judgmental way he had on the trail, as if he was genuinely interested in getting to know her. He had not only heard of Duomo Magazine, but he had read a few issues. Conversation circled naturally back to the opening.

"So what did you think of Diamond's artwork?" Jake asked.

"Over the top. I absolutely hated the bleeding trees," Ellie started. "Very clear message about paper consumption, but extremely aggressive." She scanned the show in her mind. "I also found the compostable toilets ridiculous. They belong in the forest, not here. It's not like you could introduce such simple technology in a large metropolis." Jake's eyebrows rose slightly as he listened.

"Was there anything you liked?" he asked, steadfast.

"Well, yes. Quite a few of his paintings impressed me," she responded. They discussed paintings as if they still stood in front of them. Jake listened intently as she waded through her thoughts. Each time, Jake recalled details she hadn't noticed, or brought a much more positive interpretation to the work. In the painting of a clear cut forest, he recalled the tiny new trees growing in the clearing. In the fatalistic stump sculptures that looked like bleeding trees, he saw a wake up call for change.

"And if you had to choose one as your favorite?" she asked.

"That would be Green," Jake stated.

"Green. Which one was that?" Ellie asked, taking in the hue of his eyes.

"It's the one of a half naked woman, gazing out into the city, half emerged in thick vines."

"I remember that one." The painting had disturbed her when she first gazed at it, like something that gets under your skin, threatening to slowly work away at your foundation "It was beautiful, romantic even, but depressing," she concluded, wondering how it could be his favorite.

"Depressing? How so?" Jake asked.

"It was like this woman was trapped, being devoured by nature so slowly she didn't even know it was happening," Ellie surmised. A small shiver made its way up her back.

"Interesting interpretation, but I had a different take," he responded, smiling at her across the table.

"Which was?" she questioned curiously.

"Well, I think it's about a love affair between Mother Nature and contemporary society. It's like the artist is romanticizing nature and urban life together; offering hope that the two can co-exist, given certain boundaries of course."

Ellie heard the hope in his voice. How could they both look at the same painting and see something so differently?

"Wow. We had totally different lenses on tonight," she observed.

"I guess so. I had on rose colored glasses, and you . . . blue," he teased.

Ellie realized that she was having fun; with an environmentalist.

"What?" he asked. She must have had a smirk on her face. Observant too, she thought.

"Well, it makes sense that you'd be the optimist. Otherwise, how could you be so energized as an environmentalist?"

"It's not just about being an environmentalist. Hang around me long enough and you'll see it's my approach to life; cup's half full."

They were so absorbed in conversation, that they didn't notice the restaurant was getting ready to close until the waitress dropped off the check. They started walking back the way they came in a comfortable silence, passing other groups of people on the street. Those blue eyes transfixed him and he knew he wanted more than conversation with Ms. Ashburn.

"Ellie. I live four blocks from here. Do you want to come over and just hang out for a bit?" Ellie pondered his invitation. Arno's words came back to her; *live a little.*

"I'd like that," she concluded, surprised by her choice.

"Then we need to head this way." He placed his hand on the small of her back, changing their direction. She liked the way he touched her gently, yet respectfully. His hand came back to his side as they walked down the street together.

As she walked beside him, she felt longing in her body for physical contact. She tried to focus on the present moment.

"What did Natalia mean when she said you did enough good work for today?"

"Well, we've been working day and night on a grass roots action campaign against the BP oil spill off the gulf coast."

"A total catastrophe," Ellie responded. "What sort of things are you doing?"

"We've been working on an online campaign, encouraging people to make seven environmental changes in their lives for one month in protest of the oil spill," he started. Ellie knew she was in for it. Not only was he incredibly sexy, but he was out doing good in the world for kids and for the environment.

"What are the changes? Stop driving your car, I imagine, is on there."

"Yeah. Reduce car use and use alternative transport. We can't exactly ask people to give it up, but you know. Consciously get out of your car and take the bus, walk, ride a bike, whatever it takes."

"And the other six?" Ellie asked.

"Choose local produce, use cloth bags, launder in cold water, stay within a 100 mile radius and use alternative transportation, reusable cups, seven-minute showers or less."

"That's sounds challenging, but doable." Ellie knew she was in trouble when launder in cold water sounded sexy rolling off his tongue. "Except living without my car, and the seven minute shower part," she added for good measure.

"You could still take the challenge," Jake suggested. "You don't have to do all of those things, or do the whole month—just as long as you want," he clarified.

"I could do it for a week," she remarked before giving it too much thought.

"Awesome! I'll email you the link. If we get enough people to sign up who enroll for a month, there's a potential matching grant for our program." Ellie took in his genuine enthusiasm for a cause, feeling another layer of attraction building. They stopped at a corner to wait for a light.

"Ellie, can I . . ." he leaned in, kissing her gently on the lips. She pressed into him and kissed him back. Apparently, she wasn't the only one who was preoccupied. They lingered in each other's arms, both slightly surprised. He seemed almost nervous.

"Wow. Why do I feel like a teenager right now?" Jake asked her.

"You and me both!" she responded lightly.

"So, I'm going to hold your hand all the way home," he announced.

"You're about sixteen right now!" Ellie laughed.

"That's generous. I was feeling about fourteen," he joked. Ellie liked the warmth of his hand, surprised at how easily her hand slipped into his, how natural it felt. As they walked, they talked about her impressions of California and what it was like growing up in Idaho. She had grown accustomed to editing her early life story into a more cheerful version, and the conversation flowed along until he asked about hunting.

"You actually pulled the trigger?"

"Yes. Many times," she thought back to her hunting days. "That's the sobering part of the experience—being in touch with the life force you are about to take, being fully accountable for the food you eat—not like picking up an unidentifiable slab of packaged meat in the grocery store. You intimately know each part of the deer or elk or rabbit, for that matter. And it tastes amazing."

"Wow. When was the last time you killed a deer?"

"My brothers' still hunt, but I haven't been since I was twenty-three or twenty-four," she responded. "Doesn't mean I won't do it again, given the chance." Ellie looked over at him, and noticed the creases on his forehead. "Oh wait. Are you a vegetarian? Is this like, impossibly difficult for you to hear?" Ellie exclaimed. Great Ellie. Scare off the first decent man you've met by admitting you're a cold-blooded animal killer.

"Well. Yeah, I'm a vegetarian, and I don't like hunting." Bizarre, he thought. Yet at the same time, he was genuinely impressed. This sophisticated, highly educated woman before him with an upscale job was also a hunter who could most likely survive better in the wilderness than he could. The idea worked its way through him. "I'm a vegetarian because of the way animals are treated in the industrial food chain. What you're talking about is a totally different thing."

"I'm glad you can see that," Ellie giggled.

"What's so funny?"

"Well, it's just, I've lived here for about three years and no one has ever asked me if I hunted. I don't think anyone I know here even knows that about me. And, what, I've known you for a few hours?"

"At least a week now," Jake quipped. They were approaching a beautiful old craftsman-style home made of dark wood with red detailing when Jake slowed his pace.

"We're here." Jake kissed her again, sending another wave of heat coursing through her body. His hands glided gently across her shoulders as he explored her lips. When his tongue pressed into her mouth she pressed just as eagerly back. After a few minutes they came up for air. He opened a gate at the side of the house, and Ellie paused as her mind and body fired off a barrage of conflicting messages.

"Jake, I need to be clear about something before we head into your house," she started.

"Okay. Shoot." Ellie took in a deep breath. She turned toward him so that their bodies faced one another. She felt the warmth of his large hand, still holding hers.

"I want to take it slowly. I need to let you know that, so you know, there aren't any expectations, despite that lovely dinner and that incredible kiss, and this. God; this heat I feel between us." Her body shook as she talked. "Lord, its like someone slipped a truth serum into my wine!" she laughed. "Major mixed messages, I know."

Jake looked at her with an expression she couldn't quite interpret—somewhere between desire and curiosity. He pulled her a little closer.

"Thanks for being honest, Ellie. Seriously," he squeezed her hand gently. He looked into her eyes as he continued. The soft ocher light of the streetlamp backlit her long hair, the green flecks in her eyes shimmering slightly. "I have to say that my body is in complete agreement with yours. I feel the sexual tension between us." Ellie's heart raced at his words. "But you have no idea how happy I am to hear a woman say she wants to take it slow. I think it's a good idea to get to know someone first. The rest will work itself out."

She could see a physical shift within him, as if his body was adjusting to the news. "But, kissing is okay, right? Kissing's not the gateway drug to sex," he remarked.

"I suppose we could kiss a little more," she smiled. Jake held the gate open for her and they walked down a little path hand in hand to a small bungalow in back.

Chapter 13

The bungalow was warm and had a subtle, earthy smell that reminded her of college. She dropped her clutch on the coffee table in the small front room. He kicked off his shoes and placed them in a shoe rack just inside the door, and she followed suit.

"What a quaint little place," she commented as her bare feet touched the smooth hardwood floor. Quaint wasn't quite the right word. Clearly, he lived frugally. Besides a new canvas couch, the furniture seemed old and slightly worn. Yet there was something orderly and tasteful in the way everything was placed.

"Thank you. Do you want the forty-five second tour?"

"Or, perhaps the deluxe tour?" She suggested.

"That is the deluxe tour," he laughed, taking her hand. "This is the living room with hall / galley kitchen," he pointed. "That over there is the bathroom; bedroom next to the bath, office on the other side of the bath. And back here," he said, as he led her through the kitchen and out a sliding glass door, "is the garden, back deck, garage and compostable toilet."

"Oh my God!" Ellie laughed. "Compostable toilet? You're serious? Is that even legal?"

"I didn't bother to find out. Want to try it out?" he asked slyly.

"No thanks. I already tried one earlier this evening at the art opening," she scoffed. My God. This wasn't some environmentalist poser, she mused, but the real deal. Usually this would send her running in the other direction, but the heat of his kiss still lingering on her lips seemed to be burning away her usual boundaries. An extensive vegetable garden filled the back yard surrounding a small raised deck, and a detached garage connected to the rear alley. His entire place, including the garden, was about a fifth of the size of the house she shared with Gillian.

"Seems perfect for a bachelor," she commented, trying to sound positive.

"I know it's small; 650 square feet small. But believe it or not, a family of four lived here before I did; for nineteen years."

"Wow." She tried to imagine four people cohabitating in this small of a space.

"Tea?" he asked, as he touched her arm.

"Sure," Ellie responded. He turned on his iPod before he went into the kitchen to start the kettle. A Brazilian samba filled the air as she sat on the couch in the living room and picked up a book; *The Omnivore's Dilemma, by Michael Pollan.* So what is the dilemma, she wondered. She flipped it over and read the back cover before setting it down. A guitar sat in the corner on a stand next to an extensive collection of CDs.

"Have you read it?" Jake asked as he set a steaming pot of tea and two mugs on the table.

"No, but I've seen his name all over the New York Times Bestseller list."

"You can borrow it if you'd like."

"I love meat too much," she quipped, in response to what was on the back cover.

"That's a perfect reason to read it," he responded encouragingly. "Based on the way you described your hunting experience, how you honored the animal, I think you'll relate to this book." Ellie took in his comment, surprised at how he seemed to get her. But on the other hand, she didn't want any moral lectures on what she should and shouldn't eat.

"I'll borrow it sometime," she responded noncommittally as she scanned other titles on his bookshelf. The majority of the titles were non-fiction and either had to do with politics, environmental activism or nature. Jake sat on the couch beside her. Ellie took in his wild curls, his slightly rugged appearance. As he poured her a cup of steaming hot tea, she had an overwhelming desire to kiss him. Deep inside of her, she felt a momentary connection with the appeal of a one night stand. Her body felt primal, as if she were simply an animal being driven by an inherent biological force. Have sex. Take in his seed. Reproduce. She lifted the cup of tea her lips, closing her eyes as she sipped, exploring the primal sensation.

As she sat beside him with her eyes closed, Jake took the moment to study her. She seemed particularly sensual: barefoot in her beautiful green silk dress, eyes closed, sitting on his canvas couch. He wondered what she was thinking about. If she had been a different woman, they would be on their way to his bedroom, enjoying a night of casual sex. He'd had a number of girls like that. They were attracted to him based on his looks and not really interested in any depth, yet crumbled like wilting flowers when he ended the sexual liaison, as if they thought sex equaled love and commitment.

Ellie was clearly attracted to him, but wanted more. This already felt different, respectful. He liked the way she spoke with subtle confidence. She didn't try to impress him, or pretend to be someone she was not.

"Ellie, tell me more about you."

"Just like that? Some sort of monologue?" she countered. "Sorry, you're going to have to engage in conversation if you want to get to know me." She stretched out her foot and placed her toes on his. Jake laughed. There it was again; confidence, flirtation. God, do I want this woman, he thought. But the idea that he would have to earn her over time made her that much more attractive. Just then, he thought about a way to get to know her that would add some lightness to the evening.

"Okay. Okay. How about a good old fashioned game of truth or dare?"

"Truth or dare?" Ellie frowned. "That's a little childish, don't you think?" Yes. Definitely more of a college guy then the young professionals she had been dating.

"What's wrong with that? Don't you ever explore your inner child? That's required if you live in Southern California," he teased.

He sat close to her and she caught that faint scent again, reminding her of damp pine needles and sandstone. A game of truth or dare with just the two of them could quickly lead into uncharted territory. She took another sip of her tea.

"Well, I'm a bit rusty. It's been a few decades since I played."

"Really. No truth or dare games during college?"

"Ah, well, you might have a point there," she mused.

"So?"

"Okay. Shoot!" Ellie laughed.

"Truth or dare?"

"Truth," she said.

"Did you vote for McCain or Obama?"

"Obama, but Hillary in the primaries," Ellie stated.

"Good. Good."

It was her turn. She tried to think of something she wanted to know about Jake Tillerman and wondered what she'd do if he said dare.

"Truth," he responded.

"Have you ever been arrested?" she asked.

"Yeah," Jake responded. "Lots of times. For protesting: environmental protests during college and one time protesting the Iraq war."

"A regular criminal," Ellie commented.

"Let's see, my turn. Truth or dare?"

"Truth," Ellie chose carefully.

"Are you a rugged Idaho girl disguised as an attractive, intellectual city girl?" he inquired, a serious look on his face.

"That is one of the strangest questions I've ever heard. I don't know how to answer that." She ran her fingers up the length of his arm, stopping just below his shoulder. "I am what I am. I'm both. I've lived both lives. To be honest, last Saturday was the first time I went hiking since I moved here."

"Seriously?"

"Seriously."

"But, you were clearly in your element out there," Jake stated as he brushed his finger against her cheek. Ellie took in a breath, trying to keep calm.

"I was. But that trail was pretty tame. Not like an extended backpacking trip."

"I've been camping a few times," he said, his smooth persona cracking slightly.

"Like how many times? What's the longest hiking trip you've done?" she asked coyly.

"I'm a city boy who happens to be an environmentalist," Jake dodged, "The ocean is my wilderness—right off shore."

"Have you done an overnight?" Ellie stayed on track.

"Of course."

"When was the last time?" she questioned, rising her eyebrows.

"Okay. Okay. More tea?" he dodged again.

"No thank you. Answer the question," she responded in a mock interrogational voice.

"Three nights. High school. Sophomore year with some of my buddies." Jake grinned broadly as he thought about his adventure with his friends so long ago. He'd felt invincible back then. They all had.

"How was it?" Ellie asked. She tried to picture Jake as a younger man, wondering what he was like.

"It rained on us. It was freaking cold, and although we had plenty of beer, we didn't pack enough food or water. And we didn't sleep; heard all of these strange noises all night long that kept us up."

"Sounds frightening," Ellie said playfully.

"And you? What was your longest backpacking trip?" he asked.

"Fourteen days along the Pacific Crest Trail."

"Holy shit. You don't mess around," Jake responded. How could she *not* be an environmentalist, he wondered.

They talked for hours, sharing stories, laughing, kissing. He learned that she had grown up on a farm, that she had once won a fishing competition, that she received top marks in her school. Everything about her was a contradiction. Where was the farm girl now, he wondered, as he breathed in the heady jasmine scent of her expensive perfume. He turned toward her, taking her hand. His deep green eyes shone in the candlelight as he spoke.

"You're not afraid to state your opinion. Not intimidated. I like that in a woman."

She wasn't intimidated by him, but more by the physical desire coursing through her body that seemed to be growing by the second. Live a little, she repeated to herself. She took his left hand and brought it to her breast. Jake looked at her in surprise.

"You sure you want to go there?" he whispered into her ear. The flood of messages coming from her conscience grew fainter, losing its resonance as she listened to her body.

"Yes," she responded in a whisper. He kissed her with more urgency as he ran his hand along the curves of her body, and she kissed him just as passionately back. It was clear they wanted the same thing. Jake lifted the candle from the table, accidentally knocking over one of the tea cups as he led her toward his bedroom. She made a move to pick it up, but he shook his head no as he pulled her to him. He caressed her arms and ribcage. Her hands shook as she quickly worked down the row of buttons on his shirt. Her dress was easy for him to slip off and within moments she stood in front of him in her lacy bra and underwear.

As the weight of his body pressed her firmly into the mattress, both fear and desire coursed through her.

"God you're beautiful," he said as he looked at her.

"So are you," Ellie murmured. He kissed her from head to toe, skillfully removing her panties and bra. Before long, he found himself entering her slowly; letting her body adjust to his size. He looked into her eyes to gauge her reaction. At first, she felt so tight, he wondered if it hurt her, but soon warmth and wetness enveloped him as she arched her hips toward him. She inhaled sharply as he moved deeper into her. They did not break eye contact as they fell into rhythm. Waves of excitement washed through him before he realized what he was doing.

"God Ellie. Hold on, I need to put on a condom," he said, pulling out of her. He gently worked his way back in as he watched her facial expressions in the candlelight. They moved smoothly together, working back into a rhythm. Her breaths grew shorter as she gave herself over completely to the wave forming in her body. And as it crested, she felt him pulsing within her.

She closed her eyes, aware of the heat and sweat of their bodies mingling together. So this is bliss, she thought. This is what it feels like to fully concede to desire. She looked at Jake hoping to find a mirror of her happiness, but he was twisting one of his curls, just as he had done on the trail when one of the kids got injured.

"Are you okay?" she questioned softly.

"I've never forgotten to put a condom on." There it was. Reality pulling her back down.

"Okay. That's not good. But you did end up putting it on in time, right?"

"Yeah, yeah," he sighed as he stroked her cheek. "I was just so caught up in you." Ellie's breath caught at his words.

"So was I. I didn't know it could be like this," she whispered.

"How do you mean?" Jake was still lying on top of her, looking into her eyes.

"The physicality. I disappeared into you, Jake. My thoughts, my inhibitions. Everything was gone. God knew what he was doing when he designed sex." As Jake listened, it was as if she had just described what he had gone through. The tenderness in her voice made him want her all over again.

"Sex is a biological force that keeps the human species alive," he countered, in an attempt to push the strange emotions coursing through him aside. He touched her cheek curiously. He knew so little about her. Was she religious? He traced his finger down her body, wondering if this would develop into anything. He noticed her skin was getting cool and he pulled the comforter over them. He thought again about how late he had put the condom on.

"I want you to know that I'm clean. I got tested three months ago and haven't been with anyone since. Well, until now that is."

"Thanks for letting me know," Ellie responded. "I, well, um. I'm clean too. It's been a long while since I've been with someone."

"How long?" he asked curiously.

"A little over a year," she admitted. Jake took in her full cheeks, her beautiful eyes, the full bodied curves beneath him.

"Over a year?" Jake repeated. "How is that even possible?"

"Usually I believe in getting to know someone before I jump in bed with them,' she sighed, biting her lower lip.

"So what happened with me?" he asked, as he nibbled on her earlobe playfully. An aftershock of pleasure coursed through her.

"I'm still trying to figure that out myself," she responded quietly.

"Don't think too hard about it deer hunter," he teased. "It's just sex." When she didn't respond, he kissed her gently. "I can see those gears going. Whatever it is, I hope we can talk it through in the morning. It's 2:30 a.m., Ellie. And I'm beat."

"I should call a cab," she said abruptly.

"No way! Are you kidding? Stay. I can take you home in the morning," Jake responded. She took in the gentle expression on his face. There was a tenderness there she could get used to. But then again, sex didn't mean anything to him. She couldn't blame him for thinking she felt the same way. After all, she had started it.

Jake kissed her as he wrapped the blankets around them. The warmth and newfound familiarity of his body conspired with the wine to lull her asleep in his arms.

A silvery creature breathing in and out through the water swam through a high mountain lake. Her scales gave way to human skin and she melded into the forest like a chameleon, skin morphing from bark to sky, water to prairie grass. With each transition she felt more radiant, more powerful as if she had finally stepped into herself. The dream carved an impression in her mind before releasing her into a deep sleep.

Chapter 14

Ellie reached for her nightstand to see what time it was, but her nightstand wasn't there. Her confusion only lasted a heartbeat before last night rushed back to her. She turned to see Jake lying beside her, fast asleep. She eyed him with a sense of wonderment as she thought over their evening together. Fragments of her dream came to her and she tried to hold onto the feeling of wholeness that it offered. Her thoughts wandered back to making love to Jake; the way he had explored her so gently, yet powerfully; the way he held eye contact with her the entire time and listened to her body. She had never experienced anything like it.

But who was she kidding? It had been incredible, no doubt about it. But she knew she had made a mistake. That woman last night who had passionate sex with a stranger was someone else; not who she was in day to day life. She didn't believe in casual sex and yet here she was, naked in a stranger's bed.

Yet part of her felt deeply connected to him. She knew that about herself. Usually by the time she had sex with a man, she was already committed to the relationship, and sex added the bond that made the relationship stronger. How could she explain that to him? *I know we just met, but since we had sex, I expect to be in a relationship with you.* It wasn't realistic.

And then there was the other part; he had entered her without a condom. Last night, after such incredible sex, it didn't seem to matter. But now, dread replaced the calm. She disdained women like that, who got so caught up in the moment that they threw caution to the wind. And now she was one of them. She could be pregnant, for all she knew; or have contracted an STD. Sure, he said he was clean, but how could she really know?

She tried to push the ideas out of her head as she glanced around the room. Her eyes grew wide. She hadn't even noticed her surroundings last night. A piece of driftwood decorated one corner of the room, and a pile of sea shells sat on his bureau next to an incense burner. Was that patchouli she smelled? God, he's a real hippy, she thought to herself. Just the type of guy I've looked down on my whole life.

But as she looked at him lying beside her in the soft morning light, observing the steady rise and fall of his chest, she felt something entirely other. She followed the curves of his body in her mind as if memorizing him. Would he be glad to see her when he awoke, or would it be awkward between them? She didn't want to wait around to find out. She had betrayed herself, and she couldn't look at him through those eyes.

Slowly, she crawled out of bed, dressed as quickly as possible and got her cell phone out of her purse to call a cab. As the phone rang, she realized she had no idea what address to give. She stepped outside to find the address on the mailbox just before the service answered. They would be there in 10 minutes. She was stretching in the morning light when she heard the click. She reached for the door, discovering it was locked. Her purse sat on the coffee table where she had left it and she knew her shoes were neatly tucked in the shoe rack just inside the door.

Ellie crept barefoot down the narrow path to the back yard in her deep emerald cocktail dress, and opened the wooden gate. The ghastly creak of the hinges startled her. That would have easily woken her up. Was he also a light sleeper? When she didn't hear any sounds from the house, she decided to go forward. The sliding glass door in back was also locked. She pushed at the window on the spare bedroom and it gave a little, but not enough for her to work her way in. So much for my smooth getaway, she thought to herself. She walked back around to the front of the house. Seven minutes had passed and the cab would be there any moment. She had no choice but to ring the front door.

Half awake, Jake opened the door in his boxer shorts and looked at her in confusion, but it didn't take him long to figure out what was going on.

"Forget something?" he said as calmly as he could muster.

"Yeah. My purse, my shoes . . . saying goodbye," she smiled awkwardly. He swept his arm in a motion that said to come in and she walked past him to retrieve her things.

"Sorry to run off like this. I didn't want to wake you and I have to be somewhere," she lied.

"I can give you a ride, Ellie. It's the least I could do."

"The cab will be here any minute. It's okay," she responded.

"Please. Cancel the cab," he said sleepily, rubbing his eyes.

"I can't, Jake." As they stood there in the stillness, looking at each other, she tried not to think of the feelings for him already growing inside of her.

"Okay. Uh. Can I call you?" Jake asked, folding his arms across his chest. They both heard the honk of the cab. Ellie didn't know how to respond.

"You have my email, right?" she dodged, as she slipped on her shoes.

"Yeah. Still have it," he responded coolly. She felt shaky as she started to walk past him. At the last moment, she quickly threw her arms around him. As they kissed passionately, she imagined staying, having breakfast, getting to know him a little better— something to justify what had transpired between them. The cab honked again.

"I'm sorry Jake, I have to go."

"Okay. See you."

As Jake watched her leave, disappointment settled into his chest. There had been plenty of times he had hoped that the woman who had shared his bed the night before would be gone by the time he awoke; but not today. He had expected to have at least a little time in the morning with her, relishing in the experience of a newfound lover; talking through the events of last night.

And it was clear they needed to talk about it. There was something strange about what had happened. At first she had been so strong, stating her boundaries up front. And then just like that, she melted. But he hadn't pushed, she had.

And the physical connection was undeniable. Even though part of him had wanted to wait, it was as if he couldn't contain himself. And based on what she'd said to him afterwards, what was it? *I disappeared into you.* It seemed she had the same experience.

He recognized the spark between them; the type of connection that begins a new relationship, and he had been curious, even though she wasn't the type of girl he usually went for, or met, for that matter. But this morning she was distant, awkward. Was she already regretting that she had slept with him?

The phone rang.

"Hello?"

"Jake. It's Ethan. Where are you, man?"

"Oh, shit. What time is it?" Jake asked as he ran a hand over his face.

"Ten minutes after nine. Everybody's here and we're going to start, but we're short one player. Meaning you."

"I'll be there in 20 minutes." He threw on his soccer jersey and shorts, gathered up his belongings, and headed out to the garage. He dropped his duffle bag in one of the panniers on his bike, snapped on his helmet and headed off for the match.

◊◊◊

Her tear ducts ached from trying to hold back the impending downpour in the back of the cab, but by the time she got home, the tears wouldn't come. Despite a building headache, she changed into her running clothes, slipped on her iPod and headed out for a run. She chose a song with a tenacious beat and set her pace to its rhythm. She ran until her sides ached and kept going, waiting for her second wind to kick in. Finally, the tears sprung forth and she walked until she could take a full breath again.

She switched her iPod to a folk album and continued running until her thoughts began to fall into order. Instead of the self-loathing she had felt earlier, she settled into the fact that she was just as capable as any other woman of being swept off her feet by passion. And it had felt incredible. She had always reasoned that with time and the build up of trust and respect, a couple could reach a climax of sexual experience. Yet in all the time she had been with Trevor, the man she almost married three years ago, she had never had an orgasm like she'd had last night.

But a relationship took time. That truth remained. And she had just blown that truth. And what a shame, she thought. She and Jake had started off so well. He was easy to talk to, and despite their extremely different lifestyles, they had a good rapport.

But how could he take her seriously now? He'd already had her. And not just had her; conquered her; devoured her. And even more devastating was his view on sex—or at least what she gathered by his comment last night. *It's just sex.* That sounded far from promising. She decided the best strategy was to count her losses and move forward—spend time by herself figuring out why she was in this downward spiral, and getting herself out of it.

After her run, Ellie downed a bottle of water and lay down on the couch, pulling a blanket over her. Just a short nap, she told herself, yawning. By the time she awoke, afternoon sunlight flooded the living room and she sat up in a daze. After a long shower, she made herself an omelet. As she ate at the kitchen island, she logged onto her laptop to check her email. She clicked her way through several newsletters, one reminding her of the benefit she was attending in a few weeks for the Children of Rwanda. She deleted three notifications about activity on her e-Connect profile, and made a note to remove her account. Then she noticed an email entitled Lady Ranger.

> *Ellie,*
>
> *It was a pleasure getting to know you throughout the evening. I'm so glad you spent the night. I was sorry you had to head out so quickly this morning, but based on that last kiss, I'm thinking we'll see each other again soon. We were supposed to have our first date this afternoon, if you remember. I guess we jumped the gun a bit. Not sure if that's still on the table?*

You said you were interested in signing up for the Seven Eco Steps. Here's the link.

Yours,

Jake Tillerman

She read through the email three or four times and each time, focused on his closing greeting; yours. She printed it out, folded it in half, and pinned it on the bulletin board next to the tiny piece of paper he had given her out on the trail. This is all I have of him, she thought. She clicked on the link in his email, and a well-designed website popped up.

For some reason, she had expected something more amateur looking. As she read through the motivation behind the Seven Eco Steps, she smiled at the optimism that came through the writing. She pictured him on their walk back to his place and his genuine enthusiasm as he told her about the project and before she knew it, she found herself signing up for the challenge. She might have blown it by sleeping with him, but this was something she could at least follow through on.

Almost instantly, a confirmation email arrived in her inbox, as well as an invitation to sign up for the Gaia Eden newsletter. Couldn't hurt, she reasoned, clicking on the subscribe box.

Before her head hit the pillow that evening, her thoughts poured over Gillian. At least someone was thinking about commitment. How would David pop the question? Were they on a plane to Europe, or on their way to the Lake house in Vermont? As she drifted off to sleep, visions of bridesmaid's gowns danced through her head, intermingled by images of a particularly handsome environmentalist.

Chapter 15

When Ellie arrived at work early Monday morning, she expected a run of the mill day, but she had another thing coming. As she read through the news online, someone turned the knob of her office door. Ellie spun around in her seat and stared at the door handle. No one ever came this early to the office.

"God Karen. You scared me half to death!" Ellie gasped as she looked up at her boss.

"Sorry about that. Have time for a coffee?" Karen asked.

"Sure. That would be great. The usual 10 a.m.? I have some more ideas to add to the draft I gave you Tuesday."

"Actually, how about now," Karen said rather abruptly. "I'm famished." This was perhaps one of the things Ellie liked least about Karen; she was always famished, ate whatever she wanted, and remained waif-like thin. Ellie, on the other hand, born with a sturdy build, had to watch every little crumb.

"Give me 10 minutes," Ellie responded. As the advertising manager, Ellie went to Starbucks with Karen every Monday morning for a brainstorming session. Ellie usually liked the concentrated time with Karen, who was an amazing Marketing Director, but an hour and a half ahead of schedule set her off guard. On top of that, Ellie's mind was somewhere else today, just as it had been all day Sunday.

They drove to Starbucks and sat at an inside table by the window. Karen seemed distracted as she sipped her latte, breaking little pieces from her large chocolate muffin and arranging them into well-ordered piles on her napkin.

"Can you keep a secret?" Karen asked. Ellie nodded. "My vacation isn't really a vacation. I'm interviewing with a major magazine in Chicago."

"Wow! Does anyone else know? Does Margo know?"

"No. No one. Especially not Margo. If she finds out I've been approached by another magazine, she'll flip." Karen took a large bite of her muffin, chewing voraciously.

"I won't tell a soul." Ellie instinctively glanced around the coffee shop to see if anyone had overheard them.

"So here's the thing, Ellie. It's my third interview. First was over the phone, second on Skype. Third one's in person. And from what I understand, it's more of a formality than an interview. As long as we all have good chemistry, then it's more about signing documents."

"So you pretty much have the job," Ellie responded, flabbergasted.

"I think so. If it's a go, then I'll start mid-June with online training, and beginning of July I'll be moving out." Ellie let out a sigh. Even though Karen was a bit of a slave driver, Ellie loved working with her. But one thing Ellie didn't like was surprises. The idea that Karen would be gone in less than two months unsettled her.

"You've picked up everything so quickly over the last eight months; we're a great team."

"Thank you Karen. You've taught me a lot," she responded wistfully.

"You'd make an excellent Marketing Director," Karen stated, sipping her Macchiato.

"Well. Thanks. I've never thought about it, seeing as we have an excellent one right now," Ellie responded. "Or at least for the next two months."

"Well, if you're interested, I'll do my best to see that you're my replacement." Ellie could feel Karen's eyes studying her, gauging her reaction.

"You'd do that for me?" Ellie questioned.

"You bet. If all goes well in Chicago, then I want to groom you to be Duomo's next Marketing Director! And if not, this conversation never happened."

"Of course! This is really amazing!" It was amazing, but at the same time, it was a lot to take in. Karen might think Ellie was marketing director material, but was she ready for such a move? She already missed writing her column that she handed over when she was promoted to advertising manager eight months ago. As Marketing Director, she'd certainly have a higher income, but a serious increase in workload and much less personal time. And further, did it even matter what Karen thought? Margo would ultimately decide.

"But what about Margo?" Ellie asked evenly.

"Margo will see how much you shine and they'll be no need to search outside the company. Besides, she already mentioned how impressed she is with your work."

"She did?" Ellie asked.

"Yeah. Anyway, that's all I wanted to say."

"Thank you Karen. I'm really grateful."

"Oh. And don't worry. You'll still get a chance to write once in a while. You're too good of a journalist for us to throw away that talent completely," Karen added, as if reading Ellie's mind. She'd had so many moments like this in her life where out of the blue, someone stepped up and offered her an amazing opportunity. And every time she was in the right position to accept. She wondered if this was common, or if some cosmic force was looking out for her.

When they got back to the office, Ellie opened the advertising section of the marketing report for the board of directors. After hearing Karen's secret, she tried to think of ways she could set herself apart in Margo's eyes. As she keyed through the slides, she came across the list of old clients. Pacific West Holdings was third from the top. Karen was the one who had reeled in this multi-national development company a few years back, which brought a lot of revenue to the magazine. But they hadn't advertised in that last two years. If she could figure out a way to reel them back in for next year, she would definitely win not only Margo's attention, but that of the board of directors.

She flipped to this year's advertisers. The Hope Farmers were eighth on the list in order of investment, which surprised her. This fast track company taught other companies how to be more socially and environmentally sustainable. There was clearly a lot of money to be made in this field, as they had secured full page ads for the next two years. Maybe that was a direction to take; something to do with sustainability.

Hope farmers; sustainability; environment, environmentalist, Jake. He pulled at her thoughts, just as he had all morning. Ellie dropped her head in her hands, wondering how long it would take to forget him.

Chapter 16

He changed into his wetsuit as first light broke across the corduroy-like surface of the Pacific. In an unspoken protocol, the surfers took turns catching waves that brought them gliding back to the coast. The waves were smaller today, but still provided the calming sensation of interacting with the ocean. Jake floated gently up and down on his long board waiting for the next set to come in. Patience paid off as he cut into a mounting wave, riding it gently back to shore. Minutes later he was up again, cruising back and forth along a curl of deep turquoise as the sunrise transformed the sky into a golden red.

By the time he cycled to the office, his mind was clear and focused. Ethan and Natalia already had their laptops open, surprised to have arrived before him.

"Late start this morning. Have a sleepover last night?" Natalia teased.

"Caught some waves," Jake responded. He might as well have said *went to the shrink*. Both Natalia and Ethan knew that early morning surfing sessions equated to something weighing heavily on Jake's mind. They also knew not to ask questions until they saw something give. Jake was all business.

"Two weeks running. You have some stats for me?"

"Yeah," Ethan cleared his throat. "We've had 1,700 hits. That's pretty decent, seeing that it's been up for just 10 days. Of those, roughly 550 people have registered for the Seven Eco Steps, and of those, 183 are entering daily tallies."

"So only a third of the participants are actually participating," Jake pointed out.

"Well, yeah. But considering the short time frame, that's pretty good," Natalia clarified.

"More people will start participating. It's like making good coffee. The idea has to percolate, then soak through. And eventually, they'll be doing the basic steps and then they'll want even more; go onto the advanced steps, read through the entire website." Ethan added.

"This afternoon we'll email reminders to fill in the forms with some humorous pictures. You know. 'Oh yeah. Gotta log that seven minute, thirty-four second shower.'" Natalia said.

"Okay. And with the 1,700 hits; what does that mean exactly?" Jake asked, as he scribbled on his note pad.

"1,700 people have landed on the page, but only a fraction of those have signed up." Ethan explained.

"Any chance of converting them into participants?"

"Always a chance, Jake," Natalia chimed in. "Especially with the social media marketing we're doing. We're just getting started. And we're hoping for a 200% increase this month alone." Jake nodded his head. Ethan and Natalia glanced at each other curiously as his eyes lowered down to his notepad.

"By the way, I was able to get a roster from Peterson's class. You must have given one hell of a lecture, Jake. Fifty-seven out of the sixty students signed up for the challenge," Ethan reported. Jake's eyebrows arched upward, pulling the corners of his mouth into the beginning of a grin.

"That's good news. And tell me more about this online grant competition. What is it, Causes?" Jake asked.

"It's called One Hundred Causes. We're already registered. We have 'til August 31st to reach 15,000 participants. If we do, we're in the running for the $125,000 grant from Starbucks."

"Starbucks, huh." Jake started. "I don't like the idea of being sponsored by a major multinational corporation," he twirled one curl between his thumb and forefinger.

"Starbucks isn't that bad. It's not like the money's from Pacific West Holdings," Ethan responded.

"Now if that were the case, we'd withdraw our entry. Wouldn't that be ironic if we won and one of the biggest developers in California sponsored an environmental organization that supports the very kids they displace?"

"The way I look at it dude, that's $125,000 less in their development budget, and a way to put this program on steroids; waking people up to how they're also responsible for the state of the planet," Ethan rattled.

"Yeah. I'm with you on that. But, taking money from them is like dealing drugs as a viable way of getting money to subsidize schools." Jake grimaced. Natalia reached over and brushed her hand across Jake's forehead where a set of furrows had settled in. He gave her a half smile.

"Slow down guys. In the first place, Pacific West Holdings isn't funding the competition. And even if they were, it's not like they're the anti-Christ. They have two green projects that I know of on the boards right now," Natalia argued.

"Peanuts compared to all the neighborhoods they've bought out and gentrified, further marginalizing the working poor. And don't forget about those wetlands they obliterated a few years back for the sake of million dollar McMansions," Jake argued. Natalia crossed her arms, staring at Jake.

"Think of all the kids you could help if you could have a Gaia Eden branch in every school district," she countered. "Not to mention paying some of those bills."

"Yeah. I suppose you've got a point there," Jake responded, thinking of his list of bills that came in every month compared with the amount of money they received in grants. If they only knew how hard he was working to keep this whole operation afloat. Even though he had planned to leave architecture behind when he started Gaia Eden, he was actually taking on even more design work than before to fund his non-profit.

Jake spent the rest of Friday afternoon finishing a grant application that had to be postmarked by the end of the day, and after a harrowing cycle across town, just made the last pick up at the Post Office. He stopped by O'Malley's for a beer, and joined a group of friends playing darts. Jake was happy to see Edmond among them, an old buddy he'd worked with on another campaign against clear cutting in Alaska.

"Hey man!" Edmond extended his hand. "Good to see you out." They patted each other on the back affectionately. The bar began to grow louder as the crowd grew, and before long, two young women had worked their way into the conversation, circling them like sharks. The tall green-eyed blond in jeans and strappy heels chatted up Edmond, while the lanky brunette in a mini skirt and golden tank top leaned into Jake, introducing herself. Genevieve, he soon learned, was twenty-six, doing her Master's in Nursing at UCLA, and did part time modeling for a local agency. The girls joined the dart game, and before long, they were somehow paired up. Jake had hoped to talk further with his friend, but clearly, Edmond didn't mind the interruption. Genevieve asked Jake about his work and feigned interest as he talked about Gaia Eden, but was too distracted by his eyes and physique to follow his conversation.

"Hold that thought. I'm going to buy you another beer," she doted. "Don't go anywhere." Jake had been in this situation a hundred times before: small talk, a few hours of flirtation, an excuse to leave together followed by casual sex. Jake caught her by the arm.

"Thanks for the offer Genevieve, but I've got to get going. Early day tomorrow."

"Well," she paused, gazing into his eyes, "we could skip the beers. I live in Westwood, right off campus." She was just the way he usually liked them: slender, vivacious, knew exactly what she wanted, no strings attached. But as of late, he'd had a change of taste. He just hoped that his change of taste would respond to his email in a timelier manner.

"It was nice meeting you Genevieve. Perhaps some other time." Edmond and the blonde were on their way to the dance floor as Jake headed out of the bar alone.

Chapter 17

Ellie took a long sip of her latte, trying to get used to the reusable metal cup she had purchased and once again focused on the article she was reading. Her mind had been floating away from her work over the last week and a half with dizzying memories of Jake, and she'd had to take harsh measures to pin herself down. This was especially important, given the extensive list of responsibilities she had in Karen's absence, not to mention her desire to show she was marketing director material without letting on she knew anything about Karen's very likely departure.

The days flew by, but in the evenings, she had abundant time to think over every aspect of that one night, and how she might have done things differently. Her emotions were like a ping pong ball slamming across the chasm between shame and desire. And as jury and judge, she hadn't been easy on herself.

At least she wasn't pregnant. She'd gotten her period late last week. And although she wanted to believe in Jake's integrity, she still needed to make a doctor's appointment to see if she had any other surprises waiting for her.

On several occasions she had written Jake Tillerman entire emails, sharing her state of mind, first saying why she couldn't be with him, and then explaining under what conditions she could. But in the end, she hadn't sent a single one. She came back to the same conclusion; she couldn't begin a relationship with sex, and she had to let it go.

As a sort of personal compensation, she had dived into the Seven Eco Steps, going through the extended lists of things you could do to get points. Competitive by nature, she enjoyed the small virtual prizes they had set up. If she hit 100 points within her first two weeks, she would be awarded a one acre organic farm in cyberspace.

She soon learned that shorter showers and laundering with cold water were just the tip of the iceberg. Not flushing the toilet every time, for example, could garner her three points, whereas using a reusable cup was only worth one. And the website went way beyond daily changes; it gave information on installing everything from double-glazed windows and gray water irrigation systems to photovoltaic panels and government rebates available for major home renovations. She certainly wasn't going to install solar roof panels or water her yard with gray water recycled from the shower and kitchen, but she was making progress on the daily changes. Part of her wondered if Jake could see her entries and comments, or if she was just an anonymous number in the database.

What she hadn't expected was the hold that one night with him would have on her emotions; not only her emotions, but her logic. Honestly; how could she go out with a hippy environmentalist sort? She could never bring a guy like that home to meet her family. And based on his home, he was most likely poor, to boot. As she glazed over the last paragraph of the article she was reading for the third time, she realized she had no idea what she'd just read. Instead, she pictured Jake's lips on hers, kissing her neck, sending chills down her body.

A bell went off on her computer, announcing a task she had pre-scheduled just for such a deviation. Right, focus, she chastised. She opened up her reminder list on the computer and started tackling it from the top down. She was actually making progress when Rebecca popped her head in her door.

"There's a gorgeous man here to see you," she announced in a sing song voice. "I wish I had that list you rattled off a few weeks ago when I asked you what you wanted in a man: tall, handsome, intelligent, charming. Something like that?" Ellie raised her eyebrows in surprise.

"Sounds delightful. Does this prince charming have a name?" she asked as nonchalantly as possible, as her heart pounded in her chest.

"He said he's a personal friend of yours, that's all," Rebecca responded with amusement. Ellie checked her lipstick in the mirror before walking down to reception.

"Darling!"

"Arno! What a pleasant surprise." They hugged each other and Ellie felt relief intermingled with disappointment.

"Can I whisk you away from all this drudgery for high tea?"

"It's not drudgery Arno! I love my job, and I never get out of here before 5 p.m."

"I know darling, but I haven't seen you in almost two weeks, and I really need a date with you now! Plus it's already a quarter after four!"

"It's not my fault you've been too busy for me. But I've been slammed at work, so I only minded a bit." In fact, she had minded quite a lot.

"Come with me!" Arno wiggled his eyebrows flirtatiously.

"You know all my co-workers now think you're my hot and heavy sex toy?" she scolded.

"Believe me. If the God's had only made me different, I'd be worshipping at your alter."

"My Goodness. You're quite libidinous today. What's gotten into you?" she teased.

"I have a table for two at Clementine's. And that is the only place I will give you the scoop—over finger sandwiches and a nice pot of Earl Grey." When Ellie didn't respond, he threw his hands up in the air. "Well?" he demanded. She wasn't getting any work done anyway.

"Okay. I'll make an exception this once," she decided.

Chapter 18

By the time they reached Clementine's, Arno had told her almost everything about his newfound romantic pursuit. Pierre, who would be forty-two next month, had grown up in a small rural village in the Burgundy region of France. Arno had worked on a farm one summer in this area when he was eighteen and they figured out they had been in the same town at the same time, all those years ago.

"After all, France and Holland are geographically quite close, with only Belgium in between," Arno explained. Although from different cultures, Arno and Pierre were both western Europeans who had lived in the States for the last twenty years. They had spent the last twelve days together, and Arno was already envisioning their future.

"Just think. Next time I go home to visit, Pierre could come with me. We could take the bullet train to Paris, spend a long weekend visiting Musee d'Orsay and the Louvre, sipping French wines in the cafes before heading to the countryside."

"And I thought I was a hopeless romantic. You put me to shame!" She grabbed his arm. "Do you mind if we sit out back on the terrace?"

"It's a little chilly for you, isn't it? You always like to sit indoors."

"It's summer, Arno. And today, I'd like to try the terrace." Since her hike a few weeks ago, Ellie had made an effort to find the open spaces in the city—even if it was just an outside terrace with a few potted plants. She found a table in the sunshine and settled in.

Arno was so entranced with Pierre that he didn't notice her scattered state of mind. She was thankful for this. Usually, she loved to share her romantic interests with Arno, but when she thought about telling him what happened, humiliation filled her. Yet every time her thoughts wandered to Jake, she could almost feel the electricity that reverberated between them, not to mention the pleasant conversations they had shared. The delicate chirping of birds pulled her back to the present.

"And you won't believe what he does for a living." Arno went on. "He's a vintner."

"A vintner and a wine connoisseur. A match made in heaven." Ellie exclaimed. She selected a sesame seed scone from the tray and put a small dollop of clotted cream on it before taking a bite. The scone crumbled gently in her mouth.

"Why are you eating like such a bird?"

"Habit. And, this is absolutely delicious. I want to savor it."

"Darling. I don't think you have to watch every little crumb."

"As a matter of fact, I do. Otherwise, I'd have to go shopping all over again every few months to upsize my wardrobe." Not to mention that her stomach hadn't felt right the last few days, like she was coming down with something.

"There could be worse plights! Promise, if that ever happens, that you'll take me with you. We need to expand the sass in your wardrobe. Hetero men appreciate a sensually dressed woman— including the good ones." Ellie thought about Jake for the umpteenth time that day.

"So, if you can indulge me a little further, there's even more," Arno cooed.

"Consider yourself indulged."

"Pierre drives a beautiful Porsche Boxster. Canary yellow."

"Dreamy," Ellie responded.

"What?" he asked. "I see a little smile on your lips. Do you think that's silly?"

"No. Of course not. He sounds dreamy. It's just," Ellie faltered, "I think you should take things a little slowly." She was hardly one to be giving such advice.

"Oh Ellie. Always the conservative one when it comes to romance."

"On second thought. Don't listen to me. You're glowing. Full speed ahead!"

"Now that's my girl!" Arno cheered, clearly pleased with her about face. "Oh. And I forgot to tell you, Pierre has a younger brother—single, hetero and I'm sure gorgeous. He's coming over in two weeks for a visit. Fancy a double date?"

"You are so kind to always have me in your thoughts, Arno." Ellie responded. "Always looking out for my love life." Maybe she should confide in him. Get his opinion, she thought.

"I just think it's about time you got laid again," he remarked casually, raising his eyebrows at her. "Thirteen months is a long, dry spell."

"Arno!" she piped before starting to laugh. "I've got it covered."

"Yeah. Right! Just think about it; a gorgeous French man in the country for a few weeks. You could have some fun, and then have things settled so you can concentrate on finding Mr. Right, without the distraction of built up sexual needs getting in the way."

"Been there, done that. Doesn't work," Ellie replied, biting her tongue. Arno looked at her, his eyes growing wide.

"Oh, darling. Oh, pray tell!" Ellie wiggled at his words. "Am I your best guy friend in the whole world?" he prodded.

"Yes," she croaked, as her cheeks started to burn.

"Then spill!"

"I saw Jake Tillerman again."

"Who?"

"Nature boy."

"When?"

"That Saturday at the art opening. After you ditched me."

"But he was with someone else, wasn't he?"

"Just a friend," Ellie explained. "Anyway, we talked. Went out to dinner, talked some more. I felt like myself around him. You know. I could be goofy, silly, and he got me." Warmth flowed through her at the memory.

"That's a very good sign." Arno nodded approvingly.

"Yes. And then he invited me back to his place."

"And you said yes."

"I did," Ellie responded.

"And then?"

"I was on the verge of going home. But I just gave into the moment."

"And you had sex with him?" Arno asked, his voice tilting upward in excitement.

"Yes," Ellie whispered, "and it was incredible!"

"Oh my God, girl! I'm so proud of you!"

"I go all out slut and you're proud of me?" Ellie wrinkled her forehead in embarrassment.

"Yes! You're simply glowing! I noticed it when I picked you up but I was so darned eager to tell you all about Pierre. And now I know why! What ever got into you?"

"I just decided to live a little; your words after all. I must've taken them to heart," she responded happily.

"You swallowed them whole! And then? What happened after that? Did you stay for breakfast? Do it again? When can I meet him?" Arno queried.

"No. I left first thing in the morning."

"You left?" Arno repeated as he lifted his left hand dramatically in the air. She nodded. "And then?"

"I beat myself up the last 12 days for spoiling my chances with a great guy."

"What? Where's the arch? A love affair's got to have arch!" he exclaimed. Ellie responded with silence. "Just because you had incredible sex doesn't mean its over. Oh contraire! That's just the beginning!" Ellie wondered if she could just lay part of herself down, and make it that simple. But she knew better.

"No. It's over," Ellie countered with determination.

"He didn't call you?" Arno asked.

"I didn't give him my number."

"I don't understand you darling! You're drawn to a man so completely that you dive in and then you don't even give him your number? Why not?" Ellie noted his disappointment.

"I can't start a relationship like that. I don't have sex until I'm really sure about someone. I betrayed myself."

"Ellie. We're not living in the 19th century here! Passion is a positive force in our lives, something to be embraced, not judged." Ellie took in his words, mulling them over.

"I respect that in you, but I'm having a hard time respecting myself right now."

Arno looked at his friend, shaking his head gently. She had always been on the conservative side when it came to relationships. He could only imagine how much she had been beating herself up for giving into her desires.

"I can see you're upset darling. But you did say you enjoyed talking to him."

"Yes. Absolutely."

"And you felt comfortable around him?" he asked. Ellie's eyes softened.

"Yes," she quietly responded.

"And you were physically drawn to him."

"Oh-My-God-yes." Ellie fidgeted with her napkin.

"Then the sex was a natural step! Granted, faster than you're used to, but that was nature in action, baby. And for once you didn't get in your own way." As she listened to him, her shoulders relaxed a little.

"I see what you're saying. But what I really want is for it to never have happened. That we could hit the re-start button," Ellie stated plaintively.

"Life's not some video game you get to control. There's a wild creature inside of you that has been trapped by your moral imperatives, and you finally let her out. Now you're trying to put her back in the cage, and she's going to fight you tooth and nail."

Ellie laughed at Arno's spot on description. That wild creature had certainly been reminiscing about that one night, distracting the heck out of her.

"I guarantee you the next time you see him you are going to want him all over again. Once you've had him inside you, you can't go back to pretending some sort of virginal state." Arno devilishly remarked.

"Arno! I'm hardly a virgin."

"All right. Let me try to say it in Ellie language. Hmmm . . ."

"No. I get it! I get it. You don't have to translate for me. I know we can't really start over. Not to mention that we're totally different from one another. He has driftwood and shells in his bedroom for God's sake. I even saw a tie-dye in his closet." Arno laughed congenially, as he placed his hand on Ellie's.

"Opposites attract. Now there's a nice cliché with which to launch a relationship."

"He did email me," Ellie admitted. "He wants to see me again. I just don't know what to say to him."

"Just email him back. Invite him for a coffee and you two can talk it out." Arno's words sounded so reasonable, but she fought against them.

"Honestly, I need to give it some time."

"It's almost been two weeks since the opening. That's a lot of time considering how intimate you were with the guy. Maybe even too much time. Think if the situation was reversed. How do you know you aren't breaking this poor guy's heart?"

"Oh please. I get the sense he's used to having lots of women. I'm sure he's forgotten all about me," she replied unconvincingly.

"It's your life, darling. But look at Pierre and me. We hooked up the same night you did and we're on fire. Don't deny yourself the same chance." She didn't want to think about it anymore. She wanted something light and fun to fill her head.

"I'm happy for you, Arno. But let's drop the subject of me and Jake Tillerman for now. Will you take me out to a movie tonight?"

"I'd love to, darling, but Pierre's taking me out dancing— some fab new club on Fairfax."

"I get it. All caught up in your newfound love."

"So are you, but you're in a prolonged state of Victorian denial."

"Okay Arno. Time to drop me back at the office."

As they headed inside, Arno and Ellie both froze in their tracks. There in front of them sat Javier, Arno's ex. The chair across from him was currently empty, but a delicate tea cup and a plate with a half eaten finger sandwich suggested his companion was not far away.

"Hello Javier," Arno's voice wavered.

"Arno. You look . . . fantastic. Hi Ellie."

"As always," Arno retorted. The animation and joviality drained from his face. Ellie started to move off to give them space to talk, but Arno caught her by the hand. As the two men looked at each other, Ellie stood still, as if trying to blend into the floral wallpaper of the tea shop. She was the first to see the handsome young man walking back toward the table. She must have bristled, because both men turned around.

"Enrique, just give me a little minute," Javier implored. Enrique hesitated before walking to another section of the restaurant where a series of framed photos of famous guests lined the wall. Arno's eyes widened before crinkling up.

"I guess it's good to see him in the flesh. Dumped for a younger man. How utterly common and predictable of you," Arno fired.

"It wasn't like that," Javier defended.

"It was exactly like that," Arno said coldly.

"Oh dear," Javier sighed. He stood there for another half a minute fumbling for something to say to make it all better. But no words came.

"Your little boy toy is waiting dear," Arno pronounced dismissively. He looked Javier straight in the eyes, his shoulders pushing backwards ever so slightly. "Besides, I too have moved on."

"You're already seeing someone?" Javier asked indignantly. Ellie heard someone laughing and realized it was her.

"Oh dear. Of course you are." It was Javier's turn to flinch. "Please let him know that he is a very lucky man, whoever he is. I will never forget you, Arno."

"Good bye Javier," Arno closed, as he headed for the restroom. Strange how a relationship can seem so perfect and then end so abruptly, she thought. When Arno came back she noticed the color had returned to his cheeks. They left the tea shop hand in hand and Ellie put her arm around him as they walked to the car.

"Are you okay?"

"Yes, darling. I will survive."

"You'll do much more than survive." Ellie rallied. "You are a precious person and Javier is a fool to have let you go."

"That's right," Arno said. "And you were here for me, Ellie. My golden angel."

"How do you feel right now?" Ellie asked.

"I'm relieved actually. I had no idea how I would react when I saw him. It was painful. But you know what? I didn't realize it, but I was in the wrong relationship. You know how you said you feel yourself around nature boy?"

"Jake," Ellie corrected.

"Yes, Jake. Well, that's how I feel around Pierre. Sure, I know it's new, but there's this safety between us, like he likes me for exactly who I am. I've moved on to a better situation."

"I'm so happy for you Arno."

"Me too. And I want to be happy for you, Ellie. The next time I see you I want to hear that you called this Jake Tillerman for a cup of coffee. Before it's too late."

◊◊◊

By the time Ellie got home, she had found her appetite, but she laced up her running shoes and headed out for a long run. As she got into her pace, she tried to think about other things, like the fundraiser for the Children of Rwanda she would be attending Sunday night. It was ridiculously expensive, but she figured it was a great cause and a fancy event was just what she needed to clear her head. But as she ran, she once again pictured Jake's lips on hers. God, what she'd give to have another night with him. Just one more day of work 'til the weekend, Ellie told herself, trying to reign in the sensual images coursing through her mind. Arno was right, she decided. She could call him this weekend for a cup of coffee and set things straight, whatever that ended up being. Even if they didn't end up together, it was the right thing to do.

Chapter 19

The boys were out of sorts Friday morning as they climbed into the van: quiet, moody. And after receiving a letter from the landlord of his office building yesterday announcing sale of the property, he was far from cheerful himself. It had been so hard to locate an office space he could afford that met his needs, and now he had thirty days to find a new location for Gaia Eden. As Jake parked the van next to the small, littered field that had been designated as a new pocket park, he wondered just what sort of day he was in for.

"Okay guys, we're here," he announced cheerfully. Let's do some stretches, hold our circle and then unload the trees." The boys groaned as Jake got out of the van and walked over to the dry patch of grass that offered one of the few green spaces in the more run down part of this high density neighborhood. He slowly started doing exercises and the boys begrudgingly fell into sequence, copying his movements. As they began to limber up, he noticed a slight, almost imperceptible change among the boys, as if a thin thread of connection intertwined them. They drank from their canteens before sitting in a circle.

"Let's do a basic check in; anything that's on your mind. Who wants to start?" Jake asked, picking up a rock from the ground. He glanced around the circle, meeting seven pairs of glazed over eyes.

"No takers? Okay. I'll start," he offered. Jake cleared his throat as he thought about his week. "I didn't sleep all that well last night, so I'm a little grumpy," Jake started, seeing a few boys nodding in agreement. "I'm honored to be with all of you young men here today. I feel that the work we are about to do will be appreciated by the people who live in this neighborhood." He passed the rock to his right and the boy next to him held it for a minute, bending his head down as if uncomfortable with the idea of eyes upon him.

"I'm glad to be here 'cause otherwise I'd be home right now with nothin' to do the whole day." Everyone listened quietly, a few boys nodded their heads. He passed the rock to Charles, who sat next to him. Charles held the rock for a moment, nodded silently and passed the stone to the next boy.

"I had an okay week. I don't think a few trees is gonna make a difference here, but I'm up for the challenge." As the boys spoke, Jake wondered if something bad had happened in this part of town, as both Jefferson and Charles, who lived in Harvard Heights, passed on the opportunity to speak. A cut above Charles' right eye furthered Jake's suspicion that something was amiss. They almost always had something to share, even if it was just the chance to make a joke. Jake made a note to check in with Charles when he had a moment.

"I'm looking forward to lunch," Grayson reported before passing the rock. His remark was met with a round of chuckles. Grayson, a tall skinny white kid with a bad case of acne, was always hungry.

The rest of the comments were more of the same; jokes, a bit of relief to be somewhere besides home. Just as the circle was closing, Jefferson reached for the rock.

"I like when we do shit outside the city better. You know. Get outta all this concrete and high rises. But, you da man Jake. And if you think this here's important, then just maybe it is." Jake listened to Jefferson's words carefully. He knew it was important to keep a balance of activities in the city and in nature. But his budget was pretty tight this year. He was also determined that the work these kids did would empower them and give them the confidence to do the right thing both for themselves and for the environment—especially within their own sphere of influence. What better place than their own neighborhoods?

"Thanks for your input guys. Hey. Before we begin, let's get a group shot on the vacant lot," Jake suggested. He hadn't meant to call it a vacant lot. It was a pocket park. None of the boys seemed to care, and Jake realized that was part of the problem. All they saw was a weedy, trash filled lot. Perhaps Jake was the only one who was thinking about what it would look like afterward. The lot was on a busy corner with a mix of apartment buildings and businesses and in no time Jake found a passerby to snap the photo.

As they began to unload the trees, the boys worked together, lifting, carrying and discussing a pattern of plantings. Next, they got out garbage bags, slipped on their work gloves and picked up the trash that was more prevalent than the weeds. By the time they started digging holes, people in the neighborhood started looking their way. Some kids playing a pick up game of basketball on a nearby court headed over to see what was going on. Throughout the morning, people stopped by, nodding their heads in approval. Their looks of gratitude didn't go unnoticed by the boys.

When the boys started stripping off their sweatshirts, Jake noticed two large bruises on Charles' arms. Add to that the cut above his right eye, and Jake wondered if Charles had been street fighting again. Jake nodded casually toward the bruises on his arms.

"What happened, Charles? That's a pretty nasty cut as well."

"I know you don't like fighting, but sometimes in this neighborhood, you've gotta," Charles explained coolly. Jake tried to think back to when he was thirteen. He certainly wasn't getting into fights.

"You'd know better than me about that. I trust your judgment. But don't forget that sometimes you can fight with words and your smarts as well."

"Yeah," he nodded. "First line of defense. I know," Charles responded downheartedly. "Tried that, Mr. Tillerman. Didn't work."

Two men from the city stopped by around 11 a.m. to hook a hose to a fire hydrant half a block away and watered the entire area, filling the holes they had dug with water to further soften the soil. Water was definitely going to be an issue here. Even though sprinklers had been approved by the city, everything had been delayed. Weekly water from the fire hydrant was the city's temporary solution.

The boys had lightened up and were even beginning to joke with one another. Some debated about which trees should go where, based on the shade they would create. It was clear they were beginning to see a pocket park and not a trashy lot. But when two muscle-laden men about Jake's age wandered over to the pocket park, Jake felt the boys in the group tense up beside him.

"What you boys doin' here?" one man said as he towered over the group. Jake looked at the thickness of his arms, his massive, chiseled torso visible through a thin white t-shirt.

"Planting trees," Jake answered calmly.

"With my tax dollars?" Asked the second man, arms folded tightly over his chest.

"No sir. Through donations and volunteer work," Jake answered in an even voice.

"Well now." The larger of the two men said. He looked the boys over one by one, stopping when he spotted Charles.

"You Ben Logan's kid?"

"Yes sir." Charles responded. Jake had never heard Charles say sir to anyone.

"Well now. I think this here's a fine thing you doin'. Carry on." The corners of Charles' mouth curled ever so slightly to form the beginning of a smile. As the burly men headed back to the street corner they'd been occupying, the boys noticeably relaxed.

"Is that someone you know?" Jake asked Charles, changing the subject away from his injuries.

"Everybody knows him," Charles answered calmly. "That's the preacher."

"He's a preacher?" Jake asked. His question was met by laughter.

"No man. He's a seriously dangerous man," Jefferson explained. "But he's got this good side to him; likes when people do something for the people from their heart. That's why they call him the preacher."

"Well then. I think that means our work here is appreciated," Jake smiled.

"That's for sure. And if he's down with it, ain't nobody gonna mess with this here park."

As they took a break, the boys talked freely. More people passed by, taking an interest in the trees and plants that now stood at attention in the small plot of land.

"My, what a change!" an older woman said as she pushed a stroller laden with her two grandchildren. "You boys are sure prettying up the place."

"Thank you ma'am," one of the boys deftly responded. And they were only half way done. Natalia would be here after lunch with more vegetation.

As Jake retrieved snacks and beverages from the van, he saw more people crossing the street to marvel at their work. He stepped back, letting the boys field the questions. He exhaled with satisfaction as he saw the pride on their faces.

"You boys doing community service?" someone asked.

"No sir. We are part of a non-profit called Gaia Eden, and we are doing our part to make our city greener," Grayson responded, not rising to the bait.

Jake sat down and passed out a round of snacks. The boys eagerly started eating and talking. The positive energy among them was so infectious that Jake had a hard time reconciling the fact that these were the same boys that had been dragging and uncommunicative just a few hours before. He allowed his mind to drift back to the weekend before last, and a chill of pleasure coursed through him followed by disappointment. He finally hooked up with a woman that woke him up inside, and she hadn't even bothered to email him back. He thought about all the times he hadn't followed up with a woman after a casual night of sex. Karma's a bitch, he thought. But he could have sworn their connection was far from casual. At least she'd signed up for the challenge. That much he knew. I guess part of me made an impression on her, he mused.

Chapter 20

Friday morning, there was a sharp knock on Ellie's door, and to her surprise, Karen sauntered in with a big smile on her face.

"I nailed the interview!" she whispered, even though they were the only ones in the office.

"Congratulations, Karen!" Ellie responded warmly.

"Thank you! But it's not totally in the bag. I have to do a two week online training course starting in June, and then I receive my official contract and begin in July."

"Before you could just get a job. It's getting more and more complicated these days, isn't it?"

"I totally disagree. You beat out 453 other candidates for your position, Ellie. It's not like it was ever easy," Ellie was surprised to hear Karen pull this statistic so easily from her memory.

"So I'll be giving notice in just over two weeks. And you know what that means?" Karen fished. Ellie shook her head. "That means you and I have some serious work to do to set you up for the take over! And that can only start with an espresso."

"Okay! But would you mind if we try Joey's Espresso? That locally owned coffee shop around the corner?"

"Never been there. Is the coffee as good as Starbucks?" Karen asked.

"Better," Ellie responded. "And it's organically grown."

"Okay. I'm down with organic. I'll swing by and get you in thirty."

Speaking of organically grown, this whole Seven Eco Steps was proving to be much harder than Ellie had thought. Although she had been diligently tracking her changes and enjoyed competing with other online participants, the practicalities of the changes were wearing on her. It was easy enough to switch to cloth bags, but then she kept forgetting them in the car. The coffee cup had seemed so simple, a real no brainer. But it was work. Instead of just tossing it, she had to make sure she brought it in from the car to wash it so she could use it again the next morning. And the seven-minute showers. Now that was a joke. Really, how could anyone who needed to be presentable take a seven-minute shower?

Part of her had come to the conclusion that the only reason she was doing the challenge was some sort of ode to her one evening with Jake Tillerman. As long as she did her daily entries, she hadn't entirely closed the chapter on him. Despite her change of heart yesterday about contacting him, she had begun to second guess herself. Determined to get him out of her mind for at least the rest of the day, she started working on a spreadsheet of potential advertisers. Finally she heard a knock on her door.

They settled into a booth at Joey's, and Ellie gave Karen an overview of the last few weeks, and how the report had been met with favorable remarks at the board meeting.

"I know," Karen responded. "Margo sms'd me on my vacation to say how well it went."

"That's strange. She didn't say anything to me."

"Well, we'll make sure that changes. What we need is a campaign that you start. Something that increases subscribers, brings in new advertisers. Something to spice things up."

"Something to give us a new edge," Ellie replied thoughtfully.

"This latte is pretty good," Karen commented. "Since when did you stop going to Starbucks? Or start using a metal cup, for that matter?" she asked, noticing the bright pink cup in Ellie's hands.

"Oh, well, reusable cups are on the list for this challenge I'm doing," Ellie explained.

"What challenge?" Karen asked curiously.

"I signed up for this eco-challenge that came about after the Deep Water Horizon oil spill. It provides daily ways to lessen your dependence on oil. You know: drive less, shorter showers, go local, eat organically grown food, use reusable cups, bags, etc, etc."

"You did? Wow. Is that why you chose this place? Walking distance from the office?"

"Yes. And it's locally owned, everything on the menu's organic, and they source locally as often as possible. Looked it up online."

"I didn't think you were interested in the environment all that much," Karen remarked.

"Of course I am," Ellie retorted. "I care about the environment, but I just don't usually think of it on this sort of microscopic level—like shorter showers for instance. I mean, how important is that, really?" Ellie reconnected with the annoyance she had felt this morning as she clocked in a 13 minute shower, which still felt rushed.

"Well. If it's only a few people taking shorter showers, not so important. But if a lot of people choose to reduce their water use, it could really add up." Karen commented as she bit into her chocolate muffin.

"If you put like that, I get it. Maybe you'd be interested in taking the challenge too."

"Couldn't hurt. Hey! Maybe we should send it to the whole office. Make it a competition at work. You know. Do something eco-friendly."

"Brilliant!" Ellie responded. It really was brilliant. Why hadn't she thought of it herself?

When they got back to the office, Ellie showed her the website. They clicked through the list, the registration forms and the enticing virtual prizes.

"This is fantastic, Ellie. The more I think about it, this just might be exactly what we're looking for. We've been looking for a way to green up the magazine. We should share this with Margo," Karen stated.

"Really? I was just thinking something to share with our co-workers, not something that needs to go through an official route," Ellie voiced, suddenly having second thoughts.

"No. Believe me. It shows initiative, Ellie. Come on." Karen marched off and Ellie had no choice but to follow her. Margo, the magazine editor, looked mildly happy to see them as they came in her office at a quarter to ten, as if she was looking for any distraction to close the gap before her noon appointment at Davinci's. A group of women in the office had concluded that that was where she saw Paul Pinkman, a businessman they were sure she was sleeping with.

"What can I do for you ladies?" Margo inquired with raised eyebrows.

"Ellie came up with a great idea of something fun we'd like to do in the office," Karen announced, winking at Ellie. Margo's shoulders visibly relaxed.

"We could use some more fun around here. What've you got Ellie?"

"You know how we've been looking for some ways to green up our magazine?" Ellie started.

"Yes."

"Well, I've been doing this online challenge where you make seven changes in your daily habits to have a lighter carbon footprint on the planet," she explained. Karen gave her a nod of encouragement. "The idea is that we make it an office competition. It would encourage all the girls to not only think about a greener, more sustainable lifestyle, but to put their thoughts into action," Ellie explained as she handed her a list of the challenge topics. "And the environment is a hot topic right now. Good for Duomo's image as well," she added, trying to show initiative.

"Genius. I like the way you think, Ellie." Margo looked over the list. One of her typical guttural laughs escaped her lips as her eyes landed on public transportation.

"I'd love to see any of these girls ride the bus!" Margo cackled as she scanned through the list. Although Ellie had tackled every other item on the list, public transportation was not one of them, unless that cab ride home weekend before last counted.

"I began the challenge last week and it's been really eye opening."

"You're going to do it for a whole month?" Margo asked, staring at Ellie. Up until this moment, Ellie hadn't thought about a long term commitment to the competition. I need to show drive and stamina, she thought to herself as she glanced toward Karen.

"Yes," she said with resolve. "For the whole month."

"I already wash my clothes in cold water. Except the ones that go to the dry cleaner," Karen threw in.

"Hmm. Seven-minute showers anyone?" Margo laughed. "Ellie, tell me you're taking seven-minute showers."

"No. But I'm down to about thirteen minutes now," Ellie admitted.

"Impressive. So. What do you know about Gaia Eden, the organization that's sponsoring the challenge?" Margo asked. Ellie's cheeks burned as she started to speak.

"It's a locally owned non-profit that fosters a relationship between inner city kids and the environment. They teach kids about environmental responsibility through workshops, nature hikes, community gardening and other programs," she summarized.

"Sounds great. How big?"

"I get the sense it's a small group, like a lot of non-profits, but very focused and professional," Ellie responded, trying to contain her nerves.

"Playing the devil's advocate, because that's what I'm good at, maybe we should see if the Audubon Society or Green Peace or some other well known Environmental entity is doing something like this." Margo suggested.

"Well. I see the appeal there, but Gaia Eden is based right here in Los Angeles, helping young boys in our communities," Ellie countered.

"I like the way you're thinking," Margo said once again. "Let's call a meeting. Get everyone in the board room now."

"Now? Yes ma'am," Ellie responded in surprise.

No one was pleased about a Friday morning meeting, but by the time Ellie had loaded up the Gaia Eden website and the Seven Eco Steps on the overhead screen, curiosity was growing.

"If you could work eco-retail therapy into the list, I'm in," Rebecca interjected, drawing a round of laughter.

"I'm in without the shopping. I think this is awesome!" Jared added.

"It's a great idea," Melissa chimed in.

"Let's click around their site," Margo commanded. When they got to the "about us" link, a headshot of Jake Tillerman popped on the screen and the room exploded with whistles, murmurs and exclamations.

"Those eyes are to die for. If he's part of the challenge, I'm going for the gold," someone said, followed by a round of "me-too's." Ellie felt herself turning crimson.

"If we sign up and we have an office competition, what's the grand prize?" Amber asked.

"Grand prize? Hmm. Yes. Motivation," Margo purred. "You girls do need motivation." Jared cleared his throat loudly. "And guy. Sorry Jared."

"How about a date with the founder?" cooed Bethany, drawing more laughter and giggles.

"How about a weekend at the Ritz Carlton downtown?" Margo suggested, taking back control of the meeting. The room once again exploded in excitement.

"What about a weekend getaway at Jade, that exclusive eco resort up north in Santa Barbara County?" Soo Jin suggested. Although this received less enthusiasm than the Ritz, minds were beginning to churn in the right direction.

"We could do a story about the whole thing. Talk about the office challenge and do a write up on an eco resort," Karen suggested.

"I'm seeing it. I'm seeing it," Margo started, as she brushed her hands into the air as if conducting. "Great for the magazine's image," giving a nod to Ellie. "Makes us all a bit more eco-conscientious and we promote an eco-resort, which our demographic would be all over." She swished her left hand from side to side, which usually meant she was thinking about money. "Plus, I wouldn't have to pay for the winner's stay, as the eco-resort would bend over backwards to have the write up and throw in the cost." The enthusiasm in the room was mounting and suddenly Amber, who had dropped the line about eco retail therapy was ready to sign up.

Margo's phone beeped. Suddenly she seemed eager to wrap up the meeting and several people gave each other knowing glances. It was time to meet Paul at Davinci's restaurant in Hotel Leonardo. Or was that in the hotel room?

"Okay ladies, gent. Who's in?" Ellie looked on in astonishment as every hand in the room eagerly shot into the air. You'd think they were giving away Gucci purses the way everyone was waving their arms.

"Ellie. Email everyone the registration link. Saving any pressing deadlines, I want you all signed up before you go home today," Margo dictated. "And the competition begins first thing Monday morning." Everyone grabbed their notepads and pens, readying themselves as Margo started firing off a task list.

"And Ellie. Your first week doesn't count! You'll have to see how to erase it so you can be on par with everyone else if you want to compete," she added. "And I do know you like a good competition."

"Oh, and I want you two to brainstorm on a way to market this. Our girls, and gent, taking the challenge. Think human interest, pump it up on social media, accentuate the challenge aspect—think reality adventure show competition with an eco-twist.

"Rebecca and Sarah, and whoever else is managing our Twitter and Facebook accounts, think of a way to get people to follow along on our progress while we encourage other's to join the green crusade through daily Tweets." Margo took a breath, pushing a streak of frosted blond hair behind her left ear, before barreling forward. "What's it called? Seven Eco Steps? That name has no sass. Let's come up with something zippy. Think of a new tag line and Karen, assign someone to contact this Jake Tillerman A.S.A.P for an interview. And Jared, based on the response he got in this room, a nice shot of him with some of the kid's he's helping would also be quite appealing to our female demographic. Meeting adjourned."

The room cleared out as everyone bee-lined for their computers.

"Ellie, Karen. Great idea. The board said we need to green up the magazine's image. And here you come along with this idea. Just what we needed! I feel like things are getting more exciting by the minute," Margo clamored over her shoulder as she walked toward her office.

"Thank you," Ellie swallowed, running after her. "Um. Margo. Do you have a second?"

"Actually I don't," Margo cut her off. "I've got an appointment."

Ellie's stomach suddenly cramped up and she ran to the restroom, getting to a stall just in time. She washed her face and rinsed her mouth out before riding a rollercoaster of emotions back to her office. She hadn't pictured it escalating like this. Office challenge, sure. But an online campaign tracking each employee's progress, including hers? A magazine article? Jake being interviewed?

This was definitely exciting, exhilarating even. But as the person who brought the idea into the office, was she obliged to report that she'd had a one night stand with the founder of Gaia Eden?

What I really need is a good talk with Gillian, she thought. But no. Gillian's at some rustic resort in the Tuscany region of Italy getting engaged, cut off from the modern world, Ellie thought as she headed back to her office.

"Ellie. Wasn't that fantastic?" Karen beamed as she opened her door.

"Yes!" Ellie responded as brightly as she could muster.

"And I have a special assignment for you. Even though all of the girls are dying to be the one to interview this Jake Tillerman, I'd like you to do it. Seems only fitting as you're the one who brought the idea into the office," Karen said as she sat down in her extra chair. Ellie did her best to ignore the churning sensation in her stomach. She breathed in gently, trying to remain calm.

"Oh, well. Thanks, but no. I think I should focus on the marketing aspect, I mean, given our recent conversation," Ellie stammered.

"No. I'd like you to do the interview. It's a chance to put you in charge, which will make a good impression on Margo."

"Oh, I couldn't possibly," Ellie started. "It's been months since I wrote an article."

"Nonsense. I insist. Believe me, you're an excellent writer Ellie. You don't get rusty in eight months! And you have the perfect angle for doing it. Just recently you said you wanted to jump in once in a while and now's your chance. My decision's final. Now please, call Gaia Eden and set up an interview," she commanded. Once Karen made a decision, there was no discussion.

"Of course. Thank you," Ellie responded. She swallowed hard as Karen looked on. "Just as soon as I finish up with this spreadsheet I'm working on," Ellie fumbled.

"I'm not leaving until I see you make the call!" Karen insisted.

"Okay, then. No time like the present," Ellie replied as evenly as possible. She clicked back open the Gaia Eden website to find the contact information. As she punched in the numbers, she felt a growing sense of anxiety in her stomach.

Chapter 21

"I think that's your phone ringing, Jake," Rafa pointed out as the boys took a water break. Jake reached for his backpack and answered the call just in time.

"Jake Tillerman," he answered.

"Mr. Tillerman. Hi. This is Ellie Ashburn from Duomo Magazine. Your co-worker gave me your cell number and she said it would be okay for me to call you in the field."

"Ellie Ashburn?" he responded in a formal tone.

"Yes, Mr. Tillerman?"

"Call me Jake. I'm afraid Mr. Tillerman is much too formal after all we've been through," he teased, turning out of earshot of the boys.

"Oh. Of course. Jake. Are you familiar with Duomo Magazine?" Ellie concentrated on her tone as Karen looked on.

"Yes," he responded slowly. She sounded so business-like.

"Our office has decided to take the challenge, and we'd like to talk with you about how you launched the idea," she explained formally.

"Your entire office has signed up?" Jake asked.

"Yes. All thirty-eight of us," she responded. "And, we would like to do a small article about you and your non-profit Gaia Eden, and what motivated you to launch this challenge. It will be published online."

"An interview, huh." Jake responded casually. "Well if that's what it takes to see you again."

"Great!" Ellie replied in a peppy voice as Karen looked on. "Any chance we could come visit you at your work or in the field to conduct the interview?" Ellie asked. Karen put her hands in a rectangular shape in front of her eyes, her right finger clicking away. Ellie waved at her with annoyance. "We'd also like to schedule a photo shoot. Something with you and the population you are working with would be appropriate," she explained, as Karen gave her a thumbs-up.

He looked at the boys talking to members of the community, sitting beneath the shade of the trees they had just planted as the sun began bearing down. Publicity would be good for everyone, he thought to himself.

"Today would have been a perfect day." Jake commented. "I'm working with some of our students planting trees in Harvard Heights as we speak."

"Today?" Ellie responded. "I don't know that we can get a photographer out to Harvard Heights at such short notice," she hesitated. Karen waved wildly at Ellie. "Can you hold for just a moment?"

"I know Jared's free! If you two can get down there after lunch that would be fantastic!" Karen exclaimed, giving her a two thumbs up.

"Well, it sounds like today would work for us after all," Ellie confirmed. "If you can give me an address, I can meet you at say, one o'clock?" Her heart raced in her chest, her stomach clenching.

"Sounds good," Jake agreed before he had a chance to reason otherwise. As he gave her his whereabouts, he looked at the boys. "But I'd like you to interview the boys in the group as well. Not just me. They're the reason this program is a success," Jake stated before getting off the phone. The whole conversation had been strange, as if Ellie was sitting in a conference room with a crowd of colleagues looking on. Or maybe this was how it was going to be. Whatever, he thought. I'm doing it for the kids.

Based on what he'd witnessed in the last twenty minutes, these boys were pros when it came to answering questions—polite, friendly, providing solid answers. What he hadn't thought about is how the boys might react to being photographed.

"Guys," he started. "What would you all say if I told you a reporter is coming to talk to us about the work we're doing out here?" He glanced around the circle, trying to gauge first responses.

"For TV? That'd be awesome!"

"We gonna be on Telemundo?" Ignacio asked.

"We're going to be on TV dude!" another boy repeated, catching just part of the conversation.

"No. Sorry guys. Nothing prime time. Just an online magazine."

"Oh. Well, that's still pretty cool."

The boys took turns grooming themselves in the side mirrors of the van, slicking their hair back, checking their teeth and tucking in their shirts.

"They're not coming 'til after lunch, guys, so chill. You have plenty of time to get beautiful."

◊◊◊

Now *this* is going to be awkward, Ellie thought, as she drove toward Harvard Heights. Not only was Jared coming in a separate car, but she was heading over in her BMW Sports Utility Vehicle to interview an avid environmentalist in a dodgy part of town. But that was just a tiny issue compared to the other one; the last time she had seen Jake Tillerman, he was standing sleepy-eyed in his boxers, discovering that she had unsuccessfully tried to sneak out after their wild night together. As the GPS system announced that she had arrived at her destination, she brought the car to a halt. She inhaled deeply before hopping out of the car. I can do this, she said to herself. Act casual, like nothing happened.

As she started walking toward the group, the boys turned toward her and stared.

"Now that is something to look at," Jefferson remarked, a low whistle forming on his lips. Several of the younger boys giggled as they took in the curves of the tall blonde dressed in a white business suit and high heels coming toward them. Jake turned, following their gaze.

"She's from the magazine. Be on your best behavior guys," Jake reprimanded as he walked toward her, meeting her half way. He glanced toward the shiny new SUV she had just stepped out of and a tiny smile formed on his lips.

"Hi Jake."

"Hi Ellie. Nice to see you again," he replied casually.

"You too. Thanks for taking my call."

"You look good," Jake observed.

"Thank you." She couldn't help but smile at him. "I'm sorry I didn't email you back."

"Don't worry about it. You told me when we met that you had a busy life. Water under the bridge. But now that you're here, what do you want to know about our program?" His friendliness caught her off guard. She had expected tension, not easy conversation. As he started talking about Gaia Eden, he spoke eloquently. The boys gathered round, jumping in.

"This here used to be a trash filled, weedy piece of ugliness," Charles began.

"And we transferred it into Preacher's Park," Jefferson continued.

"Transformed it," Jake corrected.

"Preacher's Park?" Ellie asked.

"That's not the real name," Grayson explained. "That's just what us guys from the neighborhood dubbed it." They hadn't even finished the project and the boys had already nicknamed the park. That had to be a good sign, Jake thought. The boys continued to interrupt each other, explaining all that they had done today to make the neighborhood a better place and to bring a little nature into the city.

"Good for the soul," added another boy. Even though she had her handheld recorder going, she still scribbled down their comments.

"Can you tell me more about the Seven Eco Steps?" Ellie asked. "I signed up last Sunday morning and I have to say it's already been an eye opening experience."

Jake nodded nonchalantly, not letting on that he had actually read some of her entries.

"It started as a way to relieve the helplessness so many people have been feeling about the Gulf Oil Spill," he began. "We wanted to give people a simple way to speak out against the oil spill that included decisive actions—daily things that just about anyone could do if they put their mind to it. So we developed the checklist of daily actions that empower everyone to lessen their personal dependence on oil." Jake brought his hands through his hair as he continued, and Ellie did her best to concentrate. She hadn't noticed the gray hairs popping up throughout his dark brown curls the last time she had seen him, or the way his nose curved ever so slightly to the left. He was definitely handsome, but not the picture perfect movie star she had created in her mind the past few weeks.

But most of all, she felt comfortable in his presence, and the queasy feeling she had experienced on the way over had disappeared. He smiled as he talked to her, and Ellie felt a gentle warmth washing through her as she realized she was smiling back. Oh gosh. What had he been saying the last few minutes?

"It's certainly not the first time someone has rallied people to make changes for the sake of the environment, but people are responding to our message and taking action because they see how simple it is to do their part," Jake concluded. Thank God for this recorder, she thought to herself.

As soon as the boys saw a man laden with cameras approaching, they started flexing their muscles as they picked up shovels and hoes. Within ten minutes of his arrival, Jared had them all posing together as they planted some drought-tolerant ground cover.

"Wait a minute. That's the same lady that helped me out on the trail."

"Yes indeed. What a coincidence," Jake responded.

"Look lady. My ankle's all better," Ignacio gloated.

"I'm glad to hear that, Ignacio," she replied. Jared looked up from his camera for just a split of a second before continuing to shoot. The interview took 30 minutes but the photo shoot went on and on, as if the photographer had never seen such handsome subjects, or beautiful foliage.

Even though Natalia had brought the extra vegetation on time, Jake was certain that they wouldn't finish planting before their time was up. He was also fairly certain no one would steal the unplanted trees overnight—especially with the Preacher watching out for his new namesake.

By the time the photo shoot had concluded and the folks from Duomo magazine had gone on their way, they were only able to plant a few rows of drought-tolerant Manzanita bushes. They could have used another blast of water from the city to make sure the groundcover took root, Jake thought as he wiped his brow.

As they did their closing circle of the day, everyone was tired and dirty, but happy. Spirits were high as talk of the day's work spilled forth from the boys, interspersed with statements of how they were all going to be famous after being in the magazine. Their excitement was on overdrive. As he listened to the conversations filling the air, Jake felt a sense of pride one might feel when listening to his or her own child boasting about an accomplishment.

As they loaded up their tools in the van, Jake smiled about something else. He not only got her phone number this time, but she had invited him out for coffee this very evening. Never mind that he didn't drink coffee. He finally had a chance to figure out what, if anything was going on between them.

Chapter 22

Ellie had changed about three times already but she still wasn't satisfied. It's just coffee for goodness sake! She told herself. She finally settled on some designer jeans that hugged her hips, a pink sleeveless shirt topped off with a long, feather-light sea foam green sweater she had purchased at a boutique in Carmel last year. She had chosen St. Martins as a meeting place, a family owned café and bakery that was within walking distance of her home. It was packed when she arrived; every seat taken by college students with their books and laptops piled high as if they planned to stay for the entire weekend. Early as usual, she stood in front of one of the bulletin boards, reading through the postings.

"Hey Ellie," his voice came from behind her.

"Hi, Jake. Thanks for meeting me. It's pretty crowded here, but the coffee is to die for."

"Well, good to know," he responded. He was wearing button down 501s and a lightweight UCLA unzipped cardigan, exposing a Greenpeace t-shirt. He could have easily passed as a grad student.

"Did you go to UCLA?" she asked.

"No. I did my undergrad at UC Santa Barbara and my masters at RISD. A UCLA professor gave me this sweatshirt after we assisted with an environmental rally."

"I hope you got more than a sweatshirt," she mused. "Road Island School of Design is a pretty prestigious architectural school. So you're an environmentalist and an architect?" Up until this moment, she had been thinking of Jake as a one dimensional character—a charming, yet poor environmentalist. Now an architect, on the other hand, seemed much more promising.

"Yeah. Keeps me busy." Jake was surprised that she knew about RISD. Most of the women he'd dated in the last few years hadn't even asked about his schooling, let alone heard of RISD. They ordered their drinks and stood next to the counter for a while before it became clear no tables would be opening up anytime soon.

They decided to go for a walk in the neighborhood, and before long, found a vacant bench. As they talked, Ellie reconnected with a feeling she had had before; she could be herself around him. But then again, she couldn't ignore the rest of what had transpired between them.

"So I think we should talk about it," Jake suggested, as if reading her mind.

"About what?" she responded awkwardly.

"That night."

"Yeah. I suppose you're right." Ellie pulled her sweater a little more closely around her body as if it were a crisp autumn evening, not a hot summer night in Southern California. Jake observed her body language with gentle amusement.

"Are you uncomfortable with what we did?" he asked. Ellie shifted on the bench, taking a sip of her latte.

"At the time I wasn't. But afterwards, yeah."

"Can you explain it to me?" he asked calmly.

"What. Here? In the middle of a busy sidewalk on a Friday night?"

"Sure. It's a perfect place. No one is really listening to us. They're all absorbed in their own realities. We're just a couple on a bench talking quietly," he remarked. But that was half the problem; she liked the idea of them being a couple.

"Okay. But bear with me here while my thoughts try to duke it out."

"Duke away. Take your time," Jake offered. He had the gentle tone of a facilitator, which cleared away her hesitation. She spoke before she lost her nerve.

"I really enjoyed our evening together. But it was like I was someone else. I've always waited to, you know."

"Have sex," Jake filled in.

"Yeah. Until I'm committed to someone. It's never been this casual thing I do with a stranger." She crossed her legs.

"Okay. So I'm guessing you feel like what we did contradicted your personal code of ethics."

"Yes. Exactly," Ellie responded, surprised by the accuracy of his words.

"Well, to be honest. It was a surprising turn of events for me too, considering the boundaries you'd laid out earlier that night. But it was clear you wanted it. We both wanted it." Ellie nodded her head in agreement, looking up into his eyes.

"And what did it mean to you?" She asked tentatively.

"Well. For starters, I've been thinking about you the last few weeks," Jake admitted. His eyebrows arched upward, a subtle smile on his face. "But not just because of the intimacy we shared. I felt we had a good connection. That it was easy to talk to you." Ellie found herself nodding once again. He was sitting close to her and she could half picture herself leaning into him, kissing the scar on his cheek.

"But as far as my views on sex, I grew up in a liberal household. Sex was something that I learned about at a young age and I was actually encouraged by my parents to explore it and embrace it, while respecting my partner's needs."

"Whoa," Ellie responded.

"What?"

"Let's just say our parents are just a little different from each other," Ellie started. "The only thing I learned about sex from my parents was that it is a sacred act between a married couple designed for procreation."

"You can't always listen to your parents," Jake countered. "Sexual intimacy is a beautiful experience. I know it can be bonding. But it's also about desire and release. It's healthy to explore your desire, as long as everyone is in agreement with what it means."

"Oh this is going to be hard," Ellie started.

"It doesn't have to be." Jake took her hand in his, pulling her fully into the moment. "Listen Ellie. Remember what you said on my doorstep before you came in that night? Where you said you wanted to take it slowly, get to know each other? We can still do that."

"And just pretend that night never happened?"

"No. We're adults here. We know what we did. We just let the sex develop naturally. Embrace it. Honor it." Ellie listened to his words. Was he someone that was into open relationships? Is that what he meant?

"I can't have sex with you and not be somehow committed," she responded. Jake crossed his arms as he looked at her. Perhaps she was right. This was going to be hard. She couldn't really expect him to commit to her at such an early stage, could she? And that wasn't all. She drove an SUV BMW for God's sake. And even in her attempt to dress casually, she had this elegance about her that suggested she should be sitting on a velvet chair in the foyer of the Four Seasons with an equally sophisticated man, not on a street bench in Westwood with him. But he couldn't help himself. He was attracted to her.

"I can commit to a third date," he compromised, turning his palms upward.

"Don't worry! I'm not asking you to be my boyfriend. That's just it. I'm in totally uncharted territory here and I don't know how to proceed," Ellie acquiesced. Suddenly she had an idea. "Maybe we could start over; as friends. You know. Get to know each other. See if we're even compatible as people?" As her words crossed her lips, she knew there was logic there—a way they could have a fighting chance to be more than friends.

"So we have incredible, orgasmic sex that has kept my mind preoccupied with you over the last few weeks and now you want to be friends?" Jake laughed, shaking his head. A group of teenage girls walking by burst into a screaming, giggling mass of energy as they heard Jake's words.

Ellie covered her face with her hands, laughing out loud as Jake pulled her toward him as if to shelter her from the barrage of attention. The warmth of his skin against hers sent a shiver down her spine. Arno was right. If he so much as put his lips on hers she was a goner.

"Where were we?" Jake asked. Ellie knew where her body wanted to be. Short term gain, or a chance at something real, she argued with herself.

"I'm just saying we could start over. Get to know each other. And then, you know. We could take it from there." This was a first, Jake thought; a woman telling him she just wanted to be friends; though her body language said just the opposite. But for some reason the idea appealed to him.

"And later, if we decide we want to be more than friends?"

"Well. I guess you'll have to ask me out on a real date."

"Okay. Deal!" Ellie felt her shoulders relax. Jake noticed a shift as well.

"I have an idea," Jake said thoughtfully. "What are you doing tomorrow?"

"Not much. Why?"

"Come with me to the Farmer's Market in the morning. I'm going to do some shopping and then some friends are coming over for brunch. You could join us."

"You just want a woman in the kitchen to help you," Ellie teased.

"'fraid not. Grandma taught me how to cook to avoid just such a situation. You know, helping raise a man who could respect feminist ideals."

"Hats off to your grandma. But I enjoy cooking," Ellie returned.

"Well then, we can cook together. You know. See if we're compatible in the kitchen." Ellie punched him in the arm.

"Dang. You've got a good punch, girl. I'll have to keep that in mind," he flinched.

"Growing up with two older brothers and two older sisters, you learn a thing or two," she smiled.

After going out for an ice cream, Jake offered to walk her to her car, only to discover she hadn't driven.

"You live in this neighborhood?"

"About six blocks away. I can give you a tour of the place." Jake walked her home, all the while fighting the desire to take her hand in his. "This is it. Thanks for walking me home." Jake looked at the large modern house that had to be at least four times larger than his.

"You live here by yourself?"

"No. I have a roommate, but she's in Italy right now with her boyfriend, most likely getting engaged," Ellie explained as she unlocked the door.

"That's exciting," Jake responded. He noticed Ellie's eyes lighting up.

"Extremely exciting. And romantic. I can't wait to hear the details." That's right, Jake remembered. Girls share the romantic stuff with one another. He remembered that about Luz; how she'd told everyone their engagement story, pointing out just how romantic a guy she was about to marry.

Ellie noticed a sudden slackness in his face as if he were far, far away.

"Are you okay Jake?"

"Yeah. Just tired." He rubbed his hands across his face while looking at her almost apologetically. "I'll pick you up at 8am, okay?"

"Okay. I guess I'll give you a tour some other time?" Ellie tentatively asked.

"Yeah. Sorry."

"Okay. Well, good night Jake."

"Goodnight." He hugged her gently before walking out into the night.

Ellie watched him go, fighting the urge to call after him. Clearly something she had said upset him, but she couldn't imagine what it could be.

Chapter 23

Ellie was up at 5:30am. After her morning run, she drank a large bottled water, logged on remotely to her work and put in an hour before showering and dressing for the day. She was finishing her second cappuccino when she heard a knock on the front door. She didn't hear a car come into the driveway and figured Jake must drive a Prius or some other silent hybrid type automobile. She stepped outside and there he was, no car in sight.

"Morning Jake," she called casually, looking around for his car.

"Oh. I biked over," he responded. "I was thinking we could catch the bus from here."

"The bus?" Ellie tried to hide her dread. A test, she thought dubiously.

"If you're not comfortable with it," Jake started.

"No. I'm game," she cut him off. "Plus, I can finally get some of my alternative transportation points for your Seven Eco Steps." They walked two and a half blocks to a bus stop Ellie had probably passed a hundred times but never really noticed. Within 15 minutes, they were dropped a block from their destination.

The Farmer's Market was packed. The few times she had made it down, parking had been a nightmare. The bus on the other hand, was a piece of cake. Jake took his time going to each booth and perusing the fresh fruits and vegetables, and Ellie had to adjust to his slow, meandering pace.

"You like zucchini?" Jake asked.

"I like it grilled with a bit of olive oil, salt and dill," Ellie responded.

"We could try that." He selected two large zucchinis.

"The small, young zucchinis are the most flavorful," Ellie remarked.

"Yeah?"

"Yeah." Confident, Jake thought. As they moved on, he was surprised to discover that she had an opinion on about every vegetable he selected.

"Hey deer hunter, how do you know so much about vegetables?"

"I grew up on a farm veggie boy. We had a year round vegetable garden that spanned three acres," Ellie fired back.

"Wow, that's so cool," Jake mused. "I would have loved that sort of experience." She didn't look much like a country girl to him in her white strappy sandals, linen Capri's and pink silk blouse. But then again, she didn't look much like a deer hunter either.

"You think so? It's hard work, Jake. We spent hours watering, harvesting, not to mention days pulling weeds because my mom didn't believe in buying pesticides. And that's not even counting all the time prepping and storing food for the winter. It's like a full time job."

"Hats off to your mom. Hard work, but worth it?" Jake asked optimistically. She heard the hope in his voice, and felt something inside her give a little. Was it worth it? She remembered the joy of biting into a sweet cherry tomato right off the vine, canning chutneys and stewed vegetables, picking wild blueberries with her brothers and sisters in the forests for jam.

"At the time I didn't think so. But yes. If I lived in a rural area again, I would definitely grow my own food." It didn't take them long to fill the cloth bags Jake had brought along with organic fruits and vegetables and hop back on the bus.

They were far more compatible in the kitchen than either had suspected. By the time his friends arrived, they had made a beautiful spread of grilled vegetables, a frittata with goat cheese and home fries seasoned with fresh herbs from his garden. Everyone gawked at the food, rubbing their hands together as they entered.

"You really went overboard this morning, Jake. This looks fantastic!" Ethan commented.

"That's 'cause I had extra help," Jake smiled. "Hey guys, this is Ellie." There were five of them, three women and two men, and they greeted Ellie enthusiastically, each taking a moment to introduce themselves. Ellie was surprised by how different they looked from anyone she regularly hung out with. They seemed wild, edgy. They soon took over Jake's back porch, crowding around the table as if they all had their regular places on the bench seats.

"You two can squeeze in here," suggested Jemma, a young woman with an impressive number of tattoos on her thin, pale arms.

"Thanks Jemma," Jake smiled. Jemma glanced at Jake through an expanse of jet black hair that partially covered her face.

"No problem," she replied, playfully looking Ellie up and down. April, a sexy redhead in knee-high boots, extremely short shorts and a woven tank top also gave her a warm smile. Ellie felt instantly jealous of this woman's ability to look so natural in an outfit Ellie would never consider leaving the house in.

After a bit more small talk over brunch, the friends dove into a heated conversation, which only took one line for Ellie to understand what it was all about.

"BP's saying 50,000 barrels a day," Ethan stated.

"Yeah. Like we can trust their numbers," April scoffed. "It's probably, like, a 100,000 barrels a day."

"Know what pisses me off? The word moratorium. How about a complete end to off shore drilling? Moratorium is like saying we're gonna take a little pause, since surveys say it's not so popular right now, with all those *oil covered pelicans* and *fishermen out of work*, but we'll be back as soon as this little Deep Water Horizon situation blows over." Jemma blew her jet black bangs away from her eyes, as if letting off steam.

"Crazy thing is, it's not a moratorium on all offshore drilling. Only deepwater drilling. So actually, it only impacts about 1% of the oil and gas platforms in the Gulf of Mexico alone. That's nothing,"

April countered, as she brushed her fingers through her long red curls.

As Ellie listened to the conversation, she simply nodded, hesitant to say anything. Everyone at the office had been extremely upset when the oil spill happened, but now that a month had passed, it seemed to elude their conversations. Clearly that was not the case here.

"This will affect the environmental health of this region for years to come," Ethan added.

"And that's exactly why, if there's enough pressure from the public and the environmental camp, this moratorium could turn into a ban of all off shore drilling that will stay put until the next republican administration comes in," Jake stated.

"Don't hold your breath, Jake," countered Edmond, a stocky man with deep brown eyes.

"Yeah. And don't forget that before the oil spill, Obama was all set to end a three decade drilling ban and open up the East coast to drilling," Ethan fumed.

"And I helped vote him in office!" Jake laughed. At least she had one thing in common with these people. Ellie tuned out of the conversation for a few moments, wondering if it had been such a good idea to come today. But then her journalistic mind pulled her attention back into the debate, just as Edmond shared some news that shocked her.

"You know what I heard from a grad student up at Claremont? If we opened all of our offshore waters to drilling, it would only supply the U.S. for one year of oil. One year! Destroy our oceans and ecosystems for what? One damned year of oil? How's that logical?" Edmond said, wrinkling his forehead.

"It's not man." Ethan responded coolly. "That's the problem."

Ellie made a mental note to find out more about this Claremont grad student. If that was actually true, she felt it was newsworthy. She sipped her juice quietly. She could imagine this conversation going on for hours. And it might have had Natalia, the woman she'd met briefly at the art opening, not arrived at that moment with her friend. The two women grabbed a few chairs from Jake's garage and marveled at the food Ellie and Jake had made together.

"Ellie. Nice to see you again. This is my girlfriend Mary."

"Hi Mary. Pleasure to meet you," Ellie said, extending her hand. Mary, a beautiful blond with tanned skin and peppered hazel eyes smiled at Ellie and squeezed her hand.

"I've heard a lot about you," she remarked coyly before letting go. Ellie glanced at Jake who raised his palms upward.

"I'm innocent," he responded. Laughter filled the table.

"Oh no. From Natalia," Mary clarified. Ellie laughed, slightly embarrassed by the attention.

"Ladies. She's kind of taken. So you might as well keep those fantasies in check now," Jake countered as he put his arm protectively around Ellie. Everyone laughed again, and the energy shifted; became lighter. Jake pulled a salad out of the fridge that Ellie hadn't helped him with.

"This salad we are about to eat was harvested from my garden, which explains all the bug bites in the lettuce."

Ellie noticed the flowers on his table had also been picked from his garden, which reminded her of something they used to do on the farm.

"You should try companion planting to get rid of the bugs," she suggested.

"What's that?" Jemma questioned.

"It's a natural way to keep the bugs out of your garden," Ellie explained. All eyes turned toward her.

"How does that work?" Jake asked, intrigued.

"Well, if you plant Marigolds next to asparagus or eggplant for example, they deter beetles that find these veggies tasty."

"Really? Cool! What can I plant next to the lettuce to keep the slugs from having first dibs?" Jake asked.

"Mint and sage repel slugs," she went on. She hadn't talked this much the whole morning. Jake's friends looked at her approvingly.

"So there's a whole methodology to it?" Mary questioned.

"Yeah. It's all about pairing. It doesn't work with all insects, but for the most part, it's pretty effective." Edmond looked at her questioningly.

"How do you know about this?" he asked.

"Well, we had a choice growing up. Buy pesticides or read up on ways to deter the insects naturally."

"So you were basically doing organic gardening in rural, conservative Idaho," Edmond concluded out loud. Ellie didn't appreciate the way he described her home state.

"Well, yeah, but we didn't think of it like that. We didn't buy organic plants or anything like that." She suddenly felt uncomfortable with so much attention from Jake's friends. She certainly didn't feel like getting into a group discussion about growing up poor.

"Come help us with our community gardens, Ellie," Ethan pleaded.

"I could do that," she responded. Before long, the guys started talking about the upcoming world cup tournament and the girls broke off into conversations of their own. It was as if her mere mention of companion planting was some sort of magical key that let her inside their world. Ellie was surprised by their genuine friendliness; something she hadn't encountered very often in L.A. Like Jake, they seemed excited about life, about making a change, although they weren't nearly as optimistic as he was. In fact, Jake seemed to be the most optimistic one among them. And even though they openly challenged his optimism, they clearly loved this about him.

Not once did someone mention fashion or movie stars, make-up or clothing, and Ellie was surprisingly relieved by the change of pace. Instead, they talked about activism, camping and hiking, great concerts they had seen and food. There was no end to the talk about food; organic of course, and fresh from the farmer's market or community garden.

They didn't ask about her work, but wanted to know what she thought of L.A. and what it was like growing up in McCall, Idaho. So Jake had done some talking after all.

"I hear you've started the Seven Eco Steps," Natalia remarked.

"Yes. And all the girls at the office signed up too," she reported.

"When?" Natalia asked.

"Well, I've been doing it for a few weeks now. But the girls signed up yesterday."

"Wow. You know how to make things happen. Must be those advertising and marketing skills."

A moment later, they were onto another topic; raw food. Ellie listened on in surprise as the women shared different recipes that sounded surprisingly delicious. There was an easiness to the group, a laid back feeling that made her a little homesick. The morning gave way to afternoon, and Edmond was soon strumming a guitar as a bottle of wine circulated around the table. A second guitar emerged in Jake's hands, and the friends sang rock ballads and even some folk songs Ellie had grown up with. When she started to sing along, the circle of friends clapped, clearly taken by her melodic voice and harmonies. Jake had gently touched her shoulder or arm more than once that day, and she had found herself placing her hand in his. It was clear his friends had all but assumed they were a couple, and neither of them did anything to contradict it.

"Do your friends hang out at your house every weekend?" Ellie asked, when they had a moment alone.

"Not every weekend, but often enough. They act like they own the place, don't they?

"They clearly love you," Ellie responded. Jake shrugged his shoulders.

"Yeah. I suppose so."

Someone accidentally knocked over a glass of wine, which splashed on Ellie's silk blouse and linen Capri's. Everyone had an opinion on how to get out the stain and before long, Ellie was wearing a pair of plaid shorts and a Gaia Eden t-shirt, offset by her rhinestone sandals as her clothes soaked in white wine and baking soda.

By the time everyone else left, it was well past dark. Jake and Ellie stood in the kitchen, leaning on the counters just across from one another. He was pleasantly surprised to see how relaxed she had been around his friends. A little quiet at first, but as the day had worn on, she had opened up.

"Did you have fun today?" he asked, smiling at the sight of her in his oversized clothes.

"I did. Your friends are great, Jake. Down to earth."

"Yeah. They liked you too. You have a down to earth side to you as well, you know."

"Thanks," she smiled, yawning. "Especially in this get up." Now that they were alone, memories of her last visit to Jake's house started filling her mind.

"Sleepy?" he asked.

"Yeah. I was up at 5:30 this morning, and it's got to be past ten by now."

Jake glanced at his iPhone. "Actually, its 8:40 p.m.," he laughed.

"Sheesh," Ellie said. "I'm wiped out. I think I should head home." Seeing her in his clothes with a sleepy look on her face made him want to sweep her off to his bedroom, but he knew better.

"Yeah. We better get you home before something happens," he flirted. She caught the look on his face, and a smirk formed on her lips. She definitely wanted to see him again.

"What are you doing tomorrow night?" she asked suddenly. Jake paused for a beat before answering.

"I'm going to see a film about the state of the oceans," Jake responded. "It's being shown on campus at UCLA." He failed to mention he was going with Clarissa, a girl he dated now and again. He felt slightly guilty about the omission.

"Oh," came Ellie's disappointed reply.

"But it's not set in stone," he responded carefully. "Why?"

"Well, I'm going to a benefit for the Children of Rwanda at the Oviatt Building and I have an extra ticket."

"The Oviatt building? Seriously? I love art deco. Did you know that's the oldest Art Deco building in Los Angeles?"

"No. I didn't. That's exciting. But the party's on the rooftop terrace."

"Sounds fancy."

"Yeah. It is. Black tie event. Are you interested in going?"

"Well. You've seen the one suit I own," Jake started.

"Your suit is fine. Just wear a tie and you're set."

"I don't own a tie," he admitted.

"Seriously? We can get you one tomorrow if you want to go. There's actually some people coming I'd like to introduce you to." Jake liked the sound of that. If she was interested in introducing him to her friends, that meant she was letting him into her life.

"Okay. I'll cancel my movie. How shall we get there?" Jake asked.

"I'm not taking the bus in my Aidon Mattix dress," Ellie warned coolly.

"Why not?" he asked. She didn't know how to respond.

"I don't want to get it dirty," she replied awkwardly.

"Business people ride the bus all the time completely unscathed. Dare I even say, clean?"

"You're like the green police, Jake! Listen. I'm doing a lot of green changes every day, but one step at a time, remember?" Ellie folded her arms across her chest, feeling the romantic moment that was forming between them slipping away.

"Sorry. I didn't mean to be pushy," Jake replied in earnest.

"Okay. So I'll drive," Ellie stated, slightly agitated.

"How about if I drive?" he offered.

"You have a car?"

"Yeah. The very chariot that will bring you to your doorstep this evening."

"I can drive myself home. I had, like, one glass of wine today, which I didn't even finish."

"I'm not doubting your ability to drive. But your car isn't here," Jake laughed.

"I totally forgot we took the bus here! I'm so used to having my car."

"Breaking habits is the hardest part," he responded. Ellie ignored his comment. Her car was hardly a habit. It was a necessity. After she gathered her things, they headed to the garage out back. Inside, there was a car under a large tarp.

"Either you have some really expensive collectible under there, or you don't drive much," Ellie quipped.

"I don't drive much." Next to the car were several bicycles. One had a bike trailer that looked like it could hold a large load of groceries or other items.

"Is that how you usually get around?" she asked, trying to keep her voice steady.

"Yeah. That one is for cross town commutes," he said, pointing to a beautiful street bike. "That one is for utilitarian trips," he remarked, pointing to the bike with the trailer, "and that over there is a Pedi cab. I used it during college. Quite a lucrative profession, I might add." A blue Toyota Prius emerged among all the bicycles as he removed the tarp.

"I guessed you'd have a Prius," she joked. For the first time, he didn't joke back.

"It was the most fuel efficient car on the market at the time, so, that's what I have. And yes, the brakes work."

"Okay." She looked at him, her lower lip slightly pulled in.

"Sorry. It's just, I'm tired of Prius jokes."

"No. I didn't mean it as a joke. I was more referencing that they're known for being so environmentally friendly. And you are definitely into the environment and . . ." she could tell she was just making matters worse.

"It's okay, Ellie," Jake recovered. By the time he dropped her off, their conversation was back to normal, and Ellie felt a little more awake.

"I really enjoyed today, Jake," she said in earnest.

"Me too." He leaned over, kissing her quickly on the cheek before she stepped out of the car.

"Goodnight."

Chapter 24

Jake made a strong impression on her friends at the Children of Rwanda charity event. And after she introduced him to the CEO of Hope Farmers, she didn't have a chance to talk to him for at least 45 minutes, as the two dove into a conversation about the future of the green movement. Ellie might have experienced a little jealousy if she hadn't had her own incredible conversation with the director of The Children for Rwanda.

And the setting was amazing. The city usually weighed her down. But from the rooftop terrace, L.A. took on an ethereal quality. She spotted Jake, finally alone, gazing toward the skyline.

"Hey," she said quietly as she leaned on the railing next to him.

"Hey," he responded warmly, glad to see her. "Thanks so much for inviting me. This has been an incredible evening. Allison thinks we can work together."

"Allison, huh. Already on a first name basis?"

"Jealous?" Jake winked. She didn't reply, but the smile on her face said enough.

"Looks like you hit it off with the Director of Children for Rwanda as well."

"Yes. He thinks I should go into non-profit. You know, join your ranks."

"An excellent idea," Jake responded.

"Maybe someday," Ellie said.

"Why not now?" Jake asked. "No time like the present to follow your heart." She tried not to read too much into his words.

"Well. Can you keep a secret?"

"Sure," he responded.

"There's a decent chance I could be promoted to Marketing Director at Duomo if things go well over the next month."

"And that's what you really want?" he asked. She thought about two applications she had recently sent to non-profits—something she did on occasion just to keep herself sharp. It was amazing how much competition there was for these low paying jobs.

"I might be more fulfilled if I was working for children's literacy, or infant healthcare," she answered honestly, "but my work at Duomo is exciting to me."

"If you really enjoy it, then you should go for it. But don't close the door on what fulfills you." She could see why his friends held him at the center of their circle; he was not only energetic and genuinely friendly, but he saw right into you, encouraging the nobler path.

◊◊◊

Over the next week and a half, they managed to see each other almost every evening, cooking together most of the time. The more they talked, the clearer it became how different their lives were. In fact, if she hadn't started the Seven Eco Steps, she would have been a complete stranger in his world. Usually, she wouldn't hesitate about bringing a bottled water for a walk on the beach, or ordering take-out. But around him, she consciously remembered to bring her new metal water bottle, or opted to cook at home, rather than creating a pile of waste with to go meals. But as different as their lifestyles were, they had the same easy communication that had been there from the get go.

She might be way behind on the whole green movement, but she knew her marketing far better than Jake. It had taken her all but ten seconds to convince him to change the name of his online campaign from the Seven Eco Steps to the Seven Change Challenge.

"It's a more concise name," she had explained. "It tells you immediately that you're entering a challenge, that it requires change, and exactly how many changes are expected of you. And it's a call to action. You pack all of that into three words."

"Wow. Fantastic tip. That's definitely an improvement," Jake had replied, texting the change to his co-workers moments after she suggested it.

A few days later when she made suggestions on his website and social media approach, he listened, but shook his head.

"I know marketing's important, but I'm not about selling to people. People have to want this on their own." For some reason, she read into his words.

"People don't always know what they want," Ellie had responded. "Sometimes they need a little convincing, especially if the concept is a bit out of their comfort zone. There's no crime in making the packaging more enticing. If they taste it, actually experience it and don't want anymore, that's their choice. At least you gave them the chance to try." Jake had smiled at her, but hadn't responded. Which was odd; he usually had an opinion about everything.

◊◊◊

When she discovered Jake couldn't relate to classical art, she viewed it as a challenge, convincing him to go to the Norton Simon Museum with her one afternoon. She felt like she won some sort of contest when he admitted to enjoying the outing, especially the impressionist art. They took turns choosing their outings, and after a night at a small theatre, it was Jake's turn to choose.

"I enjoyed the play. Thanks for taking me," Jake managed as he held her hand. "Have your hiking boots on and be ready to go by 8:30 a.m. tomorrow," he stated flirtatiously before kissing her goodnight on the cheek.

He took her hiking in Solstice Canyon in Malibu Saturday afternoon. It felt so incredible to be out in nature again that Ellie felt herself longing to kiss him on the lips. But she didn't dare. He grabbed her playfully and kissed her on the cheek, but pulled away right afterwards as he always did, as if intentionally avoiding physical contact.

Although Jake could talk endlessly about the environment and architecture, she was still uncertain of what he was looking for in a relationship, or if he wanted one at all. Whenever they went out, she couldn't help but notice other women staring at him. And based on his upbringing, casual sex was just fine in his book.

They found a clearing and she pulled out a picnic blanket, throwing it over a patch of uneven grass as the warmth of the day settled over them. As they ate their lunch in silence, Ellie decided it was time to get some answers.

"Jake, can I ask you something?" she asked, as she peeled off her lightweight sweatshirt.

"Yeah. Shoot."

"What are you looking for in a partner?"

"I don't know," he responded, caught off guard.

"You don't know?" Ellie gazed at him. Jake crossed his arms over his chest, tucking his hands into his armpits. "Looks like I've made you uncomfortable," she observed.

"No. Not really. I just don't have a checklist or something I can just rattle off, but give me a minute." Truth was, he didn't know, because he hadn't thought about a relationship for a long time; until recently. He enjoyed his time with Ellie, and the idea of having something more with her was growing on him. He knew this was an opportunity to be honest, but also to be careful. A spider crawled onto her arm and Jake prepared himself for the scream, but it didn't come. She flicked it off without flinching, as Jake looked on with amazement. Courageous; I'll have to add that to my list, he thought.

"So. Let's see. I want to be with someone I'm attracted to inside and out; someone who is independent and strong," he eyed her thoughtfully. So far, she fit the bill. "And someone who shares my lifestyle and my convictions." And there it was. Out in the open, he thought.

"So what do you mean by lifestyle and convictions?" The strange words of her e-date James Hadley came back to her: Everyone is conducting an interview.

"You've seen the work I do, Ellie. That's got to give you insight into who I am. I don't believe in sitting by on the sidelines, wondering why the world's going to hell and thinking it's someone else's responsibility to do something about it. I believe in taking action." There was a shyness about him that she recalled from their first dinner together, before things had gotten crazy.

"I admire that in you Jake," she responded. "I want to help people too. That's why I go to fundraisers; to help. I'm just not ready to dedicate my life to it." Jake did his best to stay on track. He had to be careful. Not too preachy.

"My focus is on the environment, but people are right in there, Ellie. It's all connected."

"Like the impacts global warming has on people?" Ellie asked.

"Okay. Do you want to get me started?" he warned. Ellie nodded for him to continue. He set down his sandwich on a little tin pan and sat up straight, as if preparing to make a speech. "So, let's take pollution for example. Did you know that the poorest people live in areas with the highest levels of toxicity?"

"I hadn't heard it like that before, but I can imagine that's the case," she responded. "I've seen pictures of Indian families living in the landfills, their children playing in the trash." Ellie couldn't stand seeing photos like that, because how could she, as one person, really help?

"Yes. That's a very good example. But it's also happening right here in the United States. People want their trash to go away, but they don't want a landfill in their neighborhood. People don't want to live next to the pollution of industrial plants, but they want the products these plants produce. But someone lives next to these places. And guess who? The poor. Why? These are the areas left over for the marginalized people in our society. The poor, who already have inadequate access to health care, and lack of access to education, who work more hours in blue collar jobs than the rest of us. They're exposed to a disproportionate amount of toxins in their living environments."

The playfulness slipped from her body as she took in his words. Memories of her upbringing flashed back to her. She hadn't grown up next to toxins, but her grandfather had died of lung cancer after working for years in a mine.

"I'm sorry Jake, but I don't think one person can address all of these problems, and this is just the sort of thing that makes the whole environmental movement seem, well, futile." Surprisingly, Jake smiled at her response.

"I should be the one apologizing. I warned you not to get me going." He squeezed her hand reassuringly. "I can see how that seems like a totally bleak picture. It is. But the good news is, there are millions of people across the planet actively pursuing solutions to these sort of inequities—and I'm not talking about the government or the businesses that contributed to the toxicity in the first place. I'm talking about community groups, non-profits, and citizens coming together—organizations that are demanding change and transforming our planet as we speak."

"Jake," She started.

"Yeah?"

"You are both entirely sexy and completely unattainable," Ellie stated, enunciating each word with a smile.

"Unattainable?" Jake shook his head. He always got carried away.

"Well, I'm sure a woman who shares your activism and convictions exists, but I'm not her." Ellie stated.

"Well hold on a minute," Jake countered.

"Wait. Let me finish. I mean, I care about the environment, I care about social justice. But it's not my life." She knew she was risking losing him, being so brutally honest, but she had no choice. "I like to go shopping; drive in my car to get my morning latte! You know? So, immediately, this wall goes up, where I have to become someone I'm not, even to consider a relationship with you." It had been a long time since a woman had spoken to him so honestly.

God, I'm pushing her away, he thought. Despite their differences, he loved being around her. He looked at her in earnest before responding.

"I don't know about that. I'm not saying you have to suddenly be a perfect environmentalist overnight. It's just like the Seven Change Challenge. You're totally doing it! It's a step by step process. I'm not perfect. I have a long way to go as well. I just want someone who wants to live consciously with me and who is open to seeing ways to living more sustainably."

"Well, I wish whoever you end up being with a lot of luck with that." Ellie grinned mischievously.

"So you've already ruled me out, have you?" Jake asked, his eyes boring into her.

"Not entirely." She leaned into him, placing a quick kiss on his lips. Jake used every bit of energy in him to resist the urge to pull her down on top of him and take her right there in the meadow. Instead, he leaned back on his elbows, glancing at her curiously.

"Good to know. So, now that I've given you my laundry list, what's yours? What are you looking for in a guy?" Ellie rolled her shoulders back as she thought about her long checklist.

"I have a princess list, really. I want someone who is passionate about life and about me. Someone who's honest, has integrity, beliefs. Handsome, smart and fit, of course, and wants a serious relationship, eventually marriage and children."

"Beautiful. I'm with you on all but the children." His words cut into her.

"I thought that might be the case." Ellie went quiet as she sat up a bit straighter. This could be a deal breaker. She definitely wanted children, and it would be pointless to start a relationship with a man who didn't. Jake noticed the shift.

"I love kids. Don't get me wrong. I'm around them all of the time, but from an environmental standpoint, it doesn't make any sense to make your own," Jake reasoned.

"But anything in moderation can make sense," she argued. "Just like your whole Seven Change Challenge. It's about moderation: shorter showers, driving less often, one or two children, versus six." Her arms folded across her chest as if a breeze had passed over her.

"Yes, that's definitely a good starting point." He gazed at her long legs and sun kissed skin, a combination of desire and respect running through him.

"So you know what that means, Ellie," he queried roguishly. "You'd have to convert to my environmental religion in order for us to reproduce."

Ellie smiled. The lightness of the conversation made it easier to discuss a topic that was dear to her. Jake started chuckling.

"What?" she asked.

"We're from two different factions of society—a regular Romeo and Juliet, eh?"

"I suppose we are. But that would also mean we were star crossed lovers, not friends."

"We'll just have to wait and see how that turns out," Jake responded. After lunch, they hiked up the trail, both lost in their own thoughts. Ellie breathed in the smell of damp earth and pine, triggering memories of home. She imagined showing Jake her home town, taking him on a backpacking trip into the remote wilderness of Idaho. She recalled a certain high mountain lake that was only accessible by trail, a good six miles in. It would shock his city-boy mind, she mused.

Jake was uncharacteristically quiet on the hike out. When he dropped her off, she gave him a hug as he brought the car to a standstill.

"Thanks for taking me out there today, Jake. It was beautiful." Jake looked into her eyes, taking in the warmth and kindness there. Not the type of girl to lead on, he thought, as he broke eye contact.

"You're welcome." He seemed distant, and Ellie did her best not to take it personally.

"Ellie, I wanted to let you know . . . I'm pretty busy this week," he trailed off.

"Yeah. Me too," she quickly retorted.

"Well. We'll call when our schedules lighten up?" His voice was constrained.

"Yeah. Sure," Ellie returned, trying to keep her emotions in check. She turned away as he pulled down the driveway, wondering what had gone wrong. *We'll call when our schedules lighten up.* Yeah. She didn't need an interpreter to know what that meant; he was breaking up with her before they even started dating. The tears wet her cheeks before she even got the door open. God, do I know how to screw up a relationship, she thought. First have sex with him, then ignore him and then tell him I want to be friends, and finally, push on the issue of children. No wonder I'm twenty nine and still single; great going Ellie.

Chapter 25

It was just after dark when Jake and Conrad set out on their bikes to hit up one of their favorite spots; the dumpster behind Book Stables. Most bookstores sent their discards back to the manufacturer, but as a second hand bookstore that seemed particularly sensitive to outer looks, Book Stables tossed a lot of donations that didn't meet their "good as new" promise.

As they dug through the discards, Jake found a pile of identical math books. The boys wouldn't really jump for joy about the books, but they certainly needed to brush up on their math skills. He came across a title that piqued his interest; "Marketing for Non-Profits." Ellie had given him quite a few tips on marketing over the last few weeks. But was there a special approach for non-profits? He'd have to brush up on it and surprise her with his knowledge. He picked up another book entitled "Commitment and Monogamy in a Contemporary World." He stuffed it between the math books and tossed the stack into his bike trailer before Conrad could see the title. As they made their getaway, Conrad was the one to suggest they go for a beer. They cycled to the nearest Irish pub and grabbed two stools at the bar.

"I'm buying tonight," Conrad announced.

"What's the occasion?" Jake asked. Conrad took a healthy sip of his beer before responding.

"Stephanie's pregnant."

"Wow man. I don't know what to say," Jake replied cautiously.

"How about congratulations, you idiot!" Conrad shook his head at his friend.

"Congratulations! Sorry. You never told me you were trying," Jake responded.

"We've been trying for about eight months now."

"So this is pretty big news, then," Jake acknowledged. He had no idea how long this sort of thing took, as he'd spent his life trying to do just the opposite.

"Yeah. She's two months along." Although Conrad was just two years older than Jake, there was this sagely side to him. Come to think of it, Jake had been hitting Conrad up for advice since they were friends in college. It only made sense that Conrad was the one who was married, had a solid job and was now starting a family.

"So do you think you'll ever settle down again? You know. Stop screwing around and actually have a real girlfriend. Someone like Luz."

It had been a while since he'd heard her name spoken out loud. Jake let out a heavy sigh. She had been on his mind over the last month; ever since that first night with Ellie.

"No one will ever be like Luz," he responded.

"Of course not. She was a gem, Jake. I'm sorry I brought her up." He set his hand on Jake's shoulder. "But there are a lot of other good women in the world."

"Yeah. I just may have found one that fits in that category."

"So I've heard."

"Ah. What, Natalia say something?"

"No. Ethan told me. He said she's upper crust, dignified, intelligent. Not your usual material." Jake had to smile at the description. All of his friends thought they were dating, and it was at least half true. Although he and Ellie were in this strange just-friends phase, he felt that the scales were about to tip. But the idea unsettled him.

"Truth be told, we're just friends."

"Come on. You haven't slept with her? I hear she's quite the looker."

"Well. Yeah. She is, and we did," Jake admitted. "But just once. I could actually use your advice on this one."

"I'm all ears," Conrad reassured him. Jake recounted the story from the beginning. Conrad listened carefully, letting Jake spin out the details.

"So now that you're in this friends phase, do you find yourself wanting more, or do you want to keep it just friends?"

"I totally want more, but I don't know. I don't want to hurt her. I'm completely confused." Jake let out an exhale as he took another swig of his beer.

"Well. If there's no chemistry," Conrad began.

"Oh God. The chemistry's incredible. The fact that I've been able to keep my hands off her is a miracle. It's really hard."

"Spare me the details," Conrad joked. "So the chemistry's there. Are you compatible in other ways?"

"We totally click. She makes me laugh. She argues intelligently when she disagrees with me. She's honest. Smart. We're great together."

"Then what's the problem?" Conrad asked. Jake brought his hands together in a ball, resting his elbows on the bar.

"Honestly? It's laughable how different we are."

"How so?" Conrad asked calmly. Jake quickly rattled off a list: too mainstream; all about her career, fashion-oriented; drives an SUV; clueless about the environment; yuppie lifestyle; type of girl who wants to marry and have kids.

"Sounds like you've been building up some ammunition against her," Conrad surmised. "That's not your style, Jake." Jake took in the criticism. He wanted to deny it, but couldn't.

"I hadn't thought about it like that." Usually he kept women at bay, sometimes letting weeks go by before calling them back. But with Ellie, if a day went by without seeing her, he felt disappointment. At the same time, he was keeping a list of her faults.

"Yet you're singing her praises," Conrad countered. "You mentioned how she's opening you up to new things too. That trip to

Norton Simon, for example. Seems like it made an impression on you."

"It did. She's into culture—sort of high culture, I guess." Jake tried to sort through the thoughts crowding his mind. "I don't know how to say this, but these sort of things haven't mattered to me in the last couple of years."

"I'm not following you," Conrad responded.

"You know. About a woman's beliefs and interests and whether we're really compatible." Embarrassment seeped over his face. How could he explain it to Conrad of all people? He had been married for the last six years, and he and Stephanie had dated for a long time before that. Now they were expecting their first baby. He knew nothing about playing the field.

"Jake. I'm going to be brutally honest with you here."

"Shoot."

"You won't let a woman matter to you because you've been holding onto Luz this whole time. She's gone, man. She can't come back even if she wanted to. You know that. You've been completely detaching yourself from women, because you don't want to experience love again. Because if you love again, you might experience pain and loss again."

Jake flagged the bartender for another beer. Conrad was one of his best buddies. This was a blessing, but sometimes it was a real pain in the ass—like right now.

"I'm not afraid of loving a woman again," Jake responded listlessly. His words fell flat. Conrad didn't respond, but the patient way he looked at Jake said it all.

"Okay. I'm afraid of commitment. That's true. And yes, I haven't committed to anyone since Luz. But I'd like to be in love with a woman again. You know, have something like you and Stephanie." Conrad's face lit up as he took in Jake's compliment.

"She and I aren't polar opposites or anything, but it's our differences that make us so great as a couple. We balance each other out. And if this woman,"

"Ellie," Jake interrupted.

"If Ellie balances you out, challenges you in a good way, then that's a good sign."

"So maybe that's why I'm afraid to be with her again physically," Jake admitted.

"How so?" Conrad asked. Jake ran his hands through his curls.

"It's hard to explain. Right now we're friends. We get along. We laugh all of the time. She gets me." Jake thought over their last week together, and his heart caught. "You should see how hard she's trying on the Seven Change Challenge. Then she'll do something out of habit, like grab a bottled water and she's half way through when she realizes what she's doing and her eyes get all wide. It's adorable. And at the same time, she has this fierce intelligence and drive."

"The way you're talking about her, it sounds like you're really falling for her." Jake opened his mouth to deny Conrad's assessment. But no words came. He was falling for her, and hard. And what if she never wanted to transition back to lovers?

"She'd have to do some serious changing if we were to settle down together," Jake responded. Conrad smiled inwardly at Jake's word choice. Perhaps Jake was talking more about himself.

"Give her a break, man. Not everyone is steeped in environmentalism on a daily basis like you and me. I mean, would it be a deal breaker if she was just say, who she is?"

"Deal breaker, well." Jake thought it through. One thing he never wanted to do was force his views on someone else. And Ellie was doing great on the challenge.

"This could work out if you can open up to the experience," Conrad offered. Jake let out a sigh, dropping his shoulders.

"I certainly hope so." He looked at his friend who would soon be a father. "Congratulations on the baby. You're going to be a great father."

"He's still forming, Jake. Congratulate me when I'm holding him in my arms."

Chapter 26

Last week Ellie had been swamped. She had brought in three new advertisers and Margo had given her several projects to head. Ellie approached each request with guarded enthusiasm. When Margo asked her to go to a mixer one evening with a group of developers and real estate brokers, Ellie dressed to the nines and spent her evening talking with the very people Margo had asked her to target.

When she happened to run into Darren Wales from Pacific West Holdings, he mentioned a new project called Stanton Lofts. The article she had clipped from the paper a few weeks ago as an afterthought suddenly gained significance as he told her more about the project they were slotting for an old warehouse area. By the end of the evening, Darren had asked for her business card and said he wanted to follow up with her. Ellie crossed her fingers; maybe this was just the connection she needed to bring them back as an advertiser.

When Margo invited her to join her and Karen for their weekly lunch, Ellie was filled with anticipation. But nothing special happened in the meeting. If anything, Ellie was annoyed by the way Margo and Karen carried on as if she wasn't even there. She inserted herself into the conversation as often as possible, but it only took moments before she was excluded again. Afterwards, Karen explained that Margo liked to play mind games once in a while as a test.

"And although you never know with Margo," she acknowledged, "I think your persistence was a good response." If it was indeed a test, this convoluted method disturbed Ellie. She preferred honesty and transparency over devious mind games.

And that brought her to Jake; he had gone from distant and non-communicative last Saturday, to making it abundantly clear that he wanted to spend time with her, texting and calling every day. Rather than the air of nonchalance she had become accustomed to, he seemed almost anxious when she couldn't see him, which she found far preferable to nonchalant.

And the office challenge was clearly going well. Some of the girls discovered that they lived not far from one another and had started carpooling. Almost everyone had switched to Joey's coffee and the owner was befuddled when the reusable coffee mugs, that had lain dormant on his counter for months, suddenly sold out in one day.

Someone had printed out a color photo of a tar covered pelican and taped it on the wall by the office copier. When no one was looking, she wrote in large capital letters across the top "What are you doing for Pelican Wanda?" Before long, the photo was surrounded by post-it notes with comments ranging from comedic to heartfelt. But most were pledges.

I will walk to work one day a week for you Wanda.

Wanda, I asked my congressmen to ban all offshore drilling.

I will make a donation so a relief worker can clean your wings and set you free.

It was Ellie who thought to post it on Twitter as part of the office challenge update. And it went viral. Pelican Wanda was re-tweeted over 450 times and counting, which resulted in a windfall of sign ups for the Seven Change Challenge and a slight increase in Duomo subscriptions.

Jake was beside himself when he saw the spike in numbers. But when the Seven Change Challenge got written up in the Huffington Post with both a picture of Pelican Wanda and a link to the Gaia Eden website, his team could barely keep up with the number of new participants. Ellie didn't expect to see Jake again until Thursday evening. Thus she was pleasantly surprised by a text message that arrived on her phone Tuesday morning; "You've got to meet me to celebrate."

When they met at Venice beach after work for a walk, Jake talked excitedly about the publicity and what it was doing for his program, for the kids, and for their political campaign against big oil.

"And I have a few leads on a new location for the Gaia Eden office." Perhaps these leads were the ones she had secretly emailed to Natalia. As she congratulated him on each success, she wondered if he thought about her as anything more than a friend who was good at marketing. They certainly had developed a good friendship over the last three weeks. As the setting sun played across his face, she noticed the scar on his cheek once again. He clearly knew what she was looking at, as he suddenly offered up an explanation.

"It happened on a camping trip at the beach when I was seven. We were roasting marshmallows," Jake started. "My dad was high as a kite and his metal prong slipped, slashing my face."

"That's terrible, Jake." Ellie reached instinctively, touching the scar as if to stop the pain from so long ago.

"Yeah, but it was also the best thing that could've happened," Jake responded, gently catching her hand in his.

"What do you mean?" Ellie questioned.

"My parents were so freaked out, that right then and there he and my mom threw a whole bag of pretty expensive marijuana into the fire. They quit cold turkey and not long after that, they got their acts together. Because of that one accident, my sister and I got to finally start our childhood instead of playing the adult role of taking care of them." Up until this time, Jake had only shared glowing stories about his parents. But it was the first time he'd mentioned early childhood. The news shocked her.

"You always see the bright side of things," she responded.

"I try to. And it makes me look sort of rugged, don't you think?" Jake raised his eyebrows as his usual smile returned to his face.

"It sure does," Ellie replied, looking into his eyes. He saw the longing on her face, and he bent down, kissing her gently on the lips.

"I missed you the last couple of days," he admitted.

"I missed you too." She wiggled her toes in the sand as he pulled her into his arms. He didn't kiss her again, but Ellie felt the shift. There was something forming between them and she had no intention of losing the momentum.

"Want to come over for dinner later tonight?" she asked as they walked forward.

"I'd love to."

◊◊◊

Ellie walked to her closet determined to choose something sexier than usual. But when she went to slip on her favorite tight jeans the buttons wouldn't snap. She tried on some of her other snug jeans and had the same problem. Ellie let out a sigh. She had fought with her weight her whole life and her rigid exercise program and diet had paid off in the last few years. Although she still ran five days a week, she had to admit she had been eating more than usual. Maybe that was because she and Jake had been cooking so many meals together, or perhaps because she was happy. And when you're happy, you let your guard down.

By the time Jake arrived on her doorstep, a mixture of excitement and nervousness flowed through her. She opened the door and as his eyes met hers, a large smile broke across his face.

"You look great," Jake commented, eyeing her flowing white dress.

"Thank you, so do you." Based on his damp curls and clean shaven face, he must have just gotten out of the shower.

"My contribution to the meal," he reported, handing her a bottle of red wine. "And these are for you," he added, handing her a bouquet of yellow and red tulips. Her face lit up.

"Thank you. They're beautiful." Her stomach growled audibly.

"Hungry, eh?" He teased.

"Yes. I hope you are too, because I made you a farmer's market vegetarian feast." Jake looked at her in surprise. "What? Did you think I was going to serve you tri-tip?" she responded. Jake laughed out loud as she led him to the inside table. They usually ate on the back deck, but it was uncharacteristically cold and windy this evening. Jake commented on the beeswax candles she had lit, and the cloth napkins that decorated the table. Despite an extremely busy day looking at new office spaces, applying for grants and working with the boys in the community garden, he had still managed to think about her throughout the day. They talked casually as they ate.

She went over the story of Pelican Wanda again and Jake listened attentively.

"It's like you're our vicarious marketing director," Jake responded.

"Well. Glad to help. On that note, did you call Nick Sanchez back?" Ellie asked.

"Yeah. That's my early morning meeting."

"Excellent," she responded. "I think you two will really hit it off." Nick was the sustainable development director of Hope Farmers. Ellie couldn't take all the credit for Nick agreeing to see Jake, but she had pushed him to follow up with Hope Farmers after he made such a good impression on the CEO that night at the Oviatt Building.

She had to be selective about what she shared with Jake. For example, she certainly didn't plan on sharing her recent hob knobbing with realtors and developers last week. She'd learned he had a keen distrust of just about everyone in the development industry, which she had initially found strange for someone who practiced architecture. But now that she had learned that his non-profit was being evicted to make room for a multi-million dollar development, she understood his frustration.

"Fantastic meal," Jake complimented, as he finished his plate. "You're an excellent cook."

"Thanks nature boy," Ellie smiled.

"You haven't touched your wine," he noticed, looking at her glass.

"To be honest, it tastes off to me." Jake gave a half smile in response.

"I'm afraid my palate for this sort of thing isn't that great. Tastes fine to me."

"Don't worry about it," she replied. She started making dessert as Jake cleaned up the dishes. She liked the feeling of them working together in the kitchen. It was strange how comfortable they had become with one another in the last couple of weeks, sharing home cooked meals together.

"I used to have movie night with Arno every Tuesday night, but he's been way too busy with his newfound love."

"So I'm Arno's replacement?" he asked.

"No. No one can replace Arno," she smiled. "You'll see what I mean when you meet him."

"I'm looking forward to it. And, not that I'm trying to fill his shoes, but if you'd like to carry on the tradition of movie night, I'd be glad to oblige," Jake suggested.

"No way. You'd hate it. We watch romantic chic flicks. Not documentaries on saving the world."

Jake had served his time watching chick flicks. He and Luz had watched many during their years together. Jake smiled deviously, scrunching up his face.

"I'll make the sacrifice for you babe." Ellie punched him in the arm, laughing.

"Well then, let me see what's on my movie queue." Once Ellie had selected a movie online, they settled on the couch together, pulling the blankets over them. Ellie pushed a button and the sleek black cabinet opened up, revealing a flat screen.

He put his arm around her and she nestled into him. He soon discovered it was much more fun to watch her reaction to the romance developing on the screen, than to actually watch the movie. A more fragile side of her emerged as she watched. He had seen this side come to the surface at the Children of Rwanda event and other gatherings where someone was in need. He had seen that expression when she came to help at the community gardens and worked with the boys. She always wanted the best for people; always had hope.

By the time the credits rolled on the film, Ellie's stomach growled.

"You can't possibly be hungry again," Jake laughed. Ellie nodded exuberantly. "How is that possible? We just ate like two hours ago."

"Vegetarian food doesn't have any substance to it," Ellie replied. "And ever since I started adjusting my diet for the Challenge, my stomach hasn't been right. I really need a big steak," she teased.

"You just have to get used to it."

"You're a great influence on me, but I have no plans of becoming vegetarian."

"We'll see," Jake responded. Ellie heard something crack on the second floor.

"Did you hear that?" she jumped.

"Yeah. It sounds like something is open upstairs, like a door opening and closing. I'll go check it out."

"We can go together," Ellie responded, grabbing a heavy flashlight that easily doubled as a weapon. She clicked on the lights for the stairway and followed him upstairs. The sound was coming from Gillian's room. Jake quickly opened the door as Ellie flipped the light switch on. The left window was wide open, the curtains blowing wildly. A quick tour through the room determined that nothing was missing or out of place.

"That's bizarre. Gillian's meticulous about closing the windows before she leaves."

"Yeah. But if she was on her way to see her boyfriend who was on the verge of proposing, she might have been distracted. Plus, this is the first windy day we've had in a few weeks. It could have easily been open the whole time."

"Yeah. You're probably right," Ellie agreed, still feeling more scared than she wanted to let on. "I'm just not used to being alone here."

"She'll be home next weekend, right? That's not that far away. Want me to stay over?" He asked nonchalantly. "And don't worry. I can sleep on the couch. I know we're friends and I won't be getting any. We could just, you know. Have a sleepover," he said with a sheepish grin.

"Okay. That'd be nice. I don't know why, but the house feels too big since Gillian went on vacation," Ellie commented quietly.

"This house is too big whether you're on vacation or not," Jake responded, causing Ellie to laugh. Ellie went upstairs to change. When she came back down, he was standing beside the couch.

"Shall I sleep here?" he asked, his arms by his side.

"Do you want to sleep on the couch?" she asked back. She had brushed out her long blondish brown hair and Jake could see the lace of her pajamas barely visible beneath her silk robe.

"No, I don't." He stated, looking directly in her eyes.

"I don't want you to either," Ellie admitted, reaching for his hand. Jake pulled her into his arms, closing the gap between them.

"Then I have to ask you something," his voice deepened to a whisper.

"Okay," Ellie replied as calmly as she could as their bodies touched.

"Can we consider this a real date?"

"You mean a date, as in we're no longer just friends?" Ellie questioned curiously.

"Yeah. Something like that."

"I thought you'd never ask."

Chapter 27

Ellie awoke to the sound of her phone ringing. She reached groggily to the side of the bed and looked at the number which simply said out of area.

"Hello?" she whispered, trying not to wake Jake.

"Ellie! It's Gillian! Can you hear me all right?"

"Gillian! There's a little static on the line, but I can hear you. Oh my God! Where are you now?" Ellie whispered. As her voice peaked, Jake rolled over in bed.

"I'm in Lucca, Italy. This totally awesome city surrounded by old stone walls."

"And?" Ellie queried.

"And I'm engaged!"

"That's fantastic!" Ellie whispered as she tried to sneak out of bed.

"Why are you whispering?" Gillian asked.

"It's the middle of the night here Gillian!"

"It's not like you're going to wake the neighbors. It's 5 a.m. if I did my math right. I wanted to catch you before you headed out for you're morning run." Ellie grabbed her silk robe, wrapping it around her naked body, and stepped into the hall, closing the door behind her. She looked at the clock on the wall and groaned.

"It's 4 a.m., Gillian." Ellie rubbed her eyes.

"Oh shit! Sorry!"

"No. It's okay. But oh my God! Tell me all about it!"

"I want to tell you in person, Ellie. But I wanted you to be among the first to know I'm engaged."

"Among the first?" Ellie sighed, feigning shock.

"I called my sisters before you. And mom, of course. But you're my best girl. Now don't get all emotional on me, but I need to ask you something." Her voice crackled a little on the line.

"Yes. Go ahead," Ellie held her breath.

"Will you be my maid of honor?" As Ellie heard the words, she choked up. She tried to breathe as the tears started welling into her eyes.

"Absolutely Gillian! Have you set a date?"

"No. But kind of soon. Sometime this fall. So are you crying already?"

"You know me too well," Ellie whimpered. She was crying harder than she should.

"You okay over there? Those don't exactly sound like tears of joy."

"They are. Believe me. I'm extremely happy, Gillian. I can't wait to see you next Saturday."

"Well, you'll have to be a little more patient as we're going to stop over on the East Coast instead of my direct flight back. I have to see my future in-laws in person. They wouldn't hear of waiting until my next visit."

"So when are you coming home?" Ellie asked, almost whining.

"I'm not sure yet. I'll send you the revised itinerary. Hopefully you'll still be able to pick me up at the airport."

"Of course."

"Okay. I've got to go. We're heading back to the hotel for a siesta, if you know what I mean. My God. The sex is better when you're in a romantic country. Swear by it."

As Ellie got off the phone, she headed back into the bedroom. The house was chilly in the early morning now that she'd adjusted the thermostat to a more environmentally friendly setting under Jake's suggestion. She draped her robe over the chair and crawled back into bed.

"Who was that?" he asked wearily.

"My roommate."

"Everything okay?" He spooned her, pulling her into his warmth.

"More than okay. She just got engaged. They're in a town called Lucca, Italy."

"Sounds like a very romantic place to get engaged," he murmured.

"I've always wanted to go to Italy," Ellie said, yawning.

"An international trip has quite an impact on the environment," he reported groggily.

"Oh Lord, Jake."

"Sorry, but it's true," he half-whispered as he pulled her closer. "I'm going back to sleep now darling." He kissed her, caressing her face gently before closing his eyes.

Chapter 28

Over the next week, Jake became a regular presence in Ellie's bed on the evening's they didn't stay over at his place. When the alarm went off at 5:45 Tuesday morning, Ellie was pulled back from a far away dream of hiking in the redwoods. As she hit the snooze button, she tried to hold onto the earthy sensations of the forest, but the images broke apart. She stretched her arms and legs as she opened her eyes to discover Jake watching her.

"Good morning, beautiful," she said gently.

"Good morning." He kissed her cheeks and ran his hand down her body.

"Ellie?"

"Mm. Hm?"

"I have a present for you."

"How did you manage that?"

"It's outside. I was planning to surprise you last night, but things, well. You know."

"Believe me," she laughed. "I know. Can I see my present now?"

"Now?"

"Yeah, I love presents," she smiled.

"Not so fast," he responded, pulling her into his arms. As they kissed, she imagined calling in sick and spending the rest of the day in bed with him, but she playfully pushed him away.

"My present," she demanded. Jake eyed her naked form before she slipped into her sweats. He got out of bed and pulled on his boxers and pants and Ellie followed him outside.

"Tada!" He pointed beside her car. Ellie gazed in wonder at a bright pink bicycle with shiny gears, a wicker basket and medium width tires.

"You got me my very own bicycle?"

"Looks that way," Jake replied, crossing his arms over his bare chest. "After you get used to it, you could even ride to work. You'll be blown away. You'll get there before everyone else. Even the buses."

"Does it have hidden wings I'm not seeing?" Ellie asked.

"It's a road bike, designed for city cycling. And I got a taller frame for you, so it will be easy to use."

"And why do I deserve such a lovely gift?" Ellie asked.

"Because you're doing so well on the Seven Change Challenge. Don't tell any of the other participants about this gift. I can't afford to get a bicycle for everyone."

"How could you afford this one?" Ellie asked before she thought to choose more sensitive words.

"I know people," he responded coyly. If she had offended him, she couldn't tell.

"Thank you Jake. It's incredibly thoughtful. And a matching helmet!" she observed, seeing the helmet with pink flames dangling off the handle bars. "It's pretty darned pink."

"You don't like pink?"

"I, well,"

"The color was Natalia's idea. And from a visibility standpoint, it's a good color choice. I suppose we could try exchanging it for another color," Jake began. Ellie was surprised at how much thought he had put into this gift.

"I love it, just the way it is."

As they got ready for work, Ellie had the sensation of being a married couple going about their morning routine. Jake made tea while she made herself an espresso. He chopped up fruit while she read through the paper.

Despite the short time he had spent in her home over the past few weeks, his presence could be felt. Many of the technical gadgets Gillian had constantly left on had been unplugged, and Ellie was amazed by the silence she hadn't known was missing. No longer did a fleet of little blinking red and green lights confront her, but a dormant section of gadgetry. Ellie wore layers in the house now instead of flipping on the heat in the evening. Jake had even adjusted the hot water heater a few degrees, which he said would save them both money and energy over the year. And on his suggestion, she had purchased a dozen compact fluorescent light bulbs. They had made a game of going around the house and replacing the bulbs.

Just like Gillian was caught up in the romantic, walled city of Lucca, Ellie was experiencing her own romantic escapade in the new territory of eco living. But as soon as Gillian returned, it would inevitably shift. Or would it? She knew Gillian would definitely freak out over the clothes line they had hung in the back yard, but would she even notice the more subtle changes?

As they got ready to head out the door, they lingered, kissing each other a few more times. And then came that palpable shift, filled with unspoken tension. It was like she was shutting the door on the fantasy of Ellie and Jake, the newly formed couple, and stepping back into the reality of their differences; she hopping in her BMW and going out to get more advertisers and subscribers; Jake heading out to save the planet.

Despite all the little changes she was making, she had come to recognize a certain half smile on Jake's face that she had first interpreted as patience, but now believed to be judgment. It had curled onto his face when she grabbed a plastic water bottle from the fridge for her morning run, or when she let the water run too long in the sink. Small, daily aspects of her routine as natural as breathing to her were under his environmental microscope when they spent time together.

Despite how well they were getting along this morning, she felt a combination of frustration and the desire to prove him wrong. That must have played a role in what she was planning. As Jake walked toward his bicycle, Ellie hopped on her new pink bike.

"You're not going to ride today, are you?" he asked, concern in his voice.

"Yes. Why not?"

"I thought you were afraid to cycle in the city. I was thinking we should break you in slowly."

"I bicycled all through college," she assured him.

"I'm impressed Ellie. You've got to be one of the stars of the challenge," Jake commented. Ellie smiled inwardly, not wanting to let on how much his comment pleased her, or how scared she actually was to ride in the city. Making all of these changes had been extremely hard for her, and he acted quite often like it was no big deal. She couldn't imagine how she would have faired thus far if it hadn't been for having a very sexy environmentalist in her midst, making the most tedious things—like line drying her clothes for instance—seem enjoyable.

"I'll cycle you to work," Jake decided.

"Won't you be late to your appointment?"

"No. I want to make sure you get there safely." He pulled out a bicycle map of Los Angeles and showed her the best routes to take, writing down a few bus lines that had bike racks on the front just in case. He double checked all the brakes on her bike and helped her adjust her helmet.

"You might want to grab a change of clothes and a towel," he suggested. When she was finally seated on her bike and he felt sure she was ready to go, he kissed her passionately, sending a chill up the back of her neck.

"Oh, and Jake. Don't forget. We have a dinner date at eight o'clock tomorrow night with Arno and Pierre at Endives, my treat."

"Shall we bike there too? If today goes well?"

"I want to dress up."

"I have two panniers that will hold a change of clothes for both of us and a whole lot more," Jake offered. Ellie squirmed. How could she explain that she had no intention of showing up at Endives on a bicycle? Not only was she not interested, she also knew Arno would be incredulous.

"What am I supposed to do? Change in the restroom?" Ellie demanded.

"Yeah, just like you'll have to do when you get to work today." Jake stated. He had a point. She wasn't sure how to wiggle her way out of this one.

"Well. Meet me here at 7 p.m. and we'll talk about it."

Jake was right. They zoomed along as automobiles and buses sat in bumper to bumper traffic. Jake rode in front of her, using arm signals for turning that she had long forgotten.

"You're doing great," he called to her as she maneuvered through traffic. Jake rode her to the front of her office building, and kissed her one more time before cycling away.

◊◊◊

She reached the office 20 minutes earlier than usual. She wheeled the shiny new bike through the front doors of the lobby and was about to pull it into the elevator when a security guard approached her.

"Excuse me ma'am."

"Yes?" she asked defensively. She certainly wasn't going to leave her bike on the street, even with the thick cable lock Jake had provided. It would be gone in seconds.

"We have bicycle storage and shower facilities on level B."

"We do?" Ellie asked incredulously. "Why hasn't anyone ever mentioned it?"

"We sent a letter to your office months ago," announced the security guard. "They were part of the re-design when the building was retrofitted last fall," he announced. "There's about nine people who use them regularly. But you'll be the first to break in the women's showers, if you'd like." Ellie followed the security guard to level B, a level she must have seen on her way up from the car garage a hundred times without realizing what was there.

The faux marble showers with lockers, a powder room and a carpeted ladies lounge stocked with towels reminded her of a country club she had once visited with her college boyfriend. Everything was brand new. Had the women's facilities really sat here unused for the last ten months? Ellie was flabbergasted by the idea. She took one of the fluffy white towels from the cabinet and headed into the brand new tiled shower. By the time she showered, dressed and headed up in the elevator, she felt invigorated. She stopped at the main lobby again and scanned the list of other tenants. There were at least seven other businesses in the large office complex and she wondered if the rest of them knew about the showers and bicycle parking.

As she entered the front doors of Duomo she saw that the light in Margo's office was on, which surprised her. She set her backpack in her office, stopped in the lounge for a cup of tea and walked toward Margo's open door.

"Good morning Margo," Ellie said.

"Morning," Margo responded coolly. "There's something I need to talk to you about."

"Okay," Ellie responded.

"Gaia Eden. First off. The article you wrote, great. And Pelican Wanda, genius. I'm excited about this one, Ellie. And it takes a lot to get me excited. But I need to know something."

"Yes?" Ellie started.

"How did you learn about the challenge? Did you happen to know someone from Gaia Eden?" The way Margo emphasized *know someone* scared her. Had someone tipped her off?

"Through Jake Tillerman, the founder. I met him while out hiking," Ellie briefly explained. "We ended up going on a date and he told me about it."

"So he's not your boyfriend?" Margo asked.

"Oh, no. Just someone I've gone out with a few times."

"Damn. He's hot Ellie. Nicely done," Margo remarked as she looked Ellie up and down.

"Thank you," Ellie replied tentatively. "So you don't see that as a conflict of interest?"

"If you went out on a date once, that's hardly a journalistic breach. But if you were to be, for example, the director of marketing and you intentionally garnered publicity for your boyfriend, we'd have a problem. " Was Margo on the verge of offering her the position? Or was this another test? What if she had been looking out her seventh floor window when Jake kissed her goodbye? It seemed highly unlikely, but Ellie felt suddenly nervous.

"Well he's hardly my boyfriend," Ellie lied once again. Margo must have seen the conflict on her face as she looked Ellie directly in the eyes.

"Is there something else you want to tell me?" Margo asked.

"I don't think so," Ellie responded cautiously. Maybe Margo had heard something from Karen, and that's why she'd dropped that line about if Ellie were to be the marketing director. She decided the best strategy if asked directly was to claim ignorance.

"You're doing a great job here. If Karen were to say, move on, you'd be my first pick to fill her vacancy."

"If for any reason it should open up, I would be honored to have the position," she responded carefully.

"Good to know where you stand," Margo said. "Now; I'd like you to come to a client lunch with me today. I'm meeting with a few people from the advertising department from Exxon Mobil. I'm not in the mood to schmooze today, and you're so damned smooth with the clients, that I could use your help."

A month ago she wouldn't have given it a second thought which client she was going after, but hearing the words Exxon Mobil made her shift on her heels.

"Can you drive? We'll leave about 11 a.m.," Margo questioned.

"Actually, I can't. I used alternative transportation today," Ellie admitted.

"You're certainly taking this whole Seven Change Challenge seriously, aren't you? Okay. I'll drive. Select some full page spreads to show the clients, and have our price sheets ready. Oh, and I want you to think about another concept for a green article."

"Okay," Ellie responded. As she made her way back to her office Ellie wavered between insolent and fearful. Who knew she was seeing Jake? She hadn't told anyone at the office. Apparently if Jake was just a fling, she hadn't caused a problem, but if they were serious, that was another matter. And despite their short time together, they were on their way to serious. Or at least she hoped so. On the other hand, Margo had just given her a huge compliment while also implying she knew Karen was looking at other prospects. And, she had invited her to a client lunch alone. That was a big deal.

Ellie answered a few emails and checked her voicemail. Darren Wales from Pacific West Holdings left a rather short message, asking her to come to another mixer so they could talk more about Duomo magazine. She made a note to herself to make a follow up call later. Right now Ellie had to get her mind around a schmooze session with Exxon Mobil. At least it wasn't British Petroleum. Either way, she had a feeling that the man who had cycled her to work this morning might not be very pleased.

Chapter 29

As Jake cycled into the city, a stream of images poured through his mind, almost all of them of Ellie. He recalled once again their trip to the Norton Simon Museum in Pasadena. They had spent close to an hour in front of the impressionist paintings. He still marveled at her knowledge. She wasn't an art historian by any means, but she seemed to know several paintings intimately, able to explain which artists had influenced others as new styles came into existence, as well as the historical context in which the paintings were made. And at the same time, she saw the beauty in the art.

"I could live in a place like this," she had commented of an Emile Bernard landscape painting of Brittany, "as long as I could still go to the theater now and then." Her comment had come quickly, and without much thought. But Jake held onto it as if it was a key to her inner workings—a way to explain the contradictions in her.

When she took him to see a theater production about a young boy who had lost his brother to drugs, Jake was stirred to tears. Once again, he was in the position of student as she told him about the playwright's own history.

"You're bringing my own city to life for me, Ellie," he had commented. He could tell his words had struck her by the smile on her face.

"Thank you Jake. I'm glad I'm offering a new view," she had responded radiantly. That was something else he liked about her; she knew how to take a compliment. How many women could take a compliment in stride? He'd have to add that to his list of what he was looking for in a woman.

She pushed him in ways he hadn't been pushed in a long time. There was something about her that reminded him of his grandma Jeanne; not her looks certainly, but her self-assuredness, mixed with a trust in humanity that could easily be mistaken for naiveté. It was a characteristic they shared, he decided, though he was certain she would disagree. What would it be like to settle down with her, he mused, as he waited at a major intersection for the light to turn green.

Chapter 30

As they cycled along Sunset Boulevard, Ellie was no longer embarrassed by the number of flashing lights Jake had installed on her bicycle, or the fluorescent yellow vest she wore. The traffic was crazy and more than once, a car honked angrily as they slipped through the traffic or changed lanes. And the driver of that stupid little sports car that had almost hit her had the audacity to honk and flip her off. It was as if half of the drivers in Los Angeles had no idea bicycles had the same rights as any automobile to ride down the streets.

"You're doing a great job, Ellie," Jake called over his shoulder toward her. A great job if staying alive is the objective, she thought to herself. Ellie concentrated on all of the obstacles around her while making sure to follow Jake's style of cycling through the city. By the time they approached Endives, adrenaline coursed through her body and she was wet with perspiration, her shirt sticking to her back.

"This is utterly ridiculous. I need a shower," she complained as they brought their bicycles onto the sidewalk.

"Do you feel more alive right now than usual?" he asked, not hearing her complaint. She had to admit she felt exhilarated, but also scared out of her wits; angry at all of the automobile drivers, and angry at herself for agreeing to cycle here. If only her competitive nature had not reared its ugly head, she would have told Jake from the get-go how ridiculous a proposition it was. Good thing she had a back up plan. Her friend Linda worked at Hotel W one block away. Ellie had explained the situation and gotten permission to take a shower there, given that the night manager didn't show up a few hours early.

"Jake. I'm sweating. I feel like I should be meeting some friends for a barbeque at the beach, not going out to an elegant dinner at Endives. I really need a shower, so" she began.

"I know this is a big change for you, but trust me. I have a plan." Jake interrupted. "I brought everything you need to freshen up in the bathroom." So that was his big plan; Ellie cleaning herself in the bathroom of a fancy restaurant like some beggar. Anger climbed up her spine.

"And I have a plan too," she countered, as she started wheeling her bicycle away from the restaurant. "I'm going to shower and change at the hotel. I called earlier, and . . ."

"Hold on a minute, Ellie." Jake cut her off. "You're going to drop a few hundred on a hotel room just for a shower? That's a total waste of money and resources; just clean up in the restroom." Ellie turned toward Jake and looked directly into his eyes. She was sick and tired of his greener-than-thou attitude. When she spoke her voice was calm yet icy.

"I just cycled through insane traffic and almost got taken out by a sports car. I'm dirty and sweaty. I *am* going to shower and then I'm meeting my friends for dinner, with or without you." She emphasized the last few words, presenting a clear take-it or leave-it option. Jake looked on in astonishment as Ellie walked away from him. Clearly she wasn't stopping to discuss it.

Jake followed after her in awkward silence. When they got to the hotel, he offered to lock up her bike and she rolled it toward him like something dirty she planned to toss in the rubbish bin. She asked if he was coming in too, and he shook his head. She disappeared down the hall, leaving Jake in the lobby with his thoughts.

He had to admit; the ride over had been harrowing, and a little sports car had almost knocked Ellie over at one point. Instead of giving up, she had pushed on, more determined than ever. Clearly she was more rattled than he realized. Perhaps cycling hadn't been such a brilliant idea after all. But how was he supposed to know she didn't want to cycle? He wasn't a mind reader.

Jake headed into the lobby restroom and used a small microfiber towel and a bar of soap to wash the sweat from his body before putting on fresh deodorant. He changed in the bathroom stall and splashed some water over his face. He looked in the mirror. Good as new. Why was it so much harder for a woman? And seriously, how could she justify forking over a night's lodging for a shower? Jake struggled with his thoughts. He was judging her again, just like Conrad had pointed out. He wasn't dating eco beauty queen April or bad-ass Natalia. He was dating Ellie. And there was a world of difference between these women.

He headed into the lobby and settled into a high backed leather chair, browsing through a travel magazine as he waited.

"So you're still here," Ellie intoned.

"Disappointed?" he asked as he raised his eyes to hers. Holy shit she looked amazing, Jake thought. She wore a teal dress that brought out her eyes and strappy, high heels. A white shawl was loosely draped around her shoulders.

"Not entirely," she countered. She was definitely calmer now, and based on the upward curl on her lips, had her sense of humor back.

"You look gorgeous, Ellie," he couldn't help but comment.

"Thanks. You brush up surprisingly well yourself." He did look great and it bothered her. How could he clean up so easily?

The tension was still between them as they began walking back toward the restaurant. Jake knew he needed to say something.

"Maybe it wasn't such a good idea to cycle here. I'm sorry if I pushed you too hard."

"Well. It's not that I can't do it," she countered. "It's just not appropriate for a fancy dinner. You understand?"

"Yeah. I get that now. But why didn't you just tell me?" Jake asked. Ellie chewed on her upper lip as they walked along the busy sidewalk.

"You gave me a bike, Jake! You really pushed for us to cycle here. It seemed really important to you, so I decided to do it."

"I, well, I appreciate that Ellie," Jake started. "But you've got to do things because they matter for you too."

"Jake. Certainly you've done something for someone else in your life. It's called compromise. And I'm hardly a push over. It's not like I'm snorting cocaine to please you." She wiggled her nose at him, causing a smile to wend its way across his face. "I'm competitive. I like to rise to a challenge. Sometimes my competitive nature serves me well, and sometimes it gets me into trouble. Like tonight."

"I'm sorry Ellie. I'm sorry I pissed you off," Jake admitted. Ellie was silent as they walked. "I'm meeting one of your best friends in just a few minutes, and I can't show up at a fancy restaurant with an angry Ellie on my hands." She laughed for the first time in over an hour, before giving Jake a long hug.

"And I didn't drop a few hundred to take a shower. My friend Linda works there. I arranged shower privileges after we decided to cycle here."

"Sorry I jumped to conclusions," Jake responded, his eyes searching out hers.

"Apology accepted."

CHAPTER 31

As they waited for Arno and Pierre to arrive, Jake leaned back in his chair, fiddling with the table cloth.

"So tell me more about yesterday. Margo asked if we were dating?" Jake started.

"No. Not exactly. She asked how I heard about the challenge. I figured she'd been tipped off somehow that we were seeing each other."

"So what did you say?"

"I said you told me about the challenge on our first date, and that we'd dated a few times. Technically, that's true." Jake rolled his shoulders back and smiled openly.

"I keep forgetting I've only known you five weeks."

"Over six if you count that first time we met on the trail," she interjected, reaching for his hand. "And instead of being upset, she congratulated me on scoring such a handsome guy."

"Had I been ugly, she might not have been so lenient on you," Jake winked at her with a smirk on his face. Ellie shook her head. She knew he was joking, but unfortunately, she had a feeling he was right. His good looks seemed to be half of the reason the article had gone through.

"But she did say if I was the marketing director and you were my boyfriend, then she'd have a problem."

"Ah. It's all about how close we are, and how powerful of a position you have. I see how it works." Jake mulled over the word boyfriend.

"So how was your meeting with the Hope Farmers?" Ellie asked, changing the subject.

"Awesome. He wants to come see the program. He said it's exactly the type of program they want to invest in."

"That's fantastic Jake!" Ellie started. Just then she spotted Arno and Pierre walking toward them. "Here they come," she pointed. Jake and Ellie both stood up to greet them.

"Hello Ellie," Arno's voice was warm and silky as he kissed her cheek. "And you must be Jake," he surmised as he extended his hand.

"Yes. Nice to meet you Arno," Jake replied, shaking his hand firmly. The two of them were about the same height, Ellie noticed, though Jake had a leaner build.

"And this is Pierre," Arno introduced, a subtle smile on his lips.

"Nice to see you again, Ellie. Hello Jake," Pierre responded commandingly. He was a good four inches shorter than Arno, yet his presence demanded attention. Ellie had to admire his raven black hair, despite it being noticeably tousled, as if he'd been riding a motorcycle. His large eyes looked from her to Jake and then back again.

"You two sure make a beautiful couple," he remarked.

"And your clothes, did you plan those outfits?" Arno interjected as he looked them both up and down appreciatively. Ellie glanced at Jake, wondering if he was about to embark on his first-ever conversation about coordinated clothing. Hoping to spare him, she jumped in.

"Coincidence," she explained. "Sit down already. I'm hungry and too polite to order before you've both had a chance to peruse the menu."

"Pierre. Perhaps you should order the wine," Arno demurred. Ellie looked at him in surprise. He was always the one to order the wine.

"I'll choose a wine based on our entrees. Ladies first." Although the veal sounded excellent, Ellie opted for the fish of the day, thinking of it as less offensive to her animal loving boyfriend.

"I'm going to have the Orange Roughy," she decided.

"Orange Roughy is actually on the watch list, er, um . . ." Jake started. "Never mind." He glanced at Ellie sheepishly, causing her to laugh.

"You might as well finish your sentence, since you started," she replied.

"It's on the watchlist for both over fishing and higher mercury content. Perhaps the halibut instead?" he finished.

"Well. I can hardly argue with that. Halibut it is," she acquiesced, as embarrassment coursed over her. She didn't dare catch Arno's eyes to see what sort of smirk might lay there in wait. As Jake ordered the vegetarian farmer's market special, she knew she was in for an interesting evening.

"I think the veal with rosemary potatoes and fennel sounds delightful," Arno remarked, "unless it's also on a list?" He looked at Jake curiously. Jake hesitated. He certainly didn't want to offend Ellie's friends, or piss her off again.

"I'm sure everything is on some sort of list," Jake tried.

"Yes, but?" Arno encouraged. Jake felt caught between a rock and a hard place. What was he supposed to do? Pretend he was someone else? He opted to be himself.

"Well. If you want to get me started, I can tell you all about the atrocities of how young calves raised for veal are treated," Jake began, "but I think it'd be rather, unappetizing, shall we say. But luckily, in some regions of the country, they're trying to make the process more humane." Jake began twisting one of his curls.

"Well," Arno paused, not sure how to proceed.

"Let's have fish as well, Arno. There's a wonderful Condrieu on the wine list that would be excellent with the baked halibut."

"Condrieu is made from the viognier grape?" Arno asked.

"Such knowledge of wine. Are you sure you're Dutch darling? You never cease to amaze me." Pierre's compliment seemed to wipe the discomfort from both Jake and Arno's faces.

"Are you drinking wine this evening Jake?" Pierre inquired as he perused the wine list.

"Sure. Sounds great." When the waiter came, everyone placed their orders.

"So Jake, I hear you work with kids teaching them about the environment?" Arno asked. Ellie shot a quick glance at Arno, doing her best to tell him to be good.

"Yes. I have a non-profit that works to foster a relationship between inner city youth and the natural environment," Jake responded stiffly.

"Fascinating," Pierre commented.

"Yes. He takes boys out hiking," Arno added, winking at Ellie. Ellie didn't wink back. The way Arno said these last few words made Jake's work sound like a childish hobby and she also didn't appreciate the smile that formed on Pierre's lips, as if they'd been joking about this very subject on the way over.

"He does much more than that," Ellie reprimanded. "He educates youth about the environment, works on urban organic gardens with his students, helps create new green spaces in high density areas of the city and builds integrity in young men that others seem to have forgotten about," she lectured. "Oh. And I haven't even mentioned the action campaign against deep water drilling he's organized with some of his colleagues and the students of UCLA, or that he's also an architect." A palpable silence followed her words as all three men caught Ellie's defensive tone. Calmly, Jake reached for her hand.

"Ellie. I'm still in the room," he smiled, "but thank you; I do like the way my work sounds when it comes off of your lips." Arno and Pierre sighed in unison, and just like that, Jake diffused the situation.

"When I said fascinating, I meant it in all earnestness," Pierre clarified. "I grew up in a rural area, and I know how important nature is to our souls. It's a good idea to protect the environment. It sounds like you're doing fascinating work, Jake." Ellie shifted in her seat, slightly embarrassed by her rampage.

"So. Is anyone watching the World Cup?" Arno asked.

"We watched a game last weekend," Ellie chimed in. "England vs. United States."

"Ah. Yes. A tie," Arno quipped. "But, did you see the game on Monday between the Netherlands and Denmark?"

"No. I'm afraid we missed that one," Jake responded.

"That's right you did. Because you two were snuggled comfortably in bed while Arno, here, dragged me to the pub at 3:50 a.m. If we had arrived 10 minutes later, there wouldn't have been a seat left in the house. I've never seen so much orange in one room," Pierre complained. Although his words had a scolding tone, the way he openly gazed at Arno suggested nothing short of adoration.

"Arno, I had no idea you were such a soccer fan! Or that you ever got up before sunrise," Ellie quipped. Arno looked particularly handsome this evening; his light blue cashmere showed off the contours of his arms and chest, and brought out his Dutch blue eyes.

"It's amazing what we will do for our game and country," Arno declared. "Now you darling, are positively glowing. And I can only assume that it is Jake who has placed that glow upon you." Now it was Jake's turn to color.

"I certainly can't take credit for her beauty," he responded, "but I'm honored that we've been spending so much time together. She's a very special woman."

"I couldn't agree more. I can't think of any woman I trust more," Arno said, smiling at her warmly.

"Gentlemen," Ellie laughed, "I'm still in the room."

As dinner progressed, the four of them settled into a comfortable rhythm of conversation. Even when the topics led down an environmental path, Jake presented his point of view clearly and inoffensively, and more than once, she heard Arno or Pierre agree with the point he was making. Pierre shared his knowledge of wines, and both Jake and Ellie listened attentively. When Ellie got up to use the restroom, Arno suddenly had to go as well. Arno grabbed her arm playfully as they walked toward the hallway.

"Ellie, darling. He's simply gorgeous. Those eyes! My God, girl!"

"I know!" she giggled, "and what's behind those eyes is equally beautiful." She hadn't meant to share such an intimate thought, but at the same time, it felt good.

"He is the most charming environmentalist I've ever met."

"You don't find him too pushy?" Ellie asked.

"Yeah. A bit. But he's a smooth one. Even when he was talking about automobile use in the U.S., he managed to compliment the efficiency of the Dutch and French public transportation systems while at the same time talking about the obsolescence of the automobile—all in a way that didn't offend me. He's a real charmer, this one. Next thing you know. I'll be taking the bus!" he joked.

"I rode the bus twice last week and once this week."

"Shut up!"

"No. Really."

"You rode the bus?"

"And that's not the half of it."

"Yes. I'm sure. Looks like you've been riding something far more exciting than the bus," Arno laughed devilishly. Ellie felt her cheeks flushing.

"Arno!"

"So much for Pierre's brother. I'll have to email him back and tell him the charming lady I mentioned went for the environmentalist after all."

"Well. It's so comforting to know that total strangers are being brought up to the minute on my sexual status."

"Ah! So it's true! You got back on," Arno quipped. Ellie thought about the last few evenings they had spent together.

"Yes. I got back on," she giggled. "And you and Pierre seem like an old couple already," she noted approvingly. "I can see it in how he acts that he really cares about you."

"It's wonderful. I never thought I'd feel this way. Especially so soon," Arno returned.

"I'm so happy for you."

"And I for you, dear."

To Ellie's utter surprise, both Pierre and Arno had agreed to look over the Seven Change Challenge website before dinner was over. As they all stood up to go, Ellie and Jake each pulled a pannier out from under the table and both men looked perplexed.

"Did you two *bicycle* here?" Arno asked.

"Yes," they said in unison. Now it was Arno's turn to gape in awe.

"You're some sort of green Pied Piper!" Arno declared. "I've got to see Ellie on a bike in that dress."

"That's not going to happen Arno. I have cycling clothes."

"This is just too much," Arno exclaimed. "As a Dutchman, I completely understand cycling, but not in this city. There's no infrastructure for it." That's for sure, Ellie thought to herself. Jake caught her expression, and smiled apologetically.

"Yes. It wasn't the best idea to cycle here, but you have to start somewhere," Jake countered. "And your country is an excellent example." Arno smiled, grateful once again for the compliment.

As Ellie and Jake changed into their cycling clothes, Pierre went out to the valet parking to retrieve his Porsche Boxter. When Ellie and Jake came out, Arno waited until he saw them get on their bicycles before taking out his phone and shooting a little video.

"I have to get this on record," he laughed as Ellie undid her lock and put on her helmet.

"Stop already," Ellie scolded.

"Darling. You'll appreciate this someday," he countered, as he filmed the two of them getting on their bikes and waving goodbye.

Chapter 32

Lunches with Soo Jin had a certain pattern. Ellie would do most of the talking, and Soo Jin would give polite, one or two syllable answers. But despite the simplicity of their conversations, Soo Jin was a bright and intelligent young woman, and Ellie enjoyed her company. When they settled into a booth at a vegetarian restaurant a seven-block walk from the office, Ellie started the conversation as usual. When Soo Jin asked what she'd been up to over the weekend, a barrage of experiences floated through Ellie's head. Besides Arno, she hadn't told anyone about her time with Jake, not even Gillian. She wanted to keep the experience for herself a little longer.

"So Ellie," Soo Jin started as she fidgeted with a thin gold bracelet around her wrist. "I want to ask you about something."

"Okay. Go ahead," Ellie encouraged, finally pulled into the moment. She looked into Soo Jin's almond eyes to see a glint of excitement.

"Can this be our secret?" Soo Jin asked timidly.

"Of course. I won't tell anyone," Ellie responded. Although they often lunched together, Ellie could not recall a time Soo Jin had shared a secret. She knew she had two sisters, that she was a first generation American, and that like many immigrant parents, her parents had worked hard to give their daughters a bright future. But Ellie hadn't learned much about Soo Jin's personal life, which had been kept secret just by the virtue of her being shy.

"I think I may be in love," Soo Jin began.

"Oh, Soo Jin! I didn't even know you were seeing anyone." Ellie felt suddenly foolish. It had never even occurred to her to ask Soo Jin about her romantic life.

"We've been seeing each other for six months now."

"Six months! Wow. You really can keep a secret."

"Yes. I'm good at keeping secrets," she replied in a sweet tone.

"I know that about you Soo Jin," Ellie smiled.

"Ellie, I need your advice."

"You need advice from me on romance?" Ellie questioned.

"Well. On. Well . . ." Soo Jin turned crimson as she skirted around the word and Ellie realized what the conversation was about.

"Oh," Ellie whispered. "I get it. You're having . . ."

"No!" Soo Jin whisper-shouted back. "Not yet." She looked around the restaurant as if to check if her parents might be in the next booth. "But, I think it's time. I'm very, very nervous."

"Is it your first time?" Ellie asked quietly.

"It will be," Soo Jin admitted as she sipped on an iced tea. "So, have you had many *experiences* in that way?"

"Yes and no," Ellie responded. She had never pictured in a million years she'd be having this conversation with Soo Jin. "Three."

"Only three times?"

"Oh no. I mean I've been with three men."

"So then you have lots of experience."

"Not compared to most of our co-workers, but some, yes," Ellie responded as she thought over her lovers.

"That's why I wanted to ask you," Soo Jin explained. "I guessed that you had more experience than me, but that you hadn't had so many lovers that you had become numb," she reasoned in a serious tone. Ellie had never realized she was so transparent, or that Soo Jin was so insightful. Did having lots of lovers numb you? That would explain the casual state of mind so many people held about it; sex no longer equaled intimacy.

"So what I want to know is, does it change the relationship dramatically?" Soo Jin questioned. "Right now, we're in love. He's kind, and faithful. We've even talked about future plans. I don't want to ruin that."

Ellie considered her question in earnest. She had lost her virginity to her high school boyfriend Derrick. Both of their families were active in the same church, and their budding sexual experience was overshadowed by guilt. This had turned her off to sex for a number of years until she met Trevor. They'd gone out all through college and a few years afterwards. Of course, they were going to get married and live happily ever after. She'd even had a beautiful engagement ring on her finger to prove it. But this was perhaps the worst possible time to talk about an unsuccessful engagement. Back to the question; sex had definitely made her relationship with Trevor stronger. And then there was Jake; could Soo Jin sense that a man had been in her bed just last night?

"Honestly, if he loves you and respects you, I think it will just make it better, Soo Jin. As long as you can embrace it as a good thing." Ellie thought back to her first encounter with Jake and what she had learned from it. "But if you fear it, or think its wrong for some reason, it will feel wrong." Soo Jin nodded, as if taking mental notes of Ellie's sagely advice.

"Have your parents met him?" Ellie asked.

"No. And they won't like him either." The excitement left Soo Jin's face as her thoughts switched to her parents.

"Why not? If you like him, love him, he must be a wonderful man."

"He's wonderful. Amazing. But, he's not Korean. And they won't accept anyone who's not Korean."

"I'm sorry. Let's leave your parents out of this then," Ellie suggested. She wanted to picture this man that had stolen Soo Jin's heart. "What's his name? How old is he? What does he do for a living?" Ellie realized that she sounded more like a protective, scrutinizing mother than a friend. So much for leaving mom out of it, she mused.

"His name is Frank. He's thirty-one and he's a Certified Public Accountant," Soo Jin announced, as if this would explain everything. This did sound promising, Ellie had to admit. He wasn't an irresponsible kid, and he had a serious job that necessitated an even-minded personality, someone who could spend hours on the details and persevere.

"And he's waited six months and he adores you," Ellie added for good measure. Once again, Soo Jin's cheeks lit up.

"Yes. We've already talked about marriage," she grinned.

"Wow Soo Jin. That's exciting!" Ellie's thoughts returned to her college beau Trevor and their plans to get married, and how this idea had opened her up. Better to try out the goods before you sign the lease, her sister Jody used to say. Her thoughts traveled again to Jake and what other insights she might have for Soo Jin after her handful of times with him.

"Oh. And remember to have protection," Ellie added.

"Well, certainly he will arrange for that," Soo Jin whispered.

"Yes. That's usually true, but you might want to have condoms on hand just in case."

"Okay," she responded uncertainly. Ellie tried to picture Soo Jin in the market purchasing condoms, and did her best not to smile.

"Are you on the pill?" she asked discreetly, matching Soo Jin's quiet tone.

"No," Soo Jin responded, her eyes widening. "I know it exists of course, and that it's a great thing for women's rights. I just hadn't thought about it before. I mean, for me."

"Well, with many pills, you need to be on it for one to two cycles before it's an effective form of birth control, so that might be something to consider too," Ellie explained. Although she had been on the pill when she was with Trevor, she'd gone off once they broke up. She hated the hormonal shifts she'd felt when on it and hadn't had reason to go back on. Based on how her relationship with Jake was developing, perhaps it was something for her to consider as well.

As they ordered dessert, Ellie's phone beeped. She glanced down to see Jake Tillerman's name on the screen.

"Ever heard of a place called Red's West?" Ellie asked.

"Yeah. It's a pub for cyclists in West Hollywood."

"How on earth did you know that?" Ellie asked.

"I considered doing a story on it when I used to work for the Eco LA Guide. It's very hip with the environmental crowd. Has recycled furniture, was made from reclaimed bricks they got from Edmond High school. It was so sad when they tore that school down. But anyway. Why?" Soo Jin asked.

Ellie stared at her in surprise. This was the longest she'd ever heard Soo Jin speak. Apparently the green movement was one of her topics.

"Because I'm meeting a guy there tomorrow night," Ellie confided.

"You're seeing someone too? That's exciting!"

"Yes. Let's add that to our list of secrets, so as not to jinx it."

"Okay." Soo Jin's expression changed, and she looked at Ellie thoughtfully. "Ellie, is this new guy you're seeing an environmentalist?"

"Very much so," Ellie smiled.

"Okay. Well. I don't know how to put this, but you can't drive there."

"Why not?"

"'*How did you get to Red's*' is their tag line. Everyone who goes there comes by alternative transport. So you need to figure out another means of transportation, besides your SUV."

"Like the bus," Ellie smiled.

"That's a good option. Plus, you'll get some points for the Seven Change Challenge." Soo Jin pointed out. "So, this guy. What is he like?" For a moment Ellie almost slipped and mentioned Jake's name. She knew she could trust Soo Jin, but she didn't want to take any chances of it getting around the office that she was dating the founder of Gaia Eden. At least not until the office challenge was over—especially after Margo's lecture.

"He's amazing, Soo Jin. He's so inspiring." Ellie tried to think of the words to describe how he had opened her back up to a part of herself she'd forgotten about; her love for nature, her desire to help others. She glanced around the little café filled with bamboo plants and water fountains. On the wall she saw a small clock made out of driftwood. As the tiny wooden hands ticked away, she realized what she was seeing.

"Oh Gosh! It's already ten after one! I've got to get back!"

"Oh my goodness. Sorry Ellie. I usually don't talk this much."

"I know!" Ellie laughed. "I guess we just haven't been covering the right topics. But talk about sex or the environment and you're suddenly a chatterbox!" Ellie joked. Soo Jin shifted uncomfortably in her seat, her neck flushing for the fourth time in the last hour. "Oh Soo Jin, I'm just teasing you. It's good to see this side of you. You should express it more often."

◊◊◊

It was 6 p.m. before she got out of her second meeting with Margo. Ellie had written a column about ten simple ways to make your home more energy efficient. Margo had been mildly complimentary, but told Ellie to think bigger.

"I want something that speaks to our professional demographic, but that also shows we're cutting edge," Margo pushed. Ellie thought about the camping trip she and Jake were contemplating. Maybe she could come up with something about luxury eco camping. Did such a thing exist? Her backpacking trips had been far from luxurious.

Just as she was getting ready to shut down her computer, she saw two emails from Soo Jin. The first one was a link to Red's. The second was a bus schedule that had been highlighted with the most direct route, which required one transfer. Clearly, Ellie had struck a chord in Soo Jin's heart. She thought about her friend in a new light; If Soo Jin is going to be daring enough to forfeit her virginity, I can try going back on the pill, she decided.

Chapter 33

Later that night, Ellie and Jake met at a neighborhood coffee house. Jake curiously eyed the map Ellie had in a stack of papers.

"You go first," he suggested. She opened the map on the table before Jake, who stared at the topography in awe.

"Utah?" he questioned. "That's really far away Ellie."

"The Grand Gulch wilderness is spectacular. One of the most beautiful areas I've ever seen," she responded. Jake liked the excitement in her eyes, but he couldn't justify such a trip.

"How would it look if I, as the creator of the Seven Change Challenge, majorly broke one of the categories? That would be bad press."

"I thought you might say that," Ellie replied without dropping a beat. "That's why I have plan B."

She opened another map and Jake looked on with a smile.

"Los Padres National Forest, eh? Now that's more like it."

"I was thinking of this area near the Santa Ynez Valley. It looks like we could do a seven day trip with the right back country permits."

"Seven days?" Jake repeated, not even trying to hide his exasperation.

"Too long?" Ellie asked.

"How about three days?"

"Too short."

"Five?"

"Okay. Deal."

"The only thing is, it's pretty dry this time of year. We'd have to pack in most of the water," she explained.

"That doesn't sound like much fun."

"Well," Ellie hesitated, "I'm not sure how to solve this. I suppose we could wait until the challenge is over, but I won't have time to take a vacation then. Plus, you certainly aren't planning to limit the scope of your life to a 200 mile radius?" Ellie asked as calmly as she could muster.

"No. Of course not. The idea is more to limit unnecessary travel."

"Going into nature doesn't fall into that category, does it?" Ellie asked.

"No. . ." Jake hesitated.

"Okay. What do you have?" Ellie asked.

"I have the answer to all of our problems."

"You've stopped the oil leak and know how to mellow out my over demanding boss?" Ellie quipped.

"Ha! I wish. No, darling. I have a solution for our camping trip. I spoke to my friend Gray Wolf and if we want to, we can go backpacking on their property. They have hiking trails, places for overnight camping and there are two wells on the property and a natural hot spring. And coincidentally, it's in the Santa Ynez Valley, just past the Los Padres National Forest. So you see? Great minds think alike." His eyebrows rose slightly.

"Wow. That sounds fantastic!" Ellie responded.

"Thing is, we need to go in the next three weeks."

"Is that possible in your schedule? I mean, you seem swamped right now," Ellie questioned.

"I am swamped. But every summer we shut down for two weeks in July. But I've still got this online campaign."

"But you have other people that work with you, right? I mean, an online campaign can kind of manage itself for a weekend, can't it?"

"Yeah. I suppose I can get away for a long weekend."

"Well. Actually. Me too. I have something else to tell you."

"What?"

"Things are looking up for me being the next Marketing Director."

"Wow. What happened?"

"Margo dropped a major hint about the possibility."

"That's great."

"I know. I'm totally excited! We were in this meeting with Exxon Mobil." Ellie quickly began, leaving no space for Jake to interrupt. "They want to do a full page ad. I suggested they do a full spread, focusing on any alternative energy exploration they're doing, and they thought it was an excellent idea." She came up for a breath.

"Exxon Mobil?" Jake repeated indignantly.

"Yeah. I know. Oil company. But before you flip out on me, they're doing exploration on an algae bio-fuel that would supplement use of oil and gas."

"Do you hear your own words?" Jake asked, pulling his hand away from hers.

"What?" she asked.

"Supplement oil and gas. Not replace it. Don't you think it's hypocritical to support our campaign against deep water drilling on one page and then have a full spread promoting an oil company on the next?" Jake crossed his arms over his chest.

"God, Jake! It's not like that, and you won't be in the same issue."

"That's not my point! You only see the dollars for your magazine and your ambition to be marketing director." Jake snapped.

"And you only see your nose," Ellie snapped back. "The oil corporations are in the best position to do research on alternative fuels, Jake. They have all the money and resources at their fingertips." Ellie's hands rested on the table firmly, as if preparing for a fight.

"Yeah, maybe. But they're driven by greed. And that's not a genuine place from which to start change," he declared.

"I totally disagree. If the end of oil is as near as you and your friends say it is, then it's going to be these huge, wealthy corporations that come up with the next energy source, not some hippies playing around in a commune."

Ellie and Jake sat in silence, staring at one another. His words had stung her, but she was also embarrassed. Why was she attacking him? The maps sat between them on the table. Downhearted, Ellie pushed them slightly away from her.

"Maybe we need to hold off on camping," Ellie began.

"Wow," Jake shook his head quietly.

"What?" Her shoulders tensed up.

"It's just. We're actually quarrelling," he observed.

"Yeah. And you're smiling. What is that?" she retorted.

"I'm not sorry about what I said about Exxon Mobil; but I had no right to criticize your job," he acquiesced. "There's nothing wrong with wanting to be marketing director. I just wonder if it's really the best thing for you." Ellie didn't know how to react. Was he now deciding what was best for her?

"I know I'm not saving the world, Jake. But the salary is fantastic and I know I could do a great job. If given the chance, I'll take it," she stated, leaving no room for negotiation.

"If that's what's important to you, then go for it," Jake responded. He had regained his composure, and his arms now rested in a neutral position by his sides.

"You really think so?" she questioned. She wished she could know exactly what went through his head sometimes, but now that he'd snapped at her, she felt she had a pretty good idea; he thought she was only driven by money and prestige.

"Well. For now," Jake said as his smile grew. "I could just see you working for a non-profit. You're so good with people. I mean, that fundraiser you took me to for the Children of Rwanda for example. You mingled with everyone. You made connections easily. And your heart was completely into it. I could see you running a program like that."

"Well. Thank you." Ellie tapped her fingers on the table, thinking. "It's strange you say that. Do you remember how I hit it off so well with the director? He actually approached me last week to see if I was interested in working for him."

"See?" Jake responded. "You'd be a natural. What did you say?"

"I said I'd think about it. But honestly, I was being polite. Non-profit doesn't pay."

"It pays in other ways." She searched his face for judgment, but couldn't see it. The anger that had coursed through her body had dissipated. Ellie was amazed. A few minutes ago, she was ready to walk out on him, and now she felt as if this man knew her better than herself. Why wasn't she working in a field closer to her heart? Like working with infants, for instance; or a non-profit like the Red Cross. But she didn't want to think about that right now; not when she was on the verge of making a major step up the ladder. Instead, she leaned toward him, speaking in a more conciliatory tone.

"I didn't mean that about the commune."

"Yes you did," Jake let out a breath. "This is hard for both of us, Ellie."

"By this. You mean us."

"Yeah," Jake looked into her eyes. She could smell the familiar pine scent of his body wash she had come to associate with their intimacy lingering on his skin. They sat at the table, the map between them like a crossroads.

"I feel like you think I'm too extreme," Jake started. "And that I don't make enough money for you to take me seriously." He hadn't meant to be so blunt, but based on the hesitation on her face, he had struck home.

"Jake. I admire your dedication to the environment. But yes, sometimes I feel like you're judging my every action. And that pushes me away." Ellie crossed her arms under her chest. Unintentionally accentuating her breasts.

"I'm sorry. The last thing I want to do is push you away. I'm amazed at how much you've accomplished on the challenge just in the last few weeks. You're doing so well."

"I know that's supposed to be a compliment, Jake. But it's still a judgment," she explained. Jake started twirling one of his curls between his thumb and pointer finger.

"Okay," he responded. "I have to work on that." He stared at his hands, his eyes landing on the maps on the table. Ellie gazed at the man before her, surprised by the series of emotions pouring through her.

"And as far as the money, well. I'd much rather be with a man I trust and love who was just getting by, then be with a rich man I don't relate to," Ellie admitted as much to herself as to him.

Jake reached across the table and kissed her on the forehead, trying to downplay the words that had so easily come off her lips; *A man I trust and love.* He thought back to the day he met Ellie out on the trail, how she seemed to blossom in the outdoors.

"So you still want to go camping with me?" he asked gently.

"Yeah. Do you still want to go with me?" Her eyes had softened.

"Definitely." He took her hand in his and pulled her toward him, embracing her. She hugged him back until the tight ball in her chest started unwinding.

They talked over dates and as the idea of a shorter trip settled over her, she began to think a three-day weekend was long enough for their first journey together. She hadn't been out overnight in a few years and it might be a good idea to break back in gently.

They started making check lists about supplies to take with them and she could see that Jake was already in unfamiliar territory. As she talked about a Whisper-Lite backpacker's stove, dehydrated soups, water filters and snake bite kits, Jake just wrote items down, as if thinking about them for the first time.

Although she knew Jake was the most environmentally responsible person she'd ever known, she was curious to see what he was like out in the backcountry. Sure, they'd been hiking a handful of times now, but those were just day hikes on the outskirts of city, not an uninterrupted journey into the wilderness.

"I'm excited to see you in action, Ellie." Jake ran his finger across the palm of her hand. His words made her smile, as she had just been thinking the same thing about him.

Chapter 34

Usually, when Ellie left work, she took the elevator down to the subterranean parking lot with her co-workers and said goodnight before hopping in her BMW. But today, she stepped out the front door of the lobby onto street level alone and walked to the bus stop one block away. A map behind plexi-glass showed all the bus routes in the area and a chart with times sat next to the map. The next bus would be there in six minutes. Ellie avoided the perforated metal bench. She imagined all the people who had sat there before; people who probably couldn't afford a car, in dirty work clothes. God do I sound like a bitch, she thought to herself. Save for some graffiti written in thick black marker on the wall, the plastic bus shelter was surprisingly clean.

A young man dressed in a gray suit approached and rested one fashionable shoe on the bench, glancing at the schedule while he continued talking on his cell phone. A brooding teenager with a pink backpack loaded with books stood to one side, listening to her iPod. As Bus 72 approached, everyone shifted slightly, reaching into their wallets.

Ellie chose a seat halfway back next to an older woman who was knitting. Despite the protocol of not staring at strangers, she couldn't help but look at the pink rows of perfectly formed stitches curving into a circle.

"Eighth grandbaby on the way," the woman explained. Her black and white hair closely cropped in tiny ringlets contrasted nicely with her chocolate skin.

"Congratulations," Ellie replied.

"Thank you child. I do love my grand babies. Haven't seen you on the bus before," she remarked. "This here's a regular commuter bus. I suppose you're on vacation or something."

"No. I live here. I just don't take the bus very often," Ellie explained, feeling like she had just admitted to some sort of misdemeanor.

"Bus is a good thing. You get to spend time thinking, or talking and not worrying 'bout the traffic." Clearly, this woman wasn't your average bus rider, thought Ellie, as she glanced around the bus. People of all ages and nationalities were on board; some people that even Ellie could tell were tourists, plus lots of regular commuters from high school kids like she'd seen at the bus stop to day laborers and white collar workers. One thing they all had in common was that no one was talking to anyone else. Leave it to Ellie to sit next to the one woman who talked to strangers. Ellie kept one ear on the conversation as she looked at the name of each stop, not wanting to miss her transfer.

"And then there's Daniel," she went on, as she showed Ellie a picture of a cute little boy with a front tooth missing. "He's my sixth grandchild. Son of Luther. Turns seven next month. He doesn't take too kindly to my knitting anymore, but do I have a surprise for him. Somethin' he's real fond of." Ellie nodded at the woman with whom she was now on a first name basis.

Her thoughts drifted back to her fight with Jake. He was like a moral compass in her life. If she compared herself to her colleagues, acquaintances and even her closest friends, she had always been the one to take on that role; making subtle or not so subtle suggestions about doing the right thing. And she took on this role with a sense of pride, she realized. But Jake, despite growing up without religion, seemed to have a compass that always pointed north—a man who led by example and brought out the integrity in others. She thought about her big news; news that brought joy to her heart. It wasn't until she had left the office that the doubt had worked its way into her thoughts.

And then there was her "business lunch" with Darren Wales this afternoon. She found it odd that he wanted to meet up at a restaurant instead of his office, but she knew the upscale lounge at the Centennial Hotel was a hot spot for business meetings. He listened to her eagerly when she spoke about Duomo, their shared target market and how timely it would be for Pacific West Holdings to return as advertisers. He nodded his head in agreement, saying he would give it some serious consideration. But the way he looked at her suggested he had far more than advertising in mind. He confirmed her suspicions when he'd asked if she had a boyfriend. *I'm seeing someone*, she had answered. This vague description hardly did justice for what she had with Jake. Wealthy, driven, upscale; Darren Wales was just the sort of guy she had been envisioning in her life—at least until she met Jake. *Who are you seeing?* He had asked. *Only fair for a man to know his competition.* Why hadn't I seen this coming, she asked herself. Too consumed with the idea of securing my promotion, she concluded. Maybe I've lost my true north. The idea unsettled her.

"This is your transfer, honey. Line four comes by every ten minutes or so, which means you probably juss on time."

"Thank you Cecile. Nice meeting you."

"Goodbye Ellie. See you again."

By the time she reached her final destination, Ellie had shifted her thoughts away from the awkward encounter with Darren Wales and to her late afternoon meeting with Margo. She shook her head, happily recalling the string of compliments Margo had fired off before offering her the Marketing Director position: Strong work ethic; innovative ideas, a real go getter; just what we've been looking for. She wanted to share her big news with Jake, but at the same time, she hesitated. Would he be happy for her, or give her that half smile she had come to recognize.

Chapter 35

She had meant to text Jake on the way to tell him she was running late, but now there was no point. She walked the short distance to the bar and was surprised to see valet bike parking out front.

"You come by bus?" asked the attendant.

"How did you know that?" she asked suspiciously.

"I saw you get off at the stop. If I scan your metro card, or validate your ticket stub, first drink's 50% off," he explained.

"Fantastic," Ellie smiled. She reached into the little pocket where she had stowed away the stub, and he nodded approvingly before handing her a coupon.

"Here you go. Have a good time."

Ellie pulled open the funky, stained glass door. Couches of all different shapes and sizes sat in clusters around the busy pub. A series of skylights filled the room with natural light.

The place was packed with hip young people, decked out in sexy, yet casual wear. Ellie's grey business skirt and red sweater made her stand out like someone who had accidentally walked into the wrong party, and the looks she was getting confirmed she wasn't the only one who thought so. A classic Bob Dylan song played in the background setting a revolutionary tone to the whole gathering.

Ellie glanced around the room in search of Jake, but couldn't find him. Her eyes wandered to a brick wall lined with photos she discerned to be activists: a photo of a man chained to a sequoia; a young woman holding a sign saying "If you can't trust me with choice, how can you trust me with a child?"; a protest march against big oil with hundreds of handmade signs poking into the air; kids working in an organic garden with skyscrapers in the background. She turned away from the wall of activism and headed to the bar. If she was going to be here alone for any length of time, she definitely needed something to drink. She gave the bartender her ticket and ordered a glass of chardonnay.

"Ellie. You made it." Jake suddenly appeared beside her. "I was beginning to think you ditched me." As soon as she looked into his eyes her shoulders relaxed.

"Sorry I'm late. I didn't see you," Ellie responded, giving him a kiss. He wore a button down, striped shirt and a pair of crisp jeans which hung loosely on his tall frame. She breathed in the pine scent of his body wash, and images of last night paraded through her mind, causing her cheeks to blush. She wondered if she would ever get to a point where she could just kiss him without that rush of heat invading her senses.

"Sorry. We're out back. I've been checking every so often to see if you were here. I didn't want to leave you waiting alone in a room full of environmentalists," he teased.

"Very funny. So Jake, I have some big news," she said, before they joined his friends. "I was promoted to Marketing Director today."

"Wow! Congrats, Ellie. I know how much you wanted this." He kissed her, pulling her toward him. "Let's do something special to celebrate," he suggested. Ellie smiled gratefully at his response.

"What did you have in mind?" she asked.

"Well, I could take you to an artsy film or maybe even a theater production. Something you like doing," he suggested. Ellie lingered in his arms. He was genuinely happy for her. That alone was enough. She thought again of how her initial excitement had been followed by a small wave of doubt—a doubt that didn't make any sense to her. She had wanted a position like this for years. She needed to wrap her mind around that before celebrating.

"Let's just mark it by having a fun evening that has nothing to do with my work. You know, simple, low brow fun," she suggested.

"Ah, then you're with the right crowd. Speaking of which, can I at least share the news with my friends?" Jake asked.

"You want to brag about me?" Ellie smiled.

"Yeah. I do," Jake responded as he put his hand in hers.

"It also means I'm going to be even busier than usual," she acknowledged. Perhaps that was part of the undercurrent of doubt; even more time at the office meant less time with Jake and other things she cared about.

"Can we still go camping?" he suddenly asked.

"Absolutely. I made sure I had that weekend free when she offered me the promotion," she responded. Jake smiled. That was a very good sign if she was giving their camping trip such priority.

The back deck was filled with potted plants on one side and a shuffle board on the other that was currently occupied by a group of scantily clad women playing competitively, which seemed to involve lots of high pitched squeals. Jake's friends sat on a wrap-around couch engrossed in a lively conversation, practically shouting to be heard over the noise from the shuffle board game.

Ellie was greeted by Jake's friends, who were now all familiar faces—faces that all appeared to be slightly tipsy. Jake announced Ellie's promotion and his friends warmly congratulated her.

"What's something you love doing that you haven't done in a while?" Jemma asked her. Ellie thought it over and the answer came to her in a flash.

"Swing dancing," she replied wistfully.

"Wow. Ellie. This is total serendipity! There's this supposedly fantastic swing band playing at Jamison's tonight," April announced.

"Do you guys even know how to swing dance?" Ellie asked. She watched as Jake's friends shook their heads no.

"How hard could it be?" Jemma replied. "I bet I can pick it up." Everyone was game. Jake pulled Ellie up from her seat as everyone started looking at the bill.

"Should we go get some dinner first?" he asked, as he put his arm around her shoulder.

"Dinner sounds great," Ellie agreed.

"They have chicken wings and other really disgusting food at Jamison's if you like that sort of stuff," Jemma commented. "But we could also go to Sprouts; this excellent vegan restaurant. Is everyone on bikes?" she asked. Ellie suddenly realized her dilemma.

"I took the bus here," she announced. Jake looked at her in surprise.

"That's fantastic, Ellie." He started laughing. "I thought you would drive, so I took the bus too, hoping to catch a ride home with you, umm, in your direction."

"Two stranded love birds. What shall you ever do?" Natalia smiled.

"You could rent bikes," Mary suggested.

"Rent bikes?" Ellie repeated.

"Yeah. Red's rents bikes Tuesdays through Sundays," she explained. "They're part of the bicycle coalition of Greater Los Angeles. You can rent the bikes here and check them in at two dozen other drop off points throughout the city." Suddenly Ellie's jovial mood started slipping away. It's not that she couldn't cycle. She'd cycled twice now in Los Angeles. But it was stressful, not relaxing. Jake caught the look on her face. He wasn't about to push her into cycling again, especially when she wasn't prepared.

"We don't have to cycle, Ellie. We could take the bus," Jake suggested. "But the next one isn't coming for half an hour." Ellie was thankful to hear such a reasonable response come out of Jake. But strangely enough, she wanted the excitement of cycling with his friends.

"You know, I'd actually consider it if I wasn't in a pencil skirt and 4 inch heels," she laughed.

"If that's seriously you're only concern, I have a solution," Jake smiled. "Come right this way." They entered the rental shop and Ellie saw a sparkly collection of cycling clothing for sale. She picked out a few items and tried them on. They were definitely snug, but much more appropriate for cycling and dancing, for that matter, than her work clothes. She stepped out of the dressing room.

"Damn," Jake commented as he looked her up and down in a way that made Ellie blush. Five minutes ago, she was a sexy office professional and now she was a sexy mama in tight cycling clothing. She certainly could adapt to any situation, he mused.

"How about a tandem?" Mary suggested. "If you're not comfortable cycling in L.A., Jake could take the lead, and you're just along for the ride." Mary winked, a mischievous smile on her lips.

"Okay," Ellie heard herself saying. "I'm game." Everyone cheered her on as they got on their bicycles. As the group started to cycle away, Ellie tensed up

"You sure you're okay with this?" Jake asked, catching the look on her face. In the short time that they'd known each other, he had come to recognize the way she would bite down on her lip if she felt uneasy about something.

"Yeah. Of course. It's just after our last cycling journey, I'm a little nervous, that's all."

"You can trust me Ellie," he assured her. Did he have any idea how much she already trusted him? How all of his friends trusted him?

"I know, Jake." There was something else that was bothering her as well. "I'm also used to being the one behind the wheel, if you know what I mean."

"You want to drive?" Jake asked pragmatically.

"Heck, no," Ellie laughed. "Plus I have a very nice view from here," she teased. Jake flashed her a smile as they got on the tandem. Even though it wasn't dark out, he had turned on the rear flashing light as well as the headlight.

Starting was a little difficult. They had to push down on their right pedals at the same time and cycle at the same speed, but it didn't take them long to coordinate their strokes. As they headed down the street, Ellie's nervousness gave way to excitement. Since she didn't have to worry about steering or navigating, she could just pedal and look around her. Although his broad shoulders and sculpted arms were extremely distracting, she managed to take in the city streets and watch Jake's friends cruising along with them. The air was still warm from the day, and she noticed people on the sidewalks dressed in summer-weight clothing making their way to various clubs or restaurants. There was a feeling of festivity in the air, and she wondered if it was always like that on a Friday night, or if she just hadn't noticed from the distance of her car. If she had been in a car, or even walking in the crowd, she wouldn't have this perspective.

"Turning right," Jake announced, as he slowed them down. They turned onto a busy street with bumper to bumper traffic, but slid right through, making it to the next intersection before the light even changed. They found a rhythm together, stopping and starting without the need to exchange words, and Ellie felt another level of trust unfolding. She liked the feel of the two of them together working as a team, and was slightly disappointed when they slowed the tandem and turned into a parking lot jam packed with bicycles.

Chapter 36

They headed to the front counter to place their orders and she looked at the long menu of vaguely familiar choices—tempeh burgers, tofu hot dogs, a raw food menu, kambucha.

"So does this count as eating locally grown organic food?" Ellie queried.

"Absolutely! Sounds like you're really doing it, Ellie. I'm impressed."

"Logging everything in as well," she reported. "But you're going to have to help me out with this menu. I don't see a single meaty item." Jake smiled at her, amazed how she just spoke her mind. Several women he'd dated had pretended to be vegetarian just to please him. Not Ellie.

"The tempeh tacos are pretty awesome," Jake noted. "They come with sautéed veggies, rice and beans. Filling as well. I know how you like a good meal."

Jake noticed several men checking her out and felt that sensation again; like he wanted the world to know that she was his. He wasn't ready to give her a ring, but something to make it clear they were an item.

"Any other suggestions?" She asked. He realized he must have been staring.

"Umm. Yeah. The soups are usually tasty."

"I'll take the tempeh tacos," she decided. He paid for dinner and they headed out back arm and arm.

"I've got some news too. I followed up with your real estate friend Geoff Gorman."

"Great. Did he have something for you?"

"Yeah. And it just may work. It's smaller than what we had, but it meets all of our basic needs. Room for the vans and all of our bikes and tools, fully wired for internet and has a small meeting room. We can rent it for three to six months without signing a long-term lease. That will at least give us time to work on a more permanent location."

"That's fantastic Jake!" Ellie responded, squeezing his arm. They joined his friends and immediately the conversation took a different route.

"So I hear you're doing great on the Seven Change Challenge," Mary said.

"I'm doing well compared to those in the office, but I hear I'm behind the online followers. Quite a challenge for me, actually. And you?"

"Well. Natalia and I have a sort of lifestyle where we're already doing everything on that list, and a whole lot more."

"Oh." Although she figured she should have taken this as an insult, she was too intrigued to know what "a whole lot more" meant.

"So what does a day in your life look like, based on that statement?" Ellie asked. She realized her tone sounded a bit more interrogative than she intended, as if she were conducting an interview, but Mary didn't seem to notice. She flashed a smile at Ellie as she launched in, as if she'd been waiting for the question all night.

"Well. We don't own a car. If for some reason public transport or cycling can't get us somewhere, we have a car-share—a car we pay shares for on an annual basis that is shared among fifteen people." Ellie took in her words and did her best to keep her mouth from gaping open. Besides loaning her car one time to Gillian, she had never shared an automobile in her life.

"How on earth do you manage that? I mean, certainly there are conflicts."

"Yeah. Naturally. But everyone in the car share relies primarily on their bicycles, public transport or carpooling with other people who own cars, contributing to the gas."

"So how many times have you used the car share this year?" Ellie asked.

"Three."

"Three?" Ellie exclaimed. "You're not getting a very good deal!"

"In our world, it's a great deal, because we don't want to use a car. Cars will be rendered obsolete in a 100 years. They are completely unsustainable, and someday, we'll choose the ability to breathe over the comfort of a personal automobile. Well. Actually not. People will choose the car until their last dying breath, leaving it to the next generation to do something about it." Ellie listened to Mary in a state of awe. In comparison, she made Jake seem like an environmental centrist.

"Okay. No car. And what else? I mean, in your daily life." Ellie asked. She was intrigued by Mary as one might be intrigued by a person from a totally foreign culture—deeply curious but not necessarily interested in relinquishing her citizenship to immigrate. At the same time, she recognized in Mary her friends from the Northwest; strong, independent females, highly self-efficient, with a life oriented to the outdoors.

"We've been doing a locavore diet for the last year. That means eating food that's produced within a 100 miles of where we live. We've been successful except for coffee, olive oil and chocolate. Natalia has an occasional cigarette, and I guarantee you that's not sourced within a 100 miles, but then it falls outside of something edible, even though it's consumed."

"Wow. That's got to be hard. I mean, what about that beer in your hand?" Ellie asked.

"Razor wire is from a local brewery. They get their wheat from Riverside County, which is actually 112 miles from our front door, but we give ourselves some leeway." She looked at Ellie as she took a slug of her beer. "Razor wire brewery also uses locally grown barley and hops," she added.

"You really take it seriously," Ellie relented. April joined the conversation and Ellie wished for a moment that Jake was by her side and not hanging with the guys. I guess it was good to get to know these women, if she and Jake were to become an official item. She wondered how Jake thought of them. Were they just dating? Were they exclusive? Considering their level of intimacy, she certainly hoped so.

"So you like Jake a lot, eh?" April inquired. Ellie was surprised by the sudden change of topic.

"Yes, I do," she responded carefully. "He seems very genuine."

"He's definitely the real deal," April stated resolutely. "I know that as a friend," she quickly clarified.

"He's pretty hot on you as well," Mary chimed in.

"Did he say that?" Ellie asked. Was Jake the kind of guy to chat over his relationships with the girls? She couldn't see it.

"No. I know 'cause he's never brought a girl around to meet us," April explained. Natalia honed in on the conversation.

"Plus he looks at you respectfully," Natalia added. He had been nothing but respectful to her from the get go; flirtatious, yes, but respectful. She wondered how he treated other women, or if there were still other women in the picture. They hadn't even had that conversation. I'm more naïve than I thought, she said to herself.

"You could say this is totally new territory for us, and I have to admit, he's got good taste," Natalia smiled provocatively toward Mary. Finally, Jake circled back round to Ellie's side just as the food was arriving. The group of friends sat in a circle, eating, talking and laughing, and Ellie felt incredibly out of place yet incredibly at home in this close knit group of friends. And the night was still young.

Chapter 37

Half an hour later they were on their bikes heading to Jamison's Irish Organic Pub. Ellie had lived in Los Angeles for three years and was seeing places in the city she'd never even known were there. Sure, it was a big city and it was possible to live your whole life here and not see all the bars and restaurants, but she'd considered herself somewhat savvy when it came to going out. But then again, she hadn't been going out with Jake Tillerman and his radical, eco-friends. This was a completely different circuit, she realized; a whole other branch of society. Who had ever heard of an Irish Pub that threw the word Organic in between Irish and Pub? In her experience these words were inseparable.

Even though it was 9:00 p.m. by the time they arrived, it was still considered early, which meant everyone had another round of drinks since the band hadn't started yet. Ellie wasn't much of a beer drinker, but she knew better than to switch back to wine. She ordered a bottled water, but the man behind the bar just winked at her.

"We don't carry bottled water darlin'. But you c'n have filtered water from this nice little tap here," he explained in a beautiful Irish accent. Ellie looked behind the bar to discover that everything was on tap, including the whiskey. In fact, there wasn't a bottle of anything, anywhere.

Although she was full from the tempeh tacos, she could smell something delicious cooking in the kitchen. Above the window was a sign that said "It might be greasy, but it's organic." She found the slogan to be lacking from a marketing perspective, but based on the flurry of orders coming from the kitchen, it was hitting its mark.

"You having fun, Ellie?" Jake asked as he took her hand.

"Yeah. It's great here, and I like hanging out with your friends."

"You've made a good impression on my friends as well. That's not so easy if you're not from our camp, if you know what I mean."

"Maybe it's because I'm doing your little Seven Change Challenge and they think it's sweet," Ellie mused. "I'm perhaps viewed as fresh meat that can be converted. Wait, I suppose your camp wouldn't use such an analogy. Let me see, fresh celery with the potential of being juiced."

Jake laughed openly as she turned toward him. He kissed her as they rejoined his friends on a long velvet couch along the wall. The band was doing their sound check and it was abundantly clear that no one would be having any conversations unless they enjoyed shouting.

As she looked at the musicians on stage, a twinge of homesickness plied its way through her: two violins, a banjo, stand-up base, lap steel guitar, regular guitar, full drum set and plenty of microphones for harmonies. There were at least seven musicians on stage and when they began to play, the dance floor swung into action.

"Want to dance?" Jake asked.

"Do you know how to swing?" she asked dubiously.

"I took a few lessons," he admitted.

"You're full of surprises," she beamed as they walked to the dance floor. Country dancing and swing dancing were as much a part of her upbringing as the mountains and forests. It was in her blood. The dance floor was one of the few places Ellie was willing to let a man take the lead, after he proved his ability. But it didn't take much to get used to Jake. Jake twirled her around like a pro as they worked their way through the crowd. And they were good together; as good as any couple on the dance floor. She seemed to respond to his touch as if she could read what he was thinking. Jakes friends hollered in excitement as the two of them worked their moves.

Jake had taken swing lessons on an off for a few years and only seemed to be able to dance well with more seasoned dancers. All of his female classmates had been a struggle; they were either too distracted by his looks, or too head strong to let a man be in charge. Dancing with Ellie, on the other hand, was invigorating, and he couldn't stop smiling as she met his every move, following gracefully, yet firmly. She kept her hands in place, responding to the pressure of his squeeze, turning in exactly the direction he had hoped every time. Her arms were strong, muscular even. He hadn't noticed that about her before, but in the tight pink top and spandex pants, every inch of her ample, gorgeous shape was exposed as she responded with skill and agility. As he felt their bodies working together, building up a sweat, he couldn't help but think of making love to her.

Forty-five minutes later, tired and sweaty, they headed to the bar for a drink. This time they had to stand in line, and as they waited, Jake pulled her to him. The bar was so crowded that the intimate way he held her went unnoticed. He placed his hand on the small of her back as he'd done several times before, and Ellie responded to his touch, arching slightly as she rapped her arms around him. She leaned into his chest, damp with perspiration. She kissed him on the neck, excited by the salty wetness she found there. She kissed her way up his neck until their lips met. Adrenaline shot through her as she felt his lips on hers. Their eyes met and she could see she wasn't alone in the longing she felt.

"Want to get out of here?" he whispered in her ear. Her eyes flickered for a moment before she responded.

"No way, are you kidding? I want to dance the night away with you. You're really quite good for a city boy." Jake felt like he'd missed a cue. So she wasn't thinking about the same thing he was after all. "But as far as getting home, we've still got to cycle all the way back, don't we?"

"Not necessarily," he explained. "There's a bike drop off not far from here and we could hop on the 14 which will take us a few blocks from my house."

"And my car is at work still, so somehow, I'll have to arrange to get that later too. I hadn't thought this whole thing through, really. The competitive side of me just wanted to get more alternative transportation points." Especially after being stripped of all my points for the first two weeks, she thought.

"We'll work it out, Ellie. Don't worry." Moments later his friends were next to them, bubbling with energy as they barraged them with comments and questions.

"You guys were amazing out there!" Edmond commented, saluting them with a shot of whiskey. "Maybe Ellie will give me a turn on the dance floor?"

"Not a chance, Edmond," Jake stated. "Find yourself another partner."

"Ellie, I have never seen Jake dance like that. I didn't even know he could swing. You've been holding out on us Jakey," Natalia teased.

"Dude. That was the shit," added Ethan. "Since when are you a swing dancer?"

"A guy's got to have his secrets," Jake responded. Everyone was in high spirits and Ellie couldn't remember the last time she'd worked up a sweat on the dance floor or felt so happy with a man. All she knew was that she wanted more. And she wasn't just thinking about the dancing. They had been intimate with one another ever since that windy night, but when they were on the dance floor, it had donned on her that she wanted to be with him completely; physically, mentally; the whole thing. She knew he had read her perfectly when he suggested they go home, which secretly pleased her.

It was just before midnight by the time they made it back to his house. They had to cut out of the club early to drop off the bikes and catch the last bus, which seemed like a modern day version of the Cinderella story to Ellie, except that she wasn't going back to a wicked stepmother, but to Jake's little bungalow.

They entered his home together, taking off their shoes and stepping inside its warmth. Ellie reached up and kissed him.

"You taste like the ocean," she said.

"So do you. It's all that perspiration we worked up on the dance floor. Want to shower?" he asked with the same casualness as if asking if she'd like a cup of tea. Ellie wondered if he planned to join her.

"Are you going to time me? That's one challenge I haven't been able to meet yet." Even though she was sure she had sweated out the majority of the alcohol she'd drank that evening, she was still a bit tipsy.

"Well, we could always . . ." Jake hesitated.

"Share?" Ellie finished his sentence. She was trying to smile, but she felt suddenly vulnerable as she exhaled. She was in love with Jake Tillerman and she didn't know if he loved her back. Wanted her, yes. But love?

"That would be a wonderfully sustainable solution," Jake responded coyly, taking her hand. He turned on the shower and they quickly undressed. Physically, she was beautiful, but there was now a depth to her beauty that came with knowing her that made him almost shy as they stood naked together under the stream of hot water. Ellie pulled him close and he could feel her trembling.

"God I want you Jake," she whispered in his ear. Although they had made love a handful of times now, there was a serious look about her that made Jake feel as if he were about to perform a more sacred act. After showering, they dried each other off and headed into the bedroom where he lit the candles on his dresser. As he looked at her in the candlelight, she seemed even more voluptuous than he remembered; her breasts fuller, her belly slightly rounded like a Goddess.

They took their time exploring each other's bodies. He worked into her gently, feeling her tighten around him. When he felt himself getting close, he slowed his pace, pulling her on top of him so she could lead. As he gazed at her, he knew he wanted her completely to himself. Ellie moaned as she closed her eyes, warmth spreading through her. When they finished making love, he rolled her over so they lay side by side. Jake pushed her long hair away from her eyes so he could see her face.

"I could seriously get used to this." He traced a finger across her cheeks and down the curve of her neck.

"Me too," she whispered as she stared into his eyes. His breath caught as she gazed into him, and he knew he was hooked.

◊◊◊

The next morning Jake woke up early to find his bed empty. He walked into the living room and there was Ellie sitting on the couch.

"Good morning," she beamed. She still wore his p.j's and had pulled on one of his fleece jackets. In fact, it looked like she'd settled in completely: a steaming cup of tea sat on the coffee table next to a plate covered in toast crumbs, and she was a good 40 pages into *Omnivore's Dilemma* by Michael Pollan.

"I thought you'd gone. But here you are, sitting in my living room, reading about the importance of small scale organic food. What a relief." As he looked at her, he felt his breath getting a little short. What was this strange, anxious feeling, he thought to himself?

"I suppose I could have called a cab," Ellie teased, "but I knew you had to wake up sometime."

"No more calling cabs," Jake replied, raising his eyebrows at her. "What time is it?" he asked sleepily.

"7:30." He couldn't remember the last time he had slept so well. No dreams, just solid, uninterrupted sleep.

"I've got a soccer match at 9 a.m. Want me to drop you off after breakfast?" He made his way over to the couch and sat down beside her.

"That'd be great."

"How did you sleep?" he asked her.

"I was a little sick this morning, to be honest."

"Seriously? Again? You didn't even drink that much last night. You redefine lightweight."

"I know, but I started with wine, then switched to beer. That's always been a deadly combination for me," she sighed. "But I'd say I haven't slept this well in years." Her words worked magic on him, banishing the strange insecurity that had plagued him just moments before. He leaned over to kiss her, but thought better of it, and headed into the bathroom to brush his teeth.

Ellie wandered out back and leaned over the deck. If they truly committed to each other, what would it mean in the long run to be with him? Would they get married and if she were green enough, start a little hippy family? Could they both continue with their careers without conflict? Would they stay in the city or would they be living on a commune in the middle of nowhere eating alfalfa sprouts?

Jake found her on the back deck sitting in the sunshine and was surprised to see the pensive look on her face.

"What are you thinking about right now?" he asked as he wrapped his arms around her.

"I couldn't possibly tell you that." Ellie smiled. He pulled her closer and started kissing her ear. Chills made their way down her spine, causing a small gasp to cross her lips.

"I'll take you all over again if you don't start talking," he threatened.

"Alfalfa sprouts," she relented.

"You must take your alfalfa sprouts very seriously," Jake laughed. "Because the look on your face was one of deep concentration, as if you were trying to solve the world's problems."

"No, that's your job, Jake. Remember?" she teased gently.

"No. It's not my job. It's all of our jobs. All of us together," Jake responded, the spirited look not leaving his face. Ellie figured it couldn't hurt to share at least part of her thoughts. Perhaps this was a good way to broach the subject she'd been thinking about since she woke up.

"That serious look you saw on my face a few minutes ago?"

"Yeah?" Jake asked as his eyebrows arched up in curiosity.

"That was me, picturing us living in some commune together."

"Eating alfalfa sprouts?"

"Yes." Ellie laughed.

"I'm down with that." He kissed her shoulder gently. Would she really consider such a thing? Leave the city and all of its cultural offerings? The idea both excited and scared him. "Speaking of alfalfa sprouts, let's make some breakfast. I'm starving," he suggested, changing the subject.

"Sounds great. I could really go for some bacon and eggs," Ellie suggested.

"I'm fresh out of bacon, but I have some vegan sausages and free range eggs."

"Oops. Of course you don't have bacon. Sorry." She was going to have to get used to the vegetarian thing if she was going to be with Jake.

"How about an omelet?"

"With greens and fresh herbs from the garden," Ellie added.

"Perfect." Ellie went out to Jake's garden and bent down to pluck a twig of rosemary and a handful of oregano leaves before heading over to the bed of lettuce. As she kneeled on the earth and plucked the leaves, she pictured herself in her family's garden, picking from a bounty of vegetables for a family meal. Usually such thoughts caused turmoil within her, but this morning, as she felt the wet leaves in her hands coupled with the memory, joy filled her senses. A familiar beeping sound pulled her from the moment. I hope it's not work, she thought as she headed back into the kitchen to wash the herbs and lettuce, doing her best to ignore her phone.

"You might as well see who it is," Jake suggested as he scrambled the eggs.

"All right. All right. I guess it wouldn't hurt to look." She took out the phone, glancing at the text message. Her shoulders relaxed as she read.

"It's Arno. Just a reminder that we're having lunch this afternoon. It's crazy, you know, but he and Pierre have been going out about two months and Arno's already dreaming of going on a European vacation with him."

"And here you are day dreaming of us living in a commune, eating alfalfa sprouts. He's way behind, eh?" Jake grinned. Would he still have a smile on his face if he knew the rest of her musings?

"Jake, I need to know something," Ellie started as she dried the lettuce leaves with a towel.

"Shoot."

"Are we a couple? You know, exclusive?" she asked. Jake smiled, setting down the onion he was about to chop, and took her hand.

"I'm not seeing anyone else," he responded. "Are you?"

"Of course not," Ellie stated indignantly.

"Well, then. I suppose we are."

"Just like that?" she asked. Jake thought about all of his doubts along the way, about Luz, about the feelings that had grown within him over the past two months.

"No. We worked hard for this, Ellie." She nodded in agreement. They sure had. Jake pulled her to him, elated that they had come to this decision so naturally together. He kissed her forehead, then each of her eyelids. The tension in his chest released its grip, giving way to warmth that radiated through him. They kissed for a long time, as if consummating their decision. When they finally broke apart, Jake retrieved his knife, and started mincing the oregano, its savory scent filling the air.

"So, girlfriend. Why don't you shower while I finish making breakfast," he suggested. Ellie kissed him one more time before heading into the bathroom to take a quick shower. There in the mirror she saw a woman she hardly recognized staring back at her. She looked very relaxed and casual in a Gaia Eden t-shirt and men's plaid pajama bottoms. Her long hair was slightly tousled, and she still looked decent with her make up washed off—a little bit like a hippy chick, even, if it hadn't been for the perfectly sculpted eyebrows and diamond earrings. I am Jake Tillerman's girlfriend, she said to the woman in the mirror, and she smiled back as if she'd just won the lottery.

Chapter 38

The week started in a rush. Jake was busy applying for grant applications to get his whole team to the gulf area to help with clean up of the oil spill. Not only was she slammed at work, but she was busy cleaning up the house for Gillian's return this coming weekend.

Her doctor's appointment at the women's clinic snuck up on her Tuesday afternoon and she arrived only six minutes early, having to rush through the forms. Ellie changed into the tiny pink gown and sat on the cold table. They knew patients had to strip down for their annual exam. Why then, she wondered, were the rooms always so cold?

The doctor was nice enough—a middle aged woman with gentle brown eyes who made Ellie feel as comfortable as one can while half naked on an examining table. Ellie mentioned her irregular periods over the last few months, and her desire to go on the pill. The doctor went over different doses, side effects, proper usage.

"But the pill does not protect you from sexually transmitted diseases. How many sexual partners do you currently have?"

"One. We're quite new, but we're in a monogamous relationship," Ellie responded.

"And how long have you been active with your new partner?"

"About six or seven weeks," Ellie estimated. She knew these were routine questions, but nonetheless, they made her uncomfortable.

"And have you been using protection?"

"Of course," Ellie responded.

"When we do the pap, I'll order a panel of standard tests, just in case. You should ask your new partner to do the same." But as she began to examine Ellie, she hesitated. "Ellie, did you give a urine sample on the way in?"

"Yes," she replied nervously.

"I need to get a blood sample as well," she stated, an unreadable expression on her face. "Just relax," the doctor directed, as she pressed the needle into the vein on her left arm. Ellie watched as her blood filled the little vial. Please let me be disease free, Ellie thought. Dr. Ericson pushed a button on the door and an assistant came in.

"Did you run an HCG test on of Ms. Ashburn's urine sample?" she asked.

"Yes, of course. I'll get it for you," the assistant responded with a warm smile as the doctor handed over the little vial filled with Ellie's blood. After the door was shut, Dr. Ericson turned toward Ellie, her brown eyes gently gazing at her.

"And before your current partner, when was the last time you were sexually active?"

"Over a year ago," Ellie replied. There was something about the way the doctor looked at her that worried Ellie. "What is it? Do I have something?" she finally asked. Just then there was a knock on the door.

"Here you go, Dr. Ericson," her assistant said, handing her some documents. She flipped through the reports and looked at Ellie.

"Ellie. Would you mind sitting up? Tammy just brought me the results of your urine test."

"That was quick."

"I'm afraid you can't go on the pill."

"Why not?" Ellie asked, shivering in her pink dressing gown.

"You have a very high count of HCG hormone in your urine. And that means you're pregnant."

"I'm what? That's not possible!" Ellie stammered in disbelief. "We've been so careful." Each time they had made love, they had been diligent about using protection. "Except that first time."

"All it takes is one time," the doctor stated.

"Yes. But I got my period a few days afterwards."

"Was this period shorter and lighter than usual?" Ellie thought about it for a few moments. A wave of panic crawled up her spine.

"Yes. It only lasted a couple of days. How did you know that?"

"When the embryo implants on the uterine wall, it can cause spotting. Many women mistake it for a period. And how long ago was that?" Ellie thought it through and felt her cheeks getting hot.

"About six weeks ago."

"So you were late and you didn't suspect anything?"

"Well, no. I thought I started my period again last week, but it only lasted a day and it was very light. I almost canceled my appointment."

"Did this light bleeding occur after intercourse?" the doctor asked. Ellie nodded uncomfortably.

"That is also quite common, Ellie. I realize this must be big news for you. Especially if you're in a new relationship."

"A new relationship with a man who doesn't want children." She would have expected tears; lots of them. But her eyes remained dry.

"I imagine there's a lot going through your mind right now. I would like to suggest that you take the rest of the day off from work and meet with a counselor. I can probably get you in to talk to someone within the hour."

"I'm not ready for a baby," she whispered.

"You have options, Ellie. Not that you need to make any decisions today, but there's a clinic."

"I don't believe in abortion, if that's what you're suggesting," Ellie stated. She was amazed how she had been cold not two minutes ago. And now she felt heat pulsing through her body.

"I'm not suggesting anything. I just want you to know your options, that's all."

"If I had bleeding after sex, does that mean the baby's in danger?" Ellie asked suddenly.

"No. You're baby is safe and sex during pregnancy does not affect the baby. During the first trimester, a small amount of bleeding after sex can occur. It suggests vaginal irritation." Ellie nodded her head slowly.

"But I would like to do an ultrasound to date the pregnancy and check in on development. We'll need to move you down to the other side of the clinic."

"Okay," she responded numbly. Her whole life she had wanted children. But not like this; not when she had just received a major promotion, not when she and Jake were so new.

Ellie felt disconnected, like she was watching some other young woman lying on a table, hearing she was pregnant. As Dr. Ericson moved the sonogram wand, Ellie looked on. She pointed to a small mass that seemed to be moving.

"There it is. See that movement there? That's the baby's heartbeat."

"Oh my God," she whispered, bringing her hands to her face. How could such a tiny little thing already have a heartbeat? Ellie wondered as her tears started to come.

"It is pretty amazing, isn't it?" The doctor responded carefully.

"Yes," Ellie whispered. Doctor Ericson went over a few practicalities, and scheduled a follow-up appointment for July 9th.

"We'll be able to see more at nine weeks."

Ellie placed her hands on her belly. Suddenly it all made sense; her increase in appetite, bouts of nausea, a sudden intolerance to alcohol, breast sensitivity, and that constant feeling that she was somehow inextricably bound to Jake. Perhaps it had nothing at all to do with love, but with biology.

Chapter 39

Sweat beaded across Jake's forehead, his heart racing. So many times it had gone off without a hitch, and now this.

"Hands in the air, I said!" yelled the security guard. Conrad followed his instructions. Jake dropped the potted plant in his hand, watching as it fell to the ground, the stems snapping in half. He slowly raised his hands to his head as the guard radioed for back up. Not one, but two police cars came screeching into the alley minutes after the guard radioed it in.

"Shit," Jake whispered under his breath. Conrad let out a sigh.

"Don't they have any real criminals to catch?" he whispered to Jake.

"Apparently this dumpster is top priority," Jake responded, causing both he and Conrad to laugh.

"You think this is funny?" shouted a short, burly officer as he approached them. "You'll think its real funny when you two pretty boys are in jail, locked up with some mean motherfuckers who think you're both real cute. Trespassing is a crime." Both Jake and Conrad kept their mouths shut as they were handcuffed and led to the police car.

An hour and a half passed as they waited in a holding cell to be processed. As soon as they were allowed access to a telephone, Conrad called Stephanie and described in as much detail as he could what had happened. Within 45 minutes, she had a lawyer down to get them out.

"Great to see you Larry," Conrad exclaimed, as they were led out of the holding cell.

"You too Conrad. Have to say I prefer meeting up for martinis by the pool instead of coming in here."

"Are we in trouble?" Jake couldn't help but asking.

"No. This won't be a problem," the lawyer explained. "I've determined that since the dumpster was set out in the alley for trash day that it technically was not on private property. Their trespassing charges are thus ungrounded. If anything, they owe you an apology and a future get out of jail free card."

"That could come in handy," Jake responded, thinking of a big protest coming up.

When Jake's feet touched pavement again, he took a deep breath, unaware that he had been breathing shallowly the last few hours. It wasn't the first time Jake had been arrested, but this time it felt like a violation. Now that he was reunited with his bike and cell phone, he pedaled away from the station before flipping open his phone. He discovered two texts from Ellie and one from work letting him know she had called. He was two hours late. He quickly punched in her number.

"Hello? Jake?" she answered, concern in her voice.

"Hi Ellie. Sorry I'm late. I got held up."

"You couldn't have texted me?" she asked with annoyance. "I've been worried."

"I couldn't. I just got out of the police station," he admitted before thinking it through. Shit, why did I say that?

"Oh my God! Are you okay? What happened?" Ellie wailed. The extremity of her tone caught him off guard. If there was one thing he'd learned about Ellie, it was that she kept it together under tense situations. God; he had worried her for nothing.

"I'm fine Ellie. Nothing's wrong. Conrad and I got caught going through a dumpster. A lawyer just got us out. Technically, we were in the right."

"A dumpster? Oh God, Jake. If you're ever that tight financially, I can always take you to the grocery store," Ellie winced, thinking about how much she had underestimated his financial situation.

"That's very sweet," Jake responded, feeling more insulted than anything. "But it's not about the money. I know it might sound strange, Ellie. But dumpster diving is more of a political statement. It's a whole movement. People do it all over the nation. They call it Freeganism," Jake began. Ellie could tell by his tone that he was gearing up for a long speech about the justification of dumpster diving. Great, the father of my child is a dumpster diver, Ellie screamed to herself.

"That's just gross, Jake," she stated abruptly, cutting him off. She looked at the dinner she had spent the last few hours making for them. She half listened as he went on justifying his actions while apologizing for causing her any alarm. The thing was, Ellie was frantic. She had taken her doctor's suggestion and called in sick for the rest of the day.

She had wandered the aisles of the Health Food store aimlessly searching out ingredients for the perfect meal over which to tell her boyfriend-who-didn't-want-babies she was pregnant. No dinner ingredients landed in her basket. In the end, she had only purchased pre-natal vitamins. When she got home, she ordered two vegetarian pizzas and made a salad. But when they arrived, she decided they weren't good enough; thus her launch into homemade quiche.

"You still there Ellie?" Jake's words came through the phone.

"Yeah. Sorry. I think it's best if we cancel for tonight."

"Are you upset because I got arrested?" Jake asked tentatively into his cell phone. He pictured Ellie in one of her elegant dresses she tended to wear these days and felt almost bad about his dumpster diving hobby. It would be the first night he hadn't seen her in two weeks.

"I'm upset about a lot of things. But let's save it for another time."

"Listen Ellie, don't be upset. I can come over. I'll make it up to you," he responded, remorse in his voice.

"I'm not mad, Jake. I don't support it, but I'm not mad. It's just late and I need to get a solid night's sleep," she explained. As if I'll be sleeping at all tonight, she thought to herself.

In the end, she was thankful he wouldn't be coming over, because although she knew she had to tell him about her news, she didn't know how. Although she had asked the doctor a dozen questions and made a follow up appointment, she spent hours online researching, getting her mind around what was happening inside of her body. Gillian called and postponed her return date again. It was all Ellie could do, when she had Gillian on the phone those few minutes, to keep herself together and not share her news; especially when she wasn't 100 percent certain what she planned to do.

Chapter 40

Friday was busy at work, and as luck would have it, she was nauseous. She'd been feeling a little unbalanced over the last few weeks, but she had attributed it to her switch to a primarily vegetarian, organic diet and stress from so much work. But she wasn't about to slow down, especially not with all the progress she'd been making. After Margo had announced Ellie's promotion and Karen's imminent departure, people looked at her with renewed respect. Well, at least the majority. She noticed that Jared, Amber and a few others distanced themselves from her. She didn't know what that was about, but had way too much on her mind to give it much attention.

Margo had requested Ellie's presence at three meetings this week, and was giving Ellie far more work than she could handle in an eight hour day. Thank God she had the weekend free to catch up.

The doctor had told her she could continue the same amount of exercise she had been doing, but not to increase her exercise regimen. Thus every morning, she set out to do her four mile run, though she had backed off on her pace. Her body needed the exercise, but her mind also needed the time to process the news. When she and Jake got together Friday night, he was clearly excited about something.

"I have an idea," Jake said thoughtfully. "What are you doing this weekend?" He sat beside her by the pool, their legs dangling in the cool water.

"I'd cleared my schedule for Gillian's return, but she won't be here 'til Wednesday. So I guess that makes me free, besides catching up on work," she responded as she gazed at him. "Why?"

"Maybe you'd want to come up north with me for the weekend," he offered, splashing a little water on her legs.

"It's not a dumpster diving excursion, is it?" she quipped. "Because you can add that to my list of deal breakers."

Jake heard the lightness of her tone, but he knew better than to ignore this warning.

"No. Nothing like that, Ellie. Promise. I have a meeting with a client up in Santa Ynez Valley tomorrow on the very property where we'll be camping next weekend." He draped his arm over her shoulders, softly kissing her ear. "You said you wanted to see me in action; this would be like diving in." Ellie took in his words, combined with the tingling sensation now traveling down her spine from the warmth of his breath on her ear.

"That's exciting. Is it a kid's program?" she asked, trying to stay centered.

"No. A client meeting for a project. It's really cool 'cause I get to use both my architectural design and my passion for sustainable community—a community I could even picture joining someday if it ever gets fully funded. It should only take a few hours, but the rest of the time, besides driving time of course, we'd have free. And I'd love your company." Ellie hesitated at first. They'd be making the same long drive next weekend. Did she want to do a long road trip twice? On the other hand, if they had a whole day together in the car, she would find a way to tell him.

"I'd love to go," she decided.

"Fantastic. And you're okay with an overnight?" Jake asked. They had done lots of day trips hiking, and had traveled to a number of museums, but thus far, no overnight trips outside the city.

"As long as I can bring my laptop to get some work done."

"Of course," Jake responded. He looked at her with one of his curious smiles before proceeding. "But I should warn you, if the Seven Eco Steps. I mean, Seven Change Challenge seems a little too green for you, this might be over the top green." Ellie thought about

Margo's request for something *outside the box*. Maybe she could write about it as well.

"I can handle it," Ellie stated confidently. "Oh. And I read about this great resort style B & B up in Santa Ynez," she added. "I wouldn't mind splurging for it." Jake rolled his eyes.

"As long as they aren't too wasteful." Ellie felt annoyed. He was such a kill-joy sometimes. But what could she expect from the founder of Gaia Eden? Another thought crossed her mind; she was going to have to change her spending habits dramatically if she were to bring a baby into the world.

"A regular, more affordable hotel is okay," she relented. Jake was surprised to see her waver in her opinion. "Any chance I can do an article on the experience?" Ellie asked. "I've been asked to find something that's hip, green and sophisticated."

Jake winked at her. "I don't think this is going to suit your Margo, and I doubt my client would want to be written up in a design magazine. But then again, you never know with Gray Wolf."

◊◊◊

Saturday morning at 8:15 a.m., Jake rang her bell and within a few minutes they were in his Toyota Prius heading out of the city. The roads were surprisingly quiet once they merged onto 101 North. They listened to the news the first hour, then talked a bit about work and plans for their camping trip, but Jake noticed Ellie was quieter than usual.

After they passed Santa Barbara, he took the exit for Highway 154 and headed up a mountain pass. He slipped his iPod into the port as they lost radio reception and soon Bob Marley was singing his sweet songs of revolution. Jake tapped along to the rhythm as they drove.

"You're sure quiet today," he observed. "You still upset about the dumpster episode?"

"No. Not really. I'm just a little under the weather," she lied. Ever since last night when she'd seen him, she looked at him differently. He was no longer just Jake, but the father of the baby growing inside her. The idea tantalized her. Jake looked at her with concern.

"You should have told me. I could have come alone."

"Don't worry. Nothing contagious. I wouldn't have come if I didn't feel up to it."

"Okay. Good to know. Have you ever been to the Santa Ynez Valley?"

"No," Ellie acknowledged. "But I know its wine country. Thus it's been on my list." Not that she could drink wine right now.

"It's a slice of paradise: farmlands, wilderness, small towns. Maybe it's more like you're used to growing up." Jake suggested. They crested the top of the mountain and started across a high bridge. The vistas opened up to a wide valley below edged by rolling hills and distant purple mountains. The crisp blue of the sky dappled with white clouds promised a warm day.

"This is beautiful. Not really like Idaho at all, but beautiful."

"We're headed through the Los Padres National Forest."

As Ellie looked around, she dropped her shoulders down, exhaling. It was like the city had been crowding in, compressing her soul and just seeing rolling hills and swaths of open space created room inside her. She thought back to a conversation she and Jake had weeks ago about her needing to "convert to his green religion" in order for them to bear children together. In this line of thought, she was at least an initiate at this stage. Bob Marley's Three Little Birds came on over the speakers and she felt another layer of happiness enveloping her.

"What are you thinking about right now?" That was one of his favorite questions. Now was not the time to be 100 percent truthful, she decided. But there were a few thoughts she could share.

"I was thinking about the first time I heard this song. It was the summer I turned thirteen," she recalled, thinking back to that long month at the lake with her cousin Janie. It had been the first time she'd tried a cigarette; the first time she'd been exposed to reggae, her first kiss. "This music was like my first taste of the bigger world outside." Jake smiled at her briefly, placing his hand casually on her knee, while keeping his eyes on the road. She liked the way he concentrated when he drove. So many city drivers turned from the wheel, talking casually as if they weren't steering a thousand pounds of steel.

"When was the first time you heard this song?" she asked.

"I don't know. I feel like Marley's music has been a part of my life from the beginning. Quite possible with my parents. They were probably listening to him when I was in the womb." She tried to imagine Jake as a child. "My twin sister and I came along unexpectedly, before my mom and dad were ready to be parents, you might say. And after we were born, they carried on as if nothing had changed." Jake tapped on the steering wheel as he talked. "They used to have these parties all of the time. The living room filled with the thick, skunky scent of marijuana, people dancing, talking dramatically about politics and regime change. And in the meantime, they both finished grad school, which meant less time to play catch or bake cookies with the kids. Not exactly a traditional upbringing."

"Who took care of you, then?" Ellie asked, astounded to learn that Jake had come about by accident. Instinctively, she rested her hands on her belly.

"My grandparents. They filled in a lot, but when they weren't around, we learned to take care of ourselves." Ellie looked at the scar on Jake's cheek, another reminder of just how irresponsible his parents had been.

"That sounds like a pretty hard upbringing," Ellie responded gently.

"Yeah. Not so nice to know you were a mistake."

"You're hardly a mistake, Jake."

"Yeah. I was," he snapped. "My sister and I both." His gaze leveled on the horizon, his jaw taught.

"I'm sorry. I meant, thank God your parents kept you two. They clearly made the right decision."

"I don't know. Seemed pretty irresponsible to me," he responded. Ellie panicked.

"Well if they hadn't kept you, you know. I wouldn't have a fabulous new boyfriend right now; there'd be no Gaia Eden." She started. "All those boys that you've helped, all of the other great things you're going to do in your life." The tears sprung from her eyes before she could finish her sentence.

"Hey, hey. Slow done there, Ellie. Don't cry. It's okay." Jake consoled, squeezing her knee. "I'm not traumatized by it or anything. I actually get along with my parents now that they're all grown up." As he watched her rubbing the tears out of her eyes, warmth emanated from his chest. He hadn't realized he would be able to love a woman again. He wanted to tell her his feelings, but he couldn't bring the words to his lips.

"You're an angel," he chose instead. Ellie didn't know how to respond. She was intentionally withholding news from him that would change his life forever. And further, she was beginning to question her steadfast commitment to keeping the baby. The timing was so wrong. But could she live with herself if she made any other decision?

"I'm no angel," she responded. "You mind if I sleep for a little bit?" she asked, wanting to get away from the subject. Funny. Ellie was usually pretty good at taking a compliment, Jake thought. But knowing that she was under the weather, he didn't want to push.

"Get some sleep. I'll wake you when we get there."

Forty-five minutes later, Jake nudged her gently awake. They turned off the highway and into the lot of an upscale roadside market. Tables and chairs surrounded a small playground with wooden play structures, and a large man in a stained white apron flipped baby back ribs on the barbeque. Ellie found the smell of the meat intoxicating. They went into the market and got some cold drinks before finding a table outside.

"I'm meeting Gray Wolf here. We'll go over the designs, which I'll need to do alone, and then we'll all head onto the property later. Ten minutes late. That's a record for me," Jake confided. As they sat down, he pulled a laptop out of his bag. "These folks are always late too."

She flipped on her laptop and started working. They sat in comfortable silence.

"Jake, my man. You're early," a deep voice boomed. Ellie looked up to see a massive, barrel-chested man with tribal tattoos climbing his dark arms and face. The black curving lines on his cheeks and forehead reminded her of ocean waves. The two men hugged each other firmly and the man slapped Jake's back with his large hands.

"You're looking good my friend. Happy, light energy all around you," the man commented as he looked at Jake. It was then that he seemed to notice Ellie. He turned toward her and smiled with deep brown eyes lined with wrinkles one only earns from years of laughing.

"Gray Wolf, this is Ellie Ashburn," Jake said respectfully. Gray Wolf shook her hand firmly and she could feel the strength in his massive arms.

"Another gorgeous environmentalist. God, life is good when those helping Mother Nature are so pleasing to the eyes." Usually she would be irked if someone spoke to her like this, but his manner was so friendly and warm that she took in the compliment with ease as his deep laugh filled the patio area. A few people looked up from their tables, and their faces too broke into smiles, as if there were no other response. The man behind the barbeque nodded at Gray Wolf, suggesting he was a regular.

"Ellie's actually, well, here with me on personal business," Jake clarified. Heat dappled his cheeks as he realized how his words sounded. "I mean, she came along for the ride."

"Came along for the ride, eh?" Gray Wolf laughed again. Now Ellie was blushing. "You look like two little love puppies," he remarked loud enough for the whole patio to hear, followed by another rapturous laugh.

"Okay, okay. Enough!" Jake pronounced, laughing along.

Gray Wolf was so open and friendly, that a natural response was to hug him, not chastise him. She refrained from doing either, and started packing her things to go.

"I'll leave you two to work before either of you say anything else to embarrass me. Nice to meet you Gray Wolf," she added.

"There's not a lot to do around here, Ellie. There's a winery within walking distance, but I suppose it's a little early."

"She can stay. I just want to go over the images and then I have a surprise for you, Jake," Gray Wolf said. She didn't want to make Jake uncomfortable in his client meeting and decided to move to another table anyway. Just then, three beautiful young women walked out of the market, each giving Jake an affectionate hug. What was it with gorgeous female environmentalists and Jake? In her opinion, the last woman lingered a little too long in his arms.

"I didn't know you were going to be here," Jake remarked.

"Surprise, surprise," the woman responded in an innocuous tone that revealed nothing. Was she being sarcastic? Flirtatious? The woman looked at him intensely for a moment longer before stepping away. Ellie noted the clear tension between Jake and this dark haired woman.

They were all introduced to Ellie, but were decidedly less friendly than Gray Wolf. Anna and Leah were Caucasian and based on their UCSB t-shirts and extremely tight shorts, looked more like college students than full time activists. The third woman who had lingered in Jake's arms was named Beatriz. She seemed to be in her late twenties, and although short and sturdy, her face held an exotic eloquence that was somehow familiar. Then it hit her; Beatriz's thick black hair, broad nose and high cheek bones reminded her of the Nez Pierce Indians she'd known while growing up in Idaho. Beatriz gave Ellie a quick up and down that was far from friendly and Ellie's smile was met with a flat stare. A quick gander toward Jake enforced her suspicion; this Beatriz had to be an ex-girlfriend.

She tried to focus on the spreadsheet in front of her, but she couldn't help but gaze up once in a while at the five of them working. They were all crowded around Jake's laptop as he went through a series of images. They talked quietly, almost secretively, which surprised Ellie; the booming voice of Gray Wolf did not seem like something that could be easily contained. Forty five minutes later the meeting was still not over and Ellie felt a surge of hunger. She slipped into the store and ordered baby back ribs from the counter, eating it at a small table inside along with a large glass of milk, well out of Jake's view.

She wandered around the boutique deli and noticed some hand painted wine glasses that made her think of Gillian. She bought a set, along with several bottles of wine, which she had gift wrapped. She decided a small gift for Jake was also in order, and settled on a reusable coffee cup with a silhouette of an oak tree. They had seen these massive trees dotting the landscape as they had driven over the pass, casting long swaths of shade on the golden hills.

When she headed back outside to the patio, it was Beatriz who looked up and noticed her, shooting a fiery look as she eyed the shopping bags dangling from Ellie's arms. Jake followed her gaze and a broad smile broke across his face as his eyes landed on Ellie. She felt a sense of relief as he waved her over.

"I see you've been busy," he remarked, looking at her shopping bags. "We're ready to head on over to the property. But the only thing is, it might take more time than I originally estimated as we've been invited for the whole gathering."

"Almost everyone who has invested in the community is coming except for the Berkshires." Gray Wolf added.

"I'm just along for the ride, remember?" Ellie said lightly. As they headed back to his car, Jake seemed nervous.

"This is kind of a big deal Ellie. I knew there was a workshop with some of the members. But this is the first time I've been invited to a full gathering."

"Is it awkward that I'm here? I mean, this seems like an important step for you."

"Well, it probably should be, but I don't mind at all. Really. But even stranger is that Gray Wolf specifically invited the two of us. I can't explain it, but he immediately took to you. I mean, I totally get that, but it's more that I promised a short client meeting and then time for you and me to hang out."

"No. You said I'd get to see you in action, and we'd have time to get to know each other better. And that's exactly what's happening, don't you think?"

"Yeah," he agreed as he tapped his fingertips on the back of her hand. He kissed her quickly on the lips before starting the car.

Chapter 41

They followed the other vehicles along a winding road edged by rambling vineyards and equestrian ranches. As she gazed out the window, Ellie thought of Beatriz, the exotic Native American. Since Ellie and Jake had established themselves as a couple, did she now have a right to pry? But the mere presence of this woman was already pulling at Ellie's competitive side; not that Jake was a trophy to be won.

"Jake, can I ask you something?"

"Yeah. Shoot."

"Beatriz. Is she an old girlfriend or something? I mean, I know it's none of my business. I'm just curious." Jake kept his eyes on the road, but his fingers caressed her thigh reassuringly as he spoke.

"It's complicated. I don't mind explaining it to you, but it'll take some time." He slowed the car and turned onto a gravel road. "But right now I need to concentrate on the meeting." They wound through a dry grass prairie for a good mile before they came to a stop before a barbed wire fence.

As if on cue, there was Beatriz, standing by the fence. Jake squeezed Ellie's hand. "She can be intense," he warned, "but don't let it get to you. You're my girl, okay?" He rolled down the window and a wave of stifling heat entered the car.

"You'll need me in the car to proceed onto the property," she stated. As Beatriz got into the car, the energy shifted. "Turn right in about 150 feet on that dirt road," she ordered, pointing.

They drove slowly. Two hundred yards down was a small guard house. The man inside didn't even bother to open the window as he saw Beatriz and waved them past.

"What was your name again? Jenny?" she asked in the same dry tone.

"I'm Ellie." This woman definitely had her guard up and Ellie could only guess why.

"Oh, Ellie," she repeated with undeniable coldness. They drove in silence. Beatriz stared out the window as if deep in thought.

"So how long have you two been dating?" she asked, without taking her eyes off the dry grass of the fields. "And why didn't I know about her?"

"Beatriz, let it go." Jake ordered calmly yet firmly. Beatriz reached toward the center counsel of the car.

"Got any of that mint lip balm in there?" she asked nonchalantly. Jake took in a slow breath and exhaled just as slowly, ignoring her question. Jake certainly seemed to be calm, but Ellie felt her breaths getting shorter. She and Jake had only transitioned back to lovers a few weeks ago. Had Jake been seeing other people regularly before that time? Perhaps Beatriz included? If he had, she certainly had no right to be upset about it, but the thought dug at her.

The dirt road gave way to a foot path, or perhaps an animal track leading into the middle of a prairie surrounded by oak trees. They parked the car next to a group of other vehicles in a clearing, and without another word, Beatriz hopped out and walked away.

"Don't let her get to you Ellie. It's nothing," Jake stated firmly.

"Okay," Ellie responded. Nothing? Intuitively she knew there was more to it than that, and she had every intention of following up with him the next time they were alone.

Above the long, golden grass of the prairie, thick swaths of chaparral and sage brush climbed the rolling hills, home to hundreds of small animals. In the center of the prairie, a large white tarp had been raised on massive wooden poles, and a gathering of thirty or so people milled about in its shade.

As it approached noon, stark heat settled over the prairie. Jake took Ellie's hand in his as they headed under the tarp.

"Water?" someone asked, as they came to join the group.

"Yes, please," they responded simultaneously. A woman retrieved a metal canister from a large cooler filled with ice and beverages and poured the cold water into metal camping cups. Gray Wolf spotted them and within minutes they were introduced to the group as Jake the architect and his girlfriend Ellie.

As they found a place to sit amongst the small crowd, Ellie was surprised by the diversity in the group. She saw Asian faces, Native Americans, people of African and Indian descent, Latinos and Caucasians—a rainbow of ethnicity beneath a tent in the middle of nowhere. Children sat in a circle at the far end of the tent, playing intently with little figures or drawing in the soil. Gray Wolf stood, walking to the front of the tent where a small podium was set up.

"Jake didn't know about the extent of today's gathering," began Gray Wolf in a voice loud enough for everyone to hear. "And although he's been working with us on the design, he hasn't had a chance to meet all of you," he explained warmly as everyone began to laugh. Someone signaled for everyone to sit down as Gray Wolf began to make a speech.

"The community we start here is to be a community of diversity, living together in harmony with each other and with mother earth," he began solemnly. As she sat on the red, dusty earth observing the gathering, she felt herself shifting into that slightly detached role of an observer. "We all bring our different skills and perspectives, our different beliefs and lifestyles, yet we are united by the principles laid out in our mission statement."

Ellie looked at all the diverse faces under the tarp as Gray Wolf continued talking, and tried to focus on his words. People caught her eye and smiled at her affectionately. She definitely wasn't in the city anymore. The group seemed almost entirely formed of couples, all dressed differently and clearly from different walks of life. But there was something similar in all of their peaceful faces. They had a hippy, earthy quality about them as if they had done their time smoking a peace pipe and making love in the open prairies under a full moon. Maybe they had all smoked something today.

That would explain that open look on their faces. These certainly were not her people. Yet the setting felt familiar, inviting.

Gray Wolf asked Jake to give a summary of the design concepts just brought forth in the meeting. Jake referred briefly to the notes in a report he'd made.

"We will incorporate organic building forms that date back to the early Chumash times, combining local materials with contemporary technologies resulting in respectful, aesthetically pleasing, durable and energy efficient dwellings," Jake explained. "The organic forms and hues of the buildings will blend into the landscape, minimizing the visual impact," he said, pointing toward the curves of the surrounding hills. "At the center of the village, both an open air platform and an enclosed gathering area will provide community members a place to gather together, interacting with their natural surroundings." She was surprised to realize how professional Jake could be, and how much he had put into this design.

No wonder he had been nervous. He had gone from presenting his work to a handful of people, to giving a presentation to its future inhabitants. Ellie listened to Jake with newfound respect. He was transforming before her eyes from a casual guy who ran a small non-profit to a man with big visions, influencing the lives of a whole future community.

She felt something loosen inside her as she glanced around at the rolling hills, not a single building in site. Ellie knew she felt at home. A dusting of soil settled into the creases of her crisp white jeans and stickers poked into her rhinestone sandals as if mother earth herself was trying to push the city girl away and bring Ellie back to her humble beginnings. Jake finished his presentation and came back to sit beside her. Gray Wolf started talking again.

"Nature provides all the guidelines we need to live a fulfilling, respectful existence," Gray Wolf continued.

Nature had been a prescient force in her life during childhood. She could be found out in the fields with her brothers far more often than in the kitchen helping her mother and older sisters. The shiny rocks in the riverbeds had been her jewels and wildflower wreaths her tiaras.

"This land belongs first to the animals, and as their guests, it is our job to protect this sacred space, minimizing our impact in the process of developing our future community."

She had logged so many hours quietly observing animals in the woods, that the animals stopped freezing when they saw her, and moved about in their regular routine, as if seeing her as one of them. She was such a wild, outdoorsy child, that she'd often been mistaken for a boy. At least until puberty set in.

Why had she drifted so far from nature? It was as if when she moved to the city and shed so much weight, she had shed that nature-loving part of herself along with it. Maybe it was an either-or situation; she could either be a woman who thrived in nature, or a woman who thrived in contemporary urban life. How could she blend these two worlds?

"We are the present and the future. We can be the model community that sets the standard in how to co-exist with the natural environment." Gray Wolf concluded. The group clapped vigorously, accompanied by a few whistles and hollers. People laughed and smiled, talking exuberantly about some of the points he had made. Many eyes were turned on Jake as well.

"Great job, Jake." Gray Wolf commended as he approached them. "You perform well under pressure. That trait comes in handy through life."

"Thanks. I had no idea you already had a whole community formed," Jake said.

"Sorry if you feel a bit in the dark, brother. It was not intentional. But now that you are here, you can see the bigger picture. Everyone here has been selected to be part of the pilot study for the community."

"I know you have special plans tonight at the cabin. But I'm hoping you both can come back tomorrow. It is important you get to know the people during the break-out sessions today and tomorrow. If you listen to their ideas and get to know them, it will help you understand the needs of those you are designing for." Gray Wolf stated.

"I need to talk it over with Ellie," Jake responded.

"We can absolutely come back tomorrow," Ellie blurted. Gray Wolf turned toward her. He contemplated her for a moment before speaking; "and Ellie, this process will break your heart wide open if you are willing to let it happen." It was as if he had just stripped away all her armor and peered right into her core. Ellie didn't know how to respond. She looked into his eyes and took a deep breath.

"I already feel my heart opening," she responded, as warmth settled in her chest. Gray Wolf smiled. Ellie watched him as he worked his way over to a beautiful round woman with thick braids of hair who could have popped out of a Diego Rivera painting. Ellie wondered if this could be his wife. Jake reached for her hand and led her to the coolers and snacks. Several people stopped them to introduce themselves, and Ellie marveled at how well Jake fielded their questions about his design. But what she couldn't stop thinking about was that Jake had planned a surprise for her; something to do with a cabin.

◊◊◊

The break out sessions started promptly at 2:00 p.m. The goal was to have *radically honest* conversations with other members of the community in groups of four—discussing topics relevant to living together in harmony. They had fifteen minutes in which to engage with each couple. Someone chimed a bell, and everyone moved into place. A couple dressed in bright, flowing clothing sat in front of them and started up a conversation.

"Hi, I'm Shanti," the woman said, "and this is my husband Damik. Our children are there with the others, Shanti and Nahbi." They extended their hands, and suddenly Ellie and Jake were exchanging ideas with them, as if they too were members of the future community.

"Do you have children yet?" Shanti asked. Ellie smiled, amazed that this was the first topic they were to encounter.

"No." Jake responded quickly. "No children."

"You will. Children are one of God's gifts. They teach us true humility and the depths of love," Shanti asserted. Ellie let out a small sigh at the truth of her words.

"My children. My daughters, have taught me more about responsibility and life than any university or career has so far. And they're both under ten!" Damik added, laughing. He raised his eyebrows toward Ellie, noticing that she was clearly interested in the topic. Jake shifted toward her as well. What better opportunity to test the waters, she thought.

"I definitely want to have children," Ellie stated without hesitancy. "They are the future, after all. Our legacy." She sipped from the metal water bottle in her hand, trying to dispel the heat she felt flushing her face. Jake's expression was hard to decipher, but it certainly wasn't delight.

"Children are the future. I clearly believe that," he responded carefully. "That's one of the guiding principles of my non-profit, Gaia Eden. But I also feel that there are plenty of children on the planet already that need our love. And, if we want to live in harmony with the earth, then we also need to think about how many people the planet can sustain."

"That is true. But if you personally choose not to have children, it will not save the planet," countered Damik. "It might even make the planet worse off."

"How so?" Jake questioned. "It's estimated the population will reach 7 billion by next year alone. And if everyone used that reasoning. . ."

"Ah, but consider how you would educate your children and how important they might be to future policy and stewardship of the earth," Damik wisely countered.

"Well. Nicely put," Jake said, as if he hadn't thought of it from this perspective before. Ellie smiled inwardly. This was a pro-kid reasoning she'd have to file in her memory banks.

Ellie could already tell she liked Shanti and Damik. Not only were they kind, insightful people, they were openly affectionate with one another, something Ellie hadn't witnessed in her Indian friends in the city. They covered several other topics, mainly related to the environment, before another couple moved toward them. Each conversation was just as intense and insightful on topics ranging from organic farming, the end of consumer based society, alternative energy, communal living, living off the grid and peak oil. Ellie was surprised how quickly the fifteen minute sessions passed. The bell sounded again, and Gray Wolf announced that it was time for a lunch break. People got up to stretch their legs and headed toward the coolers where various potluck dishes were retrieved and set out on blankets upon the ground.

"Hope this is not too overwhelming," Jake said apologetically as they settled down with a plate full of vegetarian food.

"Overwhelming?" Ellie mused. If he only knew what this experience was like on pregnancy hormones. "It's sort of like an uber-game of truth or dare. Without the dare, of course." Jake laughed at her analogy.

"Not a bad idea. But these conversations are pretty revealing, aren't they? And it seems to me that based on your responses, we're on the same page a lot more than I would have thought."

"Are we?" Ellie asked thoughtfully. They had both been adamant about quality education of youth and she had whole heartedly agreed about the need to find alternative fuel sources—but in both cases, how could someone think anything to the contrary? Yet at the same time, they were so different. This whole scene was something she would never have joined on her own accord, yet it tugged at something deep inside. "So would you really want to live in a commune like this? Oh. That's not it. Ecovillage?" Ellie asked.

"Ecovillage. Yeah," Jake repeated. "It's totally sustainable. Plus, you have a built in community with a common vision."

"Like a fraternity?" Ellie asked.

"Well, sure. Like a frat and sorority combined, but without all the stupidity and alcohol," he added. "Alcohol is a threat to the environment anyway. Take vineyards, for example. They use up hundreds of acres that could be better utilized for food crops."

"There's no way I'd live in your eco village unless you keep the vineyard," she retorted, "with a mix of red and white grapes." Jake put his arm around her shoulder.

"Well, then. I guess we'll keep the vineyard," Feeling his arm around her, there was nothing more in the world she wanted at that moment than to kiss him. He looked down at her as if reading her mind and kissed her openly. She had pretty much willed that kiss, but the touch of his lips shocked her out of the almost trance-like stupor she was in.

Ellie took a deep breath, as if trying to wake herself up. Although she felt alive and invigorated by all of the conversations she had had today, she was also wary. She couldn't deny that she had fought her way up that proverbial socio-economic ladder, and part of her doubted the viability of this whole undertaking.

"Jake. I love the idealism here. It's incredibly refreshing, but what I don't understand is this whole idea of ending consumer society. I mean, even in the early days of this country when people were exchanging furs for food, it was still consumerism."

"No," Jake countered, "That was survival."

"Commerce is just a civilized version of survival," she returned. "I mean, think about it. A functioning economy is necessary to keep society going. Look at all of the people who are out of work right now, losing their homes to foreclosures. The economy tanks and people are on the streets. How would a community like this survive if it weren't for the generous underwriting of Indian Casino money—a sort of consumerism in itself?" Ellie looked out toward the horizon, not a building in site.

"Okay. That would be a good point if it were true, Ellie. But this project's not funded with Casino money. It's still in the conceptual phase. They need a major supporter to make it become a reality." He straightened and turned to face her. "But regarding money, consumerism. Here's what I do know. Money can make a big difference in how comfortable you are in life, but it's not the answer. The answer is taking responsibility through community, support, interaction and living sustainably. And that's not idealism, that's the future of survival." Jake looked into her eyes, as if willing his words to penetrate her thoughts.

"I certainly hope you're right," she responded, "and that I'm wrong. Even though it doesn't make total sense to me, I can picture it working somehow." What could she picture working? Being there with him? Being a member of some earth loving, hippy community? Jake embracing her pregnancy? Part of her tried to pull back to strong, no nonsense Ellie. But another part of her was in love with the feelings coursing through her mind and body. And Jake's presence was definitely a key ingredient.

"You two enjoying yourselves?" a female voice asked. They looked up to see the rotund woman Ellie had seen earlier next to Gray Wolf.

"Sparrow," Jake said as he hugged her. Ellie smiled inwardly at her name. She was hardly a sparrow.

"Jake. So good to see you again. Feel like you know who you're creating for?" she asked.

"Yes. I'm definitely getting a sense. They seem like solid folks with strong, environmental ideologies. My kind of folks." Jake responded. "Sparrow. This is Ellie, by the way."

"Yes, I know," she said gently, yet firmly.

"This must be quite a lot to experience all at once," she commented as she looked Ellie in the eyes. "What do you think of all of this?" Sparrow asked as she circled her hand in the air. Ellie was intrigued by the deep blue-gray of her pupils.

"I could not have imagined such an insightful afternoon," Ellie responded. "Everyone I've met seems honest and kind, and I think the work you are doing here, the community you are forming, will be like no other." Her words seemed to have been pulled from that secret part within her where soft things, like sentiment and hope reside; things she thinks but does not say.

"Thank you," Sparrow gently replied. Suddenly she put her hands on Ellie's shoulders and looked at her intently. Ellie stared back, trying to sort out the mix of emotions flowing through her as this stranger peered into her eyes. Sparrow took one hand off Ellie's shoulder and hovered it over Ellie's heart and belly. Although she didn't make contact, Ellie felt a warmth coursing through her. Just as quickly, the moment was over, and Sparrow released her shoulder. She nodded at Jake with a strange smile before walking away.

Ellie's eyes popped open wide.

"What was that all about?" she asked. He smiled coyly and was about to respond when a young man with long dreadlocks approached them. Soon Jake was caught up in a lively conversation about solar based water pumping systems. Ellie used the moment to excuse herself and headed to the ice chest for a drink.

She tried to get a grasp on what had just happened. Although she had never gazed into a stranger's eyes like that, she now felt a sense of calm, rather than the initial fear that had bolted through her. She stepped outside the tent for a moment and walked toward the low lying chaparral. She carefully broke off a few leaves from a sage plant and rubbed them together between her hands, inhaling the scent as a sense of peace settled into her.

She considered the expanse of land around her, thinking about all she had learned about the property through their discussions with others. The tribe's recent purchase was not just a small ranch, but 5,000 acres of wilderness and farmland that came with livestock, a working ranch and a sizeable vineyard. She had heard of the Santa Ynez Valley, but had no idea such a beautiful, rural area existed just a few hours north of the concrete jungle in which she'd immersed herself over the past few years.

She could imagine living on this land, silently watching a deer in the meadow as she had done as a child; spending hours in the outdoors. The very thought of it made her emotional. Tears started to form in the corners of her eyes.

"If anyone would like to go for a hike, I have arranged a few hike leaders to take you around the property. This is the wilderness folks. Look out for rattlesnakes and make sure to take along plenty of water. We'll be having a closing circle at 5 p.m.," Gray Wolf's voice boomed.

"What do you say, Ellie? Shall we go for a hike?" Jake asked as he reached her. As he got closer, he took in her tear-stained face.

"What is it?" Jake asked, concern covering his face. "You look exhausted."

"I feel strange," Ellie answered weakly.

"Do you feel sick?"

"No. This feels incredible here," Ellie felt the surge of emotions, not sure how much she wanted to ride it out. "I feel drawn and repelled at the same time. And I'm exhausted, like I was up all night or something, even though I got about eight hours." He looked at her with concern, listening intently. "And why on earth am I telling you so honestly, exactly how I feel all the time? This is just weird."

"Ellie. Have a little self compassion." He squared her shoulders and looked down into her face. "For starters, I'm pretty sure Sparrow just gave you a blessing—which if you weren't expecting it can feel pretty intense." Ellie nodded, thankful for the explanation. "Two, we've been having these philosophical life conversations over the last couple of hours with strangers, which although extremely invigorating, can be tiring."

"Yeah. Totally. You, on the other hand, seem energized by it," she remarked.

"I am. Getting to know these people just makes my work so much more tangible. I can't tell you how much Nate and Allie remind me of my mom and dad."

"Seriously? I mean, they were extremely intelligent, insightful even. But really out there. I mean, I understand the idea of straw bale homes, but using cow poop to build animal shelters?"

"No. Not straight cow poop. It's a composite made out of old newspapers, recycled cardboard and a bi-product of cow manure after they process it to release methane gas." Jake explained.

"Now you're sounding like them!"

"No I'm not!" Jake laughed. "Can you believe this is where we get to go hiking next weekend? I think this place must be some sort of vortex, because the energy out here is amazing," Jake commented, taking in a deep breath.

"Oh. You're not going to go all *vortex* on me, are you?" Ellie asked, laughing.

"Can I please quote you on that? That's the funniest thing I've heard all day." Ellie hadn't meant to be funny, but she gave him a generous smile anyway.

"And as far as a hike goes, I'm pretty tired, Jake." She started sneezing incessantly and Jake pulled a handkerchief out of his pocket. She took it reluctantly, dabbing her eyes and blowing her nose.

"I can tell this has been intense for you. I'll tell you what. Let me just make contact with a few more of the members and then we'll be off."

"But this is so important to you, Jake. If I could just take a nap, maybe in the car. You could finish up?"

"Are you kidding? You'd die of heat stroke if you took a nap in the car out here!" Jake retorted. A woman sitting on the next blanket overheard their conversation.

"You can take a nap in the shade of the trees," she suggested. "There are a few cots over there set up for nursing mothers. No one's using them. It's quite lovely."

"Okay," Ellie responded. Jake seemed surprised, but Ellie waved him off.

"I feel like I have to nap this instant. Maybe someone gave me some sort of truth sleeping potion," she chided.

"Don't worry, Ellie. This is a drug free community. Lay down in the shade. You deserve a bit of rest."

"Okay. Take your time, Jake. Really." As Ellie made her way slowly toward the shaded area, she noticed the women working in the shadows of the trees. They were bundling sage in cigar-shaped rolls tied with string; smudge sticks. Her mother would buy one on occasion at the country market and spread the cleansing white smoke around the house. Beatriz was among the women, and their eyes met. Was it her imagination, or did Beatriz just smile at her? She turned instinctively away, and found herself looking for Jake as she entered the shade and lay down on a cot draped in thin cotton curtains suspended from a tree branch.

"Hey Jenny." Ellie looked up from the cot to see Beatriz walking toward her. Why the hell does she keep calling me Jenny? "Don't get up," Beatriz said as she came closer. "Here. Your very own keepsake smudge stick from a real Native American." There was definitely sarcasm in her voice, but it almost seemed like Beatriz was trying to be friendly in her own, difficult way.

"Thank you Beatriz."

"You're welcome Ellie." Beatriz raised her eyebrows as Ellie smiled.

"You feeling okay?" Beatriz asked in a voice without cadence.

"Tired, a little dizzy. I guess I'm just not used to the heat."

"You'll get used to it over time. It will only get easier. Smell the sage. It might help," Beatriz recommended before walking away. Ellie knew the conversation seemed to be missing parts. What did she mean by get used to it over time?

A slight breeze rustled through the trees and Ellie found herself idly trying to locate Jake in the crowd. She saw him standing close to Sparrow near the edge of the tent, listening intently to her words. He nodded his head with a serious look on his face. Sparrow and Jake both started looking around until their eyes fell upon Ellie. Although she wanted to look away, she couldn't divert her eyes. He didn't smile, but had the same serious stare, as if he were looking right through her. What if she's telling him that I'm not the one for him? Ellie thought wearily. What if she's telling him he is meant to be with Beatriz? That's what that smile was about, Ellie thought. But she was too much at peace in this gentle place to let her mind play that what-if game it so loved to play. She tried to re-order the words of the strange conversation she'd had with Beatriz in a way that made sense as she drifted off to sleep.

Ellie entered an imaginary land. Here, homes seemed to merge out of the earth in organic forms. Goats, sheep and chickens meandered through the small streets and a line of windmills crested the hilltop. She walked naked through the village, hand in hand with a man, and they entered a vast garden where they ate freely from the fruits and vegetables. Her nakedness did not bother her as she placed strawberries in her mouth. As they reached a covered pavilion in the town center, everyone rose, calling them by name. The man walked through circular doors of a beautifully designed building where students awaited him and she sat in the grass, writing the document that everyone followed. A child who trailed behind her with a wreath of flowers in his hair held two babies in his arms. Children danced in circles, praising the earth.

"Don't forget to feed the animals," the boy called to her. The man came back out of the building where a group of people from around the world had gathered to bestow gifts upon him. The detailed dream twisted and turned in her mind as if furrowing a deep path in her memory. The man called to her from a distance, as if over in the next valley. Slowly, his voice came closer and closer by.

Jake sat next to her on the cot, watching her sleep. She looked so beautiful; he didn't want to disturb her. That and he was remembering that first night they were together all over again. He had awoken in the middle of the night and rolled into her. He'd spent a good while staring at her in the moonlight pouring through his bedroom window, studying her features. Now he studied her soft figure in the dappled sunlight. He wondered if they would have a short time together or if they were the type of couple that lasted a lifetime. Her eyes moved quickly back and forth beneath her eyelids and it was clear that she was deep in a dream.

"Ellie, wake up sleepy head." Ellie stretched her arms and opened her eyes to see Jake sitting next to her. He had drawn the curtain back slightly, letting in a little fresh air.

"Wow. How long have I been asleep?" Ellie asked.

"A few hours."

"Oh my God. Why did you let me sleep so long?" Ellie asked.

"You clearly needed the rest."

"How long have you been sitting here?"

"Just a few minutes," he lied. "I think you were dreaming." He ran a hand across her forehead, noticing the perspiration that had developed there. She was hot to the touch.

"Yes. That's right. I was," she said groggily as the images still floated in her mind.

"When Johanna and I were little, I sometimes woke up before her and I would catch her dreaming, watching her eyes moving back and forth beneath her eyelids," Jake said quietly. Ellie liked when Jake talked about his twin sister.

"What did she dream about?"

"She rarely remembered her dreams."

"I always remember mine," Ellie admitted.

"So what were you dreaming about?"

"A contemporary garden of Eden."

"That sounds pretty peaceful."

"It was pretty detailed."

"Tell me about it."

"No. Not now," Ellie decided. "I usually like to keep my dreams to myself. But someday I'll share it with you."

Chapter 42

After participating in the closing circle they drove back to the small town of Santa Ynez where Jake took her to an expensive Italian restaurant. They talked over the day, and Ellie smiled at him in wonder. I'm falling for a hippy, she thought to herself. And clearly, by the way he held her hand and talked with her; he was falling for a deer hunter. After dinner, they drove down a windy country road and started up a long grade. Finally, he stopped the car.

"Come on, the sun is setting in about 10 minutes."

They hiked up the long grass prairie until they reached the top of a hill where a single, rustic cabin stood. It was much cooler on the ridge. Jake opened the cabin door and grabbed two wool blankets. Ellie stared at the view that opened up in front of them. The oak trees cast long shadows across the valley as the sun started dipping in the sky, its reddish light shimmering in the single paned windows of the cabin. Ellie could imagine ditching the city, and settling down right here.

"It's so beautiful," Ellie commented as she took in the deep orange and red of the sunset.

"I love this view," he responded, as he looked into her eyes. She stared back, daring herself not to be the first to break contact. Jake stared back until she couldn't help but look away. She was in love with this man. Her mind raced, fighting against the sensation. She couldn't fall completely until she knew he wanted all of her. But before she could think about that, she had to clear up some other issues that had been on her mind.

"So what was going on with Beatriz back there?" she asked.

"Well," he paused, as if searching for the right words. Ellie's mind started creating scenarios: Beatriz was his ex-girlfriend. Seeing her today had re-awakened his passion for her. He was so sorry to have to end this pleasant start with Ellie. She held her breath as he began to speak.

"Beatriz and I have a complicated past." His face looked pained as he started to tell his tale. "Her sister Luz and I had a serious relationship that lasted all through my time at UCSB. Luz and I were engaged our junior year." Ellie imagined Luz as the more beautiful of the two sisters and pictured Jake married with little half white, half Indian children. Jealousy shot through her.

"Luz was diagnosed with Leukemia my last year in college and she died fifteen months later." Tears pooled into the corners of his eyes and he reached his hand up to brush them away.

"Oh Jake. I'm so sorry." Ellie responded. Jealousy gave way to sadness as she imagined Jake young and happy, on the verge of marrying the woman of his dreams.

"And Beatriz. Well, she and I tried to be there for each other to work our way through the pain."

"As lovers?" Ellie couldn't help but ask.

"We were lovers at some point, but it was more out of our shared loss, then out of love. That was over three years ago. We've been friends ever since. But she's been telling me to stop dating floosies and get on with my life. To love again," tears rolled down Jake's cheeks as he continued. "When she saw you she was immediately defensive," Jake went on.

"But why? Does she still want a relationship with you?"

"No. Nothing like that. She wants resolution."

"Resolution?" Ellie asked, confused. The sun dipped lower in the sky.

"Do you remember in the car when she asked why she didn't know about you?"

"Yeah." How could she forget the ice in Beatriz's voice?

"When she saw us together, saw the energy between us; that I brought you along today, she assumed we were serious. She was pissed that I hadn't told her about you." Ellie had to smile; Beatriz was protective of Jake. Wanted what was best for him. Wanted to be informed when he settled down.

"But later, Sparrow set things right."

"What do you mean, set things right? Is she Gray Wolf's wife?" Ellie asked.

"No!" Jake started laughing. "Gray Wolf is not the type to settle down with one woman. Anyway, he could never handle Sparrow. She's a shaman of sorts."

"Oh." She thought again of how Sparrow had suddenly placed her hands on her shoulders and stared into her eyes, as if she was reading her soul like an open book.

"I saw Sparrow talking to you. It looked like a pretty serious conversation. What did she say? Or set right, as you put it?"

"It's not mine to share, Ellie. Believe me. It's way too much information for you right now." Ellie felt a rush of anger at being told what she could and couldn't handle.

"Try me."

"I can't talk about that," his jaw line firmed.

"Why all the secrecy?"

"Ellie, I just shared one of the greatest tragedies of my life with you. Can you give me a break here and let me keep something to myself?" his face hardened as he looked at her.

"Jake, I'm so sorry. I didn't mean to pry," she responded in earnest. "You're amazing and honest and you've shared so much. I can't imagine losing someone I loved at such a young age." She leaned into him, hugging him until she felt his shoulders loosening.

"It's okay Ellie. Don't feel sorry for me. I lived through it. She'll always be a part of who I am." Jake spread one blanket on the steps of the cabin, pulling Ellie down beside him before wrapping a second blanket around them.

As they sat in silence, Ellie felt a series of events click into place, mapping out a plan. The sacred land they had visited today was the place where she would tell him. Not tomorrow when he needed to focus on his work, but next weekend, when they would have it all to themselves for their solo camping trip. It would be a place to unite their two worlds; his environmental vision and work with her upbringing in nature, and the value she placed on the life forming within her.

"Thanks for listening to me Ellie. I'm so glad we're together." She answered him with a delicate kiss. He put his arm around her shoulders as they watched the gold of the sun melt into deep orange and then crimson before it dropped below the horizon.

Chapter 43

"Oh my God! That's got to be heavy! How can you even hold your hand up?" Ellie exclaimed. The engagement ring on Gillian's finger boasted a huge diamond surrounded by a small cluster of rubies.

"Stunning, isn't it? Almost as big as my ego," she joked.

"Oh Gillian. I'm so happy for you! Now. I want to hear how he proposed! I've been waiting for three weeks now!"

"I'm not telling you on the drive back from LAX. I want to tell you over a glass of wine at home, with my feet dangling in the pool," Gillian stated.

"You're really going to make me wait another 45 minutes?"

"Yes! And in the meantime, let's talk about you."

"About me? You just spent over a month in Italy and you want to talk about me?" Ellie shrugged her shoulders.

"Yes! Tell me about all the runs you went on, all the meals you cooked at home, the man hiatus."

"Ah. The man hiatus. I forgot about that," Ellie reminisced.

"You forgot about it? What the hell? Did you meet a guy?"

"As a matter of fact, I did."

"You've been holding out on me Ellie! You sneaky little bitch."

"Easy, Gillian. Like when did I have a chance to tell you, anyway?"

"When I called!"

"It was the middle of the night, Gillian, and I didn't want to wake him . . ."

"Oh my fucking God!"

"Gillian!"

"Sorry for swearing, but I think you just admitted to having a man in your bed."

"You're ruining my whole story. The build up. How we met. All that."

"You slept with a man! And do you still like him?"

"God yes."

"Ah ha! You call upon God as well."

"Yes. But in a positive, Alleluia sort of way."

"Don't get all religious on me Ellie. Who is he? How did you meet?"

"I'll tell you when our toes are dangling in the pool, and you've given me my present."

"Your present?" Gillian's brow wrinkled. "Sorry Ellie. I was too caught up in the whole engagement thing. It slipped my mind."

"Oh. Of course. Sorry. I didn't really expect anything."

"Joking! Of course I have a present for you. You know I always get you something when I do a big trip." Gillian remarked.

"I know. I guess I'm like a little kid at Christmas." Ellie responded as she focused on the road.

"Ah. You've finally defined your innocent side in a sweet little cliché, just at the moment you've lost your innocence to a stranger," Gillian teased.

"He's not a stranger. His name is Jake Tillerman. He's gorgeous and kind and respectful and I really like him. We've been seeing each other almost the entire time you were gone."

"Holy shit! You're really serious about this, Ellie! Congratulations!" Although Gillian's boisterous energy and loud voice felt overpowering, Ellie was caught up in her excitement. Besides Arno, none of her other friends knew about her relationship until this moment and it felt good to talk to a friend about him. By the time Ellie pulled into the driveway, she had heard about most of Gillian's trip, except for how David proposed. As they pulled into the carport, Gillian hopped out and almost knocked over a pink bicycle.

"What's that?" Gillian questioned.

"My new bicycle," Ellie explained unassumingly. Gillian shot her a strange look. Ellie was not only acting differently, she looked different to her too; she seemed like a fuller version of herself.

"You get enough exercise with all the running you do. God, you look great Ellie. I don't know if it's this new guy in your life, or if you've been on some sort of health kick, but you're really glowing." Ellie was surprised. It was uncharacteristic of Gillian to give such a soft compliment.

"Thank you, Gillian. The bike was a gift from Jake. My other car."

"Second car. Yeah, right!" Gillian chortled. "But I have to say I'm impressed that he's already buying you gifts." Ellie let the first comment slide. If someone had told her three weeks ago that she'd be biking to work instead of driving, she would have laughed as well.

As they brought her luggage inside, Gillian looked around at the house in silence.

"It feels great to be home," she sighed. She didn't seem to notice that all of her electronic gadgets had been unplugged, or that the house had been subtly changed in the weeks she had been gone. Perhaps the rustic lodging in a Tuscan villa had helped. She dropped her bags in the living room and the two friends headed to the back yard, opening a bottle of wine. As they dipped their toes in the water, Gillian saw Ellie's t-shirts and underwear flapping in the wind.

"What the hell. Did the dryer break?"

"No. I just hung up a clothesline. It's so hot this summer your clothes can dry in a few hours." Ellie informed her as casually as she could muster.

"You. You just hung up a clothesline?" Gillian asked incredulously.

"Well. Jake and I."

Gillian took in her words as a lawyer might when cross examining a witness; her eyebrows arched up as she wove the details together.

"And you're riding that bike for more than exercise," Gillian deduced. "I've got to meet this guy." That was one thing she loved about Gillian. She was quick.

"You're going to love him."

"He's not some hippy environmentalist you met at an eco-church, is he?"

"Are there eco-churches?" Ellie asked.

"How the hell should I know? I was joking. How did you meet?"

"Well, the day you were visiting your cousin, I promised myself I'd do something for me that had nothing to do with men. Something that I used to love and haven't done in a while."

"Masturbate?" Gillian commented crassly. Ellie didn't rise to the bait.

"Gillian. Do you want to hear this or not?"

"Sorry, Ellie. I love you and I want to hear every word," she responded, dipping her toes into the pool

"That's when I went hiking. I told you about it."

"But you didn't mention him!" Gillian said, taking a sip of her wine. As she watched Ellie's designer bras flap gently on the clothesline and Ellie sipping sparkling water rather than wine, she seemed resigned to the idea that anything was now possible. As she listened to Ellie's story unfold, she focused, completely engaged.

"The art opening was a week later?" she interrupted.

"Yes. And we talked for hours." She mentioned their evenings together, meeting his friends, their hikes and museum visits and finally the trip to Santa Ynez Valley last weekend and the romantic cabin. She edited out the details of the gathering. She knew Gillian loved her, but she could be so harsh and Ellie just wasn't in the mood for another rampage. As Ellie concluded her story, Gillian had finished her first glass of wine and started on a second.

"I go away for a month and you go through some sort of major metamorphoses."

"Almost seven weeks!" Ellie interrupted.

"Yeah. That's right. But anyway, I can make sense of the hiking, the cycling even, but since when are you a swing dancer?" Gillian asked, laughing.

"I grew up swing dancing," Ellie explained.

"How is it that there's this whole other side to you that I know nothing about?"

"That's because you just know L.A. Ellie." she responded coyly.

"And the Ellie I know, that I assumed was Idaho Ellie, believes in taking it slowly. Yet he was already in your bed when I called three weeks ago." Ellie nodded.

"You astound me," Gillian added. Ellie thought of the information she was withholding that was far more astounding.

"Speaking of astounding. Tell me NOW!" Ellie cried.

"Okay. Okay. I'm not done with you, Ellie. I want to know more about this Jake Tillerman. But, yes, I think you've been patient enough."

Ellie could tell that Gillian was enjoying holding onto her engagement story, just as Ellie had savored keeping Jake to herself. But sharing your story with one of your closest friends was also something to savor. Gillian flipped her hair back and started her story enthusiastically.

"So, we were in this beautiful walled city called Lucca that has a lot of old church towers. We'd hiked to the top of one already and as soon as we got to the top and looked out, David started acting weird and staring across the way, immediately wanting to leave. It was totally annoying. Well, as soon as we got down to the ground, David insisted we hike to the top of another tower. I wasn't in the mood, but he was adamant. I tagged along behind him in silence as we made our way across this ancient city and we almost got in a fight. But there was something about the look on his face, like it wasn't about this tower, but something much more important.

"A small gathering of people at the base of the next tower looked at us uncertainly as we approached. I finally backed down, and we climbed up the old stone steps of yet another tower. Higher and higher." She twisted a strand of long brown hair between her fingers as she continued.

"David barely spoke on the way up and I could see the sweat dripping down his neck. I figured he was just out of breath from all the climbing and I was still a little pissed that we were going up another set of old stone stairs. But when we got to the top, there were two girls up there." Gillian inhaled at the memory.

"Not just any girls, but two beautiful young Italian girls in white dresses. They saw David and nodded at him. He nodded back, as if he knew them. I had been on the look out for anything that seemed romantic. You know, something that might indicate a sign of a proposal, but time after time, I had been wrong. I figured I had misconstrued his friendly nod toward these young girls, because really, how would he know two young teenagers on the top of a church tower and what could they possibly have to do with anything?

"Strangely, despite it being the height of tourist season, there was only one other couple up there and they had black cases on their backs, as if out of some sort of idiocy, had decided to hike all the way up an old church tower with their musical instruments. I was about to make some sort of comment under my breath to David, but just then, the couple unpacked two violins and started playing." Gillian's face softened as she recalled the story. Ellie smiled as she tried to picture the magical scene.

"The girls started singing along to the music in two-part harmony. My Italian is so rusty, I couldn't make out all of the words, but it was definitely a love song. *Amore* was in there. *Come sei bella, ti voglio bene.* I'm not sure of the exact words, but it was a very romantic song. It was then that I saw the smile on David's face and how everyone was looking at me. Ellie, it was absolutely amazing. I was speechless. In the middle of the song, David got on his knee and held up this ring." Gillian moved her hand in the sunshine. The light caught the diamond and rubies, and Ellie stared, mesmerized as the light refracted small rainbows onto the damp edge of the pool.

"Oh Gillian. I had no idea he was such a romantic."

270

"Jesus! Me either!" she laughed. "It was the sort of fairytale moment I could picture you wanting and I actually thought of you when those angelic girls started singing."

"Did you shed any tears?"

"Not then. But later. At the hotel that night." Gillian's voice dropped to almost a whisper. "As we got undressed and climbed into bed together, the diamond ring actually glistened in the moonlight coming through the window. And I cried. I cried because he was so incredibly sweet and romantic and I had no idea that was in him. And I cried because that night, I made love to the man that will soon be my husband."

As Ellie listened to the story, she could feel the tears coming down her cheeks and Gillian did not tease her for them. She too had tears in her eyes.

"I'm so happy for you Gillian," Ellie said as she gave her friend a hug.

"Thank you Ellie. You're the only person I could share that with without making a joke out of it. My God. You're romantic nature actually helped prep me for this, you know that?"

"Good to know it's good for something," Ellie replied.

"So this Jake guy also sounds like a romantic." Ellie thought back to the candlelit dinner he had made her. A half dozen other things he had said or done over the last few weeks trailed through her mind. Ellie smiled in response, her eyebrows arching upward.

"A romantic environmentalist. You're in serious trouble, girl."

"Serious trouble," she agreed.

"So. How often do you think about having his babies?" Gillian asked, her eyes fixed on Ellie. She waved her hand at Gillian as if brushing away a fly, but inside, she felt her heart palpitating as if someone had just caught her in the act. She desperately wanted to share her news, but knew she had to tell Jake first.

"Daily," Ellie smiled. That was at least true. Gillian laughed and gave her a hug.

"So you want to go to Ono tomorrow night?" Gillian asked. "I haven't had sushi in almost a month!"

"I can't tomorrow night. Jake and I are getting together to plan the final details of our backpacking trip this coming weekend. But I kept tonight open for you "

"Backpacking? God. This is going to take some getting used to," Gillian responded. "Not only this new version of eco-Ellie, which is a total head trip, but I'm used to having you to myself—you know, when you're not out on some flop of a date," Gillian teased.

"Shut up! You're the one who's engaged. I mean, how much longer do I have you?" she asked.

"Oh Ellie," Gillian sighed. "It's inevitable. Considering I have my own company, and he works for a hedge fund, it only makes sense for me to move there."

"But the majority of your clients are here!" Ellie responded.

"Yeah. But my fiancé, who makes about five times my annual salary in three months, lives there."

"Well I guess that settles it," Ellie replied.

Chapter 44

When Gillian finally met Jake Thursday night at the house, her response was surprisingly like that of the women in the office when they saw him online.

"He's so fucking gorgeous! And, clearly, he knows he's model material, but at the same time, there's something honest about him," she surmised.

"Quiet, Gillian! He's going to hear you!" Ellie whispered as they stood in the kitchen. Jake, who was out back by the pool, was clearly out of earshot, but Ellie felt nervous for some reason.

"He's quite a catch," Gillian proceeded.

"Well so is David." Gillian smiled at Ellie's compliment as she spun the diamond ring around her finger, a habit she had developed over the last few weeks. Perhaps it was a way to get used to the weight of it.

"David's definitely a catch. Handsome as well. But not the model boyfriend like you have. God, those eyes. And that chiseled chin. Jesus."

The two women headed back to the pool and Jake stood up.

"Can I help you with anything?" he asked.

"We're fine," Ellie said.

"So Jake. Tell me how you talked Ellie into putting up this clothes line," Gillian started.

"Well. I don't know that I talked her into it."

"Yes you did. She didn't have an environmental bone in her body until she met you," Gillian remarked. Ellie glared at her. "Well, now come to think of it, that's not quite true," Gillian revised. "She was the one who started doing the recycling. And she's very particular about her vegetables. Have to be fresh. She won't let the lawn guys use any chemicals on the vegetation and gets all pissy when I leave the lights on."

"Oh God. And have you seen her charity bulletin board?" Gillian went on. "Maybe she's not out to save the environment on the level you are, but she's all about social justice."

"Okay Gillian. You can stop any time now," Ellie sighed.

"As I recall, I saw my non-profit on your bulletin board," Jake commented, flashing Ellie a smile. "So it looks like social justice and the environment both have a place in your life."

"Speaking of which, I have some Endangered Species organic chocolate. Something I discovered all on my own before you came along. Would anyone care for a piece?" Ellie asked, trying to maneuver the conversation in a different direction.

Although Gillian usually dominated any conversation, Jake held his own over the evening and more than once he had to call on his diplomacy skills to disarm Gillian's cutting remarks. As an interior designer, Gillian had a lot to say about architectural design, and their tastes differed dramatically.

"What do you mean, high ceilings are poor design? They create volumes of space that give a room grandeur, and great expanses of wall appropriate for art. Are you suggesting people live without art?"

"It's not just about the art. High ceilings might work in the temperate climates of the West Coast, but if you're going to be in Boston, where you have real winters, high ceilings don't make sense. Not only are they expensive to heat, which clients don't like, they waste energy. And as far as art goes, art can exist in smaller spaces. You see it all the time on the east coast."

"With an attitude like that, you'll be stuck with small jobs that won't get you anywhere," Gillian snapped back.

"Well, I guess it depends on what your objectives are. I believe in designing spaces people are happy to live within, but that also make environmental sense. And I'm not alone Gillian."

The debate went on and on, but in the end, Gillian was actually agreeing with some of his points, and they were laughing together. Ellie looked on in astonishment. If he could bring Gillian around to another point of view, what couldn't he do?

After Jake headed home, she probed Gillian.

"So what do you think?" Ellie inquired.

"Oh. You want me to appreciate him for something besides his body? What, like his holier than thou eco-chic lifestyle?"

"He's hardly condescending about it Gillian. Do you really think that?"

"Well, no actually. He's just so fully into the whole green scene that he breathes it. Sorry I said that greener than thou crap. To be fair, I'd have to say he was pretty diplomatic about the whole thing. He made a good first impression, Ellie. He's clearly into you, and he seems like a good guy. But he's not exactly marrying material."

"What do you mean by that?" Ellie snapped.

"Nothing. Sorry." Gillian rarely faltered when it came to stating her opinion, but when she did, she was usually holding back something big.

"No. I want to hear what you were going to say," Ellie demanded. Gillian raised her eyebrows as if double checking and Ellie nodded.

"Okay. I can see how you're attracted to him. He's kind. Genuine. He cares about kids and the environment, and he's romantic as hell around you."

"But?" Ellie asked, crossing her arms over her chest.

"He's from a different walk of life, sweetie. He's not someone that could support your tastes; someone who's in line with your lifestyle," Gillian surmised.

"I don't need a man to support me, Gillian. And as far as my lifestyle, well," she started. Well what? Was she ready to admit she was questioning the substance of the very life she had built up over the last three and a half years in L.A? That her time in nature over the last few months had been pulling at her with a ferocity she hadn't known existed within her?

"I'm not saying he needs to support you. I'm just saying it's a two income world. If you ever tie the knot, it makes a lot more sense if you both have a similar philosophy on money and lifestyle."

"Believe me. I know we have different lifestyles. But part of the reason he has so little is he doesn't believe in consumerism. His philosophy dictates it."

"And your lifestyle and work dictates the opposite. Duomo is all about people being surrounded by aesthetically pleasing things—whether it's a $1500.00 purse or a 1.7 million dollar loft—with high ceilings, thank you very much." Ellie bristled at Gillian's words. Why was she so critical? But of course Gillian didn't view it as criticism, just as a statement of the facts.

"I feel alive around Jake. Like he speaks to my heart. I know he's not some hot shot stockbroker or CEO of a multinational, but he owns his own business—a business he's passionate about. And, he's a licensed architect. He understands aesthetics."

"I'm sorry, Ellie. You know him a lot better than I do. I just don't want you to get hurt."

"That is the farthest from my concerns. I trust him. Besides, we're just starting out, Gillian. It's not like I'm tying the knot or anything." Ellie's spirits began to dampen. What would happen when she told him her news this weekend? Would he embrace her or reject her? One thing she knew about Jake was he always did the right thing. This thought calmed her.

"Tell me you haven't been envisioning marriage and family with him in that old fashioned mind of yours," Gillian commented, laughing.

"It's healthy for a woman to have a rich fantasy life," Ellie defended.

"That usually pertains to sexual fantasies, Ellie, not wedding rings and baby buggies."

"So you don't like him."

"No! No. I think he's wonderful, Ellie. I'm sorry. I didn't mean to be so critical. Honestly. I haven't seen you this happy and relaxed in a long time, and if Jake is the reason, then the rest will work itself out. Besides, you're right. You two are just starting out, and he seems great. Please. Forget about what I said."

"Thanks. I think," Ellie tried.

"Just don't forget to schedule in my wedding into that Jake-consumed agenda."

"Don't be ridiculous. I wouldn't miss it for the world!"

Chapter 45

It was early; far too early for being out of bed on a Saturday morning. But as the group of ten men stretched on the athletic field, the smell of freshly cut grass jolted Arno into familiar territory. He imagined in his muscle memory the same speed and dexterity he had 15 years ago when he'd played at the soccer clubs in Amsterdam.

"Glad you two could make it again," Jake called over to Arno and Pierre.

"It's a little premature to say whether we'll make it or not," Pierre joked.

"You'll do fine, darling. I'm more worried about me. You work out at least five days a week, where I'm a 2x a week sort of guy."

"You guys did great last time. And you saw that we're not competitive. It's about playing the game, having some fun," Jake reassured them. He'd used some of the same words when he had sold them on the idea of coming out for a skirmish two weeks ago. The team had been two men down for the last month, and the idea came to him after their dinner together.

Arno and Pierre had been lukewarm to the idea at first. But it felt as if they needed a new activity to do together that didn't belong fully to either of them. A soccer match was the perfect idea, Arno had thought, and luckily, Pierre had agreed in the end. As the ten players divided into two teams, a man in his mid-thirties named Jerry started laying the ground rules.

"Okay. We're playing a half field today so we can make it more than 15 minutes. Jake, heads or tails?"

"Heads," Jake called. The coin flew into the air.

"Tails. Your team is shirtless."

As the match started, Arno felt the power in his legs, which seemed to thrive on the field. The crisp morning air filled his lungs, as he inhaled the sweet scent of freshly cut grass.

"I'm open!" called a young man in black shorts as Arno worked the ball down the field. He passed it to him, and the man brought the ball further down field before kicking it to Jake, who slammed it into the net.

"Yeah!" called out the team members. Pierre was now on defense and as the other team worked the ball down field, Pierre slid in and nimbly nabbed the ball from a man ten years his junior. Arno watched in amazement at his speed and dexterity. Pierre must have been quite something at the French soccer clubs in his youth, he mused. Pierre, Jake, Conrad and one other guy whose name he had forgotten were now running back up field and Arno brought up the rear.

This time the other team was more prepared and already had two men on Jake. Suddenly, the ball was kicked backward and Arno sprinted, catching it just in time to kick it down field to Conrad. It was Pierre who made the goal this time. The game went on for half an hour before the men took a break. By 9 a.m., the heat was already pressing down.

"You guys are great," Jake commented.

"Sure you haven't been training?" Conrad asked.

"No. Unless watching the World Cup counts."

Conversation was easy among the men and Arno realized how much he had missed gatherings just like this. They were gathered not by age, occupation, race or sexual orientation, but out of a love for a sport. Sure, he didn't mind taking in the sleek, muscular lines of the men on the field, but it was an afterthought. But he'd have to tell Ellie just how impressed he was with Jake's physique. But then again, she didn't even know he was out here today.

"You would have loved the games in France," Pierre announced. "Boys would turn the slightest little strip of lawn into a soccer field."

"Same in the Netherlands. Whether you're from the city or the country, everyone plays."

"I'd love to play a pick up game in The Netherlands or France," Jake imagined.

"Well at our age, there aren't really pick up games anymore," Arno explained.

"The nation is very crowded and with such a heroic interest in soccer, everyone joins soccer clubs. And it's competitive. You're expected to practice regularly, even if you're a banker by day."

"That sounds so European to me," Jake laughed.

"You two should come with us this fall. We're planning a trip at the end of September," Pierre suddenly suggested.

"That's a splendid idea, Pierre," Arno confirmed. He'd love to have Ellie on vacation with them. Lord knew she needed it, with all the work she had in her new position. And although he had only met Jake a handful of times now, he already had a good feeling about him.

"That sounds awesome, but to be honest, my passport is expired." That, and the carbon footprint, he said to himself. Ellie, of course, was the type of woman who would love to take an international trip. But Jake felt differently about Pierre and Arno; these men were natives of the countries they wanted to visit, which was quite different than just a pleasure trip that didn't involve visits to family.

"Do me a favor and get your passport in order, Jake. You never know when it might come in handy. What if you get a grant to take your program to Brazil, for example?"

"Or to study the sustainable nations of Europe?" Pierre threw in.

"Sheesh. Now you guys are speaking my language."

"And don't rule out the idea of joining us on a trip. If you want to impress Ellie, take her to the French countryside."

"Or on a cycling trip in the Netherlands. You could do the entire country by bicycle, and early fall is a fantastic time of year." As the men talked, a sense of camaraderie formed, and by the second half of the game, they were working together like a team, scoring multiple goals. By 10 a.m., the men cleared out; half hopping in their cars and a handful of others hopping on bicycles.

"See you next week?" Jake called from his bike.

"Sounds good! Enjoy your camping trip." Pierre and Arno waved from the Porsche Boxter. Already, their differences were reclaiming them from the early morning of synergy. Jake headed home to shower and change, strangely exhilarated about heading into nature with Ellie.

Chapter 46

The car ambled slowly along the dusty road, and Ellie felt a strange mix of excitement and exhaustion as they approached the prairie they had visited just last weekend. The Oaks cast long afternoon shadows across the prairie and down the hillsides. Jake stretched his legs as he stepped out of the car.

"Here we are," he announced. Ellie inhaled the crisp smells of the prairie, feeling her shoulders relax. They hadn't gotten on the road until after 1:00 p.m., and they had spent over an hour in gridlock on the 405. But as they had left the city, Jake noticed the contentment in her eyes, which relieved him; she had seemed anxious over the last few weeks.

"I'm happy we're here Jake," Ellie sighed. "It's not exactly the wilderness, but it's definitely nature."

"Me too," he smiled. He was looking forward to exploring the property with her. Although the ranch was large for the Santa Ynez Valley, 5,000 acres worked out to be just under eight square miles. They could easily traverse the property in half a day's hike, and they had it to themselves for three days, a luxury that was unheard of in the middle of the summer.

"We'd better start hiking," Ellie suggested. "There's no time to waste." It was already approaching 6:00 p.m. and they had about two hours of daylight to hike in and set up camp.

"I suppose so," Jake returned. "This way," he pointed. They retrieved their backpacks from the car, locked up and started around the edge of the prairie to a sandy river bottom. A slight breeze rustled the leaves of the oak trees that covered the property. As they hiked up the river bottom, they came upon a family of deer enjoying the coolness of the sand in shadow. At first the deer froze in their tracks. Their eyes met for a few moments before the gracious animals bounded away. Ellie unconsciously stepped in front of Jake on the trail, leading the way. They hiked in silence for the next 15 minutes, noticing other little animals scurrying into the shadows as they ascended.

Jake watched her hiking in front of him, taking in the muscles in her shapely legs, her taught, golden skin. Ever since his talk with Conrad a few weeks ago, he had chosen to concentrate on things he liked about her. And as his mind worked its way around her complexity, she had unfolded before him as just the type of woman he wanted in his life: strong, opinionated, soft and soulful all mixed in one. As they headed up a sage covered hill along a small animal trail, Ellie slowed her pace to look at her compass.

"Jake, hold on a minute. Can I take a look at the map again? I think we're going the wrong way. That creek is more to the northwest. See, here," she pointed.

"You're right. We are. That's because I have a surprise for you," Jake announced excitedly. "We don't need the tent tonight."

"What do you mean?" She was looking forward to sleeping in the tent, gazing at the stars through the mesh roof. "There's not some luxury cabin up here, is there?"

"Not exactly. You'll see soon enough. If I understand the directions correctly, we just need to keep following this trail for another 10 or 15 minutes." Ellie didn't exactly like surprises, but with Jake, she had to get used to the idea. They hiked up another ridge and had to scramble over a few boulders before the trail headed upward toward a high meadow. Around the next bend Ellie came to a standstill and stared.

"Surprise!" Jake said quietly. A cluster of small animals drinking next to a water pump scattered as they entered the clearing. There in front of them were three teepees made out of heavy canvas. Ellie smiled. She hadn't slept in a teepee before.

"Wow Jake. Authentic teepees!"

"No. Not really. The Chumash aren't teepee Indians. Their homes were more like sophisticated huts made of willow branches. But these teepees were only put in six months ago. Since we were arriving so late, Beatriz suggested we stay here." Ellie was surprised to hear that Beatriz had suggested it. She smiled at the idea that she was somehow growing on her.

The area was clearly well maintained. An outhouse was placed discreetly beneath a large oak tree twenty yards to the left. A picnic table sat off to one side, not far from the water pump, and a fire ring surrounded by large rounds of wood that served as seats lay in the center. There was something romantic about this Indian camp.

"I suppose this is our transition night. Not exactly wilderness, but still out in the woods, under the stars," Jake noted. Ellie looked into Jake's eyes. That was a good description, she thought; a transition night. She knew this was the right place to tell him her news. They were completely alone in the middle of sacred land, a place she would never have known about or visited if it weren't for him. It was strange to think she was already nine weeks along. Sensing something intimate in the way she looked at him, Jake pulled her close and kissed her tenderly. As usual, he felt a pull in his loins as her body brushed against him. He hugged her tightly before breaking the embrace.

"Let's set up camp, deer hunter."

"I'll set up the kitchen and you can set up our beds in the teepee," Ellie suggested.

"That sounds egalitarian enough," Jake quipped. Ellie set up the portable camp stove on the table. As the water started to boil, she turned her attention to the fire ring. A fire would be nice later in the evening, she thought. She gathered kindling beneath the oak trees and took a few pieces of wood from the neatly stacked woodpile and expertly prepped the campfire. She glanced toward the teepee and saw Jake inside, laying out their sleeping bags. Even though she'd had plenty of snacks on the way up, she was starving. At least she now understood the reason for her constant hunger.

"Are you hungry yet?" she asked over her shoulder.

"Getting there," Jake replied from a distance. Ellie pulled out a small cutting board and started prepping the fresh veggies they had picked up at a food co-op on the way up. As she added the soup mix to the boiling water, Jake came and sat beside her.

"How's the teepee?" she asked.

"Pretty sweet. I think we'll sleep well tonight. Can I help at all?" He asked as she added seasoning to the tofu and vegetables.

"Maybe you could open that bag of chips and find our table cloth and mugs. Is that water drinkable?"

"Yes. It's well water." The sun had ducked behind the mountains and the shadows deepened across the valley. With everything set up, they sat down on the log stumps, taking in the surroundings. He lit two candle lanterns and placed them on the table as the last of the light left the sky. Ellie filled two mugs with the steaming hot soup, and then used a second pan to sauté the vegetables.

"This looks delicious," Jake commented as they sat down at the table.

"Everything tastes better when you're camping," Ellie said wistfully. "My father used to say that."

"Did he take you camping a lot?"

"Yes. Every summer we'd go on a ten-day trip. My brothers, my dad and I."

"And your mom and sisters?"

"They'd come on some of the weekend trips, but not the long trips. Did you go camping with your parents?" Ellie asked.

"Car camping quite a bit, but not where we actually hiked in."

"But the car camping was enough to get you interested in nature?" she asked.

"Yeah. I guess you could say that. It was such a major contrast to the city. I loved it. I remember this one time a deer ate potato chips out of my hand when we were visiting Yosemite. My parents were mad, because they figured I knew better than to give a deer junk food, but also because it was clear that the deer was so used to humans that it had lost its fear."

"Well, the deer in Idaho have their fear instincts well intact," she reassured him.

"I'd like to see your wild Idaho deer," he responded playfully. After they finished the meal, they worked together to clean up the dishes and placed their sundries in a lock box behind the teepees designed to keep food safe from animals. Ellie lit the fire and they pulled two logs close together, leaning in toward the heat. Slowly, the larger pieces of wood caught fire, crackling and popping before the fire settled into a steady burn.

As Jake looked at Ellie in her hiking clothes, a beanie covering the crown of her long brownish-blonde hair, he once again had a hard time reconciling the difference between her two worlds.

"How did you end up so far from nature?" he questioned.

"Like how did I end up in Los Angeles so far from home?"

"Not only Los Angeles, but everything," he said slowly. Ellie felt the heaviness of his question. She thought about how much her life had changed in the last five years. But it wasn't just the last five years. The seed had been planted years before.

"When I was young, I loved being in nature. It was as much a part of me as breathing," she began softly. "But it was also part of being poor." She had never mentioned growing up poor. In the country, yes, but she'd never told him this part. But now she wanted him to know. He listened to her without interrupting. "We lived in a run down house on a ranch that was just one step up from a trailer park. Although my mom was an avid reader, she rarely had time to finish a book because she had to work so hard taking care of five kids and working on the farm. We lived close to the land, growing most of our food and raising our own meat. Down here, people romanticize such a life, but it's extremely hard work raising your own food, canning and jarring everything for the winter, cleaning out the chicken poop from the chicken house, you get the picture." Jake was surprised by her words. It sounded like they had both had a hard childhood.

"Did you have time to play and just be a kid?"

"Yes. Lots of time to play. The forests were my playground, but like most girls, I wanted dolls and pretty store bought things, and the answer was almost always no." Jake considered the beautiful clothing she usually wore in a new light; she was making up for the past.

"That must have been hard, Ellie."

"It was. But the hardest part was I didn't want my parents to see my disappointment, so I pretended not to care. I picked flowers to decorate my hair, collected fiery autumn leaves and shiny rocks to decorate my room. Besides, there were kids that were poorer than we were. I never went hungry." Ellie poked a stick into the newly formed coals in the fire as she gathered her thoughts. "Then one summer, everything changed. I stayed with my aunt in Seattle. My mom's sister."

Ellie looked up at the moon that was beginning to crest the hill as she described her summer with Aunt Rocklynn. Instead of being tied to the land, she was exposed to culture: art museums, theater and reading—hours of reading, curled up in the bay window with books on every subject she could imagine.

"After that summer, I was never the same. I read just about every book in the library and started focusing on writing. No one seemed to get me anymore, except for my mom. She understood my quest for knowledge." Ellie rolled her shoulders back as she talked about how she began to associate urban life with opportunity and expansion; rural towns with poverty, stupidity, being stuck.

"So even though I loved nature, at the same time I knew I had to get away from it." Ellie knew she was exposing herself, sharing thoughts she'd never shared with anyone before. But he already seemed to understand her more than most of her L.A friends, and if they were going to really be together, it was important that he know this about her as well.

"How old were you that summer?" Jake asked, as he held her hand.

"Fourteen."

"About the same age as the kids that come to Gaia Eden."

"Yes. It's a great age to have a positive role model, Jake." Something scrambled behind them in the trees and Jake jumped. Ellie turned slowly, smiling.

"Just rats or mice. Nothing to be afraid of."

"It sounded much bigger than a rat or a mouse," Jake shifted uneasily.

"Trust me. Nothing to worry about," she reiterated. She couldn't help but laugh.

"Come on. Aren't you even a little bit uneasy? At first I thought it was too quiet, but now that it's dark, it's like we're in the middle of a zoo with all the animal sounds I'm hearing."

"We're in their territory," Ellie responded. "Plus, they smell our food. They're waiting for their chance to come see what's for dinner." Jake smiled. She was clearly in her element and this made him feel somehow safe. As he began to relax again, he marveled about all she had just shared with him. He loved when she opened up, which didn't happen nearly enough. It helped him understand her contradictions.

"Thanks for telling me about your aunt; about that summer," Jake said suddenly. Ellie squeezed his hand, thankful for his encouragement. It had been a while since a guy seemed interested in knowing details about her life. He kissed her forehead, smoothing a hand across her face, pleased to see her expression lighten in response to his touch. "There are plenty of cultured, well-to-do people who live close to nature, I might add."

"You mean like the people we met on this property last week?" She asked. Jake nodded. "They strike me as city folk that have an affinity with nature. It's a nice combination, but I wonder, when it comes down to it, if they can walk the talk."

"Do you think I fall into that category?" he asked.

"Well. I don't know. I mean. You're making a real impact, Jake."

"But you can't picture me milking cows or collecting chicken eggs?"

"Oh no. I can picture that. But I can't picture you mucking out the stables, pulling weeds for hours, mending a Rota tiller, or putting in an irrigation system," Ellie teased.

"Maybe not at first, but I'm a quick learner, good with my hands" Jake added as he rubbed her back.

"You make an excellent boyfriend as well."

"You just called me your boyfriend. I think that's the first time you've said it."

"I think I'm still in denial," Ellie hesitated.

"Why?"

"Because I really want us to work out Jake." Her secret burned inside her.

"We are working out," he responded earnestly. "And you're a total catch," he added. Ellie smiled softly in response as she watched the red orange flames licking around the larger pieces of wood in the fire. Jake put his arm around her, holding her as she gazed into the flames. He couldn't be sure, but there seemed to be a sadness about her.

"I was thinking. Maybe we could drive over to meet my parents next weekend."

"You want me to meet your parents?" Ellie asked.

"Well. Yeah. They're important to me. And you're important to me, so . . ." he exhaled slowly. It had been a long time since he'd even thought of bringing a girl home to meet his parents.

"I would like that. Do they have names?"

"Graham and Eden."

"Nice names. And if I recall, Graham's an atheist and Eden is a Buddhist. Hard core activists and highly intellectual?" She left the part out about their poor parenting skills when Jake and his sister were little.

"Impressive attention to detail," Jake exclaimed "And do you want me to meet your parents?" Her parents had been on her mind non-stop since her trip to the doctor's office.

"Not unless you're planning to convert to Christianity and propose to their still virgin daughter."

"I guess I won't be meeting your parents in this lifetime," Jake joked. Ellie's smile quickly vanished.

"I would like you to meet them someday," Ellie almost whispered.

"Someday?"

"When we're sure we're solid." Jake contemplated her words. He knew relationships took time, but he already knew how strongly he felt about her and this was the second time this evening she had expressed doubt.

"I know we're new, but we're solid, Ellie. What's going on? Why the doubt?" Ellie felt tears rising to the corners of her eyes as she kissed him. She had finally found a man she could trust, who excited her and challenged her. And she was scared. How would he react to the news? How long could she postpone telling him?

"I love you Jake," she responded. Jake hugged her so fiercely, it surprised her, but no words came to match hers.

The moon slowly rose in the sky as the fire died down to glowing red embers. As they threw water over the coals, the fire hissed into the darkness, a plume of steam and smoke rising into the night. Jake wrapped his arm around Ellie as they slowly made their way to the teepee.

Chapter 47

The half-full moon illuminated the clearing with its silvery light. Long, angular shadows of the teepees disappeared into the dark patches beneath the oak trees. Before stepping into the teepee, Jake's eyes followed its angular shadow into the darkness, wondering what sort of creature crouched there just out of sight. As he closed the thick canvas flap and tied it off, he felt a sense of relief. Not only was he happy to be inside, he was already anticipating being with Ellie. Even though they had made love a dozen or more times now, he felt nervous all over again as he watched her change into her pajamas and climb into the sleeping bags he had zipped together into one.

He'd seen his friends fall hard for women and he had observed their strange behavior with a healthy skepticism. He'd been there and done that. For some reason, it had never occurred to him that he could fall in love again. Yet here he was, transfixed by the sight of her.

"Jake," she whispered. "I need you under the covers. It's cold in here all alone." He quickly pulled off his fleece, stripping down to his boxers before climbing into the sleeping bag. Instead of finding her in the pajamas she had put on just a few minutes ago, he found her completely naked.

"Well this is a pleasant surprise," he murmured. She tugged at his boxers as he began kissing her fervently. Despite the cold evening air, her body felt almost hot against his.

"Make love to me, Jake," she requested. He pulled her close, looking into her eyes. He could picture staring into her eyes every night before they went to bed together, for many years to come.

As he began to make love to her, a halo of moonlight shone upon them through the top of the teepee. Her mane of hair, spread out beneath her, silvered in the moonlight, framing her face. Ellie pressed against him as he kissed her neck and worked his hands across her breasts and over her belly. He loved the fullness he felt in every curve of her sensual female form, how she responded to his touch. He didn't have to work very hard before he felt her tightening around him, her breath coming fast. He felt a spasm course through his body as he finally released inside her. I am so lucky to have this beautiful woman, this angel, he thought to himself. She pulled him down next to her, as their breaths slowly returned to normal.

"Jake. There's something I need to tell you."

"What's that, darling?" he asked as he pulled out. There was something he wanted to tell her too. But as he started to take off the condom, he could tell something was wrong.

"Ellie. Hold on. Where's the flashlight?" His voice was stern, anxious.

"Right over here." She sat up and reached for the flashlight she had tucked into a little pocket of her bathroom kit. Jake took it from her and shone it toward his hands.

"Oh fuck!"

"What?" Ellie cried, startled by his words.

"The condom. It broke."

"What do you mean? Condoms don't break."

"It's broken. Jesus Christ."

"Please. Don't swear like that."

"Ellie. We have to do something."

"Do what?"

"Go to a pharmacy. Take the morning after pill."

"I can't." She stated. He looked at her frantically.

"What do you mean, you can't? I don't want kids, Ellie. You have to take the morning after pill," he commanded, the flashlight shining across her.

"I don't have to do anything!" she responded as she pushed him away.

"Sorry. Of course. Your body. Your choice," the words came out of him automatically. "But I'm not a family guy."

"Then we might as well end this right now," Ellie responded forcefully, as she reached for her clothes.

"I don't want to end this," Jake exclaimed, his face bunching up. "I haven't felt this strongly about anyone since,"

"Since Luz," Ellie cut in. "I don't believe in abortion. It's against my faith. Against everything I am." She slipped her shirt over her naked breasts and started to put on her jacket. Jake rubbed his hands through his hair, trying to think. The teepee had seemed like the most romantic place on earth not thirty seconds ago, but now it seemed eerie, like it was closing in on him.

"Honey. Ellie. Listen. It's not abortion. If there's any chance that you're fertile right now, that sperm and egg haven't even met yet. The cells aren't even dividing. You can't think of it that way."

"I can't Jake! You can't ask that of me," she cried.

"God. Ellie. I'm sorry. I. We. We have to think." He stood up in the teepee, pulling on his underwear.

"Maybe if you shower, you know. Rinse thoroughly," his hands gesticulated.

"There's no shower up here, Jake. Besides, it's too late," she started. Tell him why it's too late, she told herself.

"I'm 33 years old. I'm not ready to have a child. It would just be in the way of everything I'm working for. I don't want to make the same mistake my parents did." Her breath constricted at his words.

"How can you say that? You wouldn't be on this planet if they'd decided to take the morning after pill," Ellie screamed. Jake was at a loss for words. He looked at the tears in her eyes and his heart seized up.

"I'm sorry," he intoned as he wrapped his arms around her. She pushed against him forcefully.

"Let go of me!" She yelled. She felt lightheaded, dizzy. She finished dressing and opened the flap of the teepee.

"Where are you going?" Jake asked. "It's the middle of the night. You can't just wander off up here."

"Yes. I can. I need to be alone right now," she stated coldly. She scrambled out of the teepee and slipped on her boots.

"Ellie, wait!" Jake called after her. "Don't do this. We need to talk this out." But she didn't wait. He watched as she quickly made her way through the moonlit prairie and disappeared over the ridge. He debated on whether or not to go after her. She'd made it clear she wanted to be alone. Yet she was clearly upset, and that's when people, even experienced people, make mistakes. There could be wolves out here, he thought. Suddenly the idea of giving her space didn't sound like such a good idea after all. He dressed quickly and headed out after her.

As he walked through the moonlight, dry grass crunched beneath his feet, causing the crickets to momentarily stop their chirping before proceeding again. Adrenaline surged through his body as he looked into the deep shadows beneath the clumps of oak trees. As he came over the ridge, his eyes scanned the valley below. He flashed his light across the prairie and suddenly a set of luminous eyes stared in his direction. He threw his hands in the air in surprise, startling the large buck, which bound up the hill and out of sight. He took a deep breath, aware of how much he was out of his element. As his eyes adjusted to the soft moonlight, he snapped off the flashlight, and tried to picture where Ellie would go.

As he thought of her, his heart filled with remorse. Why had he been so insensitive? He certainly knew she was the type of woman who would keep a baby if she got pregnant. And hadn't she openly stated that she wanted children early on in their relationship? Not to mention her views she shared just last week in the gathering on this very property. Knowing this, wasn't he playing with fire? Since the first time they had made love, he had been far less careful than ever before, which baffled him. It was like he wanted her so completely that all logic left his head. Yet he knew, despite their differences, she was the kind of woman he wanted to marry someday. For some reason, this thought calmed him.

It was then that he spotted her sitting on a large outcropping of boulders. He walked slowly toward her, making sure she could see him standing below. He stood still, waiting for her to make some sign that he could get closer. Standing in silence, he breathed in the crisp evening air. Finally, he saw her wave her hand toward him and he scrambled up the rocks, sitting down beside her. She spoke calmly when she finally found her voice.

"Jake. I can't continue this."

"Please don't say that."

"Believe me. I don't want to say it, but it's true. I can't be with someone who doesn't believe in having children."

Jake turned toward her, but she wasn't looking at him. Her gaze focused somewhere far away. Jake tried to think.

"Ellie, the chances of you being pregnant just like that are pretty slim."

"That's not the point. The point is, if I was pregnant, you wouldn't want to keep it." Jake couldn't deny her words. He simply wasn't ready. But the idea of losing her just on principle of a remote possibility disturbed him.

"The thing is, I can picture being with you. For a long time. Even getting married someday." He was undeniably in love with her. "And given the right circumstances, and a serious change of mindset on both of our parts, having a child—one, not more." The words scared him, but Ellie had finally turned toward him, her eyes soft. He hurried on.

"Even though I feel incredibly close to you, we need to grow into each other before we embark on something so life changing as having a child together. Now's not the right time."

Ellie turned away from him, gazing into the darkness once again. She closed her eyes, bowing her head as if in prayer. He did his best to give her space, to wait for her response. Finally, she broke the silence.

"You know what they say. God only gives you challenges that you can handle," she stated quietly. "And this is our challenge, Jake. It's either going to destroy us, or make us whole."

Jake felt a shiver run up his spine.

"The prophecy," he whispered, placing his hands in his face.

"What prophecy?" she asked, puzzled by his response. Slowly his hands came away from his face. As he looked into her eyes, he recited the words that had played like a riddle in his mind over the last week.

"This is the challenge you have been waiting for. It will either destroy you, or make you whole," Jake quoted. Ellie recalled the romantic poems he had read to her on several occasions.

"What are you talking about? Is that from another Hafiz poem?" she asked.

"No. That afternoon in the prairie. That's what Sparrow said to me, Ellie. That was her prophecy about you and me. You almost quoted her just now." Ellie remembered Sparrow's strange blessing, the way her hand had hovered over Ellie's belly, as if sensing the life force growing there. Not really a prophecy, Ellie thought. More likely keen intuition combined with knowing how Jake viewed the world.

As she turned toward Jake, she tried to read his expression. He sat with his legs crossed, staring out into the night.

"So what does that mean to you?"

"It means you're pregnant." Hearing him say the words so decisively, it was almost as if she had told him herself.

"Okay. Let's just say that's the case," Ellie cautiously proceeded. "And you've just told me how you're not ready for a child. Where does that leave us?" Jake didn't know how to respond. He needed time to think.

"Before we get too rapped up in this, why don't we just wait to get a pregnancy test. Then we can cross that bridge when we get there."

"There's no bridge to cross, Jake." she interrupted. "A positive test means you'll be a father. And if you don't want to be, I can't help you there. There's no other option for me. And if it were negative, I still know how you feel about having kids." Jake felt himself closing down, curling into himself. No matter what he thought to say, it didn't make things better. But Jake did know one thing. Sleeping on it always helped people clear their heads.

"Honey, I want us to talk this through and I know we can work this out. But right now, I think it would make more sense to get some sleep and talk about this in the morning, after we're rested and less emotional." Ellie nodded, wiping the tears from her eyes. He reached for her.

"Ellie, you're freezing. Shall we head back to the teepee, warm each other up?" he asked gently. She was so cold, her body was shaking. Jake helped her off the rocks and they walked slowly through the moonlit prairie, huddled together.

The teepee felt warm and inviting and it didn't take them long to change back into their pajamas and climb into the sleeping bag together. Ellie was so exhausted that she began to cry again. Jake hugged her tightly.

"It's going to work, Ellie," he reassured her. He thought again of Sparrow's words. Either Ellie was pregnant, or the challenge was their contradictory views on having children. How could they overcome such a fundamental difference in belief? And it had been there all along and he had ignored it. If she wasn't pregnant, he knew his actions and words tonight would take a major toll on their budding relationship. The idea of losing her frightened him.

"You scared me when you hiked out like that."

"I'm sorry, Jake, but you were so awful."

"I know. I'm sorry." He kissed her on the forehead and she released a little into him, letting him spoon her. They lay like that for a long time, as if regaining each other's trust.

"Let's promise each other that we'll be kind to one another through this, however it turns out, and whatever we decide." Jake suggested quietly. Whatever I decide, Ellie said to herself. Ultimately it was her decision.

◊◊◊

It was dusk as she crawled on her belly up the mountain slope. Coyotes crawled from their dens, readying themselves for the hunt. They weren't the only ones out for the kill. She focused on the herd of deer not twenty yards away, antlers bent earthward, chewing on the short mountain grass. She leveled her gun, looking through the scope. She set her sight on a buck that stood apart from the rest of the group. The yelping of coyotes came closer as she readied herself to pull the trigger.

"Ellie! Wake up!" Jake whispered, shaking her gently.

"What?" she responded groggily.

"Ssh! Don't you hear them?"

"Who?"

"Wolves!" Jake whispered urgently. Ellie snapped awake and sat up, listening to the yelping all around them.

"Not wolves, Jake. Coyotes," she whispered.

"Are you sure?"

"Yes. I'm sure. Although they're smaller, it's still not ideal to be surrounded by a pack of coyotes. If they get too close, we need to make a lot of noise to scare them off," she advised. Their yelping filled the valley.

"God. They sound eerie," he whispered.

"I know. It's a beautiful sound if you're listening from inside your house, but not from a tent. At least we're in a teepee," Ellie whispered back. "Shall we open that tiny window flap up there and see how close they are?"

"No!"

"They're not going to hop in the window," she said quietly. "I want to see them." She unrolled the small flap and peaked out into the night. They were gathered at the far edge of the fire ring, safely keeping their distance from the lingering smells of burning wood. Their silky bodies meandered in and out of the shadows as they got closer to the teepee.

"There's a drum in the next teepee," Jake whispered. "Do you think it's safe for me to go out there?"

"I've got a better idea," Ellie responded. "Where's the flashlight? I need to look for something." Jake tried to remember where he put the flashlight as he fumbled through the darkness. The coyotes came closer as Ellie felt her way through her pack.

"It sounds like they're right outside the teepee!" Jake whispered. The sounds of paws scratching at the earth sent chills down his spine.

Suddenly, a high pitched sound filled the tent as Ellie blew into the whistle she had packed for the trip. The coyotes scattered in the moonlight, disappearing over the ridge. Jake finally peaked out the window, seeing the last of the coyotes scampering out of sight.

"Okay. That was scary," he sighed.

"Don't be scared. They were just curious. Really, coyotes rarely attack humans."

"Good to know. And you! You were so calm through the whole thing," Jake remarked. He felt a little embarrassed. Wasn't he supposed to be the protector here?

"I've been around them over the years and I've learned about their behavior. They'd rather not be seen. I mean, for the most part, coyotes are afraid of humans. They only get aggressive with people when they lose their natural fear of us. Like from kids trying to feed them potato chips, for example," she smiled.

"That was a deer, not a coyote," Jake laughed, pleased that she had referenced his Yosemite story. "Anything else I should know about coyotes?"

"Well, they've been known to hunt small house pets and they sometimes try to attack small children, you know, children under five years old," Ellie added. As the words escaped her lips, she saw the expression on Jake's face change. Inevitably, she knew what he was thinking about. She pushed ahead in her description, hoping to make the topic of children seem as normal as possible.

"So parents who live in rural areas where coyotes have been spotted are always advised to keep small children inside, especially at dusk, when coyotes start to come out." Jake didn't know this sort of thing. And these are the sort of things responsible parents would know about. Determined to push the thought out of his mind, he focused on the coyotes instead.

"I have a new nickname for you; Coyote Ellie. I think that sounds much better than Lady Ranger Ellie or Deer Hunter."

"Coyotes are also known as tricksters," Ellie responded coyly. Suddenly, he remembered something striking Luz had shared about coyotes years ago. Not to be outdone, he added this rare bit of knowledge pulled from his memory banks.

"Did you know, Coyote Ellie, that the Chumash Indians have a Sky Coyote in their mythology?" Jake was confident, sure that she could not know this. "He's part of the creation story of humans." He looked into Ellie's eyes and suddenly all the humor of the situation evaporated.

"Oh, Jake. Did you hear what you just said?" she responded sleepily.

"Yeah," he sighed. "It's like the universe is teasing us."

"Weird, huh?" she yawned.

"We'll talk it out in the morning, darling," Jake said quietly. "Go back to sleep."

They snuggled together and Ellie fell asleep quickly, while Jake tried to make out her features in the darkness of the teepee. Just after they had made love this evening, he had been on the verge of telling her he loved her. He had also been mulling over the idea of her moving in with him. Now that Gillian was engaged, she would be moving to the East Coast, and Ellie certainly couldn't afford that big house on her own. It was more of a whim, he realized; a fanciful thought. But what if this woman nestled in his arms, which he'd known for just a few months, was now pregnant with his child? If he truly loved her, would this not be something to celebrate? Perhaps if he believed in having children; but he didn't.

Jake listened to the pre-dawn stillness, aware of the slightest sound. The whistle hung from a nylon rope around his neck and he fingered it gently for reassurance. It wasn't until black gave way to the graying dawn that he finally fell asleep.

Chapter 48

Saturday morning came too quickly for the young couple. Ellie was out of the teepee first and although she had slept surprisingly well those last few hours after the coyote visit, she was not blessed with the ability to sleep in. Despite her love of camping, her body was stiff, as a sleeping bag and pad could not compare to the luxurious mattress and satin sheets she had at home. What started as a few stretches turned into a spontaneous yoga session.

As she entered triangle pose, she once again recalled the story of Gillian's engagement. She pictured the old church tower, the young girls in white dresses and David, kneeling before her best friend. One thought intertwined itself with another and soon she was wondering if she was destined to be an unwed mother. Despite his words last night, Jake didn't seem like the type of man that would marry. And clearly he wasn't ready for a child. And if she knew this about him, why had she ever started a relationship with him in the first place? Tears made their way down her cheeks but she wiped them away, determined to pull herself back into the moment. Maybe it was best to tell him the whole truth. Not in words, but in pictures.

Jake woke from a restless sleep to the sensation of being too hot. He rubbed his eyes, glancing at his watch. It was only 7:30 a.m. in the morning, but the sun was already beating down on the teepee, warming the air within. He peered outside the teepee and Ellie was nowhere to be seen. Although first concerned by her absence, he was glad to have a moment alone to collect his thoughts. The kettle on the small camp stove was still warm and he made himself a cup of tea. He realized now that he had heard her in the background of his dream, moving about the teepee, filling the kettle and moving gently about the campsite.

He ran his hands through his hair, as he often unconsciously did when he was worried about something and thought about what had transpired over the last twenty-four hours.

Although he knew he felt strongly about Ellie, he couldn't get his hands around the other part. He hadn't committed to anyone in the last five years and here he was discussing the possibility of having a child with, in many respects, a relative stranger. Yes. He knew her intimately in many ways and felt comfortable in her presence, like she understood him. A part of him even believed he loved her, and had been on the verge of telling her just last night. But were they really in love? And what were her true convictions when it came to the environment? Was she just taking the challenge as some sort of distraction for the month or to impress him, or was she serious about making the changes? This was his life work after all. And if they were to have a child together, he wanted that child to grow up with a healthy respect for the environment. The idea of a child lingered in his thoughts as he began his yoga series.

As he breathed in the fresh morning air, focusing on his practice, he tried in vain to push his concerns away. He focused on the physical movements, pressing himself deeply into the poses. After finishing his practice and making himself another cup of tea, Jake began to grow anxious. He didn't like the idea of her wandering off by herself. Sure, she was capable of taking care of herself in the outdoors, but this wasn't a well traveled area. If something happened to her, it was up to him alone to find her in an expanse of five square miles of rolling hills, canyons, riverbeds and trails overgrown with chaparral. He called her name into the valley and then up into the hills, but the only answer that came was a slight breeze rustling the dry leaves of the surrounding Oak trees.

The calmness of his yoga session gave way to worry. He wrote her a note and put it on top of the table with a large rock on top of it. He decided the best thing to do was go to the car and retrieve his cell phone. That way, if he found her injured, he could at least call for help. He went to his backpack to retrieve his keys, but they were missing. He searched through all of the pockets two times before he noticed the note sticking out from under the sleeping bag. He must have rolled over it earlier.

Had to get something from the car. Be back soon.

~Ellie.

Although he was relieved to know she was okay, he also felt anger rising up, like a parent ready to scold a child who'd run off in a crowd causing worry.

He hiked in the direction of the car, and within 10 minutes, he saw her walking slowly toward him, talking on her cell phone. Apparently she couldn't be away from her cell phone for more than twelve hours, he thought. She hadn't spotted him yet, and it was so still, he could hear she was in conversation with a client.

"That's fantastic news," she was saying. "We'd love to have you advertise with us next year. Do you think the Stanton Lofts project will be ready by then?" she inquired. She talked on for a few more minutes. "I'll have Judy call you first thing Monday to get you the details." She listened closely to the phone call, in rapt attention. "I'm so glad it worked out. Oh no. No problem. Okay! Bye!"

Ellie hung up and slid the cell phone into her pocket. Cell phone out of sight, her attention switched to a small white envelope in her hand about the size of a greeting card. She was holding it gently to her chest when she suddenly saw Jake.

"Good morning," she smiled.

"I thought we agreed this was a work-free, cell phone-free weekend. What was so important?" He asked with more agitation than intended.

"I came to get something from the car that I forgot and I saw that I had three messages. I just checked and there was an important call from work."

"It couldn't wait until Monday?" Jake asked. He noticed her hair was in tangles, probably from the beanie she had been wearing most of the evening and her eyes seemed puffy from lack of sleep. Or had she been crying again?

"No. It couldn't," she retorted. They walked in silence back toward the teepees. Stanton Lofts, Jake repeated to himself. How do I know that name? And then he pictured the yellow development board that had been tied to the gate outside his old office last week, and the project name that was written in block letters across its surface.

"Pacific West Holdings," he said incredulously. "They're clients of yours?"

She glanced at him hesitantly.

"Yes. You're familiar with them?" Jake felt heat rising in him.

"Familiar with them? They're the reason we were evicted, Ellie. Stanton Lofts is the project that will go on the property after we're gone. But that's not all. They're one of the biggest developers in Los Angeles and they've been displacing the very populations I work with by buying up poor neighborhoods, gentrifying them and pushing out the poor."

"Jake. I had no idea. This is a terrible coincidence." She tried to think of something to say so Jake wouldn't take it so personally. "But, it's not just Pacific West Holdings, right? I mean, in a way, isn't that what most developers do? Take older properties and transform them into something more appealing?"

"Maybe the ones you know, but no. There are developers who keep human integrity in mind. Pacific West Holdings also bulldozed wetlands to put in million dollar condos back in 2007, before your time here in L.A. After a long battle against an environmental group who was trying to protect the wetlands, they won; basically, because they had more money. That's a little insight on your big client." His voice rasped.

Ellie wasn't used to seeing Jake like this. Usually, he was so diplomatic; presented information fairly. She had clearly hit a sore spot.

"I did know about the wetlands but I hadn't heard it like that," she countered. "I heard that they actually incorporated the wetlands into the design; a tiny wetland that wasn't very significant."

"Sounds like you heard it from the green washed mouth of the developer," Jake tersely replied. He heard the unfriendliness in his tone and saw Ellie raise her eyebrows in response.

"People need places to live too, Jake," she countered. Of course, Jake thought. She was an ambitious business woman working with big developers who advertised in her magazine. This was how she played the game. She looked the other way when it came to environmental degradation, bought into the glossed over stories that altered reality. This was the other side of her. The side he hadn't seen yet.

"That wetland was not an isolated ecosystem. It was connected to a small river and surrounding marshlands. They incorporated ten percent of the wetland into their design. Ten percent, Ellie." She looked at him in surprise. She hadn't heard this percentage before. But then again, she hadn't been researching the company for their environmental standards, either.

"That's better than nothing," she responded feebly. But clearly, it wasn't. It was terrible. Ellie started to speak, but Jake cut her off in a rage.

"Is that how you would raise your child Ellie? Tell her that doing just 10% of the right thing is okay? That money is more important than social justice? Is that the kind of mother you'd be?"

Her cheeks burned as if his words had reached out and smacked her. She was particularly caught on the words 'your child' as if Jake had already decided that the life developing inside her wasn't their child, but hers. But then again, he didn't know she was actually pregnant. She was so stunned by the coldness in his voice that she couldn't even manage a response. And apparently, he wasn't through.

"Why did you take the Seven Change Challenge?" he asked wildly. She knew this was a test. A test she didn't want to fail. But then again, maybe she did.

"I was impressed by your enthusiasm. I wanted to try it out. Just to see."

"Just to see, huh? That's just not good enough, Ellie. Not good enough at all," he responded coldly. And then he did something against his very nature; he walked away from her without uttering another word.

Ellie watched him until he disappeared over the ridge. Her hand slid into the little paper envelope and she eyed its contents. She closed her eyes, praying in silence. Please help me make the right decision. As the minutes slipped by, instead of giving into tears, she found herself calmly walking toward the sage bushes. She picked several stalks of the white powdery leaves and tucked them into her pocket before heading back to the teepee. She inhaled the scent of the medicinal leaves, thinking not only of Beatriz and the other women making smudge sticks in the shade of the trees last week, but of her childhood friends and family.

By the time Jake cooled off, and got back to his senses, he was not only embarrassed by his behavior, but disoriented. He hadn't spoken to anyone like that in ages—especially not someone he cared about; someone he loved. He knew he owed Ellie an apology, and he thought of the right words to say to her as he tried to regain his orientation. She hadn't personally chosen Pacific West Holdings as a client. She didn't own the magazine after all, she was just an employee. He wasn't mad at her. When it came down to it, he was scared. And Lord knew she'd be an excellent mother. What had gotten into him?

It took him another twenty minutes, but he finally crested the right hill and was relieved to see the three teepees. As he hiked toward the central one, he called out her name, but she didn't answer. He looked around the camp and knew right away something was different. The stove still lay out on the table but Ellie's backpack was missing from the teepee. In its place was a rock, with a neatly written note underneath in tiny handwriting on the front of a thick white envelope.

> *Dear Jake,*
>
> *This was our great challenge, and we failed. Our life views are just too different on the big issues. Despite all of this, I had hope. But I was fooling myself—I cannot be with a man who doesn't believe in my integrity and who doesn't believe in having children. I'm sorry it didn't work out between us.*
>
> *You've reconnected me with nature and for that I will always be grateful.*
>
> *Good bye.*
>
> *~Ellie*

Jake crumpled up the envelope in his hand and shouted her name, but she was gone.

Chapter 49

The hike back to the main road took her less than an hour and when she climbed over the last barbed wire fence, she stepped onto the shoulder of a mountain highway. She slipped on her sunglasses and raised her thumb in the air. The third car that passed slowed to a stop 50 yards ahead and she walked quickly in its direction. As she approached the white pick up truck, she did her best to swallow the fear welling up inside her. She had never hitchhiked before, but figured the odds of summoning a serial killer her first time were pretty low. As she got closer she peered inside the window to see a stout woman with a thick braid of salt and pepper hair coiling down her back.

"Where you headed?" the woman asked in a friendly voice.

"South," Ellie responded.

"Well that's vague. Like South America or Santa Barbara?"

"Los Angeles."

"I can give you a ride into Santa Ynez," the woman offered with a laugh. "Hop in."

"Thank you," Ellie replied.

"I'm Carrie by the way." The woman offered her hand as she pulled back onto the road with a burst of speed.

"Nice to meet you. I'm Ellie." She usually gave her full name, but today it felt good to just be anonymous Ellie. In less than a minute, Carrie was telling her all about the music scene in the Santa Ynez Valley as if gossiping with an old friend.

"A lot of country music, of course, but also a decent singer-songwriter presence. We have open mics once a month at the Jones' House." Ellie mentioned the folk music she grew up with and before she knew it, she was talking about Idaho with this perfect stranger named Carrie.

"Hot Damn! You're from McCall, Idaho? I've got family in McCall." It didn't take long to find someone in common and Ellie was shocked by how small the world could be sometimes.

"Justine Fairbanks? Yes! She worked at the library in McCall. I used to see her almost daily. I totally remember her. Stocky build, thick glasses. Totally excited about books in this reserved, clever way."

"That is the most accurate description I've ever heard of Justine's book fetish," Carrie chuckled.

"Well she was working in the right place. Every time I went in, she had another suggestion of something I might enjoy."

"You don't strike me as someone who spends hours in the library," Carrie commented. "Not that I'm saying you come across as dense or something. Quite the contrary. I can tell you're a smart one. You just strike me as the outdoorsy type."

"I used to be quite outdoorsy before I moved to L.A.," Ellie confessed, "but I also love books. It's quite possible to spend your days outside and your evening hours indoors, enwrapped in a book," Ellie explained. They pulled into Santa Ynez. The small downtown area had an old western theme, and the surrounding roads disappeared into farmland. Ellie looked at the little town with a touch of nostalgia. She and Jake had had a romantic dinner here just last week.

"Well the bus stops here," Carrie announced.

"Thanks for the ride, Carrie. Can I give you a few dollars for the gas?" Ellie asked.

"Heck no. We only drove for 15 minutes. You know, Ellie. I'm headed to a barbeque right now and there'll be some folks there from Santa Barbara. Maybe if you hang out for a while, you can catch a ride back with one of them."

Ellie hesitated. She was completely out of her element, relying on strangers. But at the same time, this woman and her small town friendliness warmed her.

"Well, if it's not too strange for me to just show up."

"Heck no. You're practically family considering you know my cousin Justine. You don't play guitar or fiddle, do you?"

"No. I used to sing, though."

"You sure use a lot of used-tos. Used to sing, used to be outdoorsy. Sounds like you need to get your priorities straight, and start doing," Carrie lectured. Now Ellie recognized the other side of small town mentality—those strong opinions which were sometimes spot on and other times enough to send someone packing to the big city. But she had to admit; Carrie had hit the nail on its head.

Within ten minutes they pulled down a long gravel driveway to a wooden home painted black with white trim. The paint curled at the windowsills and the warbled sheen of the single-paned windows bent their reflections as they walked past. Dressed in jeans, a t-shirt, hiking boots and a baseball cap, Ellie hardly recognized herself. But in this crowd, she couldn't have picked a more incognito outfit if she'd tried. She could already hear the sounds of a guitar strumming and a deep male voice singing a folksy ballad. Within a few minutes someone offered her a beer, but she asked for water instead. As she tried to push the thoughts of Jake out of her mind, she thought it best to send him a text message, so he at least knew she was safe.

As she sent him a brief text, she sat down on an old wooden bench and listened to the musician singing a sad song about love and loss. In any other situation, the predictable lyrics would have amused her, but today no laughter came. Her throat tightened as she thought of the last words Jake had said to her and she felt something inside of her break. She had believed in their love and he had betrayed her, disowned the idea of their child, and devalued her efforts of honoring his way of life.

I know better than to give myself over so completely to a man, she berated herself. Knocked up and alone; I'm like a bad country song. How am I going to get myself out of this one? She was thankful for the dark sunglasses she wore as she spiraled downward into her thoughts. She listened to the next band with her eyes closed, concentrating on the melody of a fiddle floating through the hot summer air.

"Hey. How's it going?" a young man standing next to her asked.

"Fine. And you?" Ellie responded, startled from her thoughts.

"Yeah. Good," he returned.

"Oh. Weren't you singing a moment ago? It sounded beautiful," Ellie remarked.

"Thanks. I'm Buddy by the way."

"Hey Buddy." Ellie slipped into the casual language of her college years. "I'm Ellie." Anonymous Ellie at a small town gathering.

"How do you know Carrie?"

"Oh. Well. I don't know her really, but I know her cousin Justine," Ellie fumbled.

"Well, they're good folk," Buddy stated.

"Yes. Very genuine." How was it that you can know someone for a fraction of an hour and get such a good read? Did it have something to do with people from small towns? She'd certainly missed her mark when it came to city folk, she thought downheartedly. Buddy talked to her for the next 45 minutes while he nursed one beer after another. It didn't take long to find out that he worked at the hardware store and owned a small walnut farm with his dad. She would have married someone just like Buddy had she stayed in Idaho. She wondered, in retrospect, if that would have been such a bad thing. But then Buddy kept talking, and she had her answer.

Before long, Ellie had eaten two hamburgers with ketchup and mustard on white buns, washed down with a few glasses of coke and a large handful of greasy potato chips. It was the unhealthiest meal she'd eaten in years, but she savored every last bite.

"So you gonna sing something for us today?" Carrie asked, as the open mic session of the afternoon got underway. Ellie signed up on the list, and after 20 minutes she was called up.

"Do you guys know Angel from Montgomery?" she asked the rhythm section.

"Oh yeah," they nodded. As she started to sing the John Prine song from her youth, at least twenty people sang along. The whistles for an encore demanded that she sing another, and she fell right in synch with the musicians on stage.

When Carrie found a ride for her to Santa Barbara she was almost sorry to leave. Ellie checked into a luxurious hotel across from the beach and looked through the handful of business cards and phone numbers scrawled on scraps of paper that had been shoved in her hands at the party. She would probably never be back in Santa Ynez again, or have reason to call these people, but the friendliness of the day felt like a much needed reminder of small town warmth.

As she watched the gold and fiery orange of sunset fill the sky from the balcony, her thoughts shifted back to this morning. How could she be so wrong about a man? She opened a brand new blank journal she had purchased in the lobby gift store and began to write. Everything she had been feeling and experiencing over the last two and a half months spilled onto the pages. This time she didn't fight the tears as his name, intertwined with her hopes for her future, appeared over and over again. She stayed up until the last thoughts came out of the ballpoint pen. Only then did she crawl into the crisp white sheets to get the sleep her body so desperately needed. Before turning out the light, she closed the book firmly, as if closing a chapter of her life.

Chapter 50

Jake was able to track a pair of dusty boot prints past his car and down the road until it turned into gravel, where they abruptly ended. If those were her prints, it was clear she had headed back to the highway. What was she going to do, hitchhike? He drove a short distance in both directions trying to find her and even stopped at a small country market, asking if anyone had seen her. No one had. He was sure that a voluptuous woman like Ellie wouldn't go unnoticed by the gas station attendants. He showed them a photo of her on his iPhone, but neither had seen her.

He headed back to the café and ordered a sandwich, wondering what to do. What if those weren't her boot prints? Jake asked himself. Perhaps he'd been too hasty in coming into town. He'd have to call Gray Wolf and get a search party together, just to make sure she wasn't lost somewhere on the property. When he retrieved his phone, he saw that he had a new text message.

I'm safe and on my way to Santa Barbara. Please don't try to contact me. I need to be alone right now and I hope you can honor that. Ellie.

He quickly texted her back:

I am so sorry for my words, Ellie. Please don't end this. We can find a way to work this out.

Jake checked his cell phone repeatedly, but no response came. As time wore on, he came to a realization. He'd lost one great love of his life and he wasn't about to lose another. He knew he had to win her back. Before he could do so, he would need to take his own beliefs and set them under a microscope.

Chapter 51

Gillian and Arno met Ellie on the boardwalk in Santa Monica, excited to have the mystery of this evening's secret plans unveiled. They left their shoes in a small pile on the sand and walked barefoot toward the ocean.

"Okay. So here's the deal . . ." Ellie announced dramatically. "I'm taking you both to a concert tonight. Because you are my two best friends in the entire state." Emotion cracked through her voice.

"And is your hotty environmentalist joining us?" Gillian asked. Ellie had prepared herself for this, but the reference to Jake stung her.

"Well, actually, no. We broke up last weekend."

"What? What do you mean you broke up with him?" Gillian barked.

"I don't understand, Ellie. He was not only gorgeous, but you two were great together," Arno cried. "Pierre and I even signed up for the Seven Change Challenge."

"You and 53,000 other people."

"Good gracious! Really? So many? All from the article?" Arno asked in disbelief. Ellie was thankful for the change of subject.

"Yes, and that's just the online article and campaign. It's going so well that Duomo decided to do a print version as well with more details—a full spread. People are tracking our progress online along with their own. It's over the top popular, and I'm still in first place in the office, although there's a lot of people online doing far better than me. Including a couple in Singapore."

"You're being tracked by people in Singapore? Did you even know you had an audience in that market?" Arno asked. He was still reeling over the idea that Ellie and Jake were over, but he recognized something in Ellie right now that wasn't to be questioned. Gillian, on the other hand, cut him off.

"Wait a second guys. Focus! Okay Ellie? I'm glad the challenge is going so stupendously and all, but what the hell? Just before your trip last weekend, you were telling me he was the man of your dreams. How could you change your mind about someone so quickly? What's up?" Gillian questioned as she dug her toes into the sand, causing everyone to stop.

"He's great, Gillian. But he can also be a total jerk. He accused me of doing the challenge only to impress him and he totally told me off when I mentioned one of my clients was Pacific West Holdings." Ellie explained. She didn't mention the rest of it, and without the crucial details, she knew her story fell flat.

"There has to be more to it than that. I mean, you knew he was an environmentalist, darling, and it seems you're more than willing to green yourself up," Arno chirped.

"He doesn't want kids," Ellie added cautiously.

"Well. That's definitely a deal breaker in your book," Gillian concluded. "Was this new information?"

"Well. Yes and no."

"Oh. Because of the environment. Is he one of those population zero guys?" Arno asked. She couldn't handle talking about Jake too much longer without breaking.

"Something like that. What's the point of being with someone who doesn't share your core beliefs?" In one of those rare moments in life, Gillian and Arno were silent at the same time. Their silence confirmed her point. "So. I just wanted you to both know that I'm done with him, and I don't want any blind dates, or anything else right now but to have time with my friends and focus on my work, which brings me to my next point."

"Go on," Arno encouraged, when he felt the length of her pause.

"I've been given my own column in the magazine!" Ellie smiled. "And ironically enough, it's about all things green."

"Now that is something to celebrate! First Marketing Director, and now a column," Arno chimed in. "Jake would be proud of you."

Ellie tried not to roll her eyes. Jake would be far from proud. He'd probably just call her a green washer.

"Fuck yeah! You so deserve it, honey," Gillian shouted. "We're going to go out and get smashed this evening!"

"No," Ellie quickly retorted. "No alcohol. I've been drinking too much lately, and I don't want anything to do with alcohol right now," she lied.

"You can drink your sparkling water, but I'm going to have a glass for you," Gillian responded. Arno was still quiet. He knew there had to be more to this than Ellie was saying but he knew now was not the time to push.

"I'm sorry it didn't work out, Ellie. Regardless of how great a guy he is, if he doesn't fit you, then that's the end of it." Arno watched her face carefully, and sure enough, he saw a flicker of doubt. He and Pierre would see Jake again on Saturday, and he could hear Jake's side. But the idea of doing so behind Ellie's back made him feel guilty.

"Arno, what do you think about going over up do's with me for the wedding?" Gillian asked. And that was the last of the conversation about Jake. Her friends seemed to easily accept that he was out of her life, but then again, maybe they were just trying to keep her upbeat.

They had no idea how fully she had fallen for him. Ellie felt the tears coming and in an effort to hide them she ran toward the waves, dipping her hands into the ocean and splashing her face with salt water. Gillian and Arno looked on in astonishment as her mascara ran down her cheeks.

"You're crazy, girl. That water probably has sewage floating in it," Arno remarked.

"Look at all the surfers out there, Arno. I highly doubt it," she countered.

By the time they got to the concert, Ellie had changed into a beautiful red dress and she danced the night away to the Avett Brothers. Arno and Gillian watched her, surprised by the freedom they saw in their friend. It was as if she was changing before their eyes.

Chapter 52

As Jake dialed Duomo magazine for the third time this week, he knew he had to be creative. He'd called twice before asking for Ellie and had been transferred to a reporter named Bethany. After all, supposedly he and Ellie barely knew each other, besides the one interview and a few dates, and for the sake of her job, she wanted to keep that impression up. How convenient, he thought.

Whereas Ellie wouldn't even take his calls, Bethany was like a cat in heat, buttering him up. She had informed him of how splendidly the online campaign was going and had even invited him out for a drink, which he had flatly refused. Ethan and Natalia had freaked out when they saw the online sign ups skyrocketing. And that was just the beginning, Bethany informed him. Once the print article hit, he'd be an environmental rock star.

His friends had been doubly shocked when he told them Ellie had broken up with him, but he hadn't felt right going into details, despite the worried looks on their faces. Ethan had taken him out for a drink, gently probing, but Jake remained distant. As the receptionist answered the line, he prepared himself.

"Duomo Magazine, may I help you?"

"Good afternoon. This is Eric Smith with Sonic Shoes. May I speak with Ellie Ashburn?" he asked.

"Certainly. I'll transfer you," the receptionist responded. He waited pensively for her to answer, his heart rate speeding up, but he only got her answering machine. He hadn't been prepared for this, and quickly hung up. He'd called her cell phone a half dozen times over the last few weeks, and no matter what sort of message he left, she never called back. What would be the point of leaving another one at work?

◊◊◊

By the second week, not even his early morning surfing sessions helped calm him, and he couldn't hold it in any longer. He felt angry and needed to talk to someone. So when Conrad came by his house, Jake prepared himself for the idea of opening up.

"You know you can talk to me about it, don't you?" Conrad offered, before Jake even broached the subject. Jake found it funny that he didn't even mention Ellie's name. Was his heartbreak so obvious?

"Can you go easy on me?" Jake asked, realizing how vulnerable he was feeling.

"Yeah, man. Of course." They sat down on Jake's back porch and Jake began from the beginning; how he felt about her, how quickly they had grown together, and then the condom breaking, and their falling out.

"She won't take my calls. I've been by her house a half dozen times and I never even see her car there. It's almost as if she's disappeared."

"God Jake. You're in a serious predicament. You're obviously in love with her, but you don't want the same things in life." Jake didn't like the way that sounded. True, they were extremely different, but as he had thought about her over the last few weeks, he had come to realize there was far more overlap than he had originally thought.

"I don't know. Surprisingly, we have a lot of common ground."

"But if she's pregnant, she's the type of woman that would keep it. That's a big difference."

"Yeah. Which means I'd be a dad, whether I wanted to or not," Jake thought out loud. Conrad flashed one of his wise man smiles at him.

"Children change you, Jake; whether you want them to or not. They make your world better."

"I keep hearing that," Jake replied.

"But if she doesn't want you in her life, you can't do anything about it." Even though Conrad was just stating a fact, the words pierced Jake. He lifted his hands to his face. Soon his whole body was shaking as the emotions he had been holding in over the last few weeks came tumbling out in the form of hot tears. Conrad rested his hand on Jake's shoulder, letting him cry.

"So tell me something, Jake," Conrad started gently. "Why don't you want children? Besides environmental reasons. Is there something else?"

Jake had been asking himself the same question over the past few weeks.

"I know what it's like not to be wanted," Jake responded.

"You mean those first five years, when your parents were still in denial?" Conrad asked.

"First seven years," Jake corrected. "I wouldn't wish that on anyone." Conrad stayed quiet for a while before responding.

"Jake. You're not a boozer. You don't smoke dope. You're about one of the most responsible guys I know. You wouldn't, in a million years, treat your own child that way. I guarantee you that part of history won't repeat itself."

"More than anything, I want her back."

"Then you need to come to terms with your feelings about children."

One afternoon when he and Natalia were working on a new urban garden project, Natalia caught Jake at a vulnerable moment, and her insights were not nearly as gentle.

"You've always said you don't believe in having children. I mean, in a way, maybe you're better off. She's one of those women that will keep it. And despite that sophistication she has, at her core, she probably wants a lot of them, being from a rural area, Christian, the whole thing. I realize she's beautiful, kind. All of that. And I saw the chemistry between you two. But think about the long run, Jake. Can you really picture yourself with someone like that?"

Natalia's description of Ellie was accurate on all accounts, but at the same time, it seemed to do her an injustice. Of course she was more than that.

"Yeah. I can," was his steadfast response. The sun began to set as they packed up the last of the flowers.

"Have you been tracking her progress online?" Natalia asked as they drove away from the site.

"Yeah," Jake admitted sheepishly. "I watch every day to see when she logs in, what she writes. She's supposedly doing really well as the new marketing director. I am so happy for her and at the same time, it breaks my heart," he added.

"If it's meant to be, Jake, it will work out."

Chapter 53

Soo Jin and Ellie headed to Green Garlands, their new favorite restaurant and Ellie, for the third time that week, ordered a vegetarian meal with tofu. Surprisingly, it was one of few foods, besides steak and bananas, that she craved.

"You didn't even know what tofu was a few weeks ago," Soo Jin teased playfully.

"Yeah. But it's a great source of protein," Ellie responded.

"You're really taking this challenge seriously, Ellie."

"Yeah. I am." Soo Jin shifted uncomfortably in her seat.

"Um. Ellie. I have to tell you something."

"Okay."

"Well, there are some rumors. People in the office are saying some stuff about you. I don't believe it of course, but I thought you should know."

"What rumors?" Ellie frantically asked.

"Well. One is that you've been dating the founder of Gaia Eden. That Jake Tillerman guy. I'm not asking you to tell me, I'm just saying, people have been talking."

"Like who?" Ellie responded uneasily.

"That part doesn't matter. I just wanted you to know."

"Well I was," Ellie admitted. "He was the environmentalist I was dating, but we broke up."

"I'm so sorry, Ellie. Are you sad you two broke up?" Soo Jin asked. Ellie couldn't even begin to answer the question. She had loved Jake and based on all of the messages he had left, clearly, he had loved her too. But then there was their core difference, despite what he'd said after the fact.

"Yes," Ellie started quietly. "But we just don't have the same values." Ellie explained. She knew this would make sense to Soo Jin.

"So hopefully those rumors will dwindle away," Ellie suggested, her cheeks burning.

"But that's not all," Soo Jin awkwardly replied.

"God. What else?"

"People think you're bulimic," she went on. Ellie had to laugh out loud. Was this how it was going to be as Marketing Director? Was she now a constant source of speculation? Ellie knew why the idea had surfaced. She had thrown up a few times at work, and she had been eating much more than usual. God; she hoped no other, more accurate theories were circulating.

"I know it's none of my business, but if it's true, Ellie, I know a great counselor who can help you." Ellie had to smile. Soo Jin wanted to protect Ellie. She looked at the sparkly engagement ring on Soo Jin's finger and her smile broadened.

"I'm not bulimic, and I really appreciate your concern and honesty Soo Jin. It's nice to know someone's got your back. And speaking of which, I'm so impressed with Frank. Now there's someone who believes in the same thing as you," Ellie commented. Soo Jin blushed. Frank had proposed to Soo Jin the very evening they first made love, and Soo Jin had said yes. Their wedding wasn't until next year, but it was clear the couple was strong, mainly because they shared the same values.

"He's the man I always dreamed of, sort of," Soo Jin faltered.

"What do you mean, sort of?" Ellie asked curiously.

"Well, I always thought I'd marry a Korean man, someone who was a friend of the family," Soo Jin admitted. "I thought we'd share the same cultural values, which would make things easier," she added.

"Is it hard?" Ellie questioned.

"At times," Soo Jin admitted uncomfortably. "But I think we will make it. Despite our differences, we love and respect each other. We're willing to make the effort."

"And what about your parents not talking to you anymore? That's got be hard," Ellie inquired gently. She thought of her own parents, wondering if they would still speak to her after she shared her news.

"It's awful Ellie. But Frank and I love each other, and we'll make it through, because we believe in us." Ellie listened to Soo Jin with new respect. Her shy friend, who had seemed like such a young girl just a few months ago, now seemed far wiser than Ellie.

"And are you interested in dating again?" Soo Jin asked.

"No. And I won't be interested in a very long time," Ellie answered wistfully.

Chapter 54

The call came in at 2:30 a.m. Friday morning. Adrenaline shot through him as he listened to the frenzied voice on the line.

"All right. Okay. And you're sure you weren't followed?" Jake questioned.

"Good. Good thinking. Stay put and I'll come get you guys." He dressed quickly before jumping into his car. As he drove toward Harvard Heights, he wondered if his actions were logical. What could he really do to help?

When he arrived at the small pocket park, it looked deserted. But as he got out of his car, Grayson and Jefferson cautiously emerged from the shadows. The neighborhood looked different at night, and the two boys weren't the only ones lurking around. A group of hyped up men standing on the front stoop of an apartment complex talked loudly while plumes of skunky smoke rose from their cigarettes into the night air. A homeless person slept on a makeshift cardboard mattress under the overhang of a coffee shop and half a block down, a scantily dressed woman leaned down to talk to the driver of a run down Audi. Jake heard sirens in the distance as the boys walked toward him.

"You guys okay?" Jake asked.

"I guess," came Grayson's meek reply once he was safely inside the car. "But if he knows we saw, he'll kill us."

"But he didn't see you guys, right? And even if he did, he isn't going to go after you," Jake stated as convincingly as he could.

Jefferson got into the back seat and pulled his hood over his face. When he started to talk, Jake didn't recognize the low growl in his voice.

"It's not the first time that bastard beat up Charles. He's one nasty motherfucker." If Charles' father could smack his own kid around, who's to say he wouldn't go after other kids as well?

"You did the right thing by calling the police," Jake reassured them.

"Yeah. The ambulance came 10 minutes later. Which means he's gotta be pretty messed up," Grayson commented.

Anger surged through Jake as he pictured a grown man taking his aggression out on his fourteen year old son. What kind of man would do such a thing?

"So I suppose you two aren't interested in filing a report? Telling the police in more detail about what you witnessed?"

"No way," came Jefferson's reply. And Grayson's silence was answer enough.

"Let's go to the hospital," Jefferson said. The hospital seemed like a nice alternative to being in this part of the neighborhood at 3 a.m.

When Jake pulled into the parking lot at Good Samaritan Hospital, he was amazed how busy it was for the middle of the night. Tracy Clark, a police officer he had befriended through overlapping clientele came toward him as he entered the hospital.

"Evening Jake Tillerman. What are you doing here?" she asked.

"Tracy," he nodded. "Came to check on Charles Logan; one of the boys in my program that I believe was recently admitted."

"What a coincidence. There was an anonymous tip off about Charles not 40 minutes ago," she casually remarked. Grayson and Jefferson, who didn't even flinch at her words, gazed steadily forward as if looking right through her.

"How is he?" he inquired. Jake had grown accustomed to Tracy's somber expression that kept her true thoughts and concerns safely locked away. She gave him a small nod. Jake knew she was asking if it was okay to continue in front of the boys. He tilted his chin up, and she continued.

"He's in pretty bad shape, Jake." Both of the boys looked at the police officer as she spoke. "But whoever it was that called in and reported the attack saved his life. I think he'll pull through."

"At least this time," Jake commented. Officer Clark motioned for Jake to come a little closer. The boys got the hint and found two seats in the lobby.

"The father had the boy's blood all over his hands and the initial assessment of the crime scene points to a one-sided fight. Unless he can hire a top notch lawyer, he's going to jail for three to five. It would certainly help if we had a testimony from our young eye witnesses." Jake nodded grimly before heading back to the boys.

They weren't actually allowed in to visit, since his condition was still critical, but they stayed in the waiting room for a few hours anyway, hoping for an update on his condition. And although Grayson and Jefferson were short on words, they thanked him more than once for coming to get them. Jake thought about how different their day-to-day lives were from his.

It wasn't the first time that he had come against a situation like this with his students. Rafa had come to the program one afternoon with black and blue marks on his arms. It wasn't until the marks had faded that Rafa told him his deadbeat dad had shown up out of nowhere, wanting money. Rafa tried to keep him out of the house, which resulted not only in the black and blue marks on his arms, but a black eye. And why had he fallen for Charles's story of street fighting? He should have picked up on signs of child abuse when he saw the bruises on his arms over two months ago.

Was he really helping these kids by having them plant a few trees and go on nature hikes? How did that help them stay alive on the streets? Or, in this case, in their own homes? Jefferson started to speak, interrupting his stream of thought.

"Usually, I wouldn't have even called the pigs, you know. I grew up learnin' that these are the sorts of things that are handled at home. And you don't mess with another family's privacy." Jake turned toward Jefferson, keenly aware that his voice, which had been gravelly and dark an hour ago, had returned to the smooth tones he associated with this bright young man.

"But Grayson and I talked it over, and you know. Thought about you telling us how sometimes the pigs are the good guys."

"And how we need to stand up for ourselves and our community." Grayson added.

"And then we called in the bacon," Jefferson concluded. Jake couldn't help but smile. They might not speak about the police in respectful terms, but at least they understood they were there to help them as well.

"You two saved Charles's life by choosing to make that call. You did the right thing."

It was after 5 a.m. when Jake finally made it home. As he reflected on the evening, he was humbled to know that his words were making a difference in at least two lives—or three, in this case. Charles had regained consciousness, but was still in bad shape. But there was something else that had struck him this evening; just about any man can become a father. But there are men who are cut out be fathers, and those who aren't. And for the first time in his life, he realized he was one of the former.

Chapter 55

Another one of Margo's crazy demands had surfaced its head in the office. Everyone was required to dress like a model for Monday's meeting and a make-up artist was even coming in to supervise the final touches. Thus at twenty minutes to three, Soo Jin and Ellie were among the other women crowded into the restroom, trying to get a glance at themselves in the mirror after the make-up artist had glammed them out.

"I want everyone in the boardroom in five minutes," Margo called. As the last of the women entered the room, Margo spoke impatiently.

"Everyone here? Good."

"So as you all know, that awful oil gusher in the Gulf has finally been plugged, and the office challenge has also finally come to an end." Several women let out a sigh.

"I can get back in my car!" someone giggled.

"Ah, forty-minute shower, here I come!" someone else chided.

"Although for some of you, this was only about the fame, I think some others have taken this whole green lifestyle to heart, and despite my three cars and four homes, not counting the cabin in Aspen, I applaud you." Ellie's colleagues laughed heartily, but Ellie felt her lips tighten. Was this really just a game for everyone? She pictured Jake and how earnest this whole thing was for him and despite the judgment he had cast on her that last day, she felt defensive on his behalf. But a moment later, she let it go, realizing for the millionth time that he was no longer in her life.

"Now, I bet you all want to know, just like our fans, who won first prize." The boardroom burst into excitement once again.

"But of course, I'm not going to tell you just like that. As a means of shamelessly using this opportunity to increase circulation, and further promote our magazine, we will be having a very special guest giving out the grand prize this afternoon. This mandatory meeting, the clothes, the make up, it's all part of a much bigger picture.

"In fifteen minutes, there will be a camera crew joining us downstairs, and if any of you have any other crass, anti-green comments to share, get them out now. This campaign's given the magazine a boost that has made the board of directors very happy," Margo added. "And now's the time to shine. Now ladies and gent, I'd like you to follow me down to the first floor, and I don't want to lose anyone on the way," Margo commanded.

Everyone was excited. How had Margo managed to pull off a surprise awards ceremony and where were they headed? Everyone had received the flyer about mandatory attendance on Monday because of a special board meeting, but it was hardly necessary; no one dared to miss a Monday ever unless they were deathly ill. Margo had fired someone who missed two Monday meetings in a row, and that had set precedent enough.

When they'd all made it down to the first floor, they noticed a large Duomo sign outside the convention room. As they entered, they saw tables decorated with potted plants. Instead of throw-away streamers and balloons, the decorations consisted of wooden, hand painted items from UNICEF. Everything, down to the organic cotton tablecloths had been chosen in the most sustainable means possible.

Ellie smiled for the first time all day as she looked around the room. All of this had come about because of Jake. She questioned herself again if she had been right to push him away, but as she thought about the way he had judged her, about the hatred in his eyes, she knew she was better off alone.

It was then that she saw him, standing in the front of the room, flanked on either side by his friends and co-workers, Natalia and Ethan. Ellie watched him from a distance as he scanned the crowd. It was hard to hide in a group of thirty-eight people. As Ellie was attempting to blend into the crowd, their eyes caught one another, and she took in a quick breath as if she'd seen a ghost. His gaze slowly lowered to her waist and she froze for a long moment before turning away. She didn't think anyone had seen the exchange, but she was dead wrong. Someone had seen every detail, down to the way her hand automatically went to her belly, flattening her dress that moments before had hidden the bump growing there.

"Ellie, your seat is up here!" Soo Jin called out. Ellie had no choice but to sit down at one of the front tables directly facing Jake. He was engaged in conversation with someone from the media, and Ellie took the opportunity to look him over. He was dressed in his one suit, the same he had worn to the art opening several months back, but he had a beautiful jade shirt on she hadn't seen before that brought out the green of his eyes.

Within a few minutes, everyone was seated and after Margo gave a brief introduction, Jake began to give his speech.

"On April 20th of this year the Deepwater Horizon oil platform in the Gulf of Mexico exploded, killing eleven men and injuring seventeen more. As news reports aired footage of the burning platform and the dark plumes of oil filling the ocean, our nation looked on in horror. Over the following three months, over 4.9 million gallons of crude oil gushed from the ocean floor, devastating marine life, delicate estuaries and other natural habitats. After many unsuccessful attempts, the well head was finally capped on July 15th. In just over ninety days, Americans witnessed the worst oil spill in our nation's history and the coastal and oceanic habitat along the Gulf of Mexico for both humans and animals was altered forever."

"In an effort to bring awareness to our dependence on oil, my team and I at Gaia Eden developed the Seven Change Challenge as an online rally call to show that we can all take daily steps to reduce our dependence on oil." Cameras flashed as Jake spoke, and Ellie could hear the whispers of her colleagues, not really listening clearly to his words, but commenting about his looks. Why am I working with these idiots? Ellie thought to herself.

"In our first week up, we had 183 participants. By taking our challenge to your office, Duomo Magazine helped bring attention to our cause and by week four, we had 37,000 participants."

This statistic was met with avid applause by attendees from the magazine, friends of Gaia Eden and members of the press.

"As of today, there are 183,647 people who are entering daily changes and 63 percent of those participants report that they are highly likely to carry these new habits forward in their daily lives." The applause was tremendous.

"Do any of you wonder what the bigger picture is for all these changes? If we tally all of your work together?" There were a few interested nods, as Jake continued.

"On average, you folks here at Duomo Magazine decreased your shower length by four minutes per day. That's 10 gallons per person, times 38, equals 380 gallons a day." The girls whistled and cheered as Jake went on. "Over a month, you cumulatively saved 11,400 gallons." Even Bethany seemed to wake up at that statistic.

"And if we count the cumulative efforts of our 183,000 plus participants, together we have saved over 82 million gallons of water in one month. That's enough water to fill about 125 Olympic-sized swimming pools!" Ellie glanced at Margo as Jake spoke. She clapped her hands tersely, a forced smile on her face. It seemed clear she wanted Jake to stop with the statistics, but he continued.

"If everyone in the challenge continues saving this much water for an entire year, we would be saving the equivalent of one third the water capacity of the Hollywood reservoir, just by reducing our daily shower time by four minutes." Ellie had never thought such a small change could make a difference. But clearly, it was all about the number of people participating. As Jake paused for a moment, taking a sip of water, he looked directly into Ellie's eyes.

"It is often said that an individual, taking small daily steps toward a more sustainable future doesn't make a difference. But when you think that each and every one of us is an individual human being, and that each one of us can change our ways of acting, of thinking, and realizing how our actions affect the planet and the lives of others, together, all of us united can drastically change the future of this planet; not only for ourselves, but for the future of our children and grandchildren."

Ellie clapped fervently along with everyone else, and for the first time in over a month, she thought of how good it had been to have Jake in her life.

"I'd like to ask Margo Chanaway, Editor and Chief of Duomo Magazine, to return to the stage."

Margo came up and spoke for a few minutes about the magazine's commitment to a sustainable future before thanking their readership for making such an immense change possible. She asked Jake to speak about Gaia Eden for a few minutes, and he gave a beautiful five minute synopsis, pointing to a group of teenagers at one of the front tables who waved vigorously at the cameras.

"And now, Jake, let's read what's in that recycled paper envelope," she drawled charismatically.

"And our grand prize winner within Duomo Magazine is . . .Ellie Ashburn." Ellie smiled as she was led to the stage to stand by Jake.

"Thank you Ellie, for being such an amazing participant," Jake shook her hand in earnest. He handed her the award, not taking his eyes off of her. She blushed as she returned his gaze, looking into those eyes that had melted her; this man to whom she had so completely given herself. She was getting dizzy from all of the flashes going off and Jake held her hand in a handshake, steadying her. Reporters asked them to turn and face the cameras and they were photographed together over and over again.

When she sat back down at her table with the hand-woven plaque, tears started flowing and this time she couldn't stop them. What her colleagues took as over excitement associated with winning the competition, Jake knew to be much more. He watched her from the stage before straightening himself and announcing the online winner, Isabelle Chen from Seletar, Singapore.

"Have a glass of champagne, Ellie," Amber suggested when the awards ceremony was over. "That'll calm your nerves."

"Thank you," Ellie responded. She held the glass in her hand, taking a tiny sip.

"You won a four day getaway to the Jade resort Ellie. That's incredible! You really deserve it," Soo Jin cheered.

"I'm green with envy," Bethany joked.

Ellie stuck it out and even talked to a few reporters before the day was through. She walked to the bus stop and hopped on as one last reporter caught her on film. Once she settled down, she closed her eyes.

"Well hello Ellie," called a familiar voice. Ellie looked at Cecile, sitting across the aisle from her. In her frequent trips on the bus, Ellie had decided that Cecile was her favorite local character.

"Hello Cecile."

"So when is he due?"

"Pardon?" Ellie asked.

"Him," Cecile pointed toward Ellie's stomach. Figures an old lady on the bus with a whole flock of grandchildren would be the first to notice. Ellie realized she didn't have much time before less discerning people would notice as well.

"February 6th," Ellie whispered.

"Congratulations," Cecile whispered back.

"Thank you.

Chapter 56

"Hello?"

"Hi Gillian. It's Jake Tillerman. Is Ellie there?"

"Listen Jake, how many times do I have to tell you? She doesn't want to talk to you. It's been a month already. Get over it. Please stop calling here," Gillian screamed before slamming down the phone. She sat down on the couch, shaking. She actually felt sorry for the guy. It didn't make any sense. Clearly, Ellie was head over heels with him and then all of a sudden, she changed her mind. Or not. She had caught Ellie on more than one occasion, tears in her eyes, but as soon as Gillian walked in the room, she claimed she was crying about something else. And Ellie was clearly depressed because she was also putting on weight and doing nothing about it—just letting herself go. And just last week she had seen Ellie walking, rather than running in the morning.

"Honey. Give the guy another chance," Gillian had pleaded.

"I can't," was her irrefutable answer. Arno and Gillian had gotten together on more than one occasion to conspire about the situation, and both agreed it was odd.

"What can we do to get them back together?" Arno had asked. But in the end, Gillian had been against any meddling.

On the other hand, there was something different about Ellie. She seemed stronger in a way; more focused and alive than ever, despite a complete disinterest in dating anyone. At least until that latest blow from work came. As she thought about her dear friend the doorbell rang. Gillian swung it open to discover Jake Tillerman standing in front of her.

"So you were calling from the porch?" she asked flatly.

"I know you're one of her best friends. Can we just talk for a few minutes? Please, it would really mean a lot to me. Just listen to what I have to say and if you think I'm nuts, I won't call back ever again," Jake promised.

"She's not home, she's at church," Gillian scoffed.

"That's fine. I'm here to talk to you," Jake responded. Gillian didn't stop him, so he continued. "Here's the thing, Gillian. I know Ellie and I were only together for a little over two months, but we were in love. She told me she loved me and I loved her. Everything was going beautifully between us and then we had one fight. One! And she walked out on me in the middle of a camping trip and never looked back."

Gillian had a rare moment of speechlessness. She heard the sincerity in his voice and she believed him. What was more, she had seen the way Ellie looked at his picture. Clearly Ellie was still in love with him. But even if her friend's actions didn't make a hell of a lot of sense, best friends are best friends. She couldn't betray that.

"Is our counseling session almost over?" Gillian responded.

"Almost." Jake quietly replied. "I saw Ellie on Monday at the awards ceremony. I even shook her hand. I need to ask you something about her."

"Do you think I'm going to give you anything?" Gillian countered. Ellie had mentioned she got first place in the Seven Change Challenge, but hadn't told her she'd seen Jake until Gillian threw a paper in front of her with a picture of the two of them shaking hands. Oh yeah, Ellie had said. Jake was handing out the awards. It was strange seeing him. Gillian had first taken her omission of this fact as a sign she had gotten over Jake, but more than once this week, she'd caught Ellie in an inexplicable, emotional state. Just my period, Ellie had said.

"Have you noticed she's more emotional than usual?" Jake asked.

"Well, yeah. But she's been under a lot of pressure," Gillian countered.

"Have you also noticed she's put on some weight?" Jake asked.

"What kind of question is that? She looks fine," Gillian retorted.

"Around the waist, especially. And in her breasts," Jake noted.

"Are you some sort of pervert? What the hell?" Gillian scoffed. "It's time for you to go." But Jake wasn't through.

"She's keeping a secret from everyone—including you and me." Gillian was curious; very curious. But she didn't like the way Jake was beating around the bush, and trying to reel her in.

"Whatever. I don't have time for your riddles Jake. Please go."

"Okay. Thanks for your time, but just think about it." Jake added before Gillian shut the door in his face.

Think about what? Gillian wondered. She sipped on her iced tea and thought about Jake's questions. Ellie had never been into sexy clothes, but lately, she'd been wearing longer styles and she didn't want to say it to Jake, but yes, she had definitely put on weight. Come to think of it, she hadn't seen her in her tight jeans in at least a month. As Gillian began to put the pieces together, she knew what Jake was getting at.

"Jesus Christ!" She said out loud. She opened the door and Jake was still standing there.

"Come in," she ordered.

"Thank you," he responded. It was a warm Sunday morning in August and she led him back toward the pool.

"Yeah. You're damned clothesline is still here," Gillian said sarcastically. Jake couldn't help but notice Ellie's clothing on the line, some of which he recognized from having taken them off of her on more than one occasion. He swallowed hard, trying to stay on track. They sat across from each other and Jake told her everything; about the camping trip, about the condom breaking, Jake saying he didn't want kids, the strange prophecy and finally the envelope.

"I had crumpled it up and thrown it away when I found her message. I didn't think there was anything in it, since it was well worn and she had written on the back. A few days before the award's ceremony, I was prepping my backpack for an upcoming trip, and I found it. I looked it over and that's when I noticed its contents for the first time." Jake handed her the envelope.

"Go ahead. Open it up." Gillian opened the envelope that had a rather brutal message to Jake on the back. When she pulled out the small black and white picture, she gawked.

"Jesus Christ!" she stammered for the second time.

"Not exactly," Jake responded. Gillian was amazed that Ellie had kept the whole thing to herself.

"And she clearly intends to keep it," Gillian intoned.

"Yes. And she thinks I want nothing to do with it. Him, her."

"And is she right?"

"Initially she was. I didn't want a child. But now I want everything to do with it. To do with her," Jake explained. He felt the tears coming into his eyes and Gillian looked at him with sympathy. First, her fiancé and now Jake. What was it with these teary-eyed, sentimental men?

"God! I've even heard her throwing up on a few occasions and she's been ravenous, eating way more than usual, not to mention larger emotional swings. And yes, she's put on weight. She's always had to be careful with her weight. I figured she was just depressed. What an idiot! How's it possible I didn't figure this out?" Gillian asked rhetorically before answering her own question. "I've been so caught up in planning the wedding that I bought all her little lies and didn't put two and two together." Jake smiled at this news, even though it also caused him pain. He should be there with her through this time.

Gillian recalled what Ellie had shared with her and Arno that day on the beach.

"You sure you're over all that eco-crap about not wanting any kids?" Gillian asked. Jake thought once again of Charles, who's life had almost been cut short by an abusive father.

"Like I said. I've changed my mind."

"Honey. I've got some good news and some bad news," Gillian began.

"Start with the bad news."

"Last night she told me she's made a decision to move back to Idaho," Gillian announced. Jake swallowed once again.

"But she was just recently promoted to marketing director. How's that possible? Why would she up and leave?"

"She got laid off three days after the awards ceremony, Jake. It doesn't make any sense."

"Do you think they laid her off because she's pregnant?"

"If they did, we're going to sue their asses. That's got to be illegal." Gillian looked at him with suspicion. "You are absolutely sure you love her, Jake?"

"I can see being with her for the rest of my life, if she'll have me," he responded earnestly. "You said you also had some good news?"

"She's a self-martyring fool and I'm going to help you get her back," Gillian stated. She saw Jake inhale.

"I am so thankful to hear that."

"Yeah. I know," Gillian smiled. Jake took a deep breath. His eyes were still glistening, but the tears had stopped.

"Congratulations by the way, Gillian; on your upcoming marriage. From what Ellie told me, you're marrying a very romantic man." Gillian smiled at the idea of Ellie conveying the engagement story to Jake. Leave it to Ellie to leave out the part that this was one in only a handful of times David had done something so romantic in their four years together.

"The wedding is Saturday, August 21st in Massachusetts. Two weeks away! That's why I didn't see it, Jake. I've been completely absorbed with all the details," she repeated.

"Sorry to enlist your help at such a busy time, Gillian."

"Yeah. Your timing sucks, but we have a lot of work ahead of us, Jake." As she thought of Ellie once again, she shifted. "But let's be clear on something here. It's not for you that I'm going to help; It's for her. Because unless I'm a complete jackass, she's still in love with you."

Chapter 57

The Yves country club and lodge in Ipswich, Massachusetts was a hotspot for old money weddings, and the beautiful brick buildings, expanses of perfectly manicured lawns and landscaped gardens spoke of subtle grandeur. The Atlantic glittered in the distance, just beyond the windswept grasses and clapboard beach houses that lined the shore.

By 10:00 a.m., the humidity was already wreaking havoc on the hair dos of the entire wedding party. Luckily, Arno's hotel was close by, and when Ellie texted him, he came right over to help contain the situation. As Ellie slipped on her bridesmaid's dress, she was thankful Gillian had given into her suggestion of the a-line instead of the princess cut. True, it was shorter than Ellie would have liked and the scooping neckline accentuated her breasts, but for once, this worked to her advantage, as all attention was drawn away from her waist. The last three weeks her body had expanded to the point that someone with a more discerning eye could certainly tell she was pregnant. On the other hand, the thickness in her waist fit her frame without immediately giving her away. She had confided in her mom and her sisters two weeks ago, once she was certain she was keeping it, and they had been far more supportive than she could have imagined. She would see them in person next week. And with their support, she would tell her father. The very idea of telling him made her shiver.

"Ellie, dear, are you okay?" Gillian's mom asked when she caught Ellie staring off into space. "Do you have a stomach ache?"

Ellie often found herself with her hand resting on her belly, not realizing what she was doing.

"Oh, no. I'm fine, Candace," she responded. "Thank you. Maybe just a little nervous about the wedding."

"No need to be. They're a match made in heaven and you will be a sparkling bridesmaid. There's such a nice glow about you in that dress."

Ellie had heard all too often in the last months that she had a glow about her. She wondered if the whole world knew she was pregnant and she was only fooling herself in delaying the announcement. But who would be excited about announcing she got knocked up by a man she was with only two and a half months that didn't even want his own child?

"I'm glad she got over those last minute dress jitters!" Ellie commented, trying to make conversation.

"Me too!" Candace replied dramatically. "That was just strange. The week before the wedding, no less, dragging us to every dress shop known to the greater Los Angeles area to look at new wedding gowns."

Ellie laughed. She liked Candace, who had stayed with them the last week. It felt good to have a mom around. Although Candace, with her sophisticated tastes and manners, was entirely different than Ellie's mom, she had her mother's warmth. She had also been a perfect sport during Gillian's last minute tirade. Usually a woman who knew exactly what she wanted, Gillian was suddenly asking Ellie's advice. Asking what styles she liked. Even insisting she try on a few gowns so Gillian could see them on someone else.

"And then she decides on the one she got in the first place!" Ellie laughed.

"Ellie, come in here!" Gillian called. She smiled at Gillian's mother and headed into the small foyer where Gillian fidgeted in front of the mirror.

"The train, can you pick it up so I can practice walking one more time?"

"Of course!" Ellie bent down to lift the long train of white silk off the deep red carpet of the foyer. Gillian took a few steps.

"God I'm nervous." Gillian twirled the engagement ring on her finger. "What if he morphs into someone else after we tie the knot? You know, starts demanding that I quit my job, that we start a family."

"You've known him for four years. He's not going to change overnight, Gillian."

"Then where did that hyper romantic proposal come from? I mean, if he can make a hard core feminist like me feel weak kneed and cry over something like that, what's going to happen later?"

"Maybe you're the one that's changing Gillian. Did that ever cross your mind?"

"Actually, it hadn't," she remarked, as her fingers started fiddling with her diamond necklace.

"You're both changing as you enter a new phase of your life," Ellie added.

"Since when did you become so sagely? It's not like you've ever been married."

"But I've spent a fair amount of time reading about the phenomenon, not to mention dreaming about it," Ellie admitted, managing a giggle.

"You know what Ellie? I bet, if you opened yourself to the idea, you could find the right man to marry right here at our wedding," Gillian suggested. "I saw how much attention Dan was giving you at the rehearsal dinner last night. And Phillip, my God. He can't keep his eyes off you. Did you know he's one of those God forsaken Christians? Oh, I suppose that wasn't the right way to say it."

"Nice to know, but let's just focus on the wedding at hand, Gillian."

Gillian took in a deep breath and a trickle of tears released down her cheeks.

"Oh my God! What is this foreign substance spilling from my eyes?" she laughed.

"Oh Gillian! Soon you will be Mrs. Cross."

"You know it's going to be Gillian Murray Cross. No way I'm losing my identity."

"You'll never lose your identity Gillian. Not in a million years."

The wedding began promptly at 11 a.m. At least two hundred people filled the ballroom, which David and Gillian had decided on for their wedding rather than the quaint stone chapel on the property. Elaborate glass chandeliers hung from the ceiling and candles lined the front of the room.

The classical quartet finished a Bach concerto as the last bridesmaid reached the raised stage. The quartet paused briefly before starting the wedding march, cueing everyone to stand.

Gillian looked like a princess in her long white gown. She walked gracefully down the aisle, with three flower girls adjusting the long train behind her. Set in ringlets, her long brown hair cascaded down her back, while a diamond tiara drew attention to her face.

The vows were simple yet tasteful and Ellie saw the tears in David's eyes as he said I do. Gillian's lips trembled slightly, but no tears came. Instead, she had a smile of encouragement on her face for her suddenly sentimental husband.

"I now pronounce you husband and wife. You may kiss the bride," the officiant declared. Ellie had heard these words so many times throughout her life, but today they seemed brand new as she watched her best friend joined in holy matrimony. Tears of happiness sprang from her eyes. Arno and Pierre waved at Ellie as she walked back down the aisle after her friend.

The photo shoot lasted 40 minutes and Ellie noticed how Philip, the groomsman she had been paired with, kept smiling at her. They always said weddings were the right place to meet someone and just as Gillian had pointed out, she had received a startling amount of attention in the last few days of rehearsal dinners and other outings from not only Philip, but Dan, a handsome man from Pennsylvania and Collin, one of David's co-workers at the hedge fund. But then again, who was she kidding? Even though she knew it was futile, her heart was still entangled in Jake. And more so, who would really want her if they knew her situation?

When the photo shoot was finally over, Ellie wanted nothing more than to get off of her feet. Due to all of the excitement, she had forgotten all about how poor a night's sleep she'd had, but now she was feeling it. Just then, Gillian appeared by her side.

"You are a married woman!" Ellie squealed.

"Who knows, Ellie. Maybe you'll be next," Gillian winked.

"Sheesh, can you stop with all of that?" Ellie requested. "So do you feel any different?"

"No. At least not yet," Gillian responded. As David started to approach them, Gillian quickly pulled her aside and spoke in a confidential voice.

"About that favor I mentioned. I need you to do it now."

"Okay," Ellie responded. She had been looking forward to the one hour pause, and had even hoped for a small nap, but she had promised Gillian she'd help with something. They hadn't had a chance to go over the details.

"It's sort of a strange request," she began.

"Well. Don't leave me in suspense."

"Just promise me you'll do it."

"What are you up to?" Ellie questioned with a nervous smile. Gillian had a crazy side, but Ellie hadn't expected it to raise its head on her wedding day.

"Don't worry. You're not going through sorority hazing or some bullshit. Trust me a little, okay?" Gillian teased as if reading her mind. David's progress was slow as each family member stopped to give him a hug and make some comment.

"Okay, what's my assignment?" Ellie responded.

"I need you to go out back past the tennis courts to that rose garden I showed you earlier. There's a bright yellow bench in the middle of the garden."

"Yeah. I remember it. Is this some sort of scavenger hunt?"

"Not exactly," Gillian smiled. "I need you to go to that bench and wait there. Someone will come to you and give you a package. It's part of a surprise for David. But, you have to stay until he's explained the entire contents of the package."

"Is this a romantic surprise?" Ellie asked.

"How'd you guess?" Gillian raised her eyebrows. "And who better to help me out with it than my over the top romantic friend?"

Ellie started giggling. Leave it to Gillian to try to organize romance through documents prepared by a stranger and then reviewed by a friend. Ellie yawned and Gillian looked at her sheepishly.

"Sorry to have you do one more thing. You've been running around all day."

"Don't worry about me," Ellie mustered. "My curiosity is giving me renewed energy."

"What are you two girls whispering about?" David asked as he finally reached her.

"Nothing," they replied in unison. David arched his eyebrows.

"I suppose you'll continue to whisper to your girlfriends even though we're married," David commented before kissing Gillian on the cheek.

"Ellie. You look great in hot pink. Did you know that you bridesmaids saved the day? If Gillian would have had her way, her wedding dress would have been hot pink. You ladies were the compromise."

"Glad to be of service," Ellie laughed. Gillian raised her eyebrows at Ellie and looked at an imaginary watch on her wrist.

"Congratulations David. You've married a wonderful woman," Ellie commented before excusing herself.

"I know, Ellie. I know," he responded with a dreamy smile. Ellie saw the glint of a tear forming in his right eye and marveled at how opposite these two were; Gillian strong, solid, vibrant in a winner-takes-all way; David, smart and reserved, except when it came to his newfound romantic nature. Perhaps they balanced each other out.

Chapter 58

The property was so expansive that it took Ellie ten minutes to reach the yellow bench, which was partially shaded by a trellis covered in fuchsia roses. Ellie understood why Gillian had chosen this spot; even though the rose garden was wide open with broad views, this particular bench was sequestered away from plain sight; a perfect rendezvous point to pick up a package and have the contents revealed without anyone accidentally seeing.

Ellie closed her eyes, appreciative of the shade and the opportunity to rest. When she opened them again, she noticed a handsome man in a gray suit walking across the expanse of lawn in her direction. His dark hair was closely cropped, just short of a crew cut. She admired his tall, lean form, the confident cadence of his walk suddenly familiar. As he got closer to the bench, adrenaline shot through her. He pulled off his sunglasses, revealing broad set green eyes that glistened in the sunshine.

"Hi Ellie." Not one of the handsome men she had encountered over the weekend sent heat coursing through her body as he did. She inhaled, trying to steady her breath.

"Jake, how on earth," she began. "What are you doing here?"

"I was invited. You did a fabulous job as maid of honor," he remarked.

"But you barely know Gillian," Ellie responded, starting to stand. "And besides, aren't you supposed to be in Louisiana right now with your group?" Jake took it as a good sign that she was at least keeping track of what he was up to.

"The team's all there, Ellie," he responded gently. She looked at him, a mix of fear and excitement coursing through her veins. She had thought of him so many times in the last month, and their brief encounter at the awards ceremony had been tough enough. Now he was right beside her. Had he really left in the middle of his grant funded project just to see her? But then the last words they had exchanged played through her like a mantra.

"You should have stayed there," she stated evenly.

"Ellie, please. I'm here right now because this is more important to me. I didn't spend a ton on a last minute flight to Boston and take the bus out here for nothing. We need to talk. May I sit down?" He asked gently.

Despite how different he looked with short hair, his crisp, well tailored suit and handsome leather shoes, he sounded like the Jake with whom she had fallen in love. Keeping up her guard, she gestured to the bench.

"I can't believe Gillian set me up like this," she commented as Jake sat beside her.

"I can't believe you didn't tell me, or her, that you're pregnant." Jake countered. Ellie bit her lip and looked at him. "Or have the decency to return a single call." Ellie was surprised to hear the pain in his voice, but couldn't ignore the anger welling up inside of her.

"What was I supposed to say? Oh, Gillian! Guess what? I got knocked up by a guy I knew for two months. And surprise! He doesn't even want to have a child with me."

"Yes, I do."

"But you said— "

"Yes. I do. Do you hear me?" he reached for her instinctively, but as his hand touched her shoulder, she flinched, pulling back. Clearly, she had heard what he said, but she shook her head.

"You're not making sense, Jake," she cried. "You said you didn't want a child, and on top of that, you made it abundantly clear that you don't think I'm fit to be a good mother—that my ethics are weak, that I'm not *green* enough. Even if you've suddenly changed your mind about having a child, how can you think *for a second* I'd want to be with someone who views me that way?" The tears pushed up into her eyes, and she didn't bother to wipe them away. Jake winced, as if the very sight of her tears sent pain through his chest.

"Of course you wouldn't want to be with someone who views you that way. But that's not me, Ellie. Please hear me out." His eyes were big and sullen and she noticed he looked thinner than she remembered.

"I'm listening," she responded.

"When I said those awful things and stormed away from you, I was overwhelmed. But as I walked it off and cooled down a bit, I knew what I had said was wrong."

"What part?" Ellie began, crossing her arms, causing her dress to flatten against her belly. Jake stared at her stomach, his eyes big. She readjusted her dress nervously.

"My judgment of you. I was wrong Ellie. I know that now. And I'm so sorry," he implored, taking her hand. This time, she didn't pull away, but she dared not to look in his eyes. She wanted to believe his words, but doubt filled her.

"So you've just changed your mind," she stated cautiously. "How do I know it's not going to swing back again?"

"It's not a snap decision Ellie. Life brought me to this conclusion. I want you, the baby, all of it." He looked at her belly again and this time she didn't try to cover it up.

"You didn't say anything like that in my voicemail," she responded, tenderness in her voice. He looked at her lips, curved into a sad smile. She was beautiful; flushed from the heat and in the sexiest dress he had ever seen her in. What he'd give to see her happy again.

"Those aren't the type of words you say in a voicemail, Ellie. You say them in person." A foreboding tingle crawled up his spine. What if Gillian and Arno were both wrong and she really didn't want him back? Had he come here for nothing? He hurried on. "When I finally saw you at the awards ceremony, I thought I would have my chance, but I didn't. But what I did get a chance to do was see you, and see that our baby was growing in there," he quietly remarked, gesturing toward her stomach.

"You just said *our* baby," she repeated, looking fully into his eyes for the first time.

"Of course, our baby. And I am so sorry about what I said about your integrity. You have far more integrity than I. You stick to what you believe in and what I said was just wrong. I know that." Ellie let out a sigh.

"Jake, the thing is your words stung so much because there's some truth in them."

"No there's not," Jake interrupted.

"Just hear me out here, Jake. You've had some realizations over the past month. So have I." He nodded for her to continue. "I'm not exactly living the life I'd imagined. You were my wake up call, Jake. And this whole Seven Change Challenge brought me back in line with my love of nature. I did some of it for you—to impress you, I suppose. But I did it for me, too. And after we broke up, I did it for the environment, for the future of this planet, for this baby." She gazed at the rose bush nearest to the bench; its butterscotch flower petals, the waxy green leaves and sharp thorns glistening in the heat. "It's not like I was changing the world, but for the first time in a long time, I was doing something." Jake listened as she spoke, wanting to hold her, but not daring to interrupt her. "I see all the good you are doing for this world, despite the odds, and I know I want to be making a difference too." She let out a breath.

"Then we'll make an excellent couple," Jake responded, looking in her eyes.

"Oh Jake. I wish it were that simple." Ellie broke eye contact.

"It can be," Jake half stated, half pleaded. As she took in the scent of his sweat, mixed with his earthy cologne, she remembered the last time they had made love. This intoxicating memory made it all the harder for her to share her news. Ellie took in a deep breath.

"No. It can't. There's something I have to tell you; I got laid off three weeks ago."

"I know. Gillian told me. How is that even possible? You just got promoted!"

"And I was told I was doing an excellent job."

"Then what happened?" he asked.

"Do you remember the day I interviewed you for the magazine?" Ellie asked.

"Of course. How could I forget? It was the beginning of our courtship. Besides that one night," Jake clarified. Yes, that one, fateful night, she thought. She did her best to stay on track.

"That day, before I interviewed you, I threw up in the bathroom at work. I thought it was because I was so nervous. A colleague saw me, actually confronted me and asked me if I was pregnant. I said no. Because of course, I didn't think I was." Jake squeezed her hand.

"Based on the ultrasound picture, I knocked you up our first time together," Jake commented sheepishly. Ellie shifted in the bench, slightly embarrassed.

"How long have you known?" he asked her, trying to stay calm. She explained the false periods, her decision to go on the pill, and her doctor's appointment a little over a week before their camping trip. Jake shook his head, sadness and guilt coursing through him as he thought once again of things he had said to her.

"And you got laid off because of being pregnant?" he asked indignantly.

"Yes and no. A rumor was circulating around the office that I was sleeping with you. Others suspected I was either bulimic or pregnant. Anyway, after the awards ceremony, Margo confronted me with an anonymous photo of you and I kissing on my front porch, dated well after I denied we were serious. It was creepy, Jake. She claimed it showed up on her desk the day after the ceremony. She told me I had been deceiving her and everyone else. She couldn't fire me for being pregnant, but she laid me off for being dishonest about you. At least I have benefits to cover the pregnancy."

"Damn. It's been a hard go for you Ellie. And almost all of it is my fault." He still had her hand in his and it felt good there, Ellie had to admit. "We can do this together. All of it," Jake continued.

"Oh, Jake." She looked at him, doing her best to hold back another round of tears. "I applied for a job six weeks ago for Children's Literacy. I don't know why. I did it on a whim, really. But they're interested in hiring me. I won't get paid maternity leave, but they are willing to work with me."

"But that's fantastic, Ellie. You're following your dreams!"

"Yes. But those dreams are going to take me to Memphis, Tennessee."

"Memphis?" Jake repeated. "Gillian said you might be moving back to Idaho, not Memphis." Jake felt his chest constricting. "So you're just going to up and move away? What about us, Ellie? Didn't it mean anything to you?"

"I've never been closer to a man in my entire life, Jake," she whispered.

"Then stay with me."

"But how? I move into your postage stamp sized house? You can't support me . . . us."

Jake considered carefully before continuing.

"Yes I can."

"How? On love? On hope? Babies cost money, Jake. Even though I think you would be an excellent father, I don't want my baby to grow up poor like I did. I want her to have opportunities." Guilt stabbed her as the words left her lips, but despite her feelings for Jake, she knew the baby had to come first.

"Our baby won't grow up poor, Ellie. I can promise you that." Jake stated. "There's something I need to tell you about the last six weeks. But before I do, I need to know something." He looked at her in earnest.

"What?"

"A very simple question; do you love me? Yes or no?" A most definite yes, she thought. Yet she hesitated.

"It's not that simple, I," she started.

"Just answer the question. Yes or no?" As she looked into his eyes, the fear evaporated.

"I love you so much Jake."

"If you truly love me and believe in me, then marry me, Ellie. I promise you that our baby will have everything it ever needs."

A series of images flashed before her eyes: her parents kissing in the kitchen when they thought the children weren't looking; family dinners around the table, everyone sharing about their days. It was a home full of hard work, but also full of laughter and love. Jake might not be a rich man, she thought, but he had the type of wealth she wanted—a richness of character.

"Say yes," he implored.

"Yes!" she answered, throwing her arms around him.

"Oh God I love you," he whispered in her ear. His words poured into her like a healing balm, her body softening into his warmth. Jake hugged her until he felt every bit of fear that he'd lost her inch its way from his body. When he finally let her go, they both laughed. He fidgeted with something in his pocket and pulled out a small blue velvet box.

"This belonged to my grandmother," Jake announced as he opened it up. Ellie stared at a dazzling emerald cut diamond surrounded by two bands of tiny rubies.

"You must have been pretty sure I would say yes."

"I don't know what I would have done if you'd said no." He slipped the ring onto her finger and much to her surprise it fit perfectly.

"I've missed you so much Jake," she admitted. He kissed her passionately on the lips, pulling her against him.

"I've missed you too darling. I promise you, I will never walk away again."

"Neither will I," she promised.

"And now for my big news," Jake began.

Chapter 59

She glanced more than once at the elegant diamond ring on her finger as she walked hand in hand with Jake toward the wedding reception. Her mind reeled from what he had just shared with her, and what it meant for their future; the conceptual ecovillage that Jake designed was now fully funded, and fast tracked for approval. It started when Jake was out to lunch with Gray Wolf. They ran into Allison, the director of Hope Farmers, and he invited her to join them. One thing led to another, and a partnership was born.

"Gray Wolf agreed that this first community would be a pilot study with me as the lead architect, with permission to replicate the model in other parts of the country," Jake had explained.

"So you are gainfully employed," she had responded.

"Yeah. I can finally afford you, and that baby in the oven" he teased. Besides conversations with her mom and sisters over the phone, she hadn't talked about the baby in person to anyone. To hear Jake talk so openly about their baby pulled her heart wide open. "And that's not all, Ellie; Gray Wolf invited us to be members of the community. I can design our future home if you'd be willing to live in nature with me, surrounded by kind-hearted people who believe in a better world."

Just when it seemed like her world was falling apart, it was as if everything had played out exactly as it needed to. But then the no-nonsense, career-minded Ellie demanded her say.

"Jake, this is incredible, but I can't just give up my career and live off you."

"I thought you might say that," Jake responded lightly. "If you want a non-profit job right here in California, instead of flying off to Memphis, I think I have just the thing." He told her all about Allison saying she needed a marketing expert to help her promote the idea and how they had both immediately thought of Ellie.

Ellie had taken all but three seconds to say yes, she'd like to live in a little home with Jake in an ecovillage. Yes, she could see herself marketing such a project.

By the time they had walked back to the Yves Country Club ballroom, they had missed Gillian and David's first dance and couples were slowly filling up the dance floor.

Jake hadn't finished the rest of his news. If tomorrow were to happen, she had to consent to the idea they had spent the last two weeks planning.

"There's more I need to tell you Ellie, about tomorrow," Jake began. Ellie was so overwhelmed with everything she had just shared, that she couldn't take much more.

"Jake," she cut him off, pulling him close. "What I'd really like just now is to dance with my fiancé."

"Absolutely," he responded. She looked up into his face, running her fingers gently over his short hair.

"Why did you cut it off?" she asked. "I loved your long dark curls."

"I had a very important appointment last week," he answered.

"I never thought you'd cut your curls just to impress a client," Ellie responded. By way of answer, Jake simply smiled. As they slow danced, Ellie leaned into him, closing her eyes. She didn't notice Philip looking on glumly, or Collin glancing longingly in her direction. But Jake did. And he thanked the universe he had woken up in time to make her his. He had found the diamond ring encircled with rubies a bit too glamorous to his taste, but as its brilliance caught his eye, he knew it would also dazzle the eyes of her suitors. Thus when Philip tapped him on the shoulder, prompting his turn to dance, Jake was a gentleman about it. Plus, it gave him a chance to make a much anticipated call.

Grandma Jeanne, who had caller I.D., answered the phone with a question:

"Did she say yes?"

"Yeah, she did," Jake announced, letting out a deep sigh.

"Then consider all the planes ordered my sweet boy. Want me to relay the information as well?"

"That would be great."

"Consider it done. We'll see you tomorrow."

Ellie saw a rush of white out of the corner of her eye as Gillian came bounding toward her.

"May I have a turn, Philip?" she asked, tapping him on the shoulder. He regrettably gave Ellie over to the bride.

"I think you're supposed to be dancing with men, not with your maid of honor," Ellie teased, as Gillian wrapped her arms around her.

"So, Ellie. What did you think of my mystery guest?"

"You're a complete trickster Gillian, and I love you for it," Ellie gushed, holding up her hand.

"So you said yes!" Gillian cried as she looked at the beautiful engagement ring.

"I did!"

"So today's my big day, and tomorrow is yours." When she took in the blank expression on Ellie's face, Gillian clamped her hand over her mouth. "I guess Jake didn't get that far. Jesus do I know how to screw things up." A series of seemingly unconnected events tumbled together in Ellie's mind: Gillian's last minute wedding dress jitters, having Ellie try on a dozen wedding dresses until she found one she loved; the favorite colors question; Arno asking her about her ring size; what her dream wedding would entail. And hadn't Jake just said he had more to discuss with her when she cut him off?

"Are you telling me there's a *surprise wedding* planned for me tomorrow?" Ellie gasped. Gillian nodded. "What if I'd said no?" Ellie wondered.

"Then a whole lot of us would have taken up drink for the next month to get over our heartbreaks and all the damned work we've done over the past few weeks," Gillian replied.

"Seriously?" Ellie gasped as tears tumbled from her eyes. Why hadn't she confided in her friends earlier? Reached out to them for help? Her answer came to her like a punch in the face; pride. And who else besides Arno, Gillian and Jake were on this team, she wondered. She hugged Gillian tightly.

"I love my sentimental girl, but no tears on the wedding dress," Gillian gently chided.

When Jake finally got off his cell phone, Ellie let him know the cat was out of the bag. Although Jake wanted to go over the wedding plans he had arranged for them, Ellie stopped him.

"I've tried on the dress and it fits me perfectly. Arno will be doing my hair. My best friend will be my witness. The rest, I leave up to you," Ellie decided.

"But you like to take the lead on things, be in control," Jake stated.

"You're right. That's always been my approach; but I've learned something through this, Jake. Sometimes I need to set down my pride and have a little faith in others."

Chapter 60

The day of her wedding, Ellie awoke covered in a fine sheen of sweat. She crawled out of bed in her underwear and sleeveless nightie to crack open the window of her suite, letting in the fresh sea air. Although she heard the distant waves of the Atlantic crashing on the shore and an occasional screech of a seagull, there were no sounds of people milling about.

Her first thought was of Jake. Despite a desire to take him back to her suite last night, Jake had insisted on waiting until after they were married. Sure, it was only one day away, but she knew he did this to honor her. He had lain beside her, stroking her belly gently, feeling the contours of her stomach in wonder before kissing her goodnight and heading out to his own suite.

This morning, as she looked herself in the mirror thinking about her wedding, she had two regrets: her family wouldn't be there to witness her marriage today and her father wouldn't be giving her away. Although the idea terrified her, she knew she had to make the call to Idaho and tell her father everything.

She practiced what she would say before she punched in the telephone number. It was 4:30 a.m. there, and although it was brutal to wake them up, she couldn't wait another minute. She was surprised when the answering machine picked up on the third ring.

You've reached Eloise and Bob Ashburn. We're on vacation for the next week. If you are a thief, please be informed that all of our neighbors are heavily armed, with permission to shoot trespassers on the spot.

Her lips curled upward in amusement, before sadness brought them back down again. After a quick shower, she pulled on a summer dress and headed to the main lodge where she had agreed to meet Jake for an early breakfast. She was surprised to see him sitting at a large table.

"Good morning, darling. Sleep well?" he asked as he stood to embrace her.

"I slept as well as any bride before her wedding day," she responded. Jake noted the circles under her eyes, and smiled almost apologetically. She was amazed how quickly they had transitioned back to a couple, despite six weeks apart.

"Having second thoughts?" he asked.

"Absolutely not," she confirmed. "Why such a big table?"

"Part of the wedding planning. You'll see soon enough."

As she ordered a tall stack of pancakes with bacon and eggs, Jake glanced at her with amusement.

"You're just having a fruit bowl?" she asked indignantly.

"I'm only eating for one," he responded as he folded his hand over hers. Ellie sat next to him with a sense of relief; her shattered hopes replaced by a dream come true. He was everything she had ever wanted; she just had the wrong check list all these years.

Jake looked up and suddenly stood. Ellie followed his eyes toward the lobby entrance and shrieked.

"Oh my God! Daddy! Mom! Jody! Carl too?" she cried as she rushed toward them. Ellie embraced her parents, and then her brother and sister. When more Ashburns came through the entrance, Ellie was beside herself. Jake had walked over toward them, but politely waited a few steps back.

"Jake," her father called, shaking his hand firmly. "Good to see you again." Ellie stared in wonder at their exchange.

"Thank you sir," Jake responded. "We're so glad you could make it."

"What do you mean again?" Ellie questioned.

"A proper man asks a father for his daughter's hand in marriage before proposing," her dad explained, winking at Jake. "And based on that ring, looks like you said yes."

Ellie's mom gave him a hug.

"Good to see you again, son."

"You too, Eloise," Jake returned. As they all came to the table, Ellie looked around at the faces of her brothers and sisters, her two nieces and mom and dad and the tears started spilling out of her eyes.

Jake's parents, his sister and two sets of grandparents arrived shortly after the Ashburn clan. Ellie was introduced to everyone before their families met one another.

"You're grandma Jeanne?" her mother asked of Jake's grandmother.

"That's me."

"I've never been in a private jet before. It was amazing. Thank you so much for providing us with the flights!"

"No problem. Just one of the perks of having owned a charter flight business, and being retired. No more work and all the benefits!" she shared conspiratorially. As she overheard the conversation, Ellie had at least one of her thousand questions answered.

After breakfast, Arno whisked Ellie away to do her hair, and Gillian arrived around 10:00 a.m., sleepy-eyed and content to help her into her gown. She handed Ellie a thick platinum ring, and Ellie eyed it with admiration.

"He picked it out himself. Some sort of Fair Trade ring, made in a community mine, whatever that means."

"It means he cares, Gillian. And that I'm marrying the right man," Ellie explained dreamily.

At 1:45 p.m., Ellie was led across the golf course toward a sandy trail heading to the Atlantic. Her father linked arms with her and they followed a trail of rose petals strewn on the path by her nieces. She drew in a sharp breath as she crested the dune, taking in a beautiful gauze tent blowing ethereally in the breeze. As she entered the tent, she took in each face of their families filling the twenty white folding chairs in the sand. Beautiful bouquets of flowers formed a ring around the altar, where a minister stood, Bible in hand, his gown billowing in the breeze.

At the sight of Jake dressed in a sharp black suit with an emerald button down shirt, Ellie felt warmth flowing through her. Conrad and Natalia stood on one side, Gillian and Arno on the other, tears in both of their eyes. The dark blue ocean formed a stunning backdrop as the waves licked at the sand.

Her father kissed her cheek before handing her over to Jake. Her mother read a verse from Psalms followed by Jake's mother reading a love poem by Hafiz. Ellie barely heard the sermon. She could only focus on Jake's eyes, filled with love and commitment. But when they exchanged vows and rings, every cell in her body stayed firmly in the present.

"You may now kiss the bride," the minister stated.

Epilogue

Five Years Later

It was one of those chilly mornings where the fog hung low in the valley, covering Gaia Eden ecovillage in a cold, wet mist. Ellie wanted to stay in bed, but Lucas was up before the muted sunrise even had a chance to press through the fog.

"Mama, papa. Time to feed Minnie and her friends!" he announced enthusiastically. Ellie stretched into Jake's warmth.

"It's too early. Come under the covers with us," she gently ordered. Lucas wiggled his way between them, his cold toes pressing into her stomach.

"Careful of mama's belly, Lucas," Jake warned.

"I know, daddy," he responded. Jake wrapped his arms around his son, warming him up.

"After we feed the animals, we need to make mama a special breakfast," he whispered sleepily into his son's ear.

"Is it her birthday?" Lucas asked in a boisterous voice.

"That's a good guess. But no, it's not her birthday. It's our anniversary."

"Annifissery? What's that?"

"Anniversary. It's a celebration of when Mama and I got married. Five years ago today."

"Oh," Lucas responded. "And married means you love mama."

"Yes, a lot" Jake smiled. Lucas was already quite verbal for a four year old. Jake attributed it to a combination of inheriting Ellie's smarts and the excellent school on the property.

Ellie sat up in bed, wrapping the covers around her.

"What if you guys feed the animals, and I make us some pancakes?"

"Yeah!" Lucas cheered.

"Oh wait, guys. It's Tuesday. Damik and Shanti are on the schedule to feed the animals."

"I wanted to do it, mama!'

"Honey, we get to work in the garden today. You love pulling out the weeds. Jake, can you get the raisins out of the cellar?" She'd usually do it herself, but at seven months pregnant, she had a hard time going down the earthen steps.

"You stay put, mama. Lucas and I have got it covered." Ellie thankfully lowered herself back onto the bed, wrapping herself in the warmth of the covers while her guys worked on breakfast.

"Can Shay come over after school?" Lucas asked after consuming his second pancake.

"Sorry, Lucas. We have a meeting this afternoon. Remember Charles and Ethan that came up last month from Gaia Eden Los Angeles?" Lucas nodded. "They're coming again. So you'll be doing an arts and crafts afternoon with the other kids while we meet with them," Jake explained.

The ecovillage was beginning to come to life. As other families started their morning routines, lights went on across the valley. The lights at the school and community center flickered on as well. After breakfast, Lucas ran off to the school house in the middle of the property and Ellie watched him from a distance as he plucked a few stevia leaves in the community gardens before entering the classroom. She moved slowly through their home to her office, retrieving her present for Jake.

They sat down on the glassed-in front porch, and despite the cool morning air, the room was warm from the solar heat that had been stored the day before and transferred into the radiant water heating system.

"Mrs. Tillerman," Jake began. "I am so glad you married me."

"Five years," Ellie marveled, gazing into his eyes. "I'm the luckiest girl in the world."

"I'm luckier," he mused. He massaged her feet, swollen from pregnancy as he sat in the wicker chair across from her.

"You know what I was thinking about when we woke up this morning? Our bicycling trip with Arno and Pierre in the Netherlands right after we got married," Ellie shared.

"That was amazing, wasn't it?"

"Yeah. I wonder if we'll ever get a chance to do something like that again."

"Sure we will. Right after our kids have graduated from high school," Jake teased. Ellie rolled her eyes.

"That's probably not far from the truth," she sighed.

"I promise we'll go to Europe before then," Jake responded. "I'd love Lucas to see Western Europe when he's a little older. And this little one too." Jake set down his cup and sat in the loveseat beside her. She leaned comfortably into his chest. As she gazed out the window, she saw Diane, a woman who was here for the week-long workshop on organic gardening, walking straight toward their porch.

"Incoming," Ellie warned.

Jake looked up. As he spotted Diane, an all too familiar half-smile crept across his face.

"Ah. My favorite new student," he griped.

"She's only been here a day," Ellie scolded reproachfully. "Let me handle this." She pushed herself up from the love seat and headed for the door.

"Hi Diane," she greeted. Diane's wet hair, adorned with a lather of white bubbles on one side, alerted Ellie to the situation at hand.

"Hi. Sorry to bother you, but I'm having trouble with my shower."

"Oh? What seems to be the problem?" Ellie asked.

"I was in the middle of showering when the water just shut off," she explained. "I tried to turn it back on, but there was only an icy drizzle."

"Oh. That must have been a shock," Ellie sympathized. "Perhaps you didn't see the sign in the shower explaining the eight-minute cycle?"

"Well, yeah, but I mean, I didn't think that actually meant," she faltered over her words before lilting into silence.

"It's not meant to be inhospitable. Since we're on a reservoir system out here, and we live in a drought area, every shower in the community is set on an eight-minute cycle," Ellie explained gently. She didn't mention that most of the residents here finished their showers in half that time.

"Oh. Okay. I get it," she responded downheartedly.

"You can borrow a bucket of warm water from us," Ellie offered. "We've built up a surplus of minutes." Diane gratefully took Ellie up on the offer before heading out.

"Thank you," Jake said in earnest when she settled back on the loveseat. "You're so much better at handling that than I am."

"You're welcome. Now where were we? Ah. Your present!" Ellie bubbled. She handed him a box in a beautiful cloth wrapping, along with an envelope. Jake started to unwrap the present, but she stopped him. "Wait. You have to read the letter first." He pulled open the envelope, finding three handwritten pages within.

"What's this?"

"It's from my journal, from the first year we were together."

"You kept a journal? I had no idea."

"Yeah. These pages are about a recurring dream. The first time it came to me was that day here on the property with the break out sessions. I fell asleep in the shade of the oak trees. Do you remember? Read it, Jake." As he read through the pages, he kept glancing up at her in disbelief. In Ellie's graceful handwriting was a rough description of Gaia Eden Ecovillage. Although parts of it were off—there was no wine making facility on the property, for example—it mentioned the school, the garden program and Jake's design center.

"Wow, this is a trip. Why haven't you ever shared this before?" Jake responded, sitting up straight.

"Well, I didn't think much of it at first. I mean, half of it is total nonsense. But then things kept happening that seemed familiar to me because I'd written them down here before they happened."

"You're giving me chills, Ellie. Is this all there was, or is there more?" he asked.

"There is more." Her smile grew wider. "This is where you should open your present." Jake quickly unwrapped the cloth, revealing a felt-lined box. He popped it open to unveil a beautiful watch.

"A watch? Honey, I never use a watch," he remarked.

"I know. But it's solar powered. It has a perpetual calendar, and, see that piece of paper underneath the watch? Read the next page of the journal there." Jake read through the page and he shook his head, laughing.

"Twins? That's why you agreed that this would be our last. Because you knew already." Her eyebrows arched upwards, a smile forming on her lips.

"It was just a recurring dream, Jake—a dream that I did my best to record. You can see that not everything was accurate. I've never walked naked through the community gardens, for example."

"Ah, but you never know. Maybe that's in your future," Jake teased, pulling at her robe.

"I don't think so," she responded, slapping his hand away. Jake looked at her belly with renewed interest.

"And the watch? Does that have special significance?" Jake asked.

"The watch is just a watch. You're always late, Jake." He smirked. It was true.

"I have a present for you too, Ellie, but you'll need to come inside." He pulled her up from the loveseat and led her to the main room. A white sheet hung over a rectangular shape on the wall above the couch.

"You got me a painting?" Ellie asked excitedly.

"Yeah. But I took a bit of a chance here," Jake admitted uncertainly. "I hope you like it. If I missed the mark, we can take it back."

She loved art, and she was impressed that Jake had thought to buy a painting for her. She carefully pulled the white sheet off the painting, revealing a vision from the past.

"Oh, Jake," she responded breathlessly. She took in the half-naked form of a woman leaning gently on a wall, two-thirds of her body nestled in nature. The woman gazed toward a cityscape on the horizon.

"You remember it?" he asked. "It's so romantic, it reminds me of you."

"Of course I remember it. Green," Ellie responded, a mix of emotions pulling at her. It was the same painting they had discussed on their first date together. She knew why it had felt so haunting; it was as if she was that woman gazing longingly over the wall.

But as she stared at the painting hanging before her, her mind no longer saw a woman entrapped by nature, yearning for the city. Now, it was as if nature was supporting this contemplative woman, connecting her with her roots, her source of power; giving her the strength and calm she needed to make a difference in the world. This was a painting of the woman she had become.

"I love it Jake," Ellie responded, wiping the tears away from her eyes. "It's perfect."

Jake sighed in relief. As he wrapped his arms around her, he thanked the universe for Ellie and all the other blessings in his life, while quietly pondering the idea of twins.

ABOUT THE AUTHOR

Originally from California, U.S.A., Kristin Anderson has been writing professionally for the last 10 years in the fields of architecture and sustainability and has worked as a freelance journalist for weekly newspapers and monthly trade magazines.

After moving to the Netherlands in 2011 with her husband Arie Jan and their son Ezra, she pursued a lifelong dream and invested her time, energy and creativity into the writing of fiction. **Green** is her debut novel.

Learn more about author Kristin Anderson at:

www.authorkristinanderson.com
www.facebook.com/AuthorKristinAnderson
www.twitter.com/AuthorKristin

Learn more about artist Catrin Welz-Stein who provided the cover art at **www.catrinwelzstein.blogspot.ch**

Made in the USA
San Bernardino, CA
11 October 2013